Ann

Praise for *USA TODAY* bestselling author Vanessa Fewings

"Vanessa Fewings has created an intriguingly sexy and masterful beginning to the ICON series!"
—Lisa Renee Jones, *New York Times* bestselling author, on *The Chase*

"Sultry, heart-pounding romance and a thrilling mystery make this gem by Vanessa Fewings one to chase, grab, and own! You will be clamoring for more!"
—Katy Evans, *New York Times* and *USA TODAY* bestselling author, on *The Chase*

"A sexy, intriguing romance that will keep you guessing. I can't wait to see what Vanessa has next for us."
—Louise Bay, *USA TODAY* bestselling author, on *The Chase*

VANESSA FEWINGS

The PRIZE

HQN™

ISBN-13: 978-1-335-01694-2

Recycling programs
for this product may
not exist in your area.

The Prize

This edition published by arrangement with Harlequin Books S.A.

For questions and comments about the quality of this book,
please contact us at CustomerService@Harlequin.com.

® and TM are trademarks of Harlequin Enterprises Limited or its
corporate affiliates. Trademarks indicated with ® are registered in the
United States Patent and Trademark Office, the Canadian Intellectual
Property Office and in other countries.

www.HQNBooks.com

Printed in U.S.A.

For Ida

CHAPTER ONE

I SHOULDN'T BE HERE.

My life felt unrecognizable. I was standing in a New York drawing room, and all its decadence seemed a mere extension of the grand wealth and endless secrets I'd been exposed to ever since meeting *him*.

Tobias William Wilder, the man who I'd unwittingly fallen for and the reason I was here. A man seemingly wiser than his thirty years, dangerously charismatic and a captivating inventor and CEO of the leading software company TechRule. He also owned the renowned Wilder Museum in Los Angeles. It felt as though fate itself had shot an arrow into my heart to strike my greatest weakness—my devotion to art.

Above me swept a dramatic ornate plaster ceiling and below my strappy Louboutin heels lay a brightly patterned Persian rug encompassing the entire room. The surrounding paintings from centuries past completed this grandeur within this Upper East Side mansion. The heat from the pine logs in the hearth spat orange sparks and brought a warmth that still couldn't lift the chill from my bones.

No, I wasn't meant to be here at all.

Nor should I have been draped in a shimmering Dior gown to attend a prestigious social event.

I'd left behind my dream job at Britain's distinguished art investigation firm Huntly Pierre, as a forensic art specialist, and now my world swirled in turmoil. A disarray I couldn't see how to pull back from.

Yesterday, we'd both fled LA on Wilder's private jet and evaded the FBI. Just over a week ago, I'd made the journey stateside to persuade Tobias to give up his secretive pursuit of stealing artwork and then apparently returning it to its rightful owners.

His obsession for justice touched me personally when he'd dared a heist at Christie's London auction house to steal back my own masterpiece, *St. Joan of Arc* by Walter William Ouless, a painting my father once owned and the same one that was meant to have been destroyed in our house fire. Right up until my gaze had swept over the canvas during a visit to the famous auction house. In those few seconds it took me to authenticate it my life changed irrevocably and it had been a prelude to my unraveling.

Even if his intensions were heroic, they were daringly illegal. His misadventures had earned him the title of Icon and the reputation for impressively evading the authorities. That was until he'd met me, because I was the one who'd caught him.

And he is the one who caught me.

Never had a love affair been so forbidden.

Just the thought of him sent a quake through me as evocative as I imagined opium would feel surging through my veins. Though Wilder was a deadlier addiction…

I could leave.

This was the lie I'd told myself so I wouldn't fall apart, but in reality I was a wanted woman. Exhaling an uncertain breath, the same one I'd held since leaving the West Coast, or so it felt, I steadied myself for another wave of panic and concentrated on the self-portrait by Peter Paul Rubens hanging dead ahead. Though now the artist's rendition mocked me with his hawkish brown eyes—even though I'd done nothing wrong, *not really*.

Wilder's deep, even tone rose from beyond the door in his usual masterful cadence as he carried on a conversation in French, and it made me wonder if he was on the phone with his uncle. Maybe he was telling him all that had happened to us. Maybe he was asking for help. Either way, Tobias sounded just as collected as that first evening I'd met him in The Otillie gallery in London.

The day everything changed.

My body tightened as I watched the door open and him enter. My feelings were as complex as the man who strolled toward me with that long, elegant stride exuding confidence, and his stark beauty left me breathless; his three-day stubble highlighted his dangerous edge that was perilously beguiling. He was dressed in a black tuxedo, and he always stunned with his short, ruffled dark blond hair and sharp chiseled features that were ridiculously gorgeous. A timeless masculine beauty inspiring the same wonder of a Greek sculpture by Praxiteles himself, a living, breathing Hermes. Wilder had the greenest eyes that sparkled with intelligence and kindness too, a mischievousness that was the catalyst for my falling for him.

His scrutiny fixed on me and sent shivers into my core. It hurt too deeply that I could never let him touch me again the way he once had. Our lovemaking threatened to woo me into compliance and addle my thoughts and right now I needed to remain razor sharp. The tension between us was ever more palpable.

He came closer. "Let me go alone."

I had to fight back. Rage against this loss of control. Yet who was I fighting with? The man who'd led me here after seducing me with his dangerous persuasion or with the Burells, one of America's most influential and menacing families. Perhaps I'd stumbled too far into the dark murky world of revenge. Every decision I made, every action taken decided my future.

His brow furrowed as he tried to read me. "It'll be safer if you stay here."

Safer, yes, but if I risked nothing my future would lay in another's hands. "You need me for this to work." I broke his gaze; it was easier that way. "Besides, this is my life we're talking about." I refused to descend into powerlessness.

He stepped back into my line of sight. "I get that, Zara. This is my fault. All of it—"

"I put the spotlight on you—"

"That was your job. To investigate." He shrugged. "To find me."

"Still, I understand why you did what you believed was right." Even if his deeds had been misguided. Though perhaps his grand ruse continued and my fate was yet to be realized. The thought of this possible betrayal caused ice to slither up my spine.

My legacy was within reach and owning my father's paintings was my birthright. I owed that at least to my father and his beloved memory.

And only Tobias could lead me back to them. Yet, at what cost?

"We'll find them." He'd sensed my thoughts were on them again. "We'll put this right."

Am I naive to believe him?

"Zara, have you thought any more about my suggestion?"

It was out of the question for me to surrender and let the blame fall on him. He'd been willing to throw himself onto his sword; at least he'd stated as much when he'd seen how torn up I was on the plane.

I'd gotten to a place where I could talk with him again. I wrapped my arms around myself. "I wish it was possible to let them go." Yet my agony was real when I thought of allowing my dad's art collection to fade into the past.

"Zara, this is more than us recovering them. This is getting justice for Burell destroying your home and inflicting pain on your father. On you. He believes he's won."

My gaze locked with his as I conveyed the silent message, *Revenge for you too, Tobias, for Burell bringing down your plane and murdering your family.*

He answered with a nod. "I want my life back too."

My stare caught the portrait of Rubens again and his eerie focus. "Is it even possible?"

"We proceed toward the life we want. The future we deserve." His hand rested on the lower arch of my spine. "Do you remember the plan?"

His plan was insanity.

This evening's event had fed his obsession with danger.

"Give me the chance to prove I can solve this." His tone had a husky allure.

Maybe he was right, maybe he could. "More smoke and mirrors?"

"If necessary."

I ran my fingers over my short bobbed wig, glad that it hid my long auburn locks making me unrecognizable.

"You make a stunning blonde." He reached up and ran a strand between his fingers. "Very convincing."

I marveled that my life had now been reduced to me wearing a disguise and joining forces with Icon.

I've lost my way.

No, not joining forces, I reassured myself. *I'm keeping watch over him and can turn this man in at any time.* He knew this, of course, I could see it in his gaze as that familiar veil of his secret life occluded him once more.

"Ready?" He gestured to the door.

We made our way out and into the grand foyer, and Tobias helped me with my long black coat. He grabbed his masquerade mask off the foyer table and we stepped out into the crisp autumn air. The sting of a November night made its way into my lungs. I glanced left and then right down Sixty-Ninth Street, orientating myself to this remarkable city.

We walked toward the blue Aston Martin parked out front and Tobias pressed his thumb to the passenger door to open it for me. I climbed in and sank into the luxury leather seat of his stylish Vanquish S. He rounded the car and got in beside me, starting the engine by using his thumb on the ignition pad. He steered the car away from the curb and into traffic.

"Whose house are we staying in?" I'd already asked him this but Wilder had avoided the question. "Tobias, who are you protecting?"

"It was my grandmother's." He didn't break his stare from the road. "The artwork will make its way to a new gallery I'm opening in the Bronx. Well, it was before all this."

"You didn't tell me you were opening a new gallery."

His shrug revealed he had the same wariness of me that I had of him.

"Your grandmother doesn't mind us staying there?"

"She died a few years ago."

"I'm sorry."

"Me too—she'd have liked you very much." He threw me a smile.

I sensed there might be a chance to enter through that chink in Wilder's armor if I let him open up naturally without me prying. I hoped he'd let me in again.

He parked a little way down from 432 Park Avenue, and the mirrored skyscraper that loomed was impossibly high. Peering up at its sheer height brought a wave of vertigo.

Tobias killed the engine. "It's certainly impressive."

Which was his way of saying we'd be taking the elevator whether I liked it or not.

We watched the decadently dressed guests arriving in their chauffeur-driven cars, then exiting and strolling toward the door. They were already masked and it infused an eeriness into the evening. The concierge greeted guests in the doorway and checked them in before they could proceed any farther.

"I've deactivated your phone's GPS." Tobias unclipped his seat belt. "It will be impossible to track."

I unclipped mine and turned to face him. "So I can't tell anyone I'm here?"

"Not yet. Look, once you're back online the FBI will track every email you send. They'll be aware of every purchase you make and your location if you use any of your credit cards. We only need a week."

What must they think of me back at Huntly Pierre, I

thought painfully and caressed my belly to ease the guilt for letting them down. Wilder's techno genius would keep the authorities busy for a while as they continued to hunt us. Our plane had taken off yesterday in LA and landed on a private airstrip off the East Coast with no record of us being on the flight or arriving in New York.

Tobias gave a thin smile. "I've got this."

The realization we were about to see Elliot Burell, patriarch of the infamous family and CEO of Burell Industries, sent a wave of terror cycling up my spine.

We had to pull this off. And then get the hell out of there. Alive, preferably.

"One step at a time, Zara." Tobias scrolled across his phone.

A quick glance and I saw he was tracking a blip on his screen. "Is Burell here?"

He dipped his head and looked out the window. "He's in the penthouse."

"And Eli?"

"He's in there too."

We'd both experienced how dangerous Burell's son was when Eli had tried to kill us both in Arizona. As I peered up at that high-rise I questioned my sanity for even considering entering that building.

"Why don't you stay in the car?" he reassured me.

"I'm ready."

"Say the word and I'll get you out of there." Tobias pried the masquerade mask from out of my hands.

"Let's get this over with."

"Okay, turn around."

He brought the mask to my face and I held it there as he secured the ribbon behind my head and then trailed his fingers down my blond bob to smooth it out. It made my scalp tingle.

I faced him again and reached out to press my hand against his chest, needing his affection. He caught my hand before it reached him and he gave it a comforting squeeze and then nudged it away. That one gesture proved he'd come to terms with us being over. It shouldn't have come as a surprise—I mean, there'd been an underlying tension since I'd boarded his plane.

Wilder provided our fake names to the concierge, who stood beside a tuxedo-wearing security guard with an earpiece. The concierge threw Tobias a big smile when she found our names on her list, though had she known he'd hacked into her system a few hours ago to add them and they weren't even real, she wouldn't be smiling at all.

We were granted access and made a beeline for the elevators at the back.

Once inside the elevator the steel doors slid closed and we ascended fast. I tried to remember how to exhale. I hated small spaces. Lifts, mostly.

"Almost there," Tobias said with an edge that anchored me.

The doors opened to a cacophony of laughter and clinking wineglasses: a sea of beautiful people within a sprawling modern penthouse with pink marble floors and walls that reflected the same gaudy decor we'd seen in the Burells' Arizona estate. The potent presence of heavy gold trimming and the Louis XIV–style ivory couches and chairs and classical ceiling murals were all seemingly designed to suffocate his adversaries with opulence.

Tobias led me into the thrall of beautiful masked men

and women who held themselves with the stature of the social elite. Their luxury perfumes and custom-made colognes drenched the air in a plume of extravagance. The ebullient mood was lifted further by the faint hypnotic music of a solo violinist, whose notes threatened to lull the unassuming.

After giving my hand a reassuring squeeze, Tobias gave me a firm glance to let me know he'd just seen Elliot Burell.

He was really here.

Drawing in a deep, steadying breath, my gaze followed Tobias's and fell upon our enemy, sending a jolt of terror into my core. Burell's sharp brown eyes peered through his black mask to survey his guests with a suspicious glare. He was taller than I imagined and even with his face partially covered with his mask I could see the hard lines of a worn and yet handsome face. His black tuxedo fit him flawlessly and I was unnerved to see such an athletic-looking man of seventy.

This masquerade mask may have concealed my expression but my eyes failed to hide my disgust.

A waiter hurried over to Burell carrying a single tumbler on a tray and offered the amber-colored liquor to him. Burell accepted the glass without even acknowledging the man's presence.

"Will you be okay?" asked Tobias. "I'm going to check our exits."

I gave a nod. There was no room for second-guessing.

We were inside the lion's den now.

Staring beyond at the magnificent panoramic view of New York and its striking array of sparkling lights on a backdrop of a black velvet night, I imagined it was beautiful when it snowed. Catching my reflection in the glass I hardly recognized myself. This disguise provided me with the confidence to watch Burell's reflection working the room with the arrogance of a man who had an empire at his feet. As expected he greeted his guests with a deadly precision.

My fingers trailed over the chain of my necklace and the single emerald glinted its reflection in the window before me. That it had once belonged to Tobias's mother brought some comfort and I allowed this moment of sentimentality.

Until a jarring thought swept in, warning this may well be the ultimate trap I'd willingly walked into.

Steadying my nerves, I stared out at the impressive architectural wonder of the Metropolitan Museum of Art. I hoped I'd get to visit there while I was here. My thoughts drifted to Tobias telling me about his gallery opening in the Bronx. There was so much good we could continue to do. So much at stake. If I left anything behind from the devastation of my life perhaps it would be what we achieved tonight. The kind of access that would bring down an evil empire.

My breath caught in my throat—panic-stricken to see the young man talking with Elliot Burell was his son, Eli. There he was arrogantly ruling the room as he surveyed the guests as harshly as his father with those piercing eyes, his haughty refined nose raised in judgment and that fop of dark hair brushing over his silver mask.

Never had I felt more vulnerable; alone in a room with two monsters.

When Eli's gaze swept my way, I froze and took a sip of wine to further conceal my face, and then breathed out a slow sigh of relief when his glare slid away.

I'd not doubted Tobias, *until this moment*.

A stark chill caused my forearms to prickle.

All I had to do was head toward the elevator and get in it and get the hell out of here, find my way to safety and a place where I could think straight and breathe in the autumn air that my constricted lungs needed. Still, the thought of leaving Tobias here sent a stab of guilt into my chest. I couldn't do it. We were too connected. I had to trust him implicitly.

Just breathe.

Centering myself, I glanced at the window again and saw Elliot Burell alone and savoring his drink while people watching. Eli was no longer beside him. I scanned the room but couldn't see him and was sure he hadn't recognized me. Observing his father's reflection, I saw Burell set down his empty glass on a side table and walk away. I spun round and headed in that direction and reached out for his tumbler. Another hand was ahead of mine and swept it away. I watched in dismay as the waiter made off with Burell's fingerprints.

Shit.

Tobias gave my shoulder a nudge and I breathed out a shaky exhale to see him again, widening my eyes toward the tumbler that was being carried on a silver tray toward the kitchen. He arched an annoyed brow at the waiter and we followed after him.

Tobias cut him off and said, "Excuse me. Will there be food?"

"Yes, sir." The waiter shifted his tray. "Hors d'oeuvres."

Tobias gave a nod of thanks as I darted my hand out to grab the glass.

I cringed that the glass had been touched by Burell's lips as I watched the waiter scurry off into the kitchen.

"Well done." Tobias sidled closer. "You okay?"

"I saw Eli."

"Did he see you?"

"I don't think he recognized me."

"I shouldn't have left you."

My gaze narrowed on him. "I don't need protecting."

"I know." He dipped his head in contradiction. "We have to make a small adjustment."

"Our exit?" I tried to read the answer from him.

"The fire escape's guarded. Our only way out is the way we came in. The main elevator."

"That's doable, right?"

"Let's hope no one notices we only arrived ten minutes ago. Ready to finish this?" He led me around to a quieter corner.

We weaved through the crowd of tuxedos and haute couture with both of us offering lazy smiles at the other guests who caught our attention. The people thinned out by the time we reached into what looked like a guest bedroom.

Carefully, Tobias took Burell's tumbler from me and carried it across the room and stepped behind the curtain. I discreetly glanced up at the ceiling to see if any cameras were trained on us and couldn't see any. Wilder was taking an extra precaution in case we were being surveyed. I stepped toward the window and peered down at the sheer drop. It reminded me how unnervingly high we were.

This was the proof I needed that Wilder was a master at his craft and I became riveted to the efficiency with which he used the thin piece of plastic tape he'd brought to slowly lift Burell's prints.

He tucked the strip into his trouser pocket. "Let's get out of here."

We hurried out the doorway and he set the glass down on a passing silver tray that was hoisted above an unassuming waiter. The young man with a crew cut carried our specimen into the kitchen to be washed. Wilder interlocked his fingers with mine and led me into the sea of people toward the elevator. I drew strength from him and secretly savored being this close to such a charismatic man that the crowd parted at his sheer presence.

I yanked on his arm when I saw our way was blocked. Eli Burell was standing before the lift doors and was casually vaping; puffs of air curled into nothing and he turned slowly to focus on us. My body stiffened at that stark memory of how Eli had a passion for hunting stag and how he liked to shoot them in the head.

He'd already tried to kill us once.

"Okay, then," Tobias whispered under his breath. "This way." He pulled me into the throng and we moved fast toward the back of the room.

It was imperative to remain calm and not look any more suspicious then we already did as we rushed into an anteroom. A few guests were talking privately and several more were huddled in close proximity on a studded leather couch. They gave us a passing glance from behind their masks.

Hanging on the far wall was a large painting by Carle van Loo of *The Victory of Alexander over Porus*, a dramatic battle scene where men and their horses had fallen victim and were overlooked by an arrogant conqueror riding his frisky white stallion. Tobias yanked my hand when I slowed to admire the portrait, which

I pined to spend more time with. This was my world, the one I'd left behind and I wanted to return to my beloved art world desperately.

Tobias gave a confident nod to a bouncer who granted us access into a glass elevator. When the doors closed on us I realized from the buttons on the panel the lift was only designed to ascend between this floor and the one above. I stared in horror at Tobias as the floating notes of a violin faded beneath us.

The doors opened to a night chill that I hardly felt. There was a vibrant throng of partygoers on the roof and Tobias and I stepped out onto a blue carpet and scanned the scene of guests who'd mostly discarded their masks. They looked like a younger version of the hors d'oeuvres–eating, champagne-drinking crowd from downstairs and were caught in a rave beat, leaping in the air in time with the bass. A DJ was lending an arty flair to the chaotic scene.

With my heart pounding, I pushed through the horde of dancers toward the entryway to the stairwell. I followed Tobias and the grip of his hand on mine verged on painful. The door burst open and an intimidating tuxedo-wearing guard appeared and spoke into a mouthpiece as he scanned the space.

The music slowed to a sultry "At Last," by Etta James, and the bouncing mass morphed into couples slow dancing. We sought refuge in the center of the throng with Tobias yanking me against his chest and twirling me in a circle. If he was panicked too, he was hiding it well, and his firm grip was the only sign we were under threat.

"Well look at that." Tobias seemed unafraid. "They're playing our song."

"Lovely."

He turned us in a tight waltz. "This is nice."

I scrunched my fingers into the fabric of his jacket and peered over his shoulder to see where that guard was. The man was staring at us.

"You okay?" Tobias looked so damn calm.

"Not exactly. They won't hurt us in front of all these people, will they?"

"I'm here, Zara."

I hoped he had the wits to talk us out of this situation because right now the hounds of hell were circling.

"It's actually a great view." He waggled his eyebrows.

"Eli looked angry."

"I owe you an apology."

I focused back on Tobias. "I insisted on coming with you."

"Didn't mean that."

"You mean the first night I met you half-naked in The Otillie?"

"I was half-dressed." He smiled. "Cute of you to remember me that way though."

"What do you think Eli's going to do?"

"Let's implement plan C."

No, there'd been no mention of what to do if we found ourselves stranded on a roof with sinister men surrounding us.

He gave my shoulder a squeeze. "You never asked what I was apologizing for."

"This is not your fault." I wanted to believe this.

"Forever the optimist, Leighton."

From this angle, I caught Eli rushing out of the glass

elevator and when he saw me he bullied his way to get to us.

Tobias stepped back. "I'm apologizing for this—"

A large blur appeared above my head and I strained my neck to see what it was, hearing excited yells from those around us who were seeing it too. An enormous drone was suspended directly above us.

"Jade," snapped Tobias, "down five feet."

"What the hell is that?" I ducked and shielded myself with my arm as it closed in.

"Open the door," he ordered.

The dancers scattered backward to allow the pod's descent toward us and the door flung open. Tobias spun me around, grabbed me, and hoisted me up into the floating aircraft and I grazed my knees on the way in as I scrambled forward on what felt like an unstable floor. Tobias gave my butt a shove and Etta's vocals enhanced this crazy commotion as everything went into slow motion.

I pulled myself up onto the seat and groaned at being trapped in this precarious floating glass bubble. The door closed behind me. "No, Jade, we have to get Tobias in." The drag of gravity rocked me off balance and I fell backward and hit my head with a loud smack on the glass dome as the pod ascended. Stunned, I was unable to exhale from the shock of speed with which I rose.

I slumped onto my knees, dazed and confused.

When I righted myself, I gawped at the harrowing view of the towering rooftop below and its view of dancers growing more distant. Vertigo shook me and nausea welled as I peered out aghast at the drop. I was going to plummet to my death. I crawled into a ball, too ter-

rified to move and not wanting to comprehend what
was happening.

This was worse than a damn elevator.

Tobias?

I braved to open my eyes and turned to stare out the
back window—

Terror surged through me and I sprang up and clawed
at the glass when I saw Tobias on the roof fighting for
his life with two men in tuxedos. One of them threw
a fierce punch to his stomach and Tobias bent double
in pain. Another blow came to his jaw knocking him
backward and he struggled to stay on his feet.

Eli was standing by watching the fray with a psychotic calmness. Tobias got away from the men but
they quickly grabbed him again and the scrap continued as they yanked off his jacket. Tobias ripped at his
own shirt like it was on fire.

Another blow to his face knocked him to the floor.

"Go back," I screamed. "Jade, go back!" Dread
caused me to freeze and I clutched my aching belly as
I watched on unable to do anything.

Drifting toward Central Park in this suffocating pod,
I cupped my hand over my mouth when I saw Tobias
clamber back onto his feet. He broke from their grip
and sprinted toward the edge of the roof with them closing in behind him and he took a running jump onto the
parapet and teetered peering down at the sheer drop.

Trapped.

He threw a quick glance toward my pod as though
confirming it was carrying me away from danger—

Wilder dived off the six-hundred-foot-high roof and
plummeted out of view.

When my constricted throat finally allowed air to pass, my scream echoed around me, and everything went black.

CHAPTER TWO

MY RAGGED BREATHS echoed within this upside-down drone that was hanging twenty feet in the air, caught in an enormous tree somewhere in Central Park. Shaking violently, I stared out at the branches holding me up. They were going to snap under the weight at some point and I was going to bloody well break something.

If I did manage by some miracle to remain suspended up here, once morning shone a glint of sun off this glass drone it would attract attention.

Oh, God... Tobias.

That dreadful memory—

As tears soaked my face I knew I'd never recover from this nightmare. I lied to myself by thinking I was shaking because of the cold and not because hell had unleashed around me.

Wait.

They'd find the fingerprints on Tobias if they looked closer at the strip of tape in his pocket and perhaps that might help point where the blame lay. Though the chance of Elliot Burell ever having had his fingerprints taken was unlikely. A sob burst from me as I tried to budge open the door with my shoulder.

If Burell or his son thought this was over, they were wrong. Their final mistake was hurting Tobias, my beautiful, sweet Wilder. All he'd done was try to make right some of the cruelest acts in history. One day the world would hear his story and come to comprehend the profoundness of his achievements.

A shudder of dread made me freeze when I squinted through the window and made out a sporty-looking motorcycle driving along the pathway toward me. It stopped directly before the tree line and a tall man wearing a silver helmet and black leathers extended the kickstand and looked in my direction.

He made his way down the bank toward my tree. I held my breath as though such madness would make me invisible. Crooking his neck upward, he peered through his black visor and folded his arms across his chest as though contemplating how I'd gotten up here in the first place. And probably wondered what kind of contraption I was in.

My heart raced as I considered what I was going to say. What did you say when caught in one of these? I had a vision of me running off and leaving my hell box behind me.

He removed his helmet—

I sucked in a deep breath and yelled, "You're out of your fucking mind!"

"I gave you one job, Leighton."

"I thought you were…" I couldn't say it.

"Clearly, I'm not."

I half hoped this pod would land on the bastard's head; *oh, the irony.* "Get me out."

He arched a seductive brow. "If you promise to behave."

"Wilder!"

"Jade," he ordered. "Out of the tree." He took a few

steps back and arched an amused brow as he waved the drone down.

Seriously? It was this easy?

I knelt so not to hit my head again as the pod shuddered and then lifted away from the branches and ascended with a rocky start. It landed with a thump and I tipped forward as it settled, my palms splayed on the glass for balance.

The door sprung open.

I ducked my head and climbed out as gracefully as possible. My high heels sunk into the soil but I didn't care about ruining these Louboutins. I was too focused on breathing in a deep sigh of relief. Tobias offered me his hand and I waved it off.

"You have to admit that was fun." He smirked.

I leaped toward him and struck his chest with my fists, forcing him backward against a tree trunk, my heart soaring in confusion. I scrunched his hair to bring his mouth to mine, biting his bottom lip in anger and kissing him fiercely in retaliation, punishingly so, and he reciprocated by bringing a hand up to capture the back of my neck to hold me to him. His scratchy three-day beard brushed my cheeks and it felt annoyingly arousing and sparked a delicious throbbing between my thighs. My fingers released his hair and trailed down to his shoulders, and the erotic tension rose further with the sound of rippling leather and kissing and my gruff annoyance. I'd wanted to be this close again more than air itself, this connected, to be his again—

I broke away and slapped him.

On unsteady heels I wobbled and my back hit the tree behind me. He came at me fast and pinned me between the trunk and his rock-hard body, crushing his chest to mine as he continued to devour my mouth with an unmatched passion.

I struggled to shove him away but he didn't budge. "You were wearing a parachute?" And then I realized it was why he'd stopped me from touching his chest in the car. "I hate you." I fisted my fingers to grab his hair and pulled him in for a kiss.

He thrust his pelvis against mine, sending a pang of arousal into me. "Leighton, I told you we're going to have to be smarter," he said darkly, "faster, more inventive then we've ever been."

"You should have told me."

"I didn't actually think I'd be parachuting off a high-rise tonight. I prefer elevators." He tilted his head as though to say, *Unlike you.*

"Can you imagine what it was like to watch you fall?"

"Did you really believe I'd leave you like that? I waited until you were safely out of harm's way. I made every concession to protect you."

"You're reckless."

"You have a wild imagination, Zara."

"Have you not read Shakespeare? This kind of stuff goes bad fast."

"I can see why Romeo drank the poison."

I pointed to the drone. "I could have been trapped in that thing forever."

"If only we were that lucky." He shrugged off his leather jacket, revealing a black polo sweater and jeans he now wore.

His change of clothes and that motorbike meant he'd planned for this.

Stepping forward, he wrapped his jacket around my

shoulders. "Did you even think about talking to Jade? I returned your access."

"I screamed at her to take me back to you."

"Well, she's not going to stray from her objective, now is she?"

I closed my eyes in frustration.

"That's going to hurt her feelings."

"Tobias." I shoved him. "You will never kiss me again. Do you understand?" I sucked in a sharp breath and stormed away, climbing the grassy bank unsteadily on pointed heels.

"Technically, you kissed me," he called out and turned to the drone. "You're good to go, Jade."

Jade's door closed and she rose off the ground and headed into the park.

It grew chilly as I waited for Tobias beside his bike. "I'm not getting on this thing."

"It's a Harley. And yes, you are." He came closer and grabbed the bottom of his jacket I was wearing and zipped it up to seal me inside.

An annoying whiff of heady cologne wafted up from his jacket, and I stomped my foot in rebellion to the way it made my sex throb for him.

Tobias lifted the bike's backseat and brought out a red helmet and handed it to me. He fiddled with my collar to make sure I was snug. "Are you going to play nice?"

I raised my chin. "I've never been on a bike before."

"I'm sure you've never flown over Manhattan before, either." He shoved his own helmet over his head and slapped the back of the bike for me to climb on.

I folded my arms across my chest, refusing.

Tobias took the spare helmet back from me and eased

it over my head and fastened my chin strap. He brought the visor down and curled his knuckles to tap on it playfully as though checking I was still in there.

He raised his visor. "Move with me. Don't try to get off when it's moving. Those are the basics. Got it?"

I turned my back on the bike.

"Or you can walk." He snapped his visor down and climbed on, looking ridiculously hot and masterful as he gripped the handlebars and revved the throttle, roaring the bike to life and hinting he was about to leave without me.

I huffed my disapproval even though it was pointless and lifted the hem of my dress as I climbed on and snuggled up close to his warm body, wrapping my arms around his waist and pressing my chest to his back with my thighs squeezed against his. He flinched and reached for my hands to bring them up higher, reminding me of his fight on the rooftop, and it sent a pang of guilt through me for arguing after he'd fought for his life.

And saved mine.

Still, this entire spectacle was even more outrageous than the one we'd planned, and I felt let down he'd kept me in the dark. The shock of watching him fall lingered, and I hugged him tighter—as though needing convincing he was okay.

Wilder kicked off the stand and we zoomed off to race across the park. I was grateful for the jacket. We were shielded by the beautiful trees on either side with their leaves scattered around them in a vision of autumn wonder, and I quietly cursed him for another exhilarating experience as we sped along.

This was just it; the uncertainty of every moment

was what terrified me. I'd dedicated my life to finding a certain safety within museums and galleries where all the danger, all the heartbreak, all the pain, was vicariously lived through the characters in those breathtaking paintings by masters long dead.

I'd been destined to remain in a cozy office while perusing the contents of manila files to assess a painting's provenance. Any doubt of its veracity could be settled by nestling in a serene corner of The Courtauld and conducting a series of scientific tests. There, issue solved. Matter dealt with and no safety net required. No "zooming around New York streets on the back of a crazy bike" was in my job description. My grip was so tight around Wilder's waist I'd be amazed if he could still breathe, and my thighs clung to his.

Tobias took a sharp turn and I squeezed my eyes shut as we weaved through heavy traffic where cars and cabs vied for space. Even with this helmet on I could hear the cacophony of the city's buzz. The horns of frustrated drivers and their inevitable squealing breaks, the thrum of people, music and undefined sounds merging to beat as one.

When we drove into the subterranean garage beneath the Manhattan mansion there came mixed feelings. I was glad to be getting off the bike but sad to break away from him. After removing my helmet and hugging it to my chest, I hurried toward the entry into the house and waited for him to unlock the door.

I wasn't ready to look at him.

I'd sworn off any romance between us on the flight here on his private jet, and yet back in Central Park I'd kissed him passionately and my lips weren't letting me forget it. They tingled with the lingering sensation of his fierce mouth on mine and his three-day scruff having deliciously scratched my cheeks until they'd flushed with happiness. He'd alighted my passion all over again, and I needed time to suppress these feelings.

Or I could just surrender this one time and soothe this ache, this desperate need to be taken. All I had to do was make my way to his bedroom and snuggle beneath the covers and wait for him to join me. We'd be together again and gloriously forgetting the pain we'd brought each other.

No, this wasn't happening. The truth of who he was ruined me with the potency of an unending nightmare. Icon, the world's most sophisticated art thief, had brilliantly shown off his impressive set of skills and terrified me—

Tobias thrived on this exhilaration, I could see it in his eyes after that daredevil stunt he'd just pulled off. A woman like me who lived a careful life, one who savored the sanctity of galleries and museums, would never be enough for a man like him. Not after this overdose of terror had left me dizzy and disorientated.

I placed my helmet on the foyer table and ripped off my blond wig and threw it next to it. My auburn locks tumbled over my shoulders as I made my way into the drawing room. Shaking from the cold, I neared the fireplace and held up my palms to draw the warmth from the fading fire. I made a mental note to chastise him later for having a hearth burning near these wonderful paintings.

I pined for the life I'd lost, for the illusion of love that had been fleeting. I ached to return to London where I could do all those things I'd taken for granted.

Staying in this house put off the inevitable. We were

going to get caught and dragged into a humiliating ordeal in a courtroom where our private lives would become public knowledge.

The door creaked open but I refused to even look his way.

There was a blur of movement as it swung farther out. I sucked in a breath of surprise at the brown teddy bear with cute ears sticking up that was taking short steps toward me. I let out a burst of laughter at the creature's sweetness. He was all pert ears, big brown eyes and cuddly belly; an adorable hologram convincingly real.

Tobias had rigged this room to create this. I should be angry but I was too damn tired. Too shaken.

Tobias came in and stared down at the bear. "There you are, Beasley."

I gave a thin smile and my heart ached that we couldn't be this—him inventing cute critters and me enjoying them with no complications between us.

Tobias came over. "Are you okay?"

"No," I said even as I slid into a forced smile at the way Beasley had stopped at my feet and was staring up with those big soulful eyes. The illusion would be broken if I knelt and swept my hand to expose this holographic bear.

"Want to talk?" Tobias glanced down at Beasley.

"I'm…" I was feeling lost but didn't want to let him see my vulnerability.

"Listen, about tonight—"

"You scared the hell out of me."

He let out a sigh of frustration. "I've been doing this a lot longer."

"I know."

"I shouldn't have taken you with me."

"I'm trying to take back some control here, Tobias. It's what I need."

"I respect you feel this way." He mulled over it. "If anything happens to you—"

"I want in to your world. No more secrets."

"We must agree on one principle."

"Which is?"

"You don't take any unnecessary risks."

My back stiffened. "Risks?"

"You trust me completely."

"Give me full access to control Jade." If he was going to ever utilize his drone or his artificial-intelligence system again, I wanted in on my ability to use her.

"Zara, you've had access since you stepped inside this place."

I considered his willingness to open up and hoped it would last.

"We got Burell's fingerprints," he added cheerfully. "Mission accomplished."

"It better be worth it."

"I'll use them to hack his computer."

"Start talking."

"I believe your paintings are in New York."

"That's why you had your jet bring us here?"

"Yes."

"Where?"

He hesitated and his gaze swept over the portraits. "I don't know yet."

A wave of frustration saturated my senses. "Burell knows we're here now."

"We need to stay one step ahead of him—"

"Did they see your parachute?"

He shrugged. "They can't track us but I can them."

"Care to elaborate?"

"I have a mechanism that allows me to track their movements—"

"Where is it?"

Tobias gave a nod of reluctance. "Go on, Beasley. Lead the way."

Beasley's little legs carried him over the Persian rug toward the far wall and he stared up at the life-size panel of Henry the III of France. An innocuous 1570 portrait of the young king by artist François Clouet. The artist captured the image of a young man with a black cap and feather curling to the right and a high ruffled collar, his majesty's insightful expression fused with his suspicious gaze carrying the weight of retrospect.

Beasley disappeared as he walked into the wall and my attention rose to the painting. Henry had been mistaken for his younger brother Francis of Alençon in the past—though on further inspection the inscription on the back of the paintings usually rectified this. I knew the positioning of such a canvas in here was no coincidence.

"Welcome to my man cave." Tobias strolled over and tapped the corner of King Henry's frame and it popped away from the wall. His fingers folded around the edge and he pulled it the rest of the way to reveal a doorway. "No more secrets."

I walked forward and peered through at the dimly lit hallway; this secrecy reminded me of the last few weeks where our interactions had unfolded like a wild affair played out in an elaborate game. He was clearly analyzing my reaction to what he was showing me. With him there were always layers of truths and it made me wonder if I'd ever get to the center of his authentic self. Perhaps I was destined to peel away and never actually find *him*. The way his stare assessed mine reminded me of his analytical nature and his brilliant mind that was always one step ahead.

A trap within a trap?

Two enemies were fighting it out with me caught in the middle like a shuttlecock, because I was the true owner of one of the greatest collections of art. My worth was my provenance stashed away in London and there was a treasure trove of paperwork to prove the authentication of those priceless pieces. I'd placed those papers in a safety-deposit box before leaving for Los Angeles. When those papers were handed over to Tobias what would my worth be then?

"If this is going to work—" his fingers curled around the frame "—there can be no more secrets between us." He let the quiet settle. "We need to prove our allegiance to each other."

"I'm still here, aren't I?"

"I feel you pulling away—"

"What do you want?" My words were razor sharp.

"Tell me they haven't stolen you from me, as well?" He reached up to cup my face with his palm and I closed my eyes as a part of me craved for his touch to linger.

He'd suffered terribly too and maybe he wasn't showing me how all this was affecting him so he could be strong for me. Still, he was Icon and my greatest weakness. I couldn't get those paintings back without him. He was the only one with the resources, the technology and the seeming death wish, willing to see through the maze between me and getting them back. These masterpieces deserved to be appreciated and adored and they belonged to the people.

They belonged to my father's memory.

Yet the sacrifice to get them back was asking so very much of us.

His thumb brushed over my bottom lip as though getting my attention back on him, and I let out a soft sigh of appeasement and his pupils dilated and his jaw tensed. I could see the fire alighting in his eyes as the rawest passion sparked between us. This danger stirred my intuition, warning that beyond this clandestine hallway lurked an endless array of Icon's possessions I wasn't ready to be shown.

Pivoting away from him, moving swiftly across the room toward the door as this dread of the unknown took hold. His footfalls hurried behind me but I kept going, unsteady on high heels that were leading me toward the fresh air I needed even if the sting of the cold night was inevitable.

Tobias intercepted me and I ran right into his chest. His back slammed against the front door he was guarding. He reached up and gripped my shoulders.

"Let go."

He freed me and his arms rose in surrender. "You want into my world but you won't even let me into your thoughts." He narrowed his gaze. "Talk to me."

"I'm leaving."

"They'll find you."

This was the cruelest truth of all because just weeks ago it would have been Tobias I'd have run to when my heart fractured into a thousand pieces, and yet there came the haunting sense he could be tricking me and his end game was still to be realized. Wisps of my naivety remained and yet I'd seen too much. The veil had lifted and I'd glimpsed a formidable facet of Wilder, the side of him that knowingly broke the law and yet did it for all the right reasons.

Or had I merely believed what I'd wanted to see?

Even as his lips brushed over my shoulder blade and followed the curve of my throat I yearned to feel how I once did when he'd soothed me with his affection.

Fighting this, fighting me, I needed him to remember my insistence back in Central Park that he never kiss me again. If his mouth met mine he'd persuade me to stay. Once, back when my life was simpler, I'd believed in our dazzling passion and had fallen for the promise that being love-struck equaled being safe.

"Zara, where are you?" Tobias's gaze deepened as he tried to penetrate my thoughts.

They were still mine, at least.

There came a rush of exhilaration when he yanked me forward and lifted me into his arms and carried me up the staircase and along the hallway. He kicked a door open and carried me in and lay me on the large bed. Grabbing the heavy duvet beneath me, I rolled over and scrambled across it but his strong hands wrapped around my ankles and dragged me back toward him.

I stilled and watched him because some part of me needed this intimacy to nudge out of the loneliness. Wilder kept his intense stare locked on me as he worked his way down his shirt, unbuttoning it and then peeling it off to reveal a ripped torso. There were a few emerging bruises on his rib cage, marking his fight on the skyscraper and relighting my sympathy. He kept his trousers and shoes on, maybe to reassure me he wasn't going to do anything more.

What I needed was to start over to the time before him and not allow myself to fall for this dazzling, dynamic man who stunned with his heart-stopping commanding presence. The bed dipped when he climbed on and he loomed over me and grabbed my wrists and raised them to pin them over my head and onto the mattress.

"Tobias?" I whispered.

"I won't kiss you." His gaze slid to my mouth in contradiction. "I promise."

Specs of gold glistened in his irises and I could see beyond the safeguard of his reckless beauty as I saw a flash of vulnerability that I'd never seen before. This was him letting me in and I clung to the hope this was real and something I could hold on to.

He looked sincere. "Zara, I have to think one step ahead because you're more important than any painting. This is me protecting you."

His kiss would be lethal if I let it happen and I turned my head away, grasping at these remnants of restraint not to fall.

"Lift your dress." He let go of my wrists.

This wasn't going to happen, *no*. I wasn't going to scrunch my satin skirt like I was doing now and hitch it up over my hips as though his words alone could elicit a Svengali response. Yet my fingers hooked beneath my panties and eased them down my hips and then I raised them slightly until my underwear was down my thighs, and calves, and then off my body. I hugged my panties to my chest, too awed by his devastating presence to think straight.

"Higher."

I dragged my teeth over my bottom lip, trying to anchor to this moment by distracting myself and not losing myself in him—my hands lifted my dress higher for him.

Wilder positioned himself between my thighs and with his eyes locked on mine he said huskily, "You didn't say anything about kissing you here."

The shake of my head in agreement was my consent and I reached for his left bicep and ran my hand over his ornate tattoo in admiration of its artistry—

I eased my thighs apart.

He dipped his head until his hair tickled my inner thighs and he moved my hands away and kissed my sex, and then his tongue ran along and he captured my clit with his mouth, thrumming me with the proficiency I'd become addicted to. My arousal intensified, rising higher, and my body writhed with the rhythm of his tongue, the shuddering revealing how spellbound I'd became as he possessed me with blinding pleasure. My moan echoed as he gripped my wrists and held them to my sides as he continued to ravage me, propelling me into the center of bliss until I forgot how to breathe.

Everything that mattered was focused in my core like an erotic spell cast to destroy me.

Yes, destroy me.

"I want you inside me," I pleaded.

"If I fuck you, I'll have to kiss you and that will mean I've broken my promise." Tobias climbed off the bed and it dipped as he stepped away.

I rolled onto my side and brought up my legs and hugged myself, too consumed with these emotions that ensnared me and left me starving for him. This wouldn't do. This infatuation was going to destroy me.

"Zara?" his voice beckoned.

I squeezed my eyes shut, needing a moment to catch my breath.

"Come with me downstairs and let me make you some food," he offered as he pulled his shirt back on and buttoned it.

"I'm not hungry."

His fingers brushed strands of hair out of my eyes. "I can make you tea."

"It's too late for caffeine."

"I want to show you the house. Give you the grand tour."

"There's no need because I'm not staying."

"Zara," he soothed as he played with a lock of my hair. "You don't want to see my grandmother's Bellini collection?"

I peeked out from my palms covering my face and my chest prickled with intrigue. "Giovanni Bellini?"

He gave a gentle smile. "Yes."

"Here?"

"I want to show it to you." He headed into the wardrobe and came back out with a chenille sweater. "This place gets cold at night."

I pushed myself up and dangled my legs over the bed and raised my arms and let him pull it over me. I shivered into the warmth of the softness that fit perfectly over my dress. "Whose is this?" I helped tug it down.

"Yours. I had clothes sent here for both of us."

I swallowed past the uneasiness of this revelation. Still, he was luring me with the promise of Bellini and the thought of it made my body quiver. *No, silly*, I reasoned, it was the way he'd just kissed me—where he'd kissed me—that was tingling deliciously even now.

He reached out and took my hand and led me along

the hallway and around the corner, and I felt petite beside him and a little calmer from the way he'd lulled me.

He paused before a beautifully carved oak door. "This was my grandma's room."

"Were you close?"

Tobias looked thoughtful. "I spent a few winters here. Edward, my second cousin, and I would play together." He stared off. "So many memories."

"Good ones?"

"Really good." But he frowned as though something had disrupted his train of thought.

"Where is your cousin now?"

"Not sure. Probably off hiking in Kathmandu or scuba diving in Bali. Edward's a marine biologist. He's always off on one adventure or another."

"When was the last time you saw him?"

He mulled over this. "Ten years, I think."

"You must contact him. You need to see him again."

"Yes, I should. When all this is over perhaps."

"Why did you lose touch?"

"It was my fault. I became obsessed with my work…"

My heart ached for him as I realized his heroic deeds had distanced him from his family.

I reached for the handle. "Can I go in?"

He seemed to rise from a daydream as he opened the door for me. "Of course."

This beautiful bedroom had been respectfully preserved with a large four-poster bed in the center and hardwood floors over which a red Persian rug was strewn. To the left sat a white antique vanity with an oval mirror that had slightly faded and a high-backed chair positioned before it. My gaze swept the walls that were adorned with Italian Renaissance artist Giovanni

Bellini's paintings. There were so many of them and they all hung unevenly. Yet it gave the room an unpretentious feel and revealed the classic taste of a woman who'd once lived here.

My gaze settled on a portrait of a young man in a simple frame, and the sitter's long fair hair and his garb indicated he was most likely a senator who'd commissioned the portrait to add a touch of status to his profession. I continued to wander and admire Bellini's exquisite paintings. Most of them were religious themed and reflected how he'd revolutionized Venetian painting with rich colors and sumptuous settings and a technique for realism that had even inspired Titian.

I let out a sigh of happiness, as though Bellini himself had reached out and soothed me with his authenticity.

"Feel better?" Tobias asked.

"Yes, much. Thank you."

His kindness felt like a lifeline and I loved seeing his gentle side when he let down his guard. He looked around the room and breathed out a sigh of wonder, hinting he was tempering his emotions. I sensed he'd been close to his grandmother.

"What a beautiful room."

"My casa is your casa." He sat on the edge of the bed and watched me walk around. "Let me know if you need anything."

"You own this house now?"

"Yes, she left Edward a manor on Bodmin Moor."

"Cornwall? That's wonderful. Though a little isolated."

"Yes, he should have gotten this place and me the manor. Still, who's complaining, right?"

"If you lived in Bodmin you'd be isolated."

He held my stare. "I know."

"You'd be lonely?"

"I'm well acquainted with…" He waved off that thought. "The quiet helps me to think."

Which was something he probably told himself to bear the agony of it.

I stepped forward and took his hands in mine and squeezed them, and he gave a nod to show his appreciation.

"Your grandmother was very generous."

Tobias brought my hand to his lips and kissed my wrist. "She was everything that was good in this world. She would have loved you."

"Which side of the family?"

"Mom's."

"Was she religious?"

He glanced at the artwork. "How did you guess?"

"You were close?"

"She was like a second mom to me." He broke my gaze. "Grandma Rose used to take us to the Metropolitan Museum whenever I visited."

"How wonderful."

He swallowed hard. "After the plane crash my uncle decided to hide me away. He wanted to protect me and I suppose he was trying to protect other members of my family, as well."

"So you were separated from everyone? Even your grandmother?"

"Fabienne thought it was best."

"You missed her?"

"Every time I saw Edward I was reminded of her. Reminded of what was stolen from me..." Tobias's eyelids flickered as though only now realizing this was why he'd willingly lost touch with him. "It was easier to pretend I had no family. For a long time that's how it was for me."

"How do you feel about being back here?"

"I wish she was here. There's so much that was unsaid."

"Are you okay to stay?"

"Yes, with you this place feels different." He leaned toward me and his lips came close, and then he pulled away as he seemed to remember. "Want to see the library?"

"I'd love to."

We made our way out and down the central staircase, through the foyer and along a hallway with remarkably well-preserved Art Deco wallpaper.

"What's down there?" I pointed.

"The old staff quarters." He followed my gaze. "I took those rooms because it's quieter."

"I'm pretty quiet."

"I meant—"

"More isolated?"

"There's a gym and I wanted you to feel comfortable to have the rest of the house."

"What about your bedroom?"

"I want you to have it."

Another wave of nervousness came over me as I took in this foreign place, wondering how I'd gotten here.

He frowned. "Do you regret coming here with me?"

"It was all very fast." I mean, we'd lifted off the roof

of The Wilder Museum in his helicopter and caught his jet right after. There'd been no time to discuss the plan or consider the fallout of leaving so abruptly. "You know the FBI suspects me too."

"They know you're a wrong fit for the MO. You were studying at The Courtauld Institute of Art and a quick cross-reference would prove you were probably attending a lecture or some other event when those other heists went down. They scared you to get to Icon."

"It worked."

His back stiffened. "We're one step ahead of them."

I turned to face him wary of what might come next because if there was one thing I knew it was some people kept their enemies close.

"Hopefully you'll be able to catch your breath here. Time can stand still in this place. Much of the decor is original. I want to keep it this way. Although I made a few adjustments to bring it into the twenty-first century."

Behind that door offered another glimpse into Tobias's past.

"Libraries have a way of beckoning," he said. "Lead the way."

The room was curved and all four walls were stacked with books upon mahogany shelves and the lighting was too soft for reading because several bulbs had gone out. In the corner was a burgundy chaise lounge and I wondered if his grandmother had liked to sit there and read.

"I'd bring my toys in here," he admitted, and his face brightened as though remembering.

"With your cousin?"

He gave a nod and pulled down a small book from a shelf and handed it to me.

"Winnie-the-Pooh?" I beamed at him. "You read this?"

"Yes, but we had to be very careful because it's signed by the author."

In amazement I read the inscription by A. A. Milne, who'd also been a playwright before writing his famous children's books. "This is adorable."

"See, my childhood wasn't all bad."

I smiled, appreciating him wanting to soften his past.

"I'll swap out the bulbs for you," he said. "I don't tend to come in here."

"Tobias, I have to call Abby." I hadn't mentioned her until now but we'd settled here a little and I hoped he'd let me call her. He had my phone somewhere, and so far I'd not come across a landline. I couldn't bear to think of my colleagues back at Huntly Pierre believing I'd abandoned them with no thought of the consequences.

He closed the book and slid it back. "Not yet."

"When, then?"

"Do you want to see the rest of the house?"

"Not right now."

"You're right. It's been a long day." He headed for the door and opened it for me. "I'll walk you to your room."

"How long will we be here?"

"I'm not sure."

"I can find my own way back. I'd like to stay in here awhile."

He gave a nod and turned to go before hesitating in the doorway. "I've got this, Zara. I've got you." He turned to face me as though needing to see I believed him.

After managing a nod, I watched him leave.

I felt like running away from LA was the worst mistake of my life. This dread of having let everyone down clung to my chest like deadwood. Returning my gaze to the row of children's books I knew this house would reveal even more secrets of who Tobias was and maybe I'd get to discover them if I was brave enough to stay.

CHAPTER THREE

I HADN'T SEEN Tobias since he'd left me alone in the library.

I'd dreamed all night long and woken up with the East Coast sun glaring between the blinds to jolt me back to the reality of the mess my life was in. This was not how I was meant to be starting a Thursday morning. *No*, I was meant to be getting ready for work and heading in for a job I loved.

Barefoot and wearing one of Wilder's T-shirts and nothing else, I padded downstairs to the front door and tried the handle. It wouldn't give and there was no key. At the back of the house the door appeared impressively modern with no lock which meant there'd be no access to the large garden that I could see through the window.

Trust had always been an issue for me.

I'd told myself it was first broken when my boyfriend Zach ran off with Natalia Donate, but when I dared to peer back further the truth was more painful. It was probably that car crash that took my mom from me that planted a seed for a life of fear. Even though I was too young to remember being strapped in the car seat at the time of her careening off when a drunk driver hit her.

Holding on, holding back, was the only way I knew how to survive.

I made my way back upstairs.

The hot shower warmed my bones and I reassured myself that this and a nice cup of tea would make me feel a little better. Heading out of the bathroom en suite, I stopped in the doorway to see the wardrobe was open. Inside I found a row of brand-new clothes hanging with their labels still on. In a corner were neatly staged female shoes of every kind from heels to sportswear. On the central aisle were more boxes and these were embossed on the top with Saks Fifth Avenue. When I explored them, I found new underwear. I was pleasantly surprised and a little unnerved to find everything was in my size. Either Tobias had gone out shopping or more likely he had someone working for him. I wondered if whoever they were knew we were here.

I put on the pretty lace underwear and after a few minutes had dressed in the Levi's jeans and Ralph Lauren sweater to tame the chill of this big house. I chose a pair of navy blue pumps that were comfy.

A hunch told me Tobias was in his man cave. I headed downstairs for the drawing room with the Persian rug and the panel of King Henry the III of France. With a tap the corner frame snapped away from the wall and I eased it the rest of the way.

There was a steel door at the end of the hallway and I remembered our conversation last night about him returning my access to his AI system.

"Jade, open the door." My command sounded calmer than I felt.

The door behind me slammed shut.

There came a hissing noise like pressure being released and the chrome door before me opened. I exhaled a shaky breath of wariness and peered down at a long metal ramp leading off into the dimness. The passionate voice of a tenor singing opera carried and I recognized Luciano Pavarotti's powerful "Nessun Dorma." This space went deep underground and from the street level I'd never have imagined this existed. I guessed that was the point for a secret man cave.

And what a cave it was—

At the end of the ramp I stared in awe at the enormous NASA-styled workshop packed with see-through monitors and high-concept technology devices like the glass screens with what looked like calculations written on them. Chrome benches were stacked with electronic gadgets, and strewn here and there were discarded fine tools hinting he was in the middle of making something or fixing it. This ultimate tech cave contradicted the old-world feel of the mansion above that was all classic decor and homey elegance.

Over Pavarotti's voice came a strange noise and I followed it, strolling in between the benches and glancing here and there to get a feel for what he was doing down here. This had to be where he spent his time inventing for his company TechRule. A wave of melancholy hit me when I imagined he might have to give it up if he ever got caught for his past sins.

Halfway down a hallway I paused to peer in at a room with a central console positioned to face five large flat screens secured to the wall. They were flashing a series of maps taken from a satellite. I recognized the aerial view of New York rotating through live images. I wondered if he had a similar one set up in LA.

Continuing down I found Wilder.

His face was covered by a long mask and he was directing a welding torch at the base of a large drone hanging five feet in the air, and it was the same one that had carried me off to Central Park last night.

Fine sparks glittered at the point where his torch met the base. The drone was suspended midair with wires strategically wrapped to hang it from the ceiling, allowing access on all sides. Other than Tobias's black jeans, he was bare chested and barefoot. His forearms were covered in long suede gloves smudged with grime and his well-toned torso was spotted in perspiration and ridiculously well-defined. His left shoulder tattoo shimmered beneath the soft yellow light and his pants were low enough to provide a glimpse of the inked Latin inscription trailing off beneath his belt. Those bruises on his torso were even more defined now.

"Hey," I called out.

The torch shut off and Tobias raised his visor. "Music down, Jade." He dragged his forearm along his brow to wipe the perspiration. "How'd you sleep?"

"I'm locked in?"

He set his torch on the table behind him.

"You've rigged this place so I can't get out."

"We have everything we need." He pulled his gloves off and threw them aside.

"Seriously?"

Tobias pulled his mask all the way off and placed it next to the torch. "Our security is designed to keep people out. The kind we don't want entering while we sleep. And while I'm down here I can't watch over you." He smiled to reassure me.

"I can leave?"

"Why would you?"

When I showed uncertainty it triggered something protective in him and he got amorous. The last thing I needed was his mouth on me. Seeing him half-naked and annoyingly competent with his power tool was stirring an inconvenient arousal.

I wanted to kiss him hard. "Let's talk about boundaries."

"Sure."

I became aware of my erect nipples betraying me through the sweater and folded my arms across my chest. "It's cold down here." I threw in a shiver.

His gaze slid to my shoes. "How does everything fit?"

"They'll do."

His frown deepened. "Boundaries?"

"Yes."

"You have full access to this place. You have full access to me." He followed that by a seductive arch of his brow.

"Tell me last night wasn't a waste of time."

"In what respect?"

"Have you had time to use Burell's fingerprints to hack his computer?" My voice strained as I added, "Did you find out where my paintings are?"

"*Yes* on the hacking and *no* to finding your paintings. I'm sorry. We have time."

I exhaled slowly. "So this is where you create your things?"

"For my East Coast shenanigans, yes." He broke into a cute smile but it faded when he looked over at the drone. "She tipped yesterday. I'm fixing her so she doesn't do it again."

"Great." Though my brain was actually screaming, *I'm never getting in her again so you're wasting your time!*

He moved closer to the drone and rested his palm on her side. "She did her job at least."

She reminded me of my terror-stricken departure off that high-rise and to be honest I'd be happy to never see her again.

He brushed his palm over her glass door. "I'm running an analysis on the footage she shot. Using face recognition from the images, I should have the names of Burell's men and their profiles by the end of the day."

Wilder was more than a renaissance man, he was a remarkable inventor and yet showed none of the traits of socially awkward geniuses. He looked just as comfortable down here with his toys as he did out in the world. I could see how he'd been influenced by those hours he'd spent alone in the outback when his plane had crashed in Australia and afterward when he'd been hidden away by his uncle to protect him. This seemed like the reason he came over as so controlling; he was probably trying to manage his universe to limit his vulnerability to pain. I wondered if he was aware of the reason for this trait. His thoughtful frown returned as he broke my gaze to peer up at his drone.

I sighed in frustration. "Time for that talk."

"Shall we talk over breakfast?" He gestured to his grubby jeans. "I'll take a shower."

"I can handle breakfast."

"That would be wonderful, thank you." He walked past me with his head down and his mind seemingly on something else.

We weaved our way around the long chrome workbenches.

I spotted his small drone sitting on what looked like a charging station. "How did you get Jade here?"

"Different drone. Same AI." He looked over at her with affection. "She takes seventy-two hours to charge."

"You have the same AI running through all your gadgets?"

"Yes, same consciousness."

"Consciousness?"

"You'll need top-level access before I share any more." He flashed a heart-stopping smile and continued along between the workbenches. "I have a few ideas that might set you up for such a privilege."

I rolled my eyes behind his back.

He faced me again. "So what do you think?"

"It's all very snazzy down here. How often do you visit New York?"

"Once every few months. Though with the new gallery opening I've visited more frequently."

I wondered if any of those visits had included Icon reconnaissance missions. "What are you working on?"

He led me to a glass wall and pointed to his calculations. "So with the success of the air keyboard, I'm working on a drop-down computer screen. It will be projected by voice command. Though that's top secret right now."

"Why would you need one of those?"

"Well, for hospitals it would cut down on cross-infection. No hardware means nowhere for bacteria to grow. It's more for abroad where the mortality rates are higher."

"That's incredible." I was honored to have been let in on his secret project. "How long are you from finishing it?"

"Three years, maybe."

"Wow."

"I'm glad you're here to see it at the beginning stage. Right now it's just an idea—" He pointed to what looked like a continuous line of algebra on a transparent panel.

"How many people have been in here?"

"No one else." He looked coy but quickly broke his gaze and turned to face the indecipherable calculations written on the glass.

I picked up a silver square cube and it fit snugly in my hands. "What's this?"

Tobias reached out and took it from me. "Careful."

"What is it?"

He cupped it in his hands. "A deflector. I don't want it emitting in here."

I feigned disinterest. "How do I open the front door?"

"Why would you want to?" He threw the cube in the air and it spun and he caught it on the way down.

Seriously? I folded my arms. "What if I need to get some fresh air or something?"

"Something?"

"How do I override the system?"

"What brought this on?"

"Tobias." I bit the inside of my cheek. "Am I allowed out?"

"Of course." He ambled up the ramp and secured the large chrome door behind us. Once through the short hallway he opened the door at the other end that led us into the drawing room.

I hurried forward and snatched the gadget out of his hand.

He looked surprised. "There are paintings in here. You're holding mayhem. One wrong move…"

"Probably no worse than exposing your art to an

open fireplace." I raised my chin proudly. "Tell me the plan, Wilder."

He let out an exasperated breath. "We get Burell to lead us to your paintings and then we steal them back."

"How?"

"That you won't like."

"What about Huntly Pierre?"

"My team sent an email to your boss stating I've hired you. That will keep Huntly Pierre at bay for a while."

"I imagine there's an email waiting for me stating I've been fired already."

"The commission I'll pay for your services will appease Adley. Your boss is perfectly reasonable."

"And the FBI?"

"They have nothing on me. Or you."

"They have a photo of me taken in Arizona." I pointed to him. "And you fit the MO for Icon."

"So does every other businessman with a private jet and a penchant for art. I have a museum. They're going to have to do better than that."

"How do we get Elliot Burell to lead us to my paintings?"

"We use an ingenious decoy. One he'd never suspect. We set up a private auction for a masterpiece and tip off Burell of its existence. He'll insist he bids first. No doubt bully his way in. He won't know there is no one else bidding."

"On what?"

"A priceless piece he's coveted for decades."

"Surely you're not comfortable giving him any one of your paintings from The Wilder?"

Tobias gave a forced smile and headed for the door.

I followed him into the foyer. "Not *Madame Paul Duchesne-Fournet*, right? Because she's on loan from LACMA?"

His words that I wouldn't like it fired up my intrigue and threatened to send me reeling.

Tobias spun around to face me. "Burell is willing to do anything to own this elusive piece. The same one he's spent millions searching for."

"What if we lose it in the process?"

"It will have a GPS inserted inside the canvas, so if it gets separated from the frame we're still able to follow where it goes."

"Won't that compromise the canvas?"

"Let go of your preconceived ideas, Zara." He walked off. "This is war."

Hurrying after him into the opulent formal dining room I felt my panic rising.

This was a quaint Victorian parlor with rosewood cabinets and ornate upholstered chairs, and none of this furniture was his taste because Tobias went with modern and form with a purpose. The fact he kept it the same as when his grandmother lived here emphasized what she'd meant to him.

He rested a palm to the right side of the door on a flat panel and the lock clicked. With a twist of the handle, he stepped out into the back garden. A burst of cold air stopped me in the doorway and I lingered there watching him. He didn't seem fazed that he was barefoot. An awning covered the entire patio and a few feet away was an outside rug, and beyond this space unfolded a large garden flanked by tall brick walls.

Tobias pointed to the door. "Press your palm on the keypad to get in and out. Just tell me where and when you're going. It's best if we go together. Each access point is camouflaged for both aesthetic and security purposes."

"When did you lift my fingerprints?"

"Back in Oxfordshire when I first met you." He shoved his hands into his pockets. "I admit I was overly cautious." He cringed. "I apologize if it seems a little invasive."

"Not accepted." I bit back my annoyance. "This painting—"

"Will be the crown of Burell's collection. Or so he'll believe."

"Who's the artist?"

"Rumor goes there are two others out there—"

My throat constricted from the clue that could only mean one painting.

"She's considered the rarest of finds," he added. "The holy grail of paintings."

He was referring to a portrait of the *Mona Lisa* that was now known as Lisa Gherardini, the wife of Francesco del Giocondo. *No*, this wasn't possible. There was no way he'd consider giving her over to a monster. If this other painting even existed. Rumors had circulated that Leonardo da Vinci had painted more than one portrait of Mona Lisa, who had patiently posed for him over the course of many years. Some specialists believed there'd been enough time to paint her several times over, especially given the artist's obsession with his subject.

A jolt of adrenaline spiked my veins that I might have been under the same roof as the *other Mona Lisa* at some point. "You own her?"

"Not exactly."

"Tobias, where are you going with this?"

"It's a good plan." He looked eerily calm. "Even if it turns my stomach."

Okay, this was a bad idea.

I was already riddled with guilt for how my life had turned his upside down, even if he was Icon, and there seemed no end in sight to the disruption I seemingly caused.

The original *Mona Lisa* was safely hanging in the Louvre in Paris and admired over the span of five hundred years. She was only now giving up her secrets as forensic specialists decoded her long-lost truths using state-of-the-art technology.

So distracted by the thought of another painting of her existing, I braved those few steps toward him. "You're not going to steal her. I won't allow it."

Tobias held out his hand for the cube.

I clutched it to my chest. "Wilder?"

"I won't."

"Whoever has her won't lend her out for this."

Even if the plan was to get her back afterward, along with my precious collection. Tobias seemed too calm. He didn't even seem affected by the cold out here even though all he had on were his jeans and that bad boy smile—probably because he could see how intrigued he'd gotten me.

He glanced at the cube and gestured for me to be cautious.

"Where is this *Mona Lisa*?"

"Have no idea." He leaned back against the patio table and crossed an ankle over another. "And we don't have time to find her."

I tried to hide my confusion at failing to follow his madcap scheming.

He gave a confident nod. "I'm going to re-create a version of the *Mona Lisa*. Make it look like another one turned up."

"What? How?"

"With 3-D technology."

The world spun.

"I knew you wouldn't like it," he said.

"You're joking, right?"

"No, I'm quite serious. The key is how to get the news to Burell without alerting the world. That can't happen."

"To get the hopes of the nation up? Yes, that would be a catastrophe."

"I agree."

"You do realize it took Leonardo four years to paint her!" I coughed past this dryness in my throat.

"Science has advanced quite considerably since the sixteenth century—"

"How can you ask me to do such a thing? Create a fake? I've dedicated my life to authenticating paintings. This is what I do. This is my life's work."

"Mine too."

An innocent replica was one thing, like *The Incredulity of Saint Thomas* by Caravaggio I'd seen at Wilder's friend's home in LA. It had taken me less than twenty seconds and a magnifier to confirm the handiwork of a talented student mimicking a teacher but that had been under his master's guidance.

I fisted my palms. "No."

"Think about it."

"No."

"I'm facing off with evil for you."

"Maybe we should rethink all of this."

"I've run every scenario."

"How could you even pull this off?"

"I own a three-dimensional printer."

"Of course you do." Vaguely, I remembered this technology could create a solid object from a digital file. *Insanity.*

"Don't worry about the materials." Tobias studied me carefully. "Its authenticity can be duplicated."

"You're not listening to me."

"I'm too blinded by your beauty." He flashed a smile.

I wanted to throw this cube at him.

"Zara, if I'm going to attempt to get your paintings back we have to play by different rules."

Blood rushed from my face that he was considering this as a viable option.

"I have a friend here who can help us obtain a couple of items we'll need. Theo's a professor at NYU. We have an appointment with him later this morning."

"You're out of your mind."

"My mind's firing on all cylinders."

"This is wrong."

"I'm arranging a private sale. Only Burell will see her and of course his own expert. Afterward, I will personally destroy her. You can witness it."

"I'm not unleashing a fake into the world."

"She'll be for Elliot Burell's eyes only."

"What if his expert talks? Shares with the world what he's seen?"

"Not if he's working for a man like Burell. If he values his life, that is."

"My father dedicated his life—"

"Burell has your father's paintings. We know this."

I caressed my forehead to ward off a headache.

"Zara, once he snatches up our *Mona Lisa* she'll be transported to join the rest of your collection. The GPS tracker placed on her will lead us to your paintings."

"I won't do it."

"Fine."

"Fine?"

"Yes, relax here. Make yourself at home."

"I won't let you do it."

"While inside Burell's computer I discovered disturbing intel."

"What?"

"I want to protect you from everything that is wrong with this world. Cocoon you."

"What did you find?"

"Burell is selling fighter bombers to foreign leaders who like to drop dirty bombs on villages. He's murdering kids, Zara."

He was right I didn't want to see beyond the veil of his cruelty but ignoring it was worse. "What can we do about any of that?"

"Bring Burell down."

"There must be another way."

"I'm open to suggestions. You've seen how powerful he is. The FBI knows he has your paintings and they can't touch him. He still has Rembrandt's *The Storm on the Sea of Galilee*, for fuck's sake. And they know it's stolen. His lawyers are ruthless. They're the gatekeepers to his hell."

"I agree something needs to be done."

Tobias softened his tone. "When I hacked his computer I unearthed a deleted email from Eli Burell to his dad. In it he informed his father he was taking care of the 'Leighton problem,' and ordering a large shipment to be transported to the East Coast. The assignment was code-named King."

"That's why we're here?"

"My satellite followed the shipment to this city. Then it went underground and I lost track of it."

"Do you believe we'll ever get them back? I mean, really?"

"We've seen the security measures he takes." He breathed out his frustration. "But I'm willing to do everything we can."

"What about Eli?"

"He doesn't get his hands dirty. In Arizona he panicked. The trap he sent us into wasn't finished. His impatience is our advantage."

I recalled us being trapped in that underground cavern four days ago with the modern-day wheel converting water into energy, a weird art piece he'd designed for his twisted fun. It also served as a security device and the same one that had almost drowned me.

I shook off the memory. "If we wait for a clue perhaps—"

"If your paintings are shipped on to another country...like Dubai."

I tried to think of another way. "Burell will place your fake painting through a stringent authentication process."

"Maybe you'd be open to viewing the painting before I place it under Burell's nose?"

"I think you're asking the impossible of yourself." I threw my hands in the air. "Leonardo da Vinci!"

"I've studied his work all my life."

"Tobias, I'm sorry my circumstances have led you to consider this."

"I saw the photos of those children, Zara." He brought his hands up and covered his face. "He's a monster. I have to bring him down. I know I'm crossing the line here. I'm doing it for you and for those people. Give me this, Zara. Let me leave my mark as Icon in a good way. My *Mona Lisa* will live for a matter of days and then she'll be gone from this world, and yet what she'll leave behind will be remarkable."

I drew in a sharp breath.

He stepped closer. "I would walk across the world for you if this is what it took to find you peace in your heart."

I caressed my chest to soothe the uneasiness. "I've asked too much of you."

Wilder's mouth lingered an inch from mine. "I promised to get your paintings back. Our lives too—"

"I'm grateful for the thought you've put into this. I am." I rested a hand on his chest to persuade him.

"No one will know of her existence. No one. Only Burell. He selfishly ferrets his paintings away. He won't tell anyone about her."

"How do you know he wants her?"

"Eli Burell has been on the hunt for the other *Mona Lisa* for his father. He wants to impress him. Look, the world knows there's another painting of her out there. Maybe two. Burell's psychotic over possessing her. She's his weakness. She's our in."

I narrowed my gaze on him. "Have you ever done this before? Faked a painting?"

"No." He looked offended. "You know me better than that."

Did I really know this complex and mercurial man with a mind capable of unraveling puzzles and redefining what it was to think outside the box?

"Burell is still looking for us?" I said.

He gave a nod. "He's not going to stop until the problem is resolved."

"And we're the problem." A slither of fear shivered up my spine.

He shrugged. "So far I've managed to outsmart them."

Silently I swore at him because if outsmarting them meant leaping off buildings his view of success was skewered.

"Are you in, Leighton?"

"No, I'm not."

"Come up with a better plan, then. You have an hour."

"What happens in an hour?"

"I begin."

"I'll think of something."

"I look forward to hearing it, but if you fail to think of a realistic concept that will hook Burell without question, I will proceed as planned."

I raised the cube. "Are you going to tell me what this does?"

"You're always accusing me of using smoke and mirrors. Like a demo?"

I handed it to him and he placed it on the patio table. "At some point—" he rested the tip of his finger on the cube "—I'll show you my other arsenal of tricks I have to pull off my plan. Full disclosure."

"Let's go to the FBI, please."

"Are you prepared to lose your paintings forever?"

There had to be another way and I was determined to find it.

I glanced at the cube. "Impress me, then."

"How about a little of that old Hampshire *fog*?" He emphasized the last word. "I know how much you love Emily Bronte's moody atmospheres. This will fit your spirited charm."

A stream of air hissed from the corner of the cube and I held in my breath at the shock of watching it form a blanket of thick white smoke. "Is it safe?"

He faded from view as a white cloud began to swallow him.

I tried to fathom how all this smokiness was coming out of that little box. *Oh, no*, I'd carried it into the drawing room near those paintings. Fog billowed around me and I could no longer see him. "Tobias?"

"Zara." He was behind me.

A thrill spiraled up my spine when I felt his presence. "This shields your escape if you get caught?"

"Very good."

The nape of my neck tingled. "And you have other gadgets like this?"

"I do."

"Show me."

"I'm tempted." His tone turned husky. "Are you tempted to experience more, Leighton?" His heady cologne mingled with his scent and saturated my senses.

"Yes." I sounded breathy as I recalled the way he'd seduced me in his bedroom last night and my hand trailed over my chest in expectation. If he touched me I'd be unable to resist him, because my body was on fire for this half-naked version of Tobias. If he held me firmly and spun me round for a kiss and ravaged my mouth like he did my sex last night my skin would liquefy. My entire being was tingling with anticipation of his caress that always morphed into domination. The delicious kind I resisted so I wouldn't lose my way in him.

You've already lost your way in him.

Silence lingered...

My body yearned for his touch, my breasts swelling, nipples tightening, chest rising and falling and making me light-headed as I spun round and swept my hands through the mist, ready to persuade him to see his dark scheming was not going to happen.

He was gone.

CHAPTER FOUR

WITHIN HALF AN HOUR I'd found my way around the cozy kitchen and made toast and scrambled some eggs and brewed fresh coffee. All this fresh produce was proof Wilder had someone working for him. Their discretion and ability to hide from me was uncanny.

Though the kitchen had been modernized, it reflected the spirit of the rest of the house with its white walls, stainless steel appliances and an open-plan design with a couch and sofa in the far corner to add a splash of homeyness.

I placed two settings with the silver cutlery on the granite island for us and found coasters for our drinks. In between these quiet moments of normalcy I tried to think of another way to get Burell to reveal where my paintings were. Though finding them would be the easy part. Getting them would take the kind of skill only one man could pull off.

"Ah, coffee." Tobias was dressed casually in ripped jeans and a J.Crew sweater and had a black jacket flung casually over his shoulder. He was carrying an iPad. He flung his blazer over the back of one of the armchairs and settled opposite at the central island.

He placed his phone beside his mug and peered at his plate. "This looks nice." He beamed with happiness.

I loved seeing this side of him. "Is this enough?"

"More than enough. You're spoiling me."

"I like doing it." Taking care of him made me happy and kept my mind busy.

"Did you find everything okay?"

"Yes."

"I fixed the heating. It should be warmer now."

"Great."

"Have you discovered the sitting room? There's a TV in there and music if you want to relax."

"Yes, thank you. I didn't know you like opera."

"My taste ranges from rock to classic."

"And of course you know all about mine." I reached for my knife and fork.

He held my gaze. "You're referring to your background search that I conducted?"

"I meant you confiscated my phone with all my music."

"Ah."

I blew on the surface of my coffee and the liquid rippled. "What I find baffling is you fingerprinted me unknowingly at your home."

"You touched my door handle."

"I was a guest."

"I'd hired you as a consultant. I'm thorough."

"You don't let many people in, do you?"

"I practice caution."

"Control?"

"Think of life as a game of chess. You move the pieces to your liking and if you're smart you predict the other person's moves...perhaps avert a disaster."

"What about their humanity?"

"A person's true nature always reveals itself." He sipped his coffee. "Though you're an enigma."

"In what way?"

He shook the salt cruet over his eggs. "You refuse to break the rules and yet you're here with me."

"I didn't have much choice."

He held my stare and his expression marred with confusion as he set the cruet down.

"What I meant was it all happened so fast. I flew off to Arizona and…"

He raised his hands to admit guilt. "I let you down. I have to live with my mistake that put you in harm's way."

"I take responsibility for my actions."

"Which were influenced by mine."

"You probably wish we'd never met."

"On the contrary. When I first met you, I found you inspiring. I wanted to protect you."

"And now?"

"I find myself thinking of you a lot of the time." He lifted a slice of toast and bit into it and grinned at me. "You're a living, breathing Titian."

"Does that line usually work?"

"You know as well as I do Titian favored intelligent subjects whose eyes reflected awareness of their environment."

"Oh, you're referring to Titian's rendition of Salome holding John the Baptist's head after she betrayed him?" I smirked to show I was joking.

"All of Titian's subjects reflect consciousness. I don't believe you'll betray me, no. If that's what you're hinting at."

Betray him, *no*, I couldn't imagine myself ever doing that.

"There are so many times you could have given me up to the authorities, Zara."

"I suppose."

"Jade," Tobias piped up. "Play *Requiem* by Wolfgang Amadeus Mozart. In D minor, please. Play it loud."

I laughed as the dramatic music played through hidden speakers fitting the mood. "Point made, Tobias."

"Sorry?" he shouted, cupping his hand to hear better.

"Very funny," I yelled. "Jade, take it down, please."

Tobias raised his gaze as the music lowered and then focused back on me. "I like having breakfast with you. Usually it's just me and Jade fighting over the salt."

That made me smile. "Do you think you'll ever settle down?"

He paused with his fork close to his mouth.

"That was a stupid question."

He placed his fork down. "It was a good question. Yes, I want to be with someone who is willing to stand up to me. I'm told I'm intimidating."

"Bossy."

"Yes, I admit—"

"Controlling."

"If I'm in command no one gets hurt."

"You're referring to Arizona?"

"I'm referring to anyone who steps inside my stratosphere. Look, all people who do business with me are prescreened. You were no exception so don't take it personally. All paintings I procure are carefully authenticated. I profiled you carefully for this very purpose. Any plane I board undergoes a preflight check that includes the engine."

My stare locked on his and he closed his eyes for a

beat. I realized his confession revealed the reason for his dominating nature.

Of course; it was so obvious.

"Tobias?" I coaxed him softly.

His gaze roamed the kitchen. "Maybe we could cook in here together one night?"

"I'd like that."

"Me too." He returned his focus to his iPad.

"Let me call Abby?"

"Not yet." He kept his gaze on the screen.

"This is hard on me."

"For that I'm sorry."

"Perhaps if I was permitted to explain everything?"

He peered up at me. "You already did, Zara. Abby told you they've been asked to pull back from Burell. As far as they're concerned it's over. You and I have taken the fall. Do you want it to end like this?"

"No."

"Same here."

We finished our breakfast in silence with him sweeping across the latest news as he ate his toast and eggs. I poked at my breakfast while watching Mr. Mercurial slip once more into his impenetrable shell. I wanted to say it was the loss of my life that hurt the most, but somewhere among the wreckage also lay what could have been between us. Though if we truly spent time together tonight maybe we'd regain a little of the trust we'd lost.

A phone number lit up the screen of his cell and he took the call and asked questions in between sips of coffee. The subject was about his London office.

From where I sat there was a good view of his iPad set to a news article about Icon. I wondered what he must think to be in the public's consciousness like this. He seemed indifferent and when his steely gaze rose to meet mine, he quickly swept away the evidence of what he'd been reading.

If my best friend, Clara, had any idea of what had happened to me she'd be worried sick. I needed to reassure her I was safe. I had to get a message to her.

Tobias hung up and set his phone down. "That was my lawyer."

"Oh?"

He cupped his coffee in his hands. "He's made a few calls on your behalf. Explained to Adley I hired you to track down a unique piece—"

"Perhaps I should call—"

"Not necessary. Not yet, anyway." He slipped off the bar stool and came closer, bringing his coffee with him. "Reynard Linde has implemented a stay on a police search of all my properties."

"Reynard?"

"My senior lawyer. He's also prevented the police from searching your flat. I'm afraid we can't stop them from searching your office."

"They won't find anything."

"I'll do everything I can to protect your privacy. I have a wall between me and whoever wants access to my business. My resources are at your disposal."

"Aren't we just holding off the inevitable?"

"Inevitable?"

"I failed to return to work." I caressed my brow to ease the tension. "I fled the FBI back at The Wilder."

"As far as I recall the officers walked away from you."

Ran from me, actually. Right before they tried to

bring me in for questioning when a hologram of an African lion appeared and chased them down the hallway of The Wilder Museum. I'd bolted in the opposite direction and right through the fire exit to the roof where I'd hopped into Tobias's helicopter and been whisked away. My getaway wouldn't exactly inspire confidence.

Tobias gave a reassuring smile. "Did you come up with a better plan?"

I reached out my hand for his phone. "I'm going to call the FBI."

He slid his phone across the granite toward me.

I picked it up. "Will they be able to track the call?"

"Keep an eye on the front door. That's a *yes*, if you're wondering."

I swiped my finger across his screen. "What you accessed on Burell's computer can be given to them—"

"Hacking is illegal."

I tapped the Google app to search for a number. "We can submit the information anonymously."

"Which helps us how?"

"They can use what you found to obtain a search warrant for all his properties—"

"The FBI can't touch him. They need more. Look, the moment he believes his art collection is under threat he'll move them. Your paintings will be lost forever."

My shoulders slumped in resignation. "What if we try to get our lives back? Forget all this ever happened?"

"Forget this ever happened?" He sounded incredulous.

"Yes, you go back to inventing gadgets and me to Huntly Pierre—"

"And Burell keeps your paintings and continues slaughtering the innocent. He doesn't need to steal,

Zara, did you ever think of that? He enjoys decimating lives. He's a high-functioning psychopath."

I turned my thoughts to home. "I need to call Clara."

"I'll set you up with a call later." He wagged his finger at me. "No calls for now. No emailing."

Reluctantly I slid his phone back to him. "We just used your phone."

"My activity pings away from this location."

"So what are you doing today?"

"I'm visiting Theo."

"Your friend at NYU?"

"Yes." Tobias came closer. "Your plan sucks."

"My father would want me to find another way." I cringed with how ashamed he'd be if he knew I had anything to do with the creation of a fake.

"Your father would want you to have the paintings back." Tobias reached up to my face and tucked a strand of hair behind my ear. "You were both meant to die in that fire. Think about that."

"Who got us these new clothes? The food?"

Tobias considered his answer. "Coops."

"He's here in New York?" I remembered Cooper fondly as his young driver who I'd met in Oxfordshire. A loyal American chauffeur who Tobias trusted. He'd been kind to me when he'd driven me back from Blandford Palace the night of my first adventure with Wilder.

Tobias straightened his back defensively. "I need him to lay low."

"Where is he?"

"A five-star hotel. He'll survive."

"You trust him?"

"Coops is smart. Loyal. He's worked for me for years." Tobias headed toward the door.

"Can I come with you?"

He spun round. "Sure."

"I'm going to persuade you against this idea."

"*Mona Lisa* will come through for us. Give her a chance."

"You're playing a dangerous game."

"I burned the bridge behind us, Zara. We move forward. Our reputations will be secure. Our freedom returned. All I need from you is trust."

"A fake painting in the twenty-first century doesn't stand a chance. There are too many specialists with access to the best science. And if it does slip past a review, if you believe you're that good—"

"What can I tell you? I'm glad I had a parachute yesterday."

"That doesn't excuse our actions."

"I'm no saint." He headed out. "But you already know that."

I buried my face in my palms and questioned if I had what it took to endure this for much longer. My gaze fixed on Tobias's phone and the iPad he'd left. Both of them were my windows to the world. All I had to do was be willing to risk alerting the authorities.

Ignoring the temptation, I cleaned up our breakfast plates and carried a fresh mug of tea back to my room.

I was grateful to find a parka among the new clothes that would hold off this East Coast chill and I carried it with me when I went in search of Tobias. I found him in his bedroom in the staff quarters.

He greeted me brightly. "Find everything okay?"

This was progress; he genuinely seemed to be trying to take his intimidation down a notch and from that curl at his lips he liked this new side to him.

"I'll pay you back for all this," I offered, gesturing to my coat.

"No need." He winked. "I'll take it out of your commission."

"I don't think you could afford me now. My rate went up." I winked back.

"I'll just have to sell all my worldly possessions so I can afford you." His stare held mine. "It would be my best investment by far."

"Then how would you ever fund all your escapades?"

"I'm inventive."

"So you'd never give them up?" I held his stare until he broke mine.

"If anything's an escapade it's you, Leighton." He nodded approvingly at a garment bag lying on the bed or maybe he just didn't want to look at me. "Spies buy new clothes when they arrive at their destination. Did you know that?" He unzipped the bag and withdrew a jacket. "Brands give away their country of origin. They even buy shoes."

I pretended not to be fazed by Wilder's James Bond fetish and watched him shrug into that Black Watch plaid jacket to which he added a Burberry scarf—I was being teased by this Abercrombie and Fitch take on a Scottish-styled hotness.

"How do I look?" He peered down at himself. "I think Coops was high when he bought this."

"You look hip." Actually he looked frickin' gorgeous like one of those sultry runway models. "You'll do."

He lowered his gaze on me. "You look like a hot librarian. Ready to burst out of— What is your style, exactly?"

"Warm." I zipped up my coat. "I'm going with you."

"I'm glad you've come around."

"Actually, I haven't."

"Don't slow me down."

"Oh, I intend to do more than that, Mr. Wilder."

"Looks like the entertainment for the day is set." He smirked and turned away.

When the allure of this dreamy-looking man slipped away and reality screeched back into focus, I was again reminded this illusion of us romantically hanging out together wasn't real. Still, Tobias was letting me in and I sensed his sweet nature just beneath the surface. It brought more comfort than he'd ever know.

We left the house after 11:00 a.m. in Tobias's Aston Martin and although we arrived in Greenwich together, he left me sitting in the car for a few minutes as he went on ahead. This was how he wanted us to visit his old professor Theodore Partridge.

The professor's office was tucked away on the third floor of the Silver Center, one of the many academic buildings of New York University. The home of the department of Arts and Sciences sat snugly in the heart of Greenwich Village. On the way here, Tobias had told me about its reputation as a well-loved hub of student life with its endless lectures, small classes and thriving social scene.

As I headed in to join him, I edged my way through exuberant students. It wasn't that long ago I'd been a student myself and I envied their easy access to some of the best minds in the world. There was no doubt the latest findings would be celebrated here.

Fully aware I'd have to brave the security surveillance from the street, I'd worn my blond wig again and added some round-rimmed sunglasses. It wasn't only this covert activity that felt foreign to me; it was the surrounding accents and chilly climate.

I knocked on the door of his old mentor's office and hoped Tobias had felt comfortable enough to open up to Theo and find some solace from the time spent with his old professor.

But, as I opened the door, I was stunned to see Theo lying on the floor with Tobias standing over him. I stared in horror at Wilder.

"It's his back," Tobias reassured me.

Theo raised his head. "Hello there," came his American accent with a remnant of Irish. "Fell off a horse during a trip to Puerto Natales five years ago. Seeing my chiropractor this afternoon. Tea?"

Tobias waved off his offer. "We're fine."

I shut the door behind me. "Can we get *you* anything?"

"Wilder already offered." Theo rose to his feet cautiously and his expression strained as he made it to his desk. "Apparently Wilder wants your visit here kept private? Divinely evocative. You art collectors are a secretive bunch." He peered over his spectacles at me and tucked his hands into his tweed jacket.

His office was a reflection of his academia and a familiar sense of organization that I admired Tobias for.

I sat in his corner armchair. "How do you know each other?"

"We met in Massachusetts," Theo explained. "Tobias was my student. He loved inventing gadgets back then, too." Theo eyed him affectionately. "Read in the *Times* you've created an air keyboard? What's wrong with this?" He pointed to his own. "Can't you invent something that will save the world, Wilder?"

Tobias smiled fondly. "Theo's given us the access code for the Leonardo da Vinci exhibit. There's one in this very building." He pointed to a Post-it note on the desk with a series of numbers scribbled on it.

Theo gave a nod. "Quite the collection of artifacts that once belonged to da Vinci. Wilder tells me you're also a fan?"

"His work was inspiring," I said. "To say the least."

"I hear you're an art forensic specialist, Zara?" he added.

"Yes."

"Tobias and I share a common passion." Theo lowered himself into his swivel chair. "Both of us have an admiration for da Vinci's work."

Another layer of Wilder revealed and I recalled his interactive world I'd experienced while wearing his augmented reality headset back at LACMA. I toured da Vinci's personal workspace, or at least the replica Tobias had created. It also explained his excitement when I'd shown him the *Cannon Gun* sketch I'd once kept hidden in a safe in my London home by the same artist; the drawing so respected it had survived the passing of time.

"The exhibit upstairs has a collection of da Vinci's paint brushes." Tobias broke me from my daydreaming. "Isn't that something?"

"Yes, it really is." My widening eyes told him I was on to him. "It's such an honor to meet you, Theo. I was a student back at The Courtauld and loved my time there. I've considered teaching." Especially as my job at Huntly Pierre was no longer viable probably. The thought of it made my stomach ache.

The phone rang and Theo gestured he should take

it. "Thanks, got it." He hung up and looked at Tobias. "They're advising us to save everything we're working on. Cameras are down."

Wilder gave a convincing look of concern and I kept my gaze off him assuming he was the cause. He'd assured me there'd be no record of our visit today and this was why. It also explained why he'd gone on ahead. Somehow he'd disabled their surveillance capacity from a remote and all without entering their security hub. I was equally annoyed and impressed with the rascal.

Tobias sat in the chair before the desk. "It's good to see you, Theo."

"Likewise," he replied.

"What can you tell us about this da Vinci exhibit?"

"Private collector. Wants to remain anonymous. There's no paintings I'm afraid, merely brushes, paints and whatnot."

"There's a sacredness to her," I piped up. "The *Mona Lisa*, I mean."

Theo brightened. "She was commissioned by Mona Lisa's husband. Though the mystery why this very painting was found among da Vinci's personal belongings after he died still baffles us today."

"A true mystery." Tobias gave a nod. "Because it should have hung in their home and not remained with the artist."

"Very intriguing," agreed Theo. "Which might explain there being the rumor of more than one. Leonardo was perfecting his painting and the process involved several canvases perhaps."

Tobias sighed with admiration. "The way he comprehended the light reflecting off the back of the moon is the exact same way he created the reflection of light emanating off Mona Lisa's cheek."

"Wasn't he dyslexic?" I said.

Theo agreed with a nod. "Leonardo wrote backward with mirror writing. It was first suspected to be related to his obsession with secrecy but what we know today proves he was left-handed and from the ingeniousness of his drawings—"

"He was using both his left and right brain simultaneously." I waved my apology for interrupting.

Theo looked impressed. "This lady knows her stuff."

"She certainly does," Tobias said with pride.

"So the exhibition here of a sample of Leonardo's personal items have been authenticated?" I sat forward, intrigued with this opportunity.

Theo raised his bushy eyebrows. "Yes, absolutely. A private collector generously loaned them to us for a month. I'm glad you'll get to see it. Fifth floor. Mention my name if you have an issue. You shouldn't."

I gave a nod. "I visited *Mona Lisa* in the Louvre a few years ago. She was beautiful."

"And even more has been revealed," said Theo.

I added with joy, "Art historians have discovered both tiny letters and numbers in the dark paint of *Mona Lisa*'s eyes. It's a secret message da Vinci was sharing with us. Maybe his signature. Somehow I doubt there's another painting of her out there," I muttered.

Theo smiled. "She'd be easy to authenticate. Carbon dating would help to rule out a fake."

"Thank you, yes, Professor." I threw a triumphant smile at Tobias to say, *There, someone has finally proven the madness of your idea.*

Tobias held my gaze. "Leonardo left his unique signature on Mona Lisa's dress as a final strike of possession."

I narrowed my gaze on him in response to his subtle strike back.

"Perhaps there was a romance revealed by her timeless smile," Tobias added with a glint of humor.

"Leonardo da Vinci hired musicians and comedians to entertain Mona Lisa during those long hours she posed for him." I raised my chin in defense of her reputation. "After all, she was married. So her smile is most likely her amusement from the entertainment provided to prevent boredom."

"And I thought you were a romantic?" Tobias smirked.

"Not when it comes to science, Mr. Wilder." I shrugged a shoulder. "You would know all this, Professor."

Tobias was studying me and I threw him a defiant smile.

"Of course, should another painting of her ever surface out of the blue, specialists will perform multispectral analysis on her." I turned my focus back to Theo. "This is an easy way to confirm her authenticity."

Theo shook his head. "Thank goodness for science."

"My point exactly. And of course they'd carbon date the canvas." I pushed myself to my feet in triumph. "Take paint samples and run her through infrared. How wonderful is this!" My nerves forced it out as a screech. "And the rest will be from Mona Lisa's smile—"

"The other *Mona Lisa*," said Theo thoughtfully.

"Can't see it happening myself," I added. "Not after all this time."

"I told you she's art obsessed." Tobias cut me off

and turned back to Theo. "It's been a wonderful visit. Thank you for this——" He tapped the Post-it note and left it where it lay. "I've memorized the numbers."

"How long are you in town?" asked Theo.

"Few days." Tobias glanced at me. "Perhaps longer."

Theo slowly pushed himself to his feet and grimaced.

"Please don't get up." I gestured my concern for his back.

He waved it off. "It's wonderful to see you. Don't leave it so long next time."

"I won't." Tobias leaned forward and hugged Theo.

I stepped forward to shake his hand. There was a bounce in my step as we headed out, because our meeting would have helped Tobias see sense.

Halfway down the hallway I waited for a couple of students to walk by. "We can still visit the exhibit."

Tobias hit the button for the elevator. "I am."

"And me too, right?"

He nudged me into the lift. "Wait for me in the car."

I turned to face him. "I'm going with you."

"No, you're not." He tossed me the car keys.

I caught them and stopped the sliding doors from closing. "Why can't I come?"

"We'll talk afterward."

"After what?"

"Let's play the 'shut your piehole' game. You go first." He peeled my hands off the doors and they slid closed in my face.

My jaw dropped at his cheekiness. I tucked the keys into my coat pocket and rode the elevator down as my annoyance almost won out over my phobia.

When the elevator landed on the ground floor, I hurried out before the doors opened fully and retraced my steps toward the foyer. Seriously, Tobias knew how much pleasure seeing that collection would give me. My feet jolted to a stop as my mind processed the thought he was going to steal something from the collection to help his re-creation.

He was such a rogue.

Hordes of students poured into the foyer having gotten caught in the downpour. With trepidation rising in my belly, I hurried toward the exit, ready to brave the rain, my angry monologue poised to be unleashed on Wilder.

Just before the front door to my left a young student caught her heel in the carpet and took a tumble onto her knees and dropped her books. I went to help her, first checking she was okay and then helping her pick them up and handing them back.

I reached for the one on Florence. "Have you been to Italy?" I looked up at her. "It's amazing." I'd visited the city with my dad and my fondest memories were of the time spent with him in the Uffizi Gallery.

"Not yet." She took her book back with a grateful smile. "Thank you."

I should have been allowed to see the Leonardo da Vinci collection and was seriously considering finding my way to the fifth floor.

A blur of movement to my right caught my attention. It was the vision of five men entering briskly with their long formal coats flapping behind them and they easily looked out of place—among them I recognized Eli Burell striding fast toward the elevator.

Tobias.

I sprang to my feet and bolted toward the stairwell and shoved the door open, taking two stairs at a time as I rushed back up toward the fifth floor, guessing he was still up there. Round and round I ascended the stairs with my legs burning from the strain.

I burst into the hallway—

Tobias was standing before an elevator, waiting for the doors to open. He turned and gave me a wry smile.

I pointed at the elevator and mouthed, *Eli*.

Tobias bolted toward me and an envelope slipped from his grip and fell to the ground.

The elevator pinged.

Tobias ran back for the envelope and scooped it up and sprung toward me, gesturing to the stairwell. I shoved open the door and he followed me. He slammed it shut behind us and we sped down the stairs to the ground floor. When we reached the bottom, we took a few seconds to listen out for anyone following us. He rested a finger to his lips in a warning for us to remain silent.

A fading lightbulb flickered.

"They didn't see you?" I whispered.

"No."

"How did Eli find us?"

"He's here for the da Vinci collection I imagine."

"Eli's not following us?"

"No. He must have heard about the collection. His father goes after anything by the artist. This is why the collection is private, so that bidders don't bully the collector."

My head struck the brick and I breathed out a sigh of panic. "Did we really need to see it today?"

"Yes, we're against the clock." He pressed his chest against mine protectively. "Still, that was fun, right?"

"No, it bloody well wasn't." I smacked my palms to his chest. "You like living dangerously."

"What can I tell you? Danger finds me." Tobias's irises glinted under the fluorescent light.

I dug in a fingertip below his collarbone. "You seek it out."

"Zara, keeping you safe is my priority—" His lips neared mine. "That's why I wanted you in the car. You defied me."

"I saved you." If his lips edged one more centimeter we'd be kissing and I glared my annoyance, trembling with arousal that had my breathlessness morphing into panting and my nipples hardening.

He arched an amused brow. "I'd have been fine. You, however, put yourself in harm's way."

"Neither of us should have gone up there."

"Do you have any idea how hot you are when your adrenaline spikes?"

I broke his gaze as I realized this buzz surging through me felt like my body was ignited from the jeopardy.

Tobias looked intoxicated from our escape. "We have something in common, after all."

No, this wasn't happening; I refused to become drawn into his drama-filled life.

"You're aroused, Leighton."

"This is not arousal. This is something completely different."

"I'm intrigued." He whispered something in French and it sounded dirty.

With indignation, I bit down on his bottom lip to punish his arrogance and then plunged my tongue against his, savaging his mouth with the fiercest kiss,

taking my power back and working my mouth into a
frenzy over his. At the same time I was annoyed with
his incorrigible unshaven brashness that cranked up
his sexiness, his scruff scraping my cheeks and sending me over—

He wasn't kissing back.

Oh, God, how embarrassing. I'd attacked him with
full-on lust and my calf was still wrapped around his,
holding him fixed against me. He'd revved me to the
point of coming with merely his body crushed against
mine. Letting my guard down was insanity with those
perilous men in the same building. I hated Tobias for
encouraging me to like any of this, and the loosening
of my grip was accompanied by a proud expression of
defiance as I nudged him away.

"That was all you." He leaned in and brushed his
lips across mine in a tease and stepped back. "Just so
we're clear."

I flicked a phantom stray hair out of my face. "We
should leave."

"I agree. The cameras are due to come back on." He
tucked the envelope into his jacket and led me out the
doorway leading to the foyer.

We remained vigilant all the way back to the car
parked across the street.

Once inside, I pulled my seat belt across my chest,
relieved when Tobias drove us away from the Silver
Center. I glanced back to make sure we weren't being
followed. My body was still thrumming from my one-
way kiss, and I tried to forget how incredible he felt
when pressed against me, how firm and protective, how
amazing we fit together. This self-imposed Wilder ban

was the cruelest torture of all and my body was still yearning for him.

Tobias glanced over at me. "Are you okay?"

"I'm fine." I peeked inside the beige envelope and saw nothing.

He gave a nod. "A clue they'll find during the authentication process of the canvas."

Squinting inside it I saw the tiny hair. "From a paintbrush?"

Occasionally they were discovered between layers of paint on a canvas and were very often overlooked by the human eye. I was stupefied to be looking at a hair plucked from one of Leonardo da Vinci's paintbrushes.

"It had already fallen off the brush." He glanced at me. "I promise."

"Still."

"I don't doubt its sanctity." Which was his way of saying this was hard on him too.

"Why do you need it?" But I already knew Tobias would insert it into the wet paint upon the canvas he was planning on creating. This fine hair would add a dash of authenticity when Elliot's specialists performed their analysis to his painting.

If his idea advanced that far.

"There's no other way." He glanced over at me. "Only a painting will be taken to his vault."

I focused beyond the window as we turned left on Washington Square, peering up at the skyscraper that made me feel insignificant when set against such a dramatic landscape. It made me wonder if someone like me could ever make a difference.

CHAPTER FIVE

TOBIAS WAS REASONABLE at least, and this thought brought comfort as I entered his workshop carrying him a freshly brewed mug of hot tea and a plate of Hobnob biscuits as a peace offering.

The Rolling Stones—"Start Me Up"—was playing loudly and the room was frigid, proving he'd cranked up the air-conditioning. He was probably using it to ward me off and not disrupt his shenanigans, because he knew how much I hated the cold.

He sat on a bar stool at one of his workbenches and his gaze zeroed in on a large screen on the wall in front of him, where a program was cycling different paintings and sketches by Leonardo da Vinci.

His gaze lowered to his smaller drone, Jade, positioned on the bench to his right. Between them lay a chessboard half-played. Tobias reached for one of the pieces and moved it over the black and white checkers. My jaw dropped when one of Jade's metal arms reached out and lifted a knight from his end of the board up and over Tobias's piece.

"Hey, guys," I said cheerfully. "I brought you tea."

Tobias spun round and beamed a big smile when he saw the biscuits. "I'm winning."

"Against Jade?"

He flashed a dangerous smile. "Music down, Jade."

I handed him his mug and then pointed to the screen. "That's going fast."

He reached for a biscuit. "I'm inputting data into Jade's software." He held the Hobnob between his teeth to free his hand so he could pat her.

I placed the plate near him. "How are you?"

"Good. Starving. You have perfect timing."

"Why is Jade processing that information?"

He lifted his bishop and waved it in front of Jade. "Yeah, you better be scared. I was going easy on you before."

"How can you stand those images going so fast?"

"It's relaxing. It's everything that exists related to Leonardo da Vinci." He glanced at the screen. "Jade has a fast processor."

"Are you dragging her into your scheming?"

"She's going to mimic Leonardo's technique."

"You mean his *sfumato* technique?"

He smiled with appreciation. "Evaporated brush-strokes providing transitions imperceptible to the human eye and thus creating a living breathing woman upon a canvas."

I placed my hands on my hips. "You really believe you can create a painting as magnificent as Leonardo's?"

"He knew science and transferred that awareness into what he created. I'm relighting his consciousness in a way."

I drew in a breath of disbelief.

Tobias focused back on me. "How else would we paint her?"

"I'm not sure you'd get his blessing."

"Perhaps when the work is done…"

I wasn't in the mood for existential conversations. "I know you admire him."

"He inspired me to become an inventor."

"How old were you when you saw your first da Vinci?"

"He seemed like he was always there." Tobias sighed with wonder. "Great tea, Zara. How about you? When did you first see da Vinci's work?" He reached for his jacket and stepped forward to wrap it around my shoulders.

"Thank you." I pulled it around me to ward off the chill. "*The Virgin of the Rocks*, my dad hung her in the drawing room." I shook my head as I tried to fathom she was still out there somewhere.

Tobias finished his biscuit and reached for another. "How long does it take for the auction houses to train its specialists in the old masters?"

"About six years."

"Yet you're the consummate expert."

"That's very flattering."

"We both know you have an uncanny knack."

"I had a head start with my dad."

"You have a unique gift. You're an endangered species, Zara. The collectors are turning away from the old masters and are focusing instead on contemporary art."

"They're wrong to turn away from the true masters."

"I agree." He gave a warm smile. "We had over 150 thousand visitors to The Wilder last year. Attendance remains at an all-time high with the public. The people see the value in our past. They get it. There's no greed with them. No selfishness." He stared past me. "Back at The Wilder, I like to walk among the guests and see their faces when they stroll through the museum. They have no idea who I am. And they don't need to say anything at all because their expressions of wonder restore my faith in humanity."

Damn him and his romanticism that wooed me. I tried not to get sucked into the version of Wilder I'd fallen for. "How will it work?" I pointed to the three-dimensional printer.

"I'll break down the components of a canvas—" He walked over to a microscope and stared down at the slide beneath. "Then I'll create a blueprint that adds in what we'd expect to find in the aging process of a painting from the sixteenth century. Paint pigments change over time and they're sensitive to ultraviolet. As you know."

"So you'll factor in the scientists' ability to break down a paint sample?"

"Yes, I'm obviously aware there should be no modern colors."

"Where would we obtain the paints?"

He gave a crooked smile.

"*You*, I meant you."

"I have my sources." He pointed to a tall chrome machine. "The data will be analyzed by the printer and then I'll utilize this to create our masterpiece. Pretty simple, really."

It didn't sound simple and I again wondered at the ease of which Tobias jumped from the science side of his brain to the arty side just like his hero Leonardo da Vinci.

Tobias carried his mug over to the printer. "I've developed an improved system that integrates oxygen. It's a fine balance. Oxygen can be an issue as it hardens the resin, so I have to keep it away from the chemicals."

I folded my arms in a stance I hoped would exude reluctance.

He took another sip of tea. "How are you feeling?"

"I'm still not sure about any of this."

Tobias pushed off away from the table. "We must focus on the prize." He held my stare for the longest time. "Retrieving your paintings as quickly as possible and transporting them to the National Gallery in London…" He went to say something else and changed his mind.

"What?"

"This afternoon I'm going to teach you a few tricks of the trade."

"What tricks?"

"The skills to defend yourself. You demanded your way into my world. Well, here you are. Buckle up."

"What kind?"

"Entry without observation. Camera interference. Running the fuck away from danger happens to be my all-time fave. If you still insist on being there when I extract your paintings."

"I should be there, right?"

"I'm working on something that would mean you don't have to be present when the retrieval of our paintings goes down."

"You mean involving other people in this?" Because there were so many paintings and one man couldn't handle them all.

"Not exactly."

"Then how else would you get them out?"

"I'll be inventive. It's what I do."

A stark memory crashed into my thoughts. "How long have you had this plan?"

"What plan?"

"When we were in the Burells' house in Arizona we were caught in Eli's mechanism and in there was a design inspired by da Vinci. The one that descended into their safe. Eli was using it to trap us further. What are you not telling me?"

"Every self-respecting art collector has a thing for Leonardo."

"Tobias?"

He broke my gaze.

"Why do I have this feeling you're not telling me something?"

He let out a frustrated sigh. "I may have outbid his dad a few times at legit auctions when we both went after the same piece of art by Leonardo da Vinci."

"Have you been riling him up for years?"

"There may have been some healthy teasing."

"After what he did to you?"

"I was waiting for the grand finale."

"As Icon?" I stomped my foot. "How dare you suck me into this. Getting Burell's fingerprints was one thing—"

"Are you with me or against me, Leighton?"

The moment of truth. Was I willing to go all the way with Icon and take the final leap? "Don't lower to their standard."

"Everything I have ever done has been for the sake of humanity." His voice remained steady. "I've never once stolen for my own gain. My personal collection was obtained legally."

Confliction washed over me again.

If I stay I'll be colluding with Icon.

I leaned on the back of a swivel chair and gripped the edge.

"Do you think this is easy for me?" He gestured his frustration. "Being trapped in this house with the woman who I was in a relationship with and now you won't even let me touch you?"

"We weren't in a relationship."

"Really? Because that's what it felt like to me."

Yes, we'd shared something special but I'd turned away from a love that I'd never recover from if I let it in. My body yearned for him and yet as I turned to look away I felt this familiar pull toward him.

"So the silent treatment has returned?" He headed up the ramp. "Excuse me while I take a break."

"I won't let you do this," I called after him.

He jolted to a stop. "It will help us get our lives back. There is no other way."

"It feels wrong. Even if no one will know."

He paused and kept his back to me. "I should have just gone ahead and dealt with this."

"Is this some kind of twisted revenge on me? Because if it wasn't for my interference nothing would have changed for you. You'd still be anonymous. You'd still be the almighty Icon."

"You don't believe that? Tell me you don't. Not after I've sacrificed my life's work to put your life right."

I sucked in a breath at his confession.

Until now he'd played down the damage I'd inflicted on him. Had I not flown out to LA, had I let this go and let the experts tackle this, perhaps we'd both have some peace at least. My stubbornness to see this resolved had landed me in a strange city with a man who had only begun to open up. Perhaps I was only seeing what he wanted me to see.

"Zara, what do I need to do to convince you how much I care about you?"

"I see you doing this—" I snapped a hand to the screen "—and I'm filled with doubt."

"Doubt?" He stormed back down the ramp toward me. "What am I to you really? A means to an end? I know I'm the only way for you to get your paintings back but what about afterward, Leighton, what happens when this is over?"

"In what way?"

He looked devastated. "Us?"

Us, the impossible dream that had never been a true possibility, an illusion of romance with the backdrop of our mutual adoration of art. Yet my body and soul told me we were meant for each other even if my mind doubted.

I raised my chin high. "Don't call me Leighton."

His expression softened as he slipped behind that familiar iciness. "It makes it easier." He whispered it to himself as he turned and headed up the ramp for the door.

With him out of sight, I slumped into a swivel chair and cupped my hands over my face as if it would help. I should have told him what he meant to me, should have shared my feelings, but I had to protect my heart. All I had to guide me was this quiet inner voice warning me to hold on and not burn up in his brightness.

The world was hunting for Icon and it had been my job to stop him. Yet here I was bringing him mugs of tea and offering biscuits like an eccentric Brit.

After fifteen minutes of staring at the screen, mesmerized by the complex drawings by da Vinci and amazed Tobias's drone was absorbing the information, I felt that same annoying awe for Tobias. Maybe he was right, maybe he could pull this off, and maybe using Burell's greed was the only way to finish this.

I went in search of Tobias, hoping to find the words that would lift the tension. At the south end of the house I heard shoes hitting a treadmill at full speed. The sound led me into the tricked-out gym with its rowing machine, weights and the treadmill Tobias was running on at full pelt. In front of him was a mirror covering the entire wall. He'd changed into a T-shirt, track pants and snazzy-looking Nikes and he had earbuds in. He was all primal perfection as he ran on the belt.

I waited for him to notice me.

Tobias's eyes met mine and then returned to his reflection in front of him. I deserved that, I suppose. My outburst had been infused with emotion born from my fear of everything imploding around us, and on top of all of this the thought of losing him. Only I'd not told him this or given him the chance to see how much I cared about him.

This is more than that...

He pressed a button on the panel and sprinted flat out and my heart skipped a beat at the vision of his well-toned athletic form and he didn't even look out of breath. The only hint of exertion was a trail of perspiration soaking his shirt.

Eventually, after ten minutes of pounding hard he punched the control panel again and slowed the machine to a walk, taking long strides with those lean legs as he cooled down from his run. I'd strolled around the gym, pretending to be interested in the weights and then the rowing machine and trying not to ogle the eye candy in the corner.

Tobias stopped the treadmill and stepped off.

"We need to talk." I folded my arms across my chest so I'd be ready for him.

"Sure. Anything for you. You know that." His smile softened the moment.

"I appreciate that."

"I'll come find you." He dragged a small towel around his shoulders and walked right past me and through a doorway as he eased out his earbuds. I followed him into a bathroom. It was decorated simply with an upscale elegance and at the far end displayed a gorgeously designed giant open-plan shower.

Tobias placed his iPod down and then peeled off his shirt and kicked off his shoes and socks and paused when he came to his track bottoms. "You might want to step out for this part."

"It's not like I've not seen you naked before." I swept my hand like it was nothing, instantly regretting my nonchalance when he tugged down his trousers and then underwear and stepped out of them to stand to his full height, staring at me with his beautiful sculptured body shimmering in perspiration with his cock half-erect. Those bruises looked sore.

"Do they hurt?" I pointed to them.

He ran his palm along them and broke my gaze.

Trying to keep my eyes on his and not sweep over his body, I began, "It's risk-verses-reward ratio. If you get caught forging a painting the rest of the plan falls apart."

"I won't get caught." He rested his hands on his hips and seemed to mull over it with his six-pack flexing, and his firm chest rising and falling—a living, breathing sculpture. The circles of his inked left shoulder swirled like an unspoken poem drawing me into its mystery. The Latin words on his groin a reminder he liked to win.

He caught me staring at him and arched a brow.

"At least give it some thought." *What the hell happened to my resolve?*

"I will."

He was trying to disarm me, that's what was happening here. He was purposefully entrancing me by rubbing his fingers over his mouth as though pretending to mull this over.

"Shower on, Jade." He strolled under the enormous faucet and water burst in streams and cascaded over him.

Stepping back I tried to avoid the spray. "You know you can't control everything the way you like to control your gadgets."

"I know." His neck craned as he looked up and drenched his face, seemingly unaware of the dreamy show he was putting on of an Olympian wallowing beneath the downpour. He turned away from me and provided a stunning view of his sculptured back with his refined spine curving into a pert bum. He rubbed shampoo into a lather through his dark golden hair, and his biceps bulged as his fingers massaged his scalp. Rising from this dreamy haze I came to find my right palm resting on the curvature of his upper back feeling rippling muscles beneath.

He turned his head slightly. "I'm thinking."

My hand slipped from him. "Oh?"

"The shower helps me to think."

"Oh, right, of course." I stepped back. "I appreciate that."

"We'll find a way."

Wanting to believe that, I drew on his strength and felt my loneliness lifting. There seemed no solution to this bewitchment and I didn't want to walk away because it felt like it may be the last time I'd ever be this close and the agony of this realization was unbearable. "You understand my concerns?"

He kept his back to me. "You made some valid points."

"Good."

"However, I choose to continue with the plan."

"Excuse me?"

"Leighton, you're a distraction."

"You're impossible."

Tobias turned and wrapped his fingers around my wrist and pulled me beneath the shower and said with a smile, "Sorry, Zara? What was that? Couldn't hear you over the water."

Beneath the downpour he nudged me against the tile and his hand rested on the right side of the wall near my head. "Do you want the truth?" He held me captive with those green irises sparkling with gold flecks. His eyes brimmed with passion.

I gave a wary nod peering up at him from behind soaked eyelashes.

"I seduced you. I brought you into my world. That day when you turned up at The Wilder Museum I tried to send you back to London. What did you do?"

"Refused to leave LA."

"Exactly. You refused to stop hunting me. You followed me all the way into the flame. Which means I'm responsible for your life now. Your future."

My hair and clothes were soaked and I squirmed against him. "We were having a nice conversation."

"We still are."

"No, this is what you do. You take charge and don't let me have a say."

"Have your say."

"I've led them to you."

He brushed water out of his eyes. "Do you forgive me for being Icon?"

"I don't know."

"That's your answer?"

"Yes."

"Maybe you should go use your own shower."

"Why?"

"If you stay in here one more second I'll kiss you hard on the mouth—" His gaze snapped to my lips.

"And then?" My hands reached out to grab his shoulders and I dug my fingernails into toned muscle.

"If you don't leave right now…"

Fighting this need for him, I turned my face away, refusing to show I was falling…

And falling…

I shoved at his chest because that was the problem—I cared too much and yielding was so, so easy. My eyelids squeezed shut as my entire being yearned for his touch.

"You're going to have to help me out here." He stepped aside. "Is that Zara for 'fuck me hard, please' or for 'get out of my way'?"

"I told you," I snapped. "You don't get to kiss me."

He drew near me, reading the truth. "Show me what I cannot do. So we're clear."

"You obviously need reminding." I crushed my mouth to his and I reached up to scrunch a fistful of his soaking wet hair to hold him to me. Daring to force his lips wider, I plunged my tongue against his, sweeping fiercely to make my point, our faces splashed with water.

I had to get him to see sense.

I pulled away, raising my chin proudly, having delivered my answer.

"Okay, so none of that." He grazed his lips along my neck, planting pecks all the way to the edge of my mouth.

I gave a nod to confirm I was standing strong on this issue. "We must remain focused."

"Laser focused," he agreed. "No distractions."

"Exactly."

"What about this?" His kisses trailed down my throat and glided along my shoulder, tenderly setting my skin alight with the slightest touch of his mouth, moving down along my chest, and then he suckled my right nipple through my soaked blouse.

"I'm not sure," I managed. "I have to think about that one."

Impatiently, he ripped open my blouse, popping buttons as he tugged and then eased the cups of my bra up, hitching it above my breasts, then leaning in to run the tip of his tongue around my areola.

"Oh, God," I moaned.

"And this?" He owned my other nipple with his nimble fingers, tugging and then sucking, sending shivers of pleasure between my thighs.

"We should remain platonic," I burst out.

"Quite agree. Makes perfect sense. Perhaps if you

were to show me exactly what you've forbidden your-self from doing to me."

"I won't do this." I reached down and gripped his cock and it felt like steel wrapped in silk and my jaw slackened in wonder at its hugeness and the pleasure it would bring.

He gave a nod. "Makes perfect sense."

"You understand why?" My whisper fell close to his ear as I continued to work my hand up and down his shaft, refusing to let go.

"Completely. The science behind your reasoning is flawless." His voice was husky. "Breaking your rule is reckless."

"I mean, if I were to take you in my mouth…" I blinked droplets of water off my eyelids. "You would come and everything would change between us."

"That would be—"

"Bad." I nipped his lower lip and sighed into his mouth, my sex wet and clenching, demanding this to happen, desperate to be filled entirely.

Under no circumstances is this happening, I reas-sured myself. All I had to do was walk the few steps to the door and this moment would be lost to history.

"We are quite capable of restraint." His mouth hesi-tated close to mine.

"I agree."

Water showered over us as we froze in this pose with both of us at a standoff, suspended in this sensual trance, our breaths panting against each other's, my clit throbbing, my sex aching for oneness.

"Touch me." My words were spoken so softly I was sure he wouldn't hear.

His hand resting on the tile curled into a fist and

my gaze lowered to those lips I deserved. This endless teasing of denial was cruel as the seconds passed like an eternity.

Tobias stepped back and stared off as though needing a moment to gather his thoughts. "I have the willpower of a God, apparently."

Yet mine was lost to me and I slumped to my knees and peered up at him.

"Well, I did." He looked down at me and his eyes were filled with kindness.

Dragging my teeth over my bottom lip to help endure this torment, slipping into the forbidden, unable to resist, my mouth captured his erection as I drifted further into the heady intoxication of this man, lavishing devotion over the erotic vision before me, lapping along the girth and shifting position to worship his balls with my mouth, bathed in falling water.

Tobias wiped droplets out of his eyes. "What would happen if I showed you how we shouldn't fuck?"

I continued sucking him longingly, squeezing him tight and tracing my tongue around the head, circling, flicking, and reminded again of its power, his easy seduction.

He drew in a sharp breath. "Because clarity is important."

"I would remember every moment of it," I whispered.

It was too late. We needed this closeness and I tried to find him amid the confusion, searching out the real Tobias as I worked him with my hand in unison with my sucking, my sighs echoing.

He reached down and cupped his palm to my cheek and his eyes were filled with affection. I fell into his gaze, tasting that bead at the tip and swooning that we'd found our way back to such intimacy. His head lolled when I drew him as far as possible, his cock edging my throat and my moans vibrating around his length.

His hands reached beneath my arms and he pulled me up and tore at my clothes, all fury and unbridled passion, removing all that was between us before hoisting me up against the wall. Naked, I flung my arms around his neck and wrapped my thighs around his waist demanding it, needing him inside me. He answered my silent cry by slamming into me with a desperate fury, sending spasms of pleasure, soaring me into nothingness as he pummeled me against the tile. The downpour bathing us both.

He slowed his rhythm, peering down at his deliberate tempo, watching himself slide in and out of me with a controlled discipline, his cock struck deeper and I trembled against him, needing to come but refusing for this to be over, dreading our inevitable separation and returning to the formality that forged itself at the other end of this.

When he pulled out of me I groaned my panic.

"I've got you." He eased me to the floor.

I lay with my arms stretched out in front of me and my bum raised, moaning my relief when I felt his hands clasp my hips and drag me backward in his direction, and him thrust into me from behind, with me in a position of surrender, my hair tumbling out before me. He reached around to strum my clit and I knew in this moment I was his. Rocking back on him, we became one as we gave in to each other's demands.

Weak in his arms, I felt like a rag doll as he rolled me over to lie on my back. He raised himself over me, entering with one long thrust, locking us together again, and I flung my legs around his waist and matched his pounding, lifting my pelvis to meet each strike, begging with this movement to have him drive in farther, his arms holding him off my chest and his steely gaze fixed on mine.

"Kiss me," I pleaded.

"One condition." He leaned in and nipped my earlobe.

"What?"

"Don't tell me you regret this happened."

"Why would I?"

His frown deepened as he seemed to mull over his answer.

I rested my fingertips on his lips. "Everything is okay. We're going to be okay."

"I know. I'm just glad you're looking at me how you once did."

"How did I look at you?"

He brought his mouth down on mine and I opened my lips to let him in, his tongue sweeping across mine with devotion. This was the kind of kiss I'd craved, infused with adoration. It went on and on, carrying us higher until we came together; his heat shot into me and my sex claimed him as the center of my universe.

Eventually, we broke apart and lay side by side on our backs, panting and staring up at the ceiling, and it felt good to have his hand holding mine still. The only sound was of our breathing and the water striking the tile.

"Shower off, Jade," he said. "Raise the temperature—73 degrees should be good."

"And bring coffee." I grinned at my cheekiness.

"Careful, we'll have your favorite drone in here. Anyway, I fancy something stronger and no one makes a Bombay martini quite like me. Stirred, not shaken. Though with what I've got planned for you we should probably reserve that for later."

"What have you got planned?"

"All sorts of fun."

I looked over at him. "This was a good decision, wasn't it? After everything."

He pushed himself up and offered me his hand to help me to my feet. "I'm glad we're still talking."

"That was more than talking." I smirked.

"We can reset if you like."

"To friends?"

He bowed his head and walked over to a corner closet where fresh folded towels were stacked neatly. He pulled out two of them.

Friends. Did I really want to downgrade us after that mind-blowing sex? No, but it was probably for the best and I did feel more relaxed around him, and that counted for something, didn't it? It would make finding our way back to our lives more comfortable.

I stood there soaked and with my sex still thrumming with a lingering ache of pleasure, hugging my arms to my chest, and grateful when he wrapped a white plush towel around me and he kissed my head with affection. He wrapped a towel around his waist and tucked it in.

"What happens now?" I wanted more than anything to rest my cheek against his chest as I breathed in the heady scent of expensive body wash that wafted my way.

"We find dry clothes." He smiled sweetly and it made him look so cute. "I'm glad you're feeling better." He raised his chin to indicate something was behind me.

"What is it?" Turning, I jumped when I saw Jade hovering a few feet away.

"She too can refuse you nothing. She's here to ask if you want sugar with your coffee."

"She heard me from in here?"

"Yes. When she oscillates like that she's asking for clarification." He looked over my shoulder. "I'm handling the drinks, Jade. Give us a minute, okay."

I spun to face Tobias again and stared up at his beautiful face, his dreamy smile, that gentleness replacing his steely demeanor, and I wanted to fall into his arms again.

He stepped back and I felt like I'd lost him all over again.

Our clothes were scattered here and there, drenched and discarded, a reminder of the wayward passion that had shaken us off course. I turned and looked at the open door and something compelled me to head for it.

Barefoot and alone, padding out into the hallway, I reassured myself resetting was easy… *That's it, good, keep walking until you're out of range because you just barely escaped being absorbed into the supernova that is Tobias William Wilder.*

CHAPTER SIX

I WAS GOING to fall.

Gravity pulled and my gloved hands trembled as I gripped the climbing rope, stealing a quick glance at the drop below. It was still dark out here in the garden and I was halfway down the side of this Manhattan mansion wall, feeling dazed from the unearthly hour in the morning. I wanted to be back inside tucked in bed and not dangling midair with this East Coast chill whipping around me.

Maybe Tobias had chosen this time because I'd be too sleepy to protest. Abseiling was somehow meant to prepare me for when we retrieved my paintings. Or even if a greater threat surfaced.

Stupid, stupid idea.

Tobias peered down at me from over the top of the roof where he was kneeling on the edge. "When you're ready, kick off from the wall and loosen your carabiner so you only descend a few feet. When you raise the rope again it will tighten the carabiner and you'll hold your position. Go ahead and repeat what you're doing now, resting your feet back on the wall. You've watched me do it. This is easy."

"Easy for you," I snapped. "How is this meant to help me?"

"If we get separated you must be able to take care of

yourself." He pointed to his waist. "I have you on the safety harness."

"Pull me up."

"I'll come down." He swung round and landed right behind me with his feet either side of mine and his chest pressed to my back.

Something bulged against my lower spine. "That better be your flashlight."

"Concentrate, please. We're going to move together—" He wrapped his arm around my waist and I breathed out a long sigh of relief. "I'm right here with you," he said.

"I'm not sure I'll ever need this."

"Let's hope so." He swung to my left.

With a nod to show I was ready, we swung out together taking a leap back and gliding downward in unison, both of us landing on the wall having lowered a few feet. Daring to go a little farther than before I continued to swing out, mirroring him and relieved he was with me. We found our rhythm.

When my feet finally made it to the ground I peered up at how far I'd come, amazed.

"Well?" He waited for my reaction.

"That's very high."

He followed my gaze. "It's not a bad start."

"I never imagined I'd ever do something like this."

He rubbed my back with affection. "I had a feeling you might like it."

This was so far out of my realm of experience I couldn't quite grasp I'd even agreed to expose myself to this danger, and yet as I stood here catching my breath and staring up at the dizzying height of how far I'd come, something shifted deep inside and there came a sense that this was a defining moment for me. My courage was awakening and it sparked a sense of independence.

"Wanna do it again?" he said.

"Yes, yes, I do."

He threw his head back in a laugh and we ran into the foyer, up the stairs, headed for the loft window and edged back onto the roof. This time Tobias went first.

I never knew there was this side to me that had lain dormant all this time. Hanging out in art galleries and snuggled in libraries didn't exactly inspire anyone to see me as heroic. Yet Tobias did and the way he looked at me now with pride in his gaze stirred my own. I beamed back at him, grateful to have at least tried it. These kinds of moments with him certainly weren't boring.

We descended five more times like this and the last three times I abseiled on my own.

I rewarded my bravery with a long hot shower and afterward went downstairs to see about fixing us breakfast.

Sitting at the granite countertop sipping tea and watching the sunrise out of the bay window, I smiled when I thought that Tobias had probably gone back to bed.

The memories of the last few days came flooding back and I froze with the realization that all that had happened had literally stunned me into compliance. That vision of Tobias leaping off the tall building shook me to the core. I'd found the courage to abseil down the wall and this felt like a breakthrough—

Sitting here, drinking tea and waiting for Tobias to take the lead wouldn't do. I had to take my power back. I had to get into his workshop and see what he was really doing in there. Surely I was his biggest threat and maybe this was his way of controlling me and distracting me from what was really going on.

I set my mug in the sink and hurried toward the man cave. I tapped the corner of the secret painting and felt the frame release from the wall. Easing my fingers around the back I pulled. I was in. I didn't know how much time I'd have or if Tobias would come looking for me.

It was no surprise his five computers needed a code to access them when I tried to get in to them. I concentrated instead on studying his hardware while trying to piece together what I could from his equipment. I searched for alternative motives for us being here or any hint a theft might be going down in New York, care of Icon.

To the left of the main area was a hallway and at the end was a large chrome door. I pressed my palm to the side on the panel but it didn't open. Ready to head back the way I'd come I turned—

Tobias was standing at the other end of the hallway staring at me with his hands shoved inside his pockets. "Zara?"

"I was just taking a look around." *Damn my honesty.*

"I can see that." He strolled toward me, with that long stride exuding power, and closed the gap between us and towered over me.

Gone were his black sports clothes he'd worn for climbing and instead he'd changed into his casually ripped jeans and a black T-shirt with TechRule's logo styled with bold sweeps. He scraped his fingers through his already perfectly styled hair as though thinking through how to handle this; *handle me.*

A waft of his heady cologne hit the spot and I tried to guard against the impending effect of swooning at this early morning vision of danger camouflaged as beauty.

And I was alone in a big old manor with him.

"What did I say to you when you first arrived here?" he said.

"That I could leave?"

"I also reassured you my casa is your casa." He stretched out his hands. "So this look of guilt on your face doesn't need to stay."

"What's in there?" I pointed to the chrome door behind me.

He kept his stare on mine. "Supplies."

I assumed he meant for when he was acting as Icon and breaking into homes to steal back paintings. I felt like I'd woken up from a nightmare of my own making. I went to walk past him and he pressed a hand to my chest and nudged me back against the wall.

"Did the climb scare you?" He trapped me between his arms as he rested his hands either side of me.

"At first."

"How do you feel now?"

I could see in his gaze he knew he'd awoken something within me and perhaps he regretted that jaunt down the wall.

"I feel braver," I admitted.

"Well, that's good, right?"

My senses sharpened as I tried to read sincerity in his voice.

We both knew he needed me if he was going to create this other *Mona Lisa*. After all, if anyone could guide him right on what the specialists would be looking for it would be me.

"I'm here for you." He brushed a strand of hair out of my face.

"I appreciate that."

"Zara, what's wrong?"

"I feel like you're keeping something from me."

"Like what?"

"I want full disclosure on everything. No more keeping anything from me."

"I'm not keeping anything from you." He stepped back. "Why do you think that?"

"I want to know what you're doing in here."

"I've been open about all of it—" He pointed across the room. "Over there the three-dimensional printer is waiting for me to extract chemical components to create our bait."

"And where will you find these samples?"

"Tomorrow I have an appointment with a sixteenth-century specialist."

"I'll come with you."

"If you like."

"Show me how you break into homes." I folded my arms.

He leaned in and whispered, "Are you sure?"

"Yes." My body shuddered against the pressure of his chest pressing mine, and if he kissed me I'd bite his lip.

"You want in on Icon's methods?" His mouth brushed my earlobe.

"For all the right reasons," I managed.

"And what might those be?"

"In case I need to use them." It was a bad lie but he seemed to mull it over.

He stepped away and stared down the hallway. "I promised you full access to this house and also full access to me. I want you to feel safe. I need to build your trust. So, if this is what you need to see, then fine."

"Fine?"

"Let's simulate." He waggled his eyebrows suggestively.

I swallowed hard and gave a nod. "What are you going to do?"

"Lock up the house and break into it. How does that sound?"

Boom… I'd just gotten Icon to reveal his methods.

Yes, that climb this morning had actually delivered a good outcome. This was the kind of evidence I should be going after. He could focus on his stupid painting that he'd never be able to replicate. I mean, we were talking about a sixteenth-century masterpiece that would be savagely scrutinized by one of Burell's highly trained art experts who would run a slew of precision-centered tests.

Meanwhile, I'd use this time to gather evidence on Wilder and when the time came, do what had to be done. My heart ached with the thought of it. Taking down Icon would probably mean I'd go down with him. I leaned against the wall to steady my legs.

"Are you okay?" He looked sincere.

"Of course." I refused to be a chess piece moved on a whim. No, I was going to be empowered and prove my place in the art world as someone who didn't sway when the pressure intensified. "Where would we start?"

He held my stare. "On the roof. I'll show you how I utilize that entry point—"

Uneasiness washed over me. "Show me in here."

"Shall we have breakfast first?"

"I'm not hungry."

He smiled. "Zara, your stomach's grumbling."

Right on cue it grumbled again and I rubbed my stomach to tame it.

"Jade," Tobias snapped—making me jump. "Bring us two bowls of fruit salad and two mugs of coffee."

His small drone rose and headed up the ramp and I watched the door swing open for it.

"Ready?" Tobias broke into a cheeky grin.

He showed me how he placed interference on surveillance cameras by using an app he'd designed on his watch; how to turn on the night-vision mechanism while wearing snazzy-looking goggles, and with the same lenses how to recognize infrared lights when abseiling into a pitch-black building.

Half an hour into my lesson we took a break to eat and Tobias leaned back against the chrome workstation and scooped in mouthfuls of fruit salad. I sat a few feet away and finished off mine and drank my coffee, all the while memorizing in detail everything he had showed me.

We kept going and I learned how Tobias navigated sensitized floor tiles by hooking up a suspended system so that he'd not touch the ground but could swing with full movement and grab a painting without touching the ground. There was also a knack to rolling through invisible laser beams to prevent their activation and I learned that too. The final piece of the puzzle came together to add to what I'd already learned from the Icon break-ins that I'd studied back in London.

I'd descended into the center of the hive.

Tobias pulled out a large chrome case and tapped it. "This contains everything I need when I'm traveling."

I stared at his large box of tricks waiting to be discovered.

"Give me a second, okay." I waved off seeing it and plopped down on a bar stool and leaned on the workstation. This had been a fascinating insight and as an art investigator these skills would take my career to the next level—I'd seen behind the curtain.

Tobias came toward me and knelt before me, resting a hand on my knee. "It's a lot to take in."

I tried to catch my breath as my head swirled with all I'd seen. Every moment that unfolded had provided me with indisputable evidence he was Icon. I'd been provided with a step-by-step process of how he pulled off his heists.

"Jade," he snapped, "bring water."

"I'm fine."

"Want to talk about it?"

"Not right now."

"I made something special for you."

"I just need a minute."

"We've been trapped in here for days, and I want to prove to you my inventing capabilities can be put to better use."

What was I doing allowing him to just lead me off like this across the room? Yet with my hand in his I walked beside him. Perhaps this was what it felt like to be in shock even if it was self-inflicted.

"Close your eyes," he said when we reached the back door.

"Why?"

"I want it to be a surprise."

"What is it?"

"Zara." Tobias smiled. "Close your eyes."

This was insanity, and to prove it each breath that followed was inhaled with a wary sharpness as I listened out for what was coming next. The sound of the lock of the door. A cool breeze on my face. His hand taking mine again as he led me into the garden…

"I put this together for you." Tobias nudged my side.

My vision cleared as I took in the garden. The landscaping had changed from a lush green lawn to places layered with turf with a geometric layout consisting of obstacles—small ramps, tubes, a minibridge—and all of these led to small holes ready for golf balls.

"You designed a miniature golf course?" I was stunned.

"Do you like it?"

"Why?" I turned to him.

"So we can play." He pointed to the house. "I thought we'd have some fun. I realized what was so special about this place was how I'd waste the day playing."

"When did you create this?"

"Edward and I built it years ago. I found it in the storeroom. My aunt never got rid of it."

I squeezed my eyes shut for a beat, realizing he'd set it up while I'd been distracted in his workshop. "Do you have golf clubs?"

"Over there." He walked over to the edge of the garden and picked up two golf clubs.

"Do you play regular golf?"

"Any self-respecting businessman knows deals are done on the green." He handed me a club. "You?"

"No, I've never even played crazy golf."

He grinned, realizing that's what we called it in England. "Would you like a couple of pointers?"

We stood at the far left of the garden with Tobias

standing behind me, his arms wrapped around my body to show me how to hold my club. Strong hands came over mine and I followed his lead with a long sweep of my club. My head swirled with how fast we'd come back to him wooing me. This felt annoyingly right, almost nudging out my doubt.

"Look at the ball and imagine the line you want it to follow before you hit it." He kissed my shoulder. "This is fun."

"Tobias." My voice sounded shaky. "I'm scared."

He let go and walked around to face me and gripped my shoulders. "You have every right to be."

"What if everything goes wrong? I mean, more than it has already?" The club slipped from my grip and fell to the ground.

He pulled me into a hug. "This was me proving my transparency. The part of me I've never shown to anyone. I scared you and I'm sorry."

My face squished against his chest. "You never felt guilty?"

"Returning the art to the original owner who had tried and failed to get it back seemed fair. I stole from the thieves." He pulled back to look at me. "I never thought that I'd meet someone like you, Zara. Perhaps things would have been different. Maybe I'd have not taken so many risks."

"I'm afraid for you."

"Don't be."

"Promise me you'll give this up."

"I have." He tipped up my chin. "I need you to believe me."

Sincerity reflected in his gaze and he looked troubled as though deeply affected by all this soul-searching.

I pointed to the house. "You have to get rid of all of that equipment."

"We'll need it to get your paintings back, but afterward it all goes."

My gaze swept over the golf course and I marveled at how well it was built. "Did your dad help you create this?"

He smiled. "Yes."

"Come on, then." I knelt to pick up the golf club. "I'll putt first."

I was close to getting through to him, I could feel it. All I needed now was to hear him say he'd find another way to locate my paintings. Perhaps we'd both come up with something better.

My aim was way off when I hit the ball, though when it was Tobias's turn he hit a hole in one. By the time we'd finished the first round we'd fallen into fits of laughter. My thoughts carried me back to a young Tobias hanging out with his father out here. I wondered if his mom had watched on with joy.

"Do you ever think of how all this will end?" I watched his reaction.

He held my gaze. "It's hard to think about that now."

"Why?"

"I've made the kind of choices that may never see a normal life for me."

My heart shuddered as I broke his gaze, not wanting to see his uncertainty.

"You must be starving." He tapped my arm to get my attention. "Do you want some lunch?"

"Yes, please." I stared down the garden again at his genius golf course and smiled at how much fun I'd had.

"Let's cook together."

"Sure." I followed him into the kitchen.

Within a few minutes we'd set about preparing the ingredients for salmon burgers. It was fun to watch Tobias washing the lettuce and then grilling the fish fillets on the stove as I buttered the buns and found the plates. I imagined this could once have been us all the time if circumstances were different, preparing meals and giggling at each other's jokes and even planning a life together.

We settled at the granite island. I bit into my burger and moaned at how good it tasted, and Tobias burst into laughter.

"What?" I dabbed my mouth with a napkin, assuming I was covered in sauce.

"I don't think I've ever seen anyone eat like you," he said. "You devour your food like it's your last meal."

"That comes from my days growing up with a dad who got so distracted he forgot to feed me." I recalled those days fondly even so. "I had to be an adult early on and cook for us."

"You grew up fast?"

I shrugged off the memory. "After our house fire my dad changed. It was depression but I was too young to recognize it then. Anyway, I found some old cookbooks of my mom's and learned how to cook from those. I liked seeing my dad eat a hot meal. I roasted chickens and beef, that kind of thing. Things easy to prepare. It's not like we didn't have the money but sometimes all we had in the house was bread and cheese."

"You were brave, Zara." He licked sauce off his fingers. "I imagine you gave him so much joy."

"I hope so."

"My uncle whisked me off to France initially and

then when I turned fourteen we moved to Plymouth in Massachusetts where my mom was born, and where I was born too, hoping to give me the best childhood despite my loss."

"Why didn't he keep you in France?"

"My parents asked him to take care of me if anything happened to them." He raised his hands. "I'm sure not once for a second did they believe it would. I found myself living in the home I grew up in, surrounded by familiar rooms and belongings, and I'm grateful my uncle gave me that stability."

"He was a good uncle."

"As close to a father as you can get. He took me out fishing once. I must have been twelve. I caught this tiny mackerel. You could fit it in your palm. Anyway, I was so damn proud. He cooked that fish on the skillet and ate the whole thing right there in front of me. From the noises he made you'd have thought he was eating a meal cooked by a top chef."

"That's adorable."

"He's the reason why I have my head on straight."

"Do you miss him?"

"We talk often. Come with me to see him in Paris."

I wiped my hands on my napkin. "That would be lovely."

"You don't sound too sure."

"Tobias, you and I…"

He pushed his plate aside. "I see."

"I need you to tell me you've changed your mind. Tell me you won't try to fake a painting. Certainly not one as prestigious as the *Mona Lisa*."

"I've created a template. I was going to show it to

you. Reassure you this is possible. We can get Burell with this."

My stomach turned and I regretted eating so much food. "I'm trying to reason with you here."

"We've come this far."

"You just told me you believe you have your head on straight. Yet we spent the day with you showing me how you break into houses. This is not normal, Tobias. This is not okay."

"When I stayed here my grandmother would take me out and buy me comics. I'd sit right over there and read them from cover to cover. I even wrote a few of my own. In those comics justice was always served. Always. I was nine when I realized that's not how the world really works."

"Do you see yourself like those superheroes, Tobias? Men who took justice into their own hands and got away with it? Because those men don't exist."

"It's better than being a victim."

"That's unfair, I've done everything in my power to restore my father's reputation." I slid off the bar stool. "Every good decision I ever made was threatened when you and I met."

"Zara—"

"Creating the other *Mona Lisa* is impossible."

"Jade's helping me." He gave a sweet smile. "Don't underestimate Jade's talents."

"I'll be right back," I lied and headed away from him and off to goodness knows where, though walking out the front door seemed reasonable. Instead, my crazy side went for the lounge.

I needed to put some space between us so I could think straight.

This was a gorgeous room with its wall-to-wall rosewood paneling and artwork providing an old-world feel. A plush green carpet and low hanging chandelier hinted it had hosted parties once and probably with influential guests. This Art Nouveau theme made me feel like I'd been transported to a simpler time.

Tobias burst through the door. "Why are you mad at me?"

"Where do you keep the Bombay thingies?"

"Zara, it's only 3:00 p.m."

"I deserve a treat."

"Why did you walk away?" He read my angry glare. "Okay, step aside. The mixologist is in the house."

I folded my arms and stubbornly stuck to my spot behind the bar and let him work around me, quietly seething at him for the insanity he'd unleashed on me. I considered how to best deliver what was going to sound like uncensored screaming.

Tobias filled two glasses with ice, poured a dash of vermouth into each one, grabbed a bottle of Bombay Sapphire gin and poured that in too. He stirred it and then tipped it through a sieve into two fresh cocktail glasses, leaving the ice behind. His fingers deftly squeezed lemon into each one. "Olive?"

"I'm freaking out here."

"I can see that." He handed me the glass, then rested his hand on the bar looking suavely confident.

"What was that really?" I pointed toward his workshop.

"In what way?"

I took a gulp of my cocktail and it burned my throat but it was a good burn, the kind that took my mind off my terror for all of five seconds.

He gestured to my glass. "Slow down."

I set my drink down. "You think you're training your protégé. Is that it?"

"This is what protection looks like." He sounded stern. "This is me looking out for you. You demanded into my world. There's a caveat."

I lifted my glass and swigged several more gulps and was pleasantly struck with the way my body flushed with warmth, and it went straight to my head.

Tobias's brow arched as he watched me take another sip and he lifted his own glass to his lips. "Damn, that's good."

"What's next? Weapons?"

"Okay, Annie Get Your Gun, take a breath. I've never used a weapon. I've never hurt anyone."

"Why does everything you do feel wrong?"

"I thought you liked my crazy golf." He held out his hands. "Come here."

"No."

"Don't you think I'd rather be taking you to a museum—" he waved his hand through the air "—strolling through Central Park with you—"

"You mean instead of forging a painting?"

"We're against the clock, Zara." Tobias caressed his brow. "This is happening with or without you."

My sharp intake of breath revealed my horror.

He turned away to stare at his reflection in the mirror behind the bar as though needing a moment to weigh his answer. "This is the only bait that will work."

Tobias set the bar too high with his rascally exploits and yet I understood his need to right those dreadful acts. This was who he was and what he had always done to find meaning to his life, restoring paintings to their rightful owners.

So far I'd stayed because of my belief I could find a way to untangle my life and have a say in how my future unraveled. I'd demanded to be shown more of his world, and perhaps it was time to explore why I was resisting the inevitability of my life changing minute by minute. I had to find a way out of this.

I reached for my drink and took a large gulp.

Justice only worked when the law played along and proof of this was the authorities turning away from me in favor of protecting Elliot Burell. He had blood on his hands like the mark of a warlord. The cruelest stain.

Eli had revealed that his family prided themselves on taking what they wanted and when they wanted it. Perhaps we were the only ones daring enough to stop them.

Tobias plucked an olive out of his drink. "I'll have my jet fueled and made ready for you. Just say when you're ready to leave and I will make it happen." He popped it into his mouth and chewed while offering a reassuring smile. "I'll miss you."

"And what about you? What will you do?"

"Nothing changes."

My shoulders slumped with frustration. "Do you really believe you can pull this off?"

He relaxed a little. "Do you want to see what Jade's come up with?"

"No."

"Yes you do." Tobias gestured toward the center of the room. "Bring her up for us, Jade."

Hanging midair in the center of the room was a hologram of the painting of *Mona Lisa*, and even her measurements appeared to match the thirty inches by twenty-one inches of the original, and she looked stunningly compelling. I couldn't look away. "This is her?" I'd been holding my breath.

"This is the template."

My gaze shot to his. "You're really going through with this?"

"Yes. I'll incorporate what I've learned about Leonardo's techniques. The way he utilized light, his knowledge of anatomy, how he transitioned from one area to the next without detection."

"This invention must never be shared, Tobias."

He shrugged. "You can watch me delete the program when this is over."

"You really believe she'll pass scrutiny?"

He looked over the hologram. "You tell me."

I set my half-finished drink on the bar and approached the life-size hologram hovering midair, bewitched by her beauty and mesmerized he'd managed to capture her. Instinctively, I reached out to touch the canvas and my hand went through her. The detail was extraordinary. This was almost as good as being in the room with her and I didn't want the spell to break because this felt like home.

"There's a slight variation from the original in the Louvre," I realized.

"A minor difference to reflect an evolution from the one he gave the Giocondos. This one feels more intimate, don't you think?"

"It's subtle." My heart fluttered with the realization Tobias had blended in the differences so well. "You've captured his technique."

Tobias came toward me and shoved his hands into his pockets. "I'm working on my fake collector's provenance. I need decent clues to her origin if I want to pique Burell's interest."

"Like?"

"Perhaps the seller's family once lived in Florence?"

"That would work." I couldn't believe I was even saying this.

"Maybe his relatives lived near the wealthy Florentine silk merchant Francesco del Giocondo."

"Giocondo commissioned the real painting to celebrate the birth of their second son, Andrea." I looked over at Tobias. "Mona Lisa's glow is quite possibly because she'd just given birth and was breast-feeding. Maybe she was lulled by the oxytocin in her bloodstream released during feeding."

"Okay, wow, that's a first for me."

"Look at her. She's radiant." I leaned in.

"Or maybe my collector is somehow related to Salaì." He gave a shrug at his suggestion. "Leonardo's assistant? After all, his master gifted Salaì with many of his paintings."

"A clean provenance inspires confidence."

He smirked.

I shot him a glare. "Did you get me tipsy on purpose?"

"I may have eased the cogs a wee bit." He looked amused.

And I'd fallen right into his trap by sipping his cocktail like Alice in Wonderland, and then deliriously diving down the rabbit hole after him.

Tobias was incorrigible.

I spun round to face him. "Leonardo da Vinci's uncle helped raise him, Tobias." I gave him a knowing smile. "You have so much in common. He had a challenging childhood with a lot of pain and betrayal. He adored math, science, botany, engineering, oh so many things but especially inventing."

Tension caught in his jaw.

I could see I'd gotten to him. "His biological parents were never married."

"Leo was a survivor."

"Organized, dependable and controlling."

"Ah, you've got me."

"Bossy, hard to keep up with and annoyingly brilliant."

"I have my moments."

"I'm still talking about da Vinci." I turned back to the frame. "The columns are not finished just as in the original in the Louvre. Not bad, Wilder."

"Thank you."

"I'm not done."

He looked amused. "Do you think Mona Lisa's husband demanded the painting from da Vinci because he was taking so long?"

"Maybe he thought da Vinci was dragging out time with his wife. Four years is a long time to spend company with a married woman."

"She's enigmatic."

"Lisa Gherardini Giocondo," I whispered to her. "Will they believe you were painted by the same hand as your sister in the Louvre?"

He stepped closer to her. "Fess up, Lisa."

"She lived across the street from Leonardo's father." I read his smile. "Of course you knew this."

"When I saw that sketch in your London flat—" He dragged his hands over his eyes to say the rest.

"Your reaction was adorable."

"You eccentric English broad."

I deserved that as most women didn't have priceless artwork tucked away in their bedrooms.

My gaze returned to the hologram. "I think I'd have liked her very much." My eyes wandered over her face, those kind eyes and that smile, and I pulled back a little to take in the canvas, recognizing the detailed touches and enthralled by the idea it would be re-created by using da Vinci's exact methods garnered by Tobias's AI. "I need to go back to the Louvre so I can spend time with the real *Mona Lisa*." I let out a sigh. "Leonardo only worked on a classic Renaissance ground of white. So you will have to find paint that matches that era. No small task."

"I know."

"Look at her. She's sensual. Carries a certain wisdom." My gaze locked with his and a moment passed between us, a deep connection contradicting our current standoff, and I read what could have even been love.

Love, from the man whose presence burned me up from the inside out, and this more than anything scared me.

My stare shot back to *Mona Lisa*. "What was your first instinct when you saw her just now?"

He looked thoughtful. "Hard to describe."

"She beckoned you?"

"Yes, she's mesmerizing."

"There's a subtlety stirring an instinctual feeling hard to articulate. I always trust this. In the original painting hanging in the Louvre, *Mona Lisa* conveys aloofness. Her smile belongs to her."

"Impressive."

I strolled around the portrait, surprised to see Tobias had managed to capture a realistic backing. "Can you increase this?"

He flicked his fingers over the image and enlarged it to such an extent it looked like it had doubled in size.

I pointed to the edge. "How did you capture this backing?"

"I accessed photographic records from the Louvre. The backing doesn't have to be exact. Different painting. Different frame."

"Same master." I threw him a disapproving glare.

"I'm enjoying watching you look at her. There's awe in your expression, Zara. Coming from you, that is a compliment."

I strolled around to face her again and breathed in an admiring sigh.

Tobias straightened his back. "Burell will be falling over himself to own her."

"Because she's one of history's greatest treasures."

He brought our drinks back over. "What's the verdict, Leighton? Will she pass if we create her from this?" He raised his glass in a toast.

I accepted my cocktail from him. "There's a flaw."

He stared at me for the longest time. "What's the issue?"

"I'm not going to tell you."

"If it's because of the eyebrows and eyelashes being present, I'll be making sure those have disappeared from sight due to either overcleaning or time passing."

Just as the original—where most people didn't even notice Mona Lisa's eyebrows were missing.

"I guessed you'd know that. However, that's not the issue. If your painting is created off this image it will not pass scrutiny."

"Why?"

I took a long deep sip. "Look at her again and tell me what you sense."

"The uncanny valley?"

That small inner voice warning something isn't quite what it seems, eliciting a sense of uneasiness when you look at it.

"Tell me so I can fix it."

I handed him my glass and walked toward the door. "Good afternoon, Mr. Wilder." At least when I fell asleep tonight my conscience would be clear.

CHAPTER SEVEN

SITTING ON THE edge of the wall I stared beyond at the monastery within walking distance, those ancient pillars looked like they'd barely survived the surrounding city. It saddened me to see the weather had ravaged the roof and caused tiles to fall away.

I drew in a wary breath of early morning air, glad for my parka with its fur hood and my Ugg boots. My heart beat faster when I heard Clara's dialing tone and my fingers tightened around Tobias's phone.

He stood a few feet away and, though he'd offered to let me chat with her alone, I'd told him I felt comfortable having him overhear us. He looked relaxed in his jeans and was now clean shaven, making him extra suave in that black blazer and scarf.

He'd not mentioned our conversation last night over the flaw I'd found in his hologram, though despite the subtlety of Mona Lisa's expression eventually he'd see it.

I went to hang up.

"Hello?" Clara's voice sounded reassuringly familiar.

"Hey, it's me." I forced the cheeriness.

"Are you okay?"

A rush of homesickness came at me and a well of guilt for disappearing without a word.

"How are you?" I kept my voice even.

"For God's sake, tell me you're not in any danger?"

"I'm fine. What do you know?"

"You may be connected to the suspect Icon who has been mentioned in the news. He sounds dangerous, Zara. I'm worried about you."

"Clara, I'm fine." I glanced up at Tobias. "I'm working on the Icon case and it seems our paths have crossed."

"Come home."

"I've been hired by a client of Huntly Pierre on a very special commission. I've done nothing wrong. Please don't worry. The money's fantastic."

Tobias rolled his eyes with amusement.

"Give me a sign you've not been kidnapped," she said.

I hated being a source of worry for her.

"Zara," she snapped. "What have you gotten yourself into? Abby Reynolds wants you to call her."

"I can do that." Though when I looked at Tobias he was shaking his head.

Everyone was overreacting because my job was waiting for me when I got home, and after I got my paintings back we'd all laugh about this...

Same old lie.

Her silence lingered. "Remember, you did this last time to me? Scared the shit out of me."

I tried to drag that memory back. "When?"

"You pissed off to Tunisia without me."

She was warning me her phone was either bugged or she suspected it was because it had been her that had flown off to Tunisia without me back in our college days. I'd been fine with it because I had exams. She'd ridden on a camel in the desert and snogged an Arabic Berber with bright blue eyes.

"I'm fine," I reassured her.

"Where are you?"

"Let me call you back. It's a bad line." I hated lying to her.

Tobias read my confliction and gestured for me to end the call.

"I'll come to you," she said.

My gaze shot to Tobias.

"Clara, I have to go. I love you."

She sighed heavily. "I love you. Be careful. Call again soon."

I hung up and dropped my phone into Tobias's outstretched hand. I couldn't work out if I felt better for having spoken with her. At least she knew I was thinking of her and I was safe.

"You okay?" Tobias tucked the phone away.

"It went as expected." I pushed myself to my feet. "Actually, I feel a little sick."

"Can I do anything?"

"I'm okay."

He gave me a sympathetic smile. "I get it."

Trying to calm my anxiety from just having called home, I blew out a wary breath. Hearing Clara's voice was yet another reminder of how far out of my comfort zone I'd come.

I followed Tobias along the well-worn pathway with its uneven tiles. We continued down a sprawling archway with stone pillars to our left and it gave this place the flair of a cathedral.

"Why are we here?" I managed to keep up with his purposeful strides.

"There's someone I need to talk with."

"You're not seriously dragging a church into this?"

"Monastery."

"I'm not doing this."

"Doing what?"

"Whatever you're up to."

"Go wait in the car, then."

I followed him through the door and we were greeted by the scent of incense and melting candle wax. This small chapel reminded me of the days when I'd gone to church with my dad. There was a bucket at the front to catch the leaks from the imminent rain.

This place was no less holy for its dilapidated state, and I broke away from Tobias to lean on a pew and genuflect toward the nave. Bowing my head in respect I whispered a small prayer. When I rose and turned to look at Tobias, he was bathed in the morning light streaming in from the stained-glass windows and he was gazing up at the frescoed ceiling.

I crossed the space between us and followed his gaze, admiring the fading fresco detailing monks in prayer with Christ in the center offering his blessing. There was a sacredness to this place; a humility. From the look of the images above someone had begun to restore the artwork and had brightened the colors and lovingly tried to repair the damage.

"Let's just go." I reached up to adjust his scarf.

He replied in a language I'd never heard before and it sounded lyrically complex and caused the fine hairs on my forearms to prickle.

"That wasn't French. What was that?"

"You spoke to your god. I spoke to mine."

"What language was that?"

"Djinang." Tobias towered over me. "I asked God to let you see my side of things."

I grabbed his lapels and rose onto my tiptoes. "My side is rational."

"I see you, Zara Leighton. Right inside your soul." His lips lingered close to mine. "I feel what you feel. Sense what you sense. You're close to a breakthrough."

"Breakthrough?"

"You're realizing the world is not perfect." He arched a brow.

"I know."

He shook his head. "You're in denial."

"We mustn't do any wrong here."

"The only law I follow is gravity."

My icy glare held his, and then settled on his lips which were annoyingly kissable.

A deep voice boomed from across the chapel. "We don't do weddings."

I broke away and gestured my apology toward the middle-aged monk who was walking toward us.

Tobias extended his hand to him. "Brother Lawrence?"

"Yes." He beamed a welcoming smile as they shook hands.

"We have an appointment with you."

"Mr. Wilder?" Brother Lawrence looked amused. "I thought you'd be older for some reason."

He shook my hand enthusiastically too and seemed happy to see us, and I couldn't help but squint my disapproval at Tobias.

We walked through the nave all the way to his office that was a cozy space. He poured us two cups of coffee. "You found us without difficulty?" he asked.

"Yes, thank you." Tobias wrapped his hands around his mug. "Thank you for seeing us on such short notice."

"My pleasure, of course."

"You're familiar with my gallery in LA?"

"Yes. Your collection rivals the Getty, Mr. Wilder. Quite the accomplishment." Brother Lawrence adjusted his belt. "Over the phone you mentioned you're opening a new gallery in the Bronx?"

"I'm hoping to open it next month." Tobias straightened in his seat. "We're putting together a collection of both ancient and modern pieces, and I want to showcase artists who are undiscovered."

"And you'd like us to consider showing Brother Bay's paintings?"

"His work's remarkable."

"We're very proud of him." He gestured his earnestness. "He remains modest nevertheless."

"He uses the same techniques as the old masters?" said Tobias.

"Yes, how did you hear about his work?"

"I read the article on him in *Time* magazine," said Tobias. "I'm surprised more people haven't heard of him."

"We don't use social media." Lawrence turned his attention to the garden. "When Brother Bay sells a painting it helps keep the lights on here. Bringing more attention to his work would be beneficial for all of us."

Tobias smiled his approval. "With your blessing, I'd very much like to showcase a few of his paintings at The Plaza later this week. I'm arranging a charity ball there, and I'd be delighted to present his art. If a collector shows an interest in purchasing a piece, I'll refer the buyer to you. Though you might consider Christie's in the future when his popularity picks up."

"This is extraordinarily kind of you."

"I'm all for supporting young talent. I take a certain

pride in discovering modern masters. Though Brother Bay's work is already receiving attention."

Brother Lawrence looked impressed. "Thank you, Mr. Wilder."

Tobias set his mug down on the coffee table and pushed himself to his feet. "May we meet with him?"

"Of course." Brother Lawrence led the way out.

We headed across the courtyard and along the cloister. I tugged on the back of Tobias's jacket to warn him I was watching his every move. He turned and flashed a megawatt smile back at me and raised his brows playfully. We stopped before an old wooden door with a metal ring for a handle.

Lawrence knocked once. "Here we are."

We stepped inside the chilled room and I sucked in a breath of awe—

The walls were adorned with modern portraits that were remarkably real, and what stunned me most was the artist had captured his subjects using a technique adapted from the old masters. I moved closer to one of them in a golden frame and realized if this man ever wanted to become a forger the art world would be in trouble.

Each painting reflected the soul of the individual who had posed. My gaze followed the rows of frames that led to a larger room where daylight flooded in. In the center a monk was standing before an easel and painting with the same style of the others.

We were in the company of a genius.

The monk turned and looked back at us with kindness in his expression, a young man of no older than thirty.

Tobias nudged my arm and I followed his gaze toward the stack of canvases resting in a wooden tray.

I pointed to them. "He even makes his own canvases?"

Brother Lawrence nodded. "Bay uses paints from ingredients he either grows or creates from scratch. He's obsessed with the sixteenth century." He reached for one of the canvases and handed it to me. "He'll tell you all about it. Don't let him talk your ear off." He winked. "If you'll excuse me." Brother Lawrence threw us a wave as he headed out.

I turned over the canvas and marveled at the smoothness of it, assuming Tobias knew the *Mona Lisa* had been painted upon a handmade linen cloth of tight warp and loose weft, just like this one. If studied under a microscope the weave would appear irregular. It was the kind of hemp the specialists would look for.

Tobias held his hand out for it. "May I?"

I gave it to him. "Can we talk?"

"Will you excuse us?" He smiled over at Brother Bay and led me toward a corner. "I'm not doing anything wrong, Zara."

"Are you really going to showcase his paintings?" I whispered.

"Yes, they're incredible. I'll be proud to show them off."

"What are you up to?"

"I'm here to learn." He narrowed his gaze on me. "What are you up to?"

I ignored his cheekiness. "Learn what exactly?"

"Why don't you take a walk in the garden?"

I pointed to him. "And leave you alone in here. No way."

He leaned toward my ear. "Just don't distract me with your fidgeting."

"Everything okay?" Brother Bay called over.

"Yes, sorry." Tobias ignored my glare and strolled back toward Brother Bay. "I imagine making this canvas by hand is a form of prayer for you?"

Brother Bay nodded. "Would you like to keep it?"

"I would love that." Tobias rolled it up and tucked it into his jacket. "How long have you been painting?"

"Since I was a boy."

He reminded me of those protégés who seemed to be born with a brush in their hand just knowing how to paint.

"Brother Lawrence has approved us showcasing your paintings at my charity ball at The Plaza," said Wilder. "If this sounds like something you'd be interested in?"

"How many other artists are collaborating in this event?"

"Just you," he replied with a glint of pride for him.

Brother Bay seemed to mull over this. "What's the catch, Mr. Wilder?"

"Catch?"

"Yes, we may be men of God but we're not naive. Why me?"

Tobias caressed his jaw thoughtfully. "Are you familiar with my work in London? This is what I do. I save places of historical importance and keep history alive. It's a passion of mine. The past teaches us so much. Brother Lawrence is a man of pride. This monastery has been self-sufficient for over one hundred years. I respect that. This is a self-sufficient endeavor. All I do is show your work. It must speak for itself."

"What do you get out of restoring old places?" he pushed.

Tobias turned to face Brother Bay's painting on the

easel. "The same joy you get from creating that, I imagine. Only this is a God-given gift that you have. We all have our passions. Art history is mine. I'm currently showcasing the Qin Terra-Cotta Army in LA."

"I bet that is quite something," he said wistfully.

"It really is."

"We'll keep all the profits?"

"Yes, of course."

Brother Bay glanced over at me. "If Brother Lawrence signs off on it. I just won't be there. We don't engage in acts of ego."

"You have my word your work will be honored," I piped up.

"Thank you." He smiled and seemed to brighten at the thought.

I'd personally seen Tobias's philanthropic work in London and knew he had enough integrity to honor his word to these monks. They might even be able to restore their gorgeous fresco in the chapel, which would take a team of specialists who wouldn't come cheap.

"I hear you use Rembrandt's technique?" Tobias sounded impressed. "I can see it in your work."

"Yes, I use a blurring technique." He placed his brush down and turned to Tobias.

"These imperceptible transitions are called *sfumato*," said Wilder.

"You know your art, then. It's how I ensure soft transitions." Bay pointed to the canvas. "No harsh outlines ensure there is no way of seeing that the person on the canvas isn't real."

Tobias sighed in respect. "The father of the technique was Leonardo da Vinci."

"And Raphael also perfected it," I said, realizing where this was going.

Bay pointed to his canvas. "The *sfumato* technique mellows colors and our imaginations fill in the rest."

"Which is why Mona Lisa smiles when you look into her eyes," said Tobias.

"And her smile drops when you look at her mouth," said Bay, flashing me a smile. "If only I was that good."

"Trust me, you are," said Tobias. "I'd also very much like to show your work in my new gallery."

"I would like that very much," he said. "Do you paint, Mr. Wilder?"

"Only dabble in watercolors," he said. "Though I wouldn't pass up the opportunity to watch you work. If you don't mind?"

"Of course not," said Bay. "Anything in particular you're interested in?"

Tobias pulled up a bar stool and sat. "Tell me more about the *sfumato* technique?"

"What about it interests you?"

"Everything," said Wilder.

CHAPTER EIGHT

I'D NOT SEEN Tobias for two days.

He'd warned me he was heading into "the zone" and would be isolating himself as part of his process by getting absorbed into his project. I'd failed to dissuade him. This time apart should have been good for me but I missed him. Even if he was hidden away in his man cave working away on *her*.

I'd tried to settle in the library where I'd pulled book after book off the shelves but found nothing to hold my attention. I couldn't concentrate, couldn't wrap my head around my colleagues at Huntly Pierre being disappointed in me.

I couldn't hold back any longer and went in search of my iPhone. I began in the most logical place, his bedroom. I was reminded that this had once been the maid's quarters. Tobias had told me he preferred it down here because it was quieter. Or maybe it was because there was less in here to remind him of his grandmother. There was really nothing in here to make the place homey and as I turned around in the center I wondered if this was Wilder's way of punishing himself. There were no luxuries in here and nothing to bring comfort.

The gym was a few doors down so it was convenient in that way but other than this it reflected Wilder's desire for isolation. Unlike me he'd made his bed and his possessions were well organized too, from the way he'd hung his clothes in the wardrobe and lined up his shoes in an orderly fashion. I searched the top drawers of the dresser and found my phone—only it had been dismantled and was in pieces; unusable. He knew I'd come looking for it.

No doubt if I left the house to go and find a phone to call Huntly Pierre, Tobias would probably know I'd left and he'd come after me. I mulled over how far I'd have to get away from the house before I made the call so as not to compromise this place. I paced trying to think this through. If I unwittingly led the FBI here they'd search the house—

That would be a disaster.

I stopped before a painting of a woman on the beach with her two children who were playing in the sand. I wanted to climb through the canvas and be transported into the happy scene. I wanted to wade into the ocean and swim off.

My grit was wavering.

I realized I'd not eaten anything since yesterday afternoon and was actually pretty hungry. Heading back the way I'd come I returned to the kitchen. I rummaged around in the fridge and settled on some provolone cheese and fresh tomatoes and then found some whole-wheat bread to make sandwiches. At least when Tobias took a break there'd be something waiting for him to eat.

Settling at the central island I reached for the remote control and directed it at the walled TV and CNN came on. The world still turned without us no matter what. I wondered if Tobias's grandmother had ever felt lonely here. I imagined she'd once looked forward to his visits. Her heartbreak at losing her daughter in the plane crash must have been unbearable and then having Tobias whisked off to France by his uncle would have cut deep. I wished I'd had the chance to know her. She'd decorated this place beautifully and had elegant taste. Maybe she'd bought some of these pieces of furniture during her travels.

Tobias and I had both lost our parents young and I wondered if it was also what had drawn us together. Although he'd been kept isolated I'd watched him with his friends and coworkers in that London pub and he'd reveled in their company. There was a complexity to him and this was why it had taken me this long to understand him. Tobias was a good man but life had distorted his sense of right and wrong.

A noise came from the upper part of the house, revealing he was out of his man cave. I slid off my bar stool and went in search of him. On the top floor along the hallway was a ladder coming down from what looked like an attic. Taking one rung at a time I gripped the bars and climbed, and at the top peeked into the loft with its low beams and dusty particles twinkling in a stream of sunlight. Tobias was in the corner kneeling over a box.

"Hey there," I called out. "What are you doing?" It was so good to see him.

"Hi, I'm taking a break." His two-day scruff was back.

"I made you a sandwich."

"What time is it?"

"Two." I trod carefully around a stack of boxes. Some were open and others still sealed to hold their secrets. "This looks like fun."

"My grandmother's things. I wish I could go through them all."

"Because you have to get back to LA at some point too?"

"Right." His tone was infused with uncertainty.

"Did your grandmother have any other relatives who might help with these?"

"Maybe my cousin Edward."

"Why didn't your mom want her to look after you instead of your uncle?"

"My grandmother was a photojournalist. Lots of traveling. I'd have slowed her down." He threw in an admiring smile. "She wrote to me. I wrote back. I bet the letters are here somewhere."

"Looks like adventure runs in your blood."

"You might be right."

"She sounds amazing. We could go through these together?" I peeked into one and ran my fingers over the records. "There's a first edition Beatles LP. Look, it's *Sergeant Pepper*. It's probably worth something." Then I remembered who I was talking with. "It has sentimental value."

"There's a record player over there."

"What's that?" I pointed to the video cassette near his feet.

"It's a video of a birthday party I had in the garden here."

"Your party?"

"That's what it says. Though it could have been re-corded over."

"Shall we watch it?" I tried to read how he felt about finding it.

"If you like." He blew out a wary breath and looked over at me.

I stepped cautiously across the attic. "Look, there's a Sony player, we can watch it on this." I picked it up. "Can I help up here?"

He brushed dust off his trousers. "I'd love a cup of tea."

"I knew I'd convert you."

He beamed at me and guarded his head as he rose to avoid the low beams.

We brought down the Sony player into the main house along with the tape. While Tobias worked on setting up the '80s cassette player in the sitting room, I made us tea and brought in our sandwiches. We huddled close on the sofa. It was nice being this close to him, and I sighed contentedly as I sipped my mug of tea.

"The footage has probably degraded," he warned.

There came the flickering color image of a garden and I recognized it as this one. The camera scanned over the partygoers wearing paper hats and settled on a three-tiered cake on a table decorated with party favors. A young boy sat behind the table wearing a paper hat and waved at the camera. It was Tobias; I recognized his sweet face, those big green eyes full of wonder and his innocence shining brightly. There was a beautiful woman beside him who I recognized as his mom from the photos I'd seen. She was wearing a summer dress and her face lit up with joy when she talked to Tobias. A dashing man stepped into the frame and he had a French accent and from the way he hugged Tobias with pride it was obviously his dad. This footage was sacred and I knew it must hurt him to see it.

"Did your grandmother film this?" I gave him a comforting smile.

Tobias swallowed his uneasiness. "Yes."

"Your mom's beautiful." She was enigmatic and had his smile. The camera panned to another dashing man watching them with fondness. "Is that your uncle?"

"That's Fabienne." Tobias gave a nod. "I should call him."

"You look just like your dad."

He really did with that charismatic smile and a sharp intelligence exuding through his eyes sparkling with joy.

Tobias blew out a stream of air as though that alone would help him hold back on showing emotion. Laughter and cheers came from the screen as his dad handed Tobias his wrapped birthday present.

His mum beamed at the camera and said, *He's going to open it and then blow out the candles.*

My face flushed with the thought that this could be like us one day, filming our child's birthday party, and I let out a sigh of wonder at their shared happiness.

His parents looked cute together.

I sensed Tobias's disquiet and threw him a concerned glance. If I found this footage moving, then he must be spinning.

"You were adorable," I whispered. "See how your mom looks at you. See how loved you are."

"Were."

I ignored his correction. "They're watching over you. Keeping you safe."

Tobias gave me a look of discomfort and I recognized the pain he carried. My gaze went back to the screen. This felt like the first time I'd gotten to share a sacred piece of Wilder's past.

And then I realized—

There are nine candles.

"Tobias, this was your ninth birthday?" I swallowed hard as my gaze snapped back to see the way he stared at the screen. "Oh, Tobias."

"Three months later they were gone." He flicked the remote and the screen went blank. He rose to his feet. "Do you want me to put a movie on for you?"

"I'm so sorry."

"I knew what was on the tape."

"Thank you for sharing it with me."

"Not one of my better decisions." He shook his head as though trying to shake off the pain.

I watched him stroll off with his head bowed. "What about your sandwich?"

"I'll have it later. Thank you for making it."

I stared at the place where he'd sat seconds ago and then turned my gaze back to the TV and my heart ached for him. This had reminded him of what he'd lost. A childhood decimated—after that crash there'd been no more Christmas mornings running into his parents' bedroom to wake them up. No more birthdays with them to celebrate, no chance of them being at his graduation or sharing his remarkable achievements and no more love that only a mother can bring. I knew what this pain meant and it changed everything, life would always be seen through a lens of survival, with no belief in fairy tales to help you to find peace.

I ran after him across the foyer and through the drawing room, managing to catch the door to his workshop before it locked. My hands gripped the banister when I saw him standing still in the center seemingly shaken.

I closed the gap between us and leaned against his

back, wrapping my arms around his waist, and gave a reassuring squeeze as I breathed in his familiar cologne.

His body stiffened against mine. "I'm fine."

"What do you need?" And then I saw *her*—

My arms slipped from his waist as I stepped back.

She rested upon an easel and looked back at me with that mesmerizing smile—

No, she wasn't real. I knew this but as I made my way toward her I could see her remarkable resemblance to the original portrait and she was dazzling. Her smile, those infamous lips curling subtly yet disappearing when your eyes met hers, and when you looked down at her mouth again that smile was gone from the enigma that was *Mona Lisa*.

I gazed upon this seeming living person and struggled with my conscience as I soaked in her beauty while confusion swept over me.

Tobias walked toward her. "Forgive me father for I have sinned."

His words were raw with truth.

"You've yet to varnish her?" My voice wavered.

Wilder's gaze moved over the canvas. "That's next."

I wanted to say she was beautiful, enthralling even, and that she was everything that was pure and mystical as one would expect from such a talented artist.

Tobias broke the spell. "It was her smile, wasn't it?" He watched me watching her. "I would ask you what you think but your face tells me everything."

Her knowing eyes, her beautiful face created with the *sfumato* technique providing a flawless finish. All that was left was the varnish and she would be perfection.

"I can't…*breathe*…" I hurried away from the lie that wanted to swallow me.

Dazed, I continued up the central staircase toward my bedroom and stripped off my clothes and left them trailing behind as I walked naked into the bathroom.

Within the hot shower I tried to wash off these feelings of guilt that tasted like the ash of my past and the bitterness of all that was wrong with me. Wash off this misery and find a way back to my life. This agony was of my own doing, my motivation skewered because I'd reassured myself I was doing it all to save *him*.

And to save my paintings.

I couldn't see straight, think straight, and this disorientation swept me up into its vortex. A sob burst from me and I pressed my hand to my mouth to prevent another, terrified that if I let go I'd never pull back from breaking down. I'd been holding on for so long, stayed strong for both of us, though as my thoughts cleared I saw the end of me.

Irrevocably lost.

Tears melded with water and I swiped at them, tilting my face toward the stream to hold them back—

Tobias stood inside the doorway and he was holding a towel. "I brought you this." He offered it to me.

My eyes flittered over to the fresh towels already in here.

He threw it onto the countertop. "Seeing you like this… I'm so sorry, Zara."

This was what shock felt like—the inability to talk, or think, or know what to do next. All I knew was that art was in my blood. I'd been destined to continue the Romanov legacy, and it hurt that this was the only way.

Tobias stepped forward. "Can I join you?"

I watched him pull open the shower door and step in

with me even though he was still fully dressed. "You hate me?"

"I'm scared of the feelings I have for you because I don't trust them."

"Trust mine."

I knew what he'd done was his way of finding his own pathway, setting a trap so ingenious he could bring down an empire. This wasn't just about art or revenge or taking our lives back, this was also about us changing the fate of thousands and preventing more atrocities, but first we had to walk through hell because that was the only way to get to the other side.

He tipped up my chin. "Is the painting that bad?"

I let out another sob. "She's beautiful, Tobias. That's the problem. I didn't really believe you'd pull it off."

"If this means I'm losing you I will destroy her." He looked earnest. "Tell me what to do."

"Hold me."

He came toward me and wrapped his arms around me. I fell against his soaking wet shirt and heaved sobs against him.

"I've got you." He kissed my forehead and pulled me firmly against him, rocking me in his arms as cascading water drenched us.

"I knew I should have gone with a Disney sketch," he said.

My nervous laughter failed with another sob. "She's spectacular."

"This falls on me. All of it." He crushed his lips to mine and kissed me fiercely, and I opened my mouth for him, letting him in, no less tortured by what he'd done, my chest aching with the impossibility of being part of this. I'd believed he'd fail and once he'd created her we'd both see this truth in her illusion…

But she was everything.

"What do you want from me?" he said. "Ask and it's yours."

"You. I need you." Because only in his arms did I know the truth; *both his and mine.*

He pulled my arms above my head and pinned them to the glass and shoved his body against mine, kissing me with need as he reclaimed me, stepping back just long enough to peel off his T-shirt and kick off his shoes. His body taut and virile and powerful, all hard muscle and curling biceps, as he discarded the rest of his clothes.

How much I had wanted him like this over the last few days and it felt like we'd waited an eternity to be together again. In his eyes I saw the truth; this time there'd be no holding back for either of us.

He slammed his body against mine and it was the closeness I'd pined for, this longing for him so intense it equaled the air I breathed. I sighed when he reached around my back and grasped my butt to lift me upward, and swiftly positioned my legs to wrap around his waist, plunging into me with one strike and penetrating me deeply, burying himself inside me. This was what I'd yearned for—him inside me and proving there was still an *us* and we would survive this wreckage of what was left behind. He reached me in the heart of the storm. The only man who could silence this agony inflicted by life's cruelty.

His lips bruised mine, savaging me with the thrusts of his pelvis rendering me his. Each strike sent a coursing pleasure into my sex as my body trembled, nipples beaded tight and my thoughts spiraling out of control from the pleasure of seeing him just as impassioned.

"I would never hurt you intentionally," he soothed. "You are the air I breathe. You are the universe I belong in, the only person who matters. I've done this for you. I want to see peace in your heart, Zara. I need you to believe me."

My body weakened as I tried to focus on his words.

"Say you believe me?"

"Yes…" I moaned through this rising climax.

As I locked eyes with his, staring deeply into his endless green irises, falling and falling until I was captured and then carried away by my powerful climax. Tobias's eyelids were heavy as he stilled and moaned roughly, his heat shooting into me and sending me into the abyss of coming.

We stayed locked together for what felt like an eternity with him inside me. I refused to be parted, my muscles clenching him tight as the ripples of bliss finally faded. This endless bond would never be enough. He was my addiction and I was willing to fight for him.

He lifted me off himself and eased me to my feet, and my thighs trembled with their unsteadiness. Tobias pulled me into a hug and pressed his lips to the top of my head in a gesture of affection.

He broke into a heart-stopping smile. "We always find our way back to each other."

Yes, destiny always ensured our souls reconnected.

He massaged shampoo into my hair and took his time to tenderly indulge me beneath the hot shower. With my eyes closed I swooned into relaxation, savoring his fingertips roaming my scalp and lulling me into a delicious stupor.

"Zara." His voice was low. "We'll find another way."

Burying my face against his chest, all I could do was hope we'd make it.

"I dare to believe I'm doing my bit to balance out the evil in the world," he said softly.

His words sent a shiver through me.

Together, we lowered to kneel on the tile facing each other and I rested my head on his shoulder. It was the stillness we needed and the calm my soul yearned for.

After a few minutes he pulled away and he gave me an endearing smile of reassurance.

Tobias kissed the end of my nose. "This is what I do."

Looking up at him, at his beautiful face and his kind eyes, I knew he saw what this battle was doing to me. This going against everything I believed.

With me in his arms on the floor of the shower, he kissed me passionately again and again. I fell against him and held him to me beneath the falling water.

After a final kiss to my forehead he rose to his feet and stared down at me. "You know I'd do anything for you." He stepped out of the shower.

He didn't even bother to reach for a towel. He just left the room seemingly not caring he was naked.

I felt the loss of him.

I climbed to my feet and turned the shower off. After stepping out I reached for a towel and wrapped it around myself, and then the fog in my mind cleared and there came an unsettled feeling at how quickly Tobias had left—

No, he wouldn't...

A flash of terror swept over me and I bolted out of the room, hurried down the stairs and sprinted across the foyer. I burst into the drawing room and almost tripped over the rug—

Tobias was naked still and knelt before the large open fireplace. He'd rammed his portrait of *Mona Lisa* amongst the chopped wood in the hearth and was trying to light the fire.

"No!" I flew toward the fireplace and reached in and grabbed the frame.

He rose up onto his heels. "I'll find another way."

"Not like this." My hands shook as I clutched her to my chest. "Not by fire."

Flames licking at the paintings, turned around, disorientated, my heartbeat thumping violently against my rib cage as I sucked in scorched air.

The hearth whooshed up in orange flames and exuded heat.

Tobias pushed himself to his feet and the dampness from the shower shimmered over his body. "How, then?"

This painting muddled everything I knew about art because as I turned her around I was staring at the face of the *Mona Lisa*.

CHAPTER NINE

I STIRRED AWAKE to the scent of waffles and freshly brewed coffee wafting into Tobias's bedroom that I'd made my own. Stretching beneath the covers, I was caught in the twilight of waking, and the promise of seeing him teased me into consciousness.

After pushing myself up to rest against the rosewood headboard, I wiped the sleepiness from my eyes. Tobias entered carrying in a tray stacked with two plates of waffles and two mugs balanced beside them. He strolled toward me wearing that cute grin I'd not seen for days, with his hair combed neatly, and he was alluringly dressed in a black J.Crew sweater and jeans.

I let out a grateful sigh when he rested the tray on the bed. "Oh, look, it's the coffee fairy."

"Spoiling you is my greatest pleasure."

My head snapped toward the dresser and I saw the painting was gone.

Yesterday, I'd hugged that portrait after having barely saved it from the flames. Perhaps that moment would be remembered as my greatest weakness, but her beauty, her brilliance, her profound existence and the reason for it were too far-reaching. I wasn't ready to do what had to be done.

We'd lain in bed together last night with the *Mona Lisa* sitting on the dresser over there, and we'd just stared at the ceiling with the weight of her existence on our shoulders.

Tell me she isn't real, I'd whispered in the darkness.

Tobias had shaken his head, proving he knew this was no small deed.

He seemed a little calmer this morning. Offering me a mug and turning the handle for me to grasp.

"Does she still exist?" I asked softly.

"For now."

"You've hidden her from me?"

"You reserve the right to change your mind." Tobias's knee met the mattress and it dipped as he leaned over to plant a kiss to the top of my head. "One day at a time, Zara."

The week's residue seeped in and caused a wave of melancholy. Distracting myself, I reached for a crispy strip of bacon and chewed on the saltiness, moaning in appreciation.

He unscrewed the syrup bottle and raised it in a gesture to see if I wanted some and then trickled it over our waffles. "Just say the word and she will no longer exist." He held my gaze, searching for the answer.

If anything went wrong with his plan he could quite possibly lose The Wilder Museum and for me, it would mean the end of the possibility of ever owning my paintings again. Even my Michelangelo in The National Gallery was under threat. My reputation would be decimated.

"This is what we'll tell Huntly Pierre." Tobias sat beside me. "I'm in New York hunting down a rare painting and you're helping me. They won't need to know what it is. I'm also here to host a charitable ball that will be held in the Terrace Room at The Plaza tomorrow evening. The invites went out late but that shouldn't be an issue."

I took a bite out of a waffle and it melted on my tongue. "So it will look like business as usual for you?"

"Exactly."

"What if the Burells take your *Mona Lisa* and stash her in one of their other homes not connected to our paintings?"

"His father has consistently kept his stolen paintings together in one place." Tobias set his mug on the tray. "That's why they found Rembrandt's *The Storm on the Sea of Galilee* under the same roof as your collection."

"The FBI saw them and just walked away. They did nothing."

"He has powerful friends."

"I hope your satellite was right and they really are in New York." I dragged my fingers through my hair, feeling my frustration rise. "I can't get over that he still has Rembrandt's painting." I'd seen it personally, and though I'd stood a little way back, everything pointed to it being authentic.

Tobias shrugged. "His lawyers claimed it was fake."

I closed my eyes in frustration. "The Burells don't entertain fake paintings. They're obsessed with owning the real thing."

"That works to our benefit this time round."

"You saw my paintings when you stole the Titian in France?"

Tobias bit into a slice of bacon.

"I just need to hear you say it."

He mulled that over. "I rappelled into the rotunda and deactivated the floor tiles. The raven didn't fly in on my descent. It flew in when I was trying to get out."

This very case had piqued my interest and I'd read the records taken by the French police but hearing it from the man himself was riveting.

He gave a nod and continued, "There was a secret door in the rotunda that the authorities didn't discover. Once on the ground I searched the room and a panel gave way. I used a sound detector to boom off the wall and it indicated it was hollow. It didn't take me long to find the entry to their second vault. Your paintings were in there. I had enough time to look around and that was it. I snapped several photos of the paperwork and that's why the dates you saw on the photographs indicated they were taken a few months ago."

I recalled how he'd shown me the evidence my paintings hadn't been destroyed in that childhood fire when we'd visited his downtown LA penthouse. Those photos had stirred both panic and exhilaration at the same time and a hope I'd never imagined. "How did they look?"

"Breathtaking."

"You recognized what you saw?"

"I'd heard the Romanov collection had been destroyed in a fire. I knew what I was looking at. I was heartbroken for the previous owner, considering the circumstances."

"You'd entered the rotunda as Icon." I reached out and touched his arm to thank him for sharing this with me. "Reporting what you found had the greatest risk to you."

Yet he'd shared this secret with me anyway, knowing I'd eventually connect such knowledge with Icon.

He looked conflicted. "I knew the danger to you was extraordinary should you find out about them. As I got to know you I trusted you. Right up until you gate-crashed Elliot Burell's granddaughter's wedding. Telling you about them put you in harm's way."

"I put myself there."

"You brought our agenda forward."

"You're always so forgiving, Tobias."

"When it comes to you."

I broke his intense gaze. "Did you get any sleep last night?"

"A few hours. I got up early to finish the painting." He cringed as though hating mentioning it. "When the time comes you won't have to worry. I have what it takes to destroy it."

"I should be there when you do it."

"If you want." He pushed the tray aside. "Do you want to sleep in?"

"No. I'm awake now. Did you go for a run this morning?"

"Yes, and worked out with Jade."

"Jade?"

"She helps me do pull-ups."

"Seriously?"

"She's capable of lifting a person off the ground." He rubbed my tummy. "You should try it sometime."

I laughed as he tickled me. "My stomach is fine, mister."

"Yes, you're perfect. We just don't want to remind you and have you running off with Mr. Perfect." He dipped to kiss my belly button.

I giggled. "Careful, you'll spill the coffee."

He patted the mattress. "It's built to withstand quite a lot. As you've discovered."

"You are Mr. Perfect."

"I'm the man your mom warned you about…" He grimaced.

I reached up and ruffled his hair. "She'd have loved you. So would my dad."

"After all the trouble I've gotten you into?"

I smiled to reassure him. "I've been thinking."

"Oh?"

I exhaled a shaky breath of doubt. "Maybe we should just let them go, Tobias." On his look of protest I added, "We have each other and if we go to the police now—"

"We're closer than you think."

"We're taking on a monster."

"Yes, but someone has to."

This felt like the walls between us were finally coming down.

Tobias looked resilient. "What Elliot did to me made me stronger. I became more than I was. And now I'm coming for him."

"You want to end this?"

"Him, Zara, I'm ready to end Elliot Burell."

"Just be careful, that's all I ask. If anything happened to you—"

He pressed his forefinger to my lips to silence me and I bit it playfully.

"Careful. You're already in the danger zone."

"Danger zone?"

"If you're standing within feet of me. Anything can happen when you're taunting me with your beauty." He brought my hand to his mouth and kissed my wrist, pressing his soft lips against my skin.

I let out a contented sigh. "Thank you for breakfast."

"I made something else for you." He pulled me up. "Want to see?"

"What is it?"

He walked over to his bedside table, reached in and pulled out a virtual reality headset. "I thought this might be fun for you."

I clambered off the bed, eager to see what he'd designed.

He slid the headset over my head. "Comfortable?"

"Yes."

"Hold your breath."

"Why?"

"Jade, run program for Zara."

As the visor cleared I was looking out at an underwater view and instinctively held my breath. I jolted when an enormous great whale swam by me and I reached out to run my hand over his body as adrenaline surged through me.

Tobias caressed my back. "One day I'll take you to Hawaii."

"This was filmed there?"

"Yes."

I could almost feel the sand between my toes as I looked down at my feet that were firmly on land now. The image had changed to surrounding lush green foliage and just above me a waterfall cascaded into a lagoon. The sound of water whooshed in my ears.

"As the Met is currently out-of-bounds I wanted to bring the gallery to you. Jade, run 'Met on Fifth Avenue.'"

I peered up at the splendor of the front of the gallery with its tall marble pillars before the architecture grandness of the New York building. "How do you create these?"

"I visit the gallery and film it. What would you like to see first? Medieval art? Greek or—"

"Old masters."

"Jade, comply."

I stood within the center of a room surrounded by exquisite art adorning pristine walls with a Renoir to my right and a Monet to my left, and straight ahead was Michelangelo's 1506 *Saint John the Baptist Bearing Witness*, the painting first attributed to Francesco Granacci but later discovered to be created by Michelangelo. It was a colorful portrayal of St. John the Baptist standing in the center of a sparse landscape surrounded by a crowd who had come to hear him speak, including Christ's disciples.

My gaze fell on the portrait beside it by Francisco de Goya and I remembered this artist was a favorite of Wilder's. Not that long ago in London, Tobias's passion had fueled our adventure at Blandford Palace where we'd run down endless hallways on a mission to discover a long-lost 1800 *The Nude Maja* hidden behind another painting. She'd been beautiful, a young woman lying naked on a bed and holding the viewer's eyes with a relaxed confidence.

Stepping forward to view another painting by Goya, I marveled at the image of a small child standing center stage within the canvas. The child was dressed in an orange costume and holding a small pet magpie secured on the end of a string. Three cats loomed close to the bird in a sinister display of danger. To the boy's right sat a cage full of finches. Goya masterfully stirred a sense of danger by reminding us of the frail boundaries of evil threatening our innocence.

These were beautiful, all of them, but nothing came

close to being near the real paintings and I eased off the headset and turned to look at him.

He gave a nod as though he'd read my mind. "I'm working on getting us to a real gallery. I didn't want you to go cold turkey on me."

He made me smile. "You're always thinking of me." I wrapped my arms around myself. "How long do we have before we have to face the authorities?"

"Not long."

My thoughts swirled as I realized our time here was at an end. "What did you do?"

"I called Adley two days ago. I told your boss we're in New York."

A jolt of fear hit me. "Abby Reynolds probably flew out with him to try to find us."

"They won't have to try too hard, Zara. I've set a meeting with them. I also need to schedule a meeting with the FBI."

"But they suspect you're quite possibly Icon?"

"That's why this meeting is so important. I must convince them of your innocence."

"And you?"

"Icon no longer exists."

I exhaled a steady breath. "What about the Burells?"

"It's time for me to step into their line of fire. There's no other way."

Terror shot up my spine. "What?"

"It's time to open Pandora's box. In other words, the mind of Eli Burell."

"I'm coming with you."

"It's best you don't, Zara."

"What are you going to do?"

"I need to lay a trap with the bait. It must be done in person. He must believe he has one up on us."

"I'll come with you."

"You'll be safer here." Tobias took my hand and led me toward a watercolor of the English countryside hanging on the far left wall. He lifted it off its hanger and revealed a safe. "Press your thumb here." He accessed it with his own thumbprint and the door clicked open. He reached in and removed a British passport. I recognized the dog-eared corner that proved it was mine.

He handed it to me. "If anything happens to me go back to London. Wait for me."

"What do you mean?"

"If I don't come back here by the end of today."

"I'm not staying in this house while you're running around putting yourself in harm's way."

"Burell is unpredictable. I need to know you are safe." He gave me a reassuring smile.

Tobias carried out the tray of food and I was left staring at my passport in stunned silence.

I burst into action and within the wardrobe quickly found a smart black skirt and white blouse and pulled over it a Chanel jacket. If the meeting with my boss was today I'd be ready. I just hoped they believed the party line that billionaire Tobias Wilder had hired me to authenticate a rare piece he'd hunted down. It wasn't too much of a lie if you counted in the fact we were searching for my paintings.

I rummaged within the shoe boxes until I found the kind of pumps I could run in.

Tobias wasn't going alone.

CHAPTER TEN

THE CAB DRIVER dropped us off at Central Park.

Tobias and I leisurely strolled the urban sanctuary with its sprawling trees, pretty fountains and beloved monuments. It was nice to be outside but at the same time I knew we were vulnerable, and time seemed to speed up as we careened toward the inevitable.

We huddled on a park bench watching the early morning joggers, the mothers pushing their prams and tourists eagerly moving on to their next sightseeing spot.

Tobias leaned forward and rested his elbows on his knees and buried his face in his palms.

"This is a good idea," I said.

He sat up and stared at me. "Let's agree to disagree."

"I can watch your back."

"Zara, when it comes to meeting with Eli, he's unpredictable."

"I handled him in Arizona."

He frowned at me. "You mean right before you fell through his trapdoor?"

"I suppose there was that."

He shook his head. "You're predictably stubborn."

No, I wasn't going to just stay indoors while Tobias ran into the center of danger.

He turned to look at me. "Let's talk about the *Mona Lisa*."

"Let's not."

"Perhaps when I bump into enemy number one it would be a good idea to know if I'm using the bait or not."

I folded my arms. "I'm undecided."

"Right." He rubbed his jaw thoughtfully. "This should be interesting, then."

I followed Tobias's gaze and saw Coops riding toward us on a bicycle. He wore a baseball cap and round-rimmed glasses and it made him look covert as he pulled up behind our bench.

He removed his rucksack and came over. "How's it going, boss?"

Tobias rose and met him halfway. "Good. How's things?"

Coops glanced over at me as though checking it was safe to talk.

"It's okay," he reassured him.

"Ms. Leighton." Coops gave a nod in greeting and raised his rucksack as he turned back to Wilder. "Once you turn on the app you'll appear on the grid. Burell will locate you using his satellite. You'll have twenty minutes until he gets to you. Turn off the app—"

"And I'm invisible." Tobias gave a nod of approval. "Well done, Coops."

"We're invisible," I added as I walked toward them, realizing Coops was in the loop with all of this.

Tobias had planned on bringing the enemy to us. That was scary but I knew there was only one way through this and that was forward.

He took the rucksack from Coops, rummaged around

inside and pulled out his smartphone. He dug around further and removed an iPhone and handed it to me. "It's a burner phone. In case we get separated. There's one number programmed in. Mine." Tobias tucked his phone into his pocket.

I slid the phone into my handbag. "What happens when Eli finds us?"

"The biggest game of cat and mouse will ensue." Tobias gave a confident smile. "We know how much he loves those."

He was referring to the contraption Eli had created called *Mousetrap for the Inevitable*, an art-inspired device to trap those who'd trespassed into his safe in Arizona. We'd learned the painful lesson ourselves that Eli had a penchant for torture when we'd gotten caught in it.

I reached into my handbag. "Coops, I have something for you. They say these deteriorate with time." I pulled out the videotape of Tobias's birthday party.

Tobias recognized it, and then his gaze rose to meet mine.

"This has great value," I told Coops. "Can you please get this converted to a digital file? We need to preserve it. No one must see it. It pertains to a private moment in Mr. Wilder's life."

"Yes, ma'am." He glanced over at Tobias, who gave a smile of resignation and handed the rucksack back.

"Thank you, Coops." He shook his head at me, and yet I could see it touched him that I cared enough to see this precious piece of his past preserved. Coops slid the videotape into his bag.

"Tomorrow night is all set." Coops arched his eyebrows playfully. "A Wilder charity ball always attracts the best guests. I made this one a five-thousand-dollar-ticket event. You gave me full reign so I chose your charity dedicated to helping orphaned immigrants."

"Thank you, Coops, well done." Tobias's tone was kind. "Tell everyone that's why I'm in New York."

"Adley Huntly was surprisingly pleasant," said Coops. "Though he does want you to call him personally."

"I'll be seeing him in person tomorrow."

"He wanted to know what this painting is that you're hunting down," he said.

Tobias shoved his hands into his pockets. "All I'll say is that it has a Russian origin."

Coops snapped his gaze to mine, realizing he was talking about my paintings. "Best keep that under wraps, then, boss?"

"My thoughts exactly," he agreed.

"Okay, good. Well, I have everything set up. The Plaza's usually booked years in advance so we got lucky. A wedding was canceled at the last minute. The deposit was huge so I feel for whoever paid for it."

"I'll need a dress for it," I said.

Wilder stared at me and it was the kind of glare that told me I wasn't invited.

"They miss you back in London," said Coops. "They want to know when you'll be back."

"Next week if I'm lucky."

Coops pointed across the park. "Your Lexus is over there."

"Great." Tobias gave a nod of approval. "Call me if you need anything, Coops."

"See you later." He hopped back onto his bike and sped off.

"We're meeting up with him again?" I watched him cycle off across the park.

"Yes."

"How much does he know?"

"Very little. That's my way of protecting him. Once my phone is activated we'll be tracked by Burell."

"What happens when he finds us?"

"We set the trap." He interlocked his fingers with mine and we walked to the chauffeur-driven Lexus. "If you'll allow me to do the honors and lay the groundwork."

He wanted me to give him the permission he needed to use that painting. I answered with silence. The cruelest answer of all, but the only one I could live with.

Once inside, Tobias asked the driver to take us to Westchester Avenue in the Bronx. He reached over me, pulled my seat belt across and clicked it in. "I've been dying to show you this place."

"We're going to see your new gallery first?"

"Yes." He leaned over and kissed my forehead. "I'm glad to be out of that house for a while."

"I like it."

"Yes, but it's not *our* home." He took my hand and squeezed it.

Staring at his face I tried to read the truth and see how he really felt about me tagging along. I needed proof he'd left his old life behind—though right before my eyes he was morphing into the legendary Icon.

His body language exuded a raw confidence, his focus intensifying, and his grip on my hand was almost unbearable as he held it in his lap and stared out at the passing scenery.

Resting my head back I took in the exquisite architecture, admiring the skyscrapers and opulent stone buildings designed by master craftsmen decades ago.

Our journey to the Bronx was slowed by traffic but within half an hour we'd pulled up to a curb and were immersed in the aliveness of an eclectic neighborhood. Tobias led me to the front of a beautiful building that stood out among the others. Its stonework revealed it had historical significance. He opened the door and gestured for me to go on ahead.

I looked around the empty space that had so much potential. The low ceiling with its soft lighting exuded a cozy and unpretentious atmosphere. I walked in farther, wanting to will this place into existence, and envisioned the walls adorned by art and the visitors awed by the emotions they evoked.

A twenty-something pretty black woman who was smartly dressed approached us and reached out to shake my hand, and then Tobias's. "Mr. Wilder. Hi, Ms. Leighton, welcome."

"Samantha." Tobias smiled brightly. "How are you?"

"Good. Excited. We're getting close to opening next month." She gestured to the other room. "We're almost there with the electricity." Sam turned to me. "This is an old place. There is lots to do to get it up to code."

Tobias added proudly, "There's history here. We saved it from being torn down and an apartment building in its place."

"The locals could be pushed out," explained Sam.

"We intend on bringing art to the people." Tobias looked so at home here.

"I have the catalogs ready." Sam led the way.

Tobias wrapped his arm around my waist and it made me smile that he felt comfortable to show affection. "Sam's an art graduate from Berkeley," he said. "We are lucky to have her."

"Oh, shut up," she said playfully. "You know I fought for this job."

Tobias gestured for us to go through to the arched partition first. "I knew immediately she'd be a great fit for us."

Sam beamed with happiness. "We're calling this 'A Wilder Gallery.'"

"I love it." I followed her.

This next room was just as empty except for the long table and lying upon it were catalogs.

"I have everything ready for you." Sam walked over to one of them. "These are the ones I love the most. I just need you to sign off and we'll purchase them."

"Recognize these, Zara?" Tobias peeled open the front page of one of the binders. "This is the Terrance Hill collection. Remember his paintings from The Broad?"

"Oh, my goodness." I peered down at the familiar artwork I'd seen showcased in the LA gallery during a special evening celebrating that young man's work.

Sam pointed to the colorful collection of images. "We'll showcase them as the main feature opening night. We're in the process of setting up strategic seating areas and establishing a room for free lessons for those who want to learn to paint."

I let out a sigh of wonder at Tobias's respect for bringing art into this thriving neighborhood, and Sam exuded the kind of warmth that would make visitors feel welcome.

"Ms. Leighton's going to help us choose our wish list," said Tobias, looking at me with a hopeful smile.

"I'd love to."

"I had a meeting with Brother Bay," he told Sam.

"Oh, I love his work." She lit up. "He's like a modern-day Rembrandt. How did it go?"

"He's donating ten of his paintings. They'll be for sale and all proceeds will go to the monastery."

"Great job, boss." She beamed at him.

Over the next hour we took an album each, choosing the paintings that spoke to us. Afterward, we conferred about our choices and managed to whittle them down. The gallery was destined to exhibit both old masters—which his aunt's collection would also become part of—to more modern pieces that would give rising artists their break.

Being surrounded by all this potential helped me to forget the threat looming. Tobias had a way of making me feel safe despite that storm whirling closer.

"Why don't you take the rest of the day off," Tobias invited Sam. "We can lock up."

"Are you sure?"

"Yes, you've got this place straightened out and worked hard. Take a personal day."

"Thank you, Mr. Wilder."

We returned to the main exhibit room until Sam was ready to leave. She looked happy about taking time off. She secured the front door behind her on the way out.

"Let me show you the office." Tobias led me up a winding stairwell and along a hallway, turning off the lights as we went.

The room he led us into reflected his easy style of simple and cozy, with a desk in the center and a computer set up. On the far end sat an in-tray, a penholder and stacks of empty folders. There was a yearly calendar fastened to the back wall to round out the business design.

Tobias locked the door behind us, and then leaned against it and held my gaze. I pretended not to be fazed by the intensity of his stare following my every move as I strolled around the room. I examined a glass paperweight, trying to steady myself against Wilder's all-consuming presence and that alpha power he exuded.

He reached into his pocket and held up his phone. "Ready?"

I pushed myself up on the edge of the desk. "We'll first be seen here at your new gallery?"

"Exactly." His green eyes narrowed on me as though judging how I felt about this. "There's nothing in here so they can't do too much damage. It will look real, though. And not staged."

Was he sure he wanted to bring down hell on us here in this beloved place? A gallery he was working on creating.

Still, I knew there was no other way but forward and I gave him a nod to let him know I was ready.

"Close the blinds." His order made me jump.

I slid off the desk and walked toward him. "Is this some kind of diversion tactic? Because if it is—"

"Take off your panties. You can either take them off with the blinds open or closed. Your choice."

"What if Burell's men get here?"

"We have time." His thumb pressed the button on his phone.

A jolt of arousal alighted my senses and I knew one more command from him would make me wet and craving him. This was just it. Wilder loved danger and as my gaze fixed on him I knew he'd just turned the app on.

A rush of fear surged through me too and the adrenaline made my nipples bead. "Fine." I removed my Chanel jacket and threw it onto the back of the swivel chair as I walked toward the window. "If I close these we won't be able to see them arrive."

"I won't ask you again."

My fingers twisted the pole and the blinds threw the room into darkness.

Keeping my back to him I hitched up my skirt and slid my thong off my hips and down, turning slightly to experience that dark edge of pleasure of having him watching me.

With peril looming, my heartbeat quickened and I fought against the trepidation. Gone was that young girl from London who yearned for safety, and in her place had risen a siren wanting more of this crackling electricity between me and *him*, the only one who mattered.

I strolled over to the desk and bent over it with my hands gripping the edge as I offered my butt to him with an arching back and my thighs spread a little; my sex clenching in need for this touch.

First the sound of his footfalls behind me and the feel of my skirt being hitched up to expose me, and then his strong hand squeezed my buttocks—

Slap.

I shot forward at the shock of his palm meeting my flesh and again coming down firmly sending a shock of bliss. "Oh, God." I inhaled sharply at the stunning realization he was taking my mind off this uncertainty.

He grabbed my hips and dragged me back into position and ran his hand along my cleft. "Nice and wet, Zara, very good. Did you like that?"

"Yes," I said breathlessly, desperate for him to touch me again.

This was him trying to scare me off, I was sure of it, but instead I felt more defiant than ever.

He spanked me and the jolt of pleasure intensified when his other hand found my sex and he began fingering me and working me into a frenzy. The sting lifted from my heated skin and pleasure flooded into my cheeks. Thighs trembling, hips grinding, muscles clenching, I rode his hand deliciously while letting out a moan of want, desperate for another erotic slap that riled me up and nudged out my good-girl side.

"Fuck me," I demanded.

"All in good time," he said darkly as he slid his fingers out and found my clit and strummed.

Squeezing my eyes shut I concentrated on not coming.

I leaned forward over the desk with my bum in the air and my head low and my arms outstretched, my hair spilling before me. My heart soared with this sense he was proving he could protect me. A quick glance back and I saw him kneeling close. This was his show of power, his careful manipulation to let me feel safe as he repositioned my thighs—a jolt of pleasure as his mouth met my sex and he devoured me, suckling my clit and sending me into an erotic trance where all thoughts dissipated and all I knew was this serenity, forgetting time and place, forgetting everything...

He rose to his feet and spun me around and sat me on the edge of the desk and I watched him free himself. The vision of his cock rising out of dark blond curls was mesmerizing and he tapped my sex with it and then buried himself deep inside me, beginning a leisurely pace of fucking me into submission; his steely gaze locked on mine.

I leaned back until I was lying on the desk and

reached low to touch myself but he grabbed my wrists and held them together with his left hand, and with his right he gave me what I yearned for and played with my clit, thrumming furiously in time with his thrusts. My spine arched, my orgasm capturing me and stealing me away for what felt like forever, body rigid and my sex massaging him with forceful spasms, rocking against him through waves of ecstasy as my moans echoed around us.

I was consumed by him entirely.

When his heat shot into me I flung my thighs around him, pulled him down onto me and buried my face into the crook of his neck. I gripped him and fell into a place where it was easy to forget.

"Zara." His voice stirred me back to consciousness and I opened my eyes to see him wiping me down there with a tissue in an intimate act of tenderness.

He walked away, strolled toward the window and peered out.

I pushed myself onto my elbows. "Are they here?"

"How do you feel?"

"Relaxed." Invigorated actually, my body tingling from my postclimax buzz. "How about you?"

"I'm displeased that someone's disrupting my time with you." Tobias reached for my panties and slid them partway. "Up."

I raised my hips as he finished sliding my underwear back on. He smiled as he leaned in, tugging aside my panties to suckle my clit. "I will be thirsty for you for the rest of my life, Leighton." He kissed me there, sending ripples of arousal.

I froze midlift and let him lavish his tongue along me again. I felt the loss of him too severely when he stepped back, and my sex throbbed exquisitely as though we still had time for his teasing.

"Are they here?" I managed breathlessly.

He repositioned my panties and pulled my skirt down. "Yes."

A jolt of fear caught in my throat.

Someone was banging on the front door downstairs.

I stared at Tobias, in awe of his eerie calmness. "What happens now?"

He helped me off the desk. I straightened my clothes and shrugged into my Chanel jacket. He grabbed his jacket and led me out and along a hallway all the way to a dead end.

Tobias's thumb slid along the screen of his phone and he went into settings. "I turn the GPS off."

I could hear the door giving way downstairs and footsteps heading fast our way.

"Time to lose them." Wilder was playing a deadly game.

"Why did you lure them here?"

"If they fail to catch us this will frustrate Eli Burell and he'll personally try to find us himself. Without him at our meeting our ruse is useless."

"How do you know Eli isn't here?"

"Coops is tracking him."

"Of course he is." I kept the dread out of my tone.

"If this was chess our move would be considered a Zugzwang, which is German for influencing the other player with a compulsion to move. It makes him weaker."

"We're drawing him out?"

"Exactly." He removed a key from his pocket and tried it in a door at the end of the hall and I breathed a sigh of relief when it turned. We hurried into another hallway and he secured the door behind us and tucked away the key. We weaved around shoppers browsing racks of clothing and they gave us a passing glance as we hurried by.

We descended a staircase onto the main floor of the store and burst out through the front door onto the street. A little way down to our right, two large SUVs were parked and a man in a black suit lingered near them.

Tobias grabbed my hand and we ran in the opposite direction until we came to a familiar-looking motorbike parked curbside. It was the Harley Tobias had used to pick me up just days ago in Central Park after his drone had crashed in a tree with me in it.

Yeah, that should have been your first warning Wilder loved dabbling in crazy, I chastised myself.

"I'm wearing a skirt," I snapped.

"I'm sure New York has seen it all before, Leighton. Get on." He shoved a helmet onto my head and then pulled me into a kiss as though we weren't being chased. He shoved his own helmet on, and we climbed onto the bike with him in front revving the engine and me hugging his chest. We sped away, merging into traffic, and he opened the throttle and zoomed off.

I didn't glance back.

When we finally parked at a curb I climbed off and stretched to ease the tension in my limbs, relieved we'd made our escape. Tobias signaled to someone and I turned to see Coops climbing the steps toward us.

Tobias placed my helmet in the back of the bike and handed his to Coops, and then he threw him the keys. I stared back to make sure we weren't being followed.

"Zara." Tobias got my attention and with my hand in his we hurried up the rest of the way toward the impressive building with the grand sign hailing this as The New York City Ballet.

With a flash of Wilder's ID, we were granted access and continued into the foyer. After walking for a few minutes, we passed under a curtained doorway. This was an empty auditorium except for the stage where two ballerinas looked like they were rehearsing.

I shot Tobias a confused look.

"Come on." He guided me down the side aisle. "Just because we have the hounds of hell on our heels doesn't mean we can't enjoy a little culture."

We settled a few rows back from the stage and I rested my head on his shoulder, lulled by the piano music which was an exquisite accompaniment to the dancers' elegant movements. I was mesmerized at the dreamlike fluidity contrasted to our recent turmoil.

"You're full of surprises," I whispered.

He turned in his chair to face me. "You have no idea."

"Oh, I think I do."

He shook his head. "We both know how dangerous the Burells are."

There came a sinking feeling. "What do you mean?"

"I must protect you at any cost."

My stare shot forward toward the dancers pirouetting beautifully.

Tobias reached for my hand and brought it to his chest. "I want us to be in a place where we can be honest with each other."

"Don't do this."

"I work better alone."

"You just tried to scare me, is that it?" I rolled my eyes. "Just close enough to have them approach but not engage?"

"That was a taste of how fast they can be on us, Zara. These men are determined to find me."

"I'm not leaving you."

"I'm not giving you any choice."

I pushed myself up and turned my back to the stage to prevent the serenity of the dancers from distracting me. "I won't let you do this."

"Sit down, please." He gestured to my seat.

"No."

He reached for my hand and pulled me into my seat. "Listen to me."

I felt like he'd let me in at the beginning of the adventure but was now dropping me off when the heat intensified. But my body still buzzed from a sense of pride that I could handle this. "I won't let you face them alone. You need a witness."

"Zara, you know what they're capable of—"

"I can protect you."

"No one can. Look, you'll be safer if you stay here. Marshall will take you home."

I felt my chest constrict. "Marshall's in New York?"

"Yes. Marshall and Coops have both worked for me for years. I trust them with my life."

And I'd been through hell and back with him too. "You trust me too, right? I feel like you're still holding back on telling me things—"

"If anything happens to you—"

"You don't get it."

"No, *you* don't," he snapped. "You are my greatest

obsession. There are times when I sense how easy it would be to love you."

I broke his gaze, not wanting him to see how his words hurt me.

He reached over and grabbed my chin to bring my attention back on him. "Zara, have you no idea how fond of you I am?"

I'd needed to hear him say that he *loved* me and this was worse than him not saying it at all. I bit back my words to let him see I was handling this.

My family had saved our paintings and they'd not hidden behind anyone. They'd accomplished what had to be done. Placed themselves in the pathway of peril for a greater purpose. I'd come this far with Wilder and I refused to back down. "I'm going with you."

"Zara—"

"You need me. If they hurt you, then your plan is screwed. So get your butt out of that chair and let's get this over with."

"I'm going to regret this."

Leaning into him, I grabbed his tie and pulled him toward me until our lips almost touched. "Negotiations are over."

"What have I done to you?" he whispered.

"We have somewhere to be. Personally, I'm eager to find out where we're going."

He pushed himself to his feet. "Careful, or I may just throw you over my shoulder and carry you off and punish your feistiness."

"Mind on the prize, Wilder." I slapped his butt and turned to make my way along the row of seats. "Mind on the prize."

He followed me down the aisle. "The prize is even more priceless than you can possibly imagine."

"Let's focus on what we can control."

"Leighton." He smirked as he pointed to the side. "Back door!"

I rolled my eyes and headed toward the right of the stage. Tobias followed and together we strolled down a dark hallway toward the exit.

Within ten minutes we were sitting in the back of an SUV and Marshall was speeding us along the FDR Drive. Seeing his driver from LA should have rattled me, but I was determined to go with this and, anyway, staying together felt right.

"Are you going to tell me where we're going?"

Tobias dragged his gaze away from the river to look at me. "I thought something Iconic was in order."

CHAPTER ELEVEN

WHEN WE ARRIVED at the South Ferry station I realized we were boarding a boat.

"It'll take us to Liberty Island," Tobias told me. "We're going to see the Statue of Liberty."

"Seriously?" Though when I remembered our threat, being trapped on an island wasn't the best idea and it sucked all joy out from seeing the famous monument.

"Why are we going there?" I all but dug in my heels.

Tobias folded his arms. "Let Marshall drive you back to the house."

"You better not turn your app on while we're on that island."

"Because that would be insanity." He widened his eyes to make his point.

He was trying to scare me so I'd leave. Instead, I flicked a stray hair off of my face and stomped off toward the ferry.

We bought two tickets and boarded just before the ferry pulled away, and a burst of the horn announced our departure from shore. We found a place where we had privacy from the tourists and both leaned on the balustrade, staring out at Brooklyn Bridge.

With the dramatic view of the city behind us, we turned and faced our destination. I remembered when Tobias had taken me out on his yacht in Malibu and it seemed so long ago. That early morning trip out on his boat to watch the sunrise, with me lying beside him as he recited ballads by William Wordsworth, would remain one of my happiest memories of us.

It was the time before everything changed irrevocably.

Tobias shrugged out of his jacket and wrapped it around my shoulders. "Do you want to go inside?"

"I like it out here." I stared ahead at the Statue of Liberty looming larger, not wanting to look at him because his beauty felt like a strike to my reason. I tried to guard my heart for what lay ahead of us. There was so much uncertainty. When this was over I wondered how we'd be once I resumed my life back in London. I pondered him ever being able to give *this* up, this adrenaline-seeking existence that would mean an end to his life's purpose.

Something told me he'd get bored of me after a while. I was the careful type, the kind of woman who gave a great deal of thought to every decision. The kind of person who never took unnecessary risks. This cold breeze cleared my thoughts and reminded me I was taking the biggest risk of my life by insisting I join Wilder on this perilous jaunt.

When our boat docked on Liberty Island, we waited in the back so the crowd disembarked first. Hand in hand, Tobias and I strolled along toward the inspirational statue and Tobias told me what he knew about her including how she was a symbol of freedom and democracy given to America by the French.

How fitting it was for us to visit this place and draw on her historical significance; she was a symbol of freedom and righteousness. Tobias also told me her height was over 305 feet and that in 1986 her flame was covered in a thin film of gold.

Of course, he'd booked our visit in advance which allowed us to enter her and climb the double spiral staircase with 377 steps all the way from the lobby to her crown, and when we reached the top we caught our breaths and laughed at how strenuous our ascent had been.

A moment of doubt hit me when I realized Tobias might very well run off and leave me up there stranded. Staring at him, I tried to read what he was really up to.

My throat tightened with dread when he pulled out his phone. Tobias turned it on and posed beside me to take a selfie of us.

"I hope that thing isn't on." I shot him a glare.

"I'll wait until we're down." He tucked his phone away.

"So they'll see we visited here?" That made sense and I relaxed a little as I stared out through the statue's crown and admired the view of water stretching out to meet New York. I mean, logistically, by the time we were off the island they'd have missed us if they tried to follow us now.

The trek down was harder and by the time we made it to the ground, my thighs were shaking. I was glad when we reached the Crown Café where we could get a drink and quench my thirst. We sat at a corner table sharing a large bottle of water and sipping tea and reviewing the photos he'd taken.

"We're coming back here." His thumb swept to another photo. "So we can enjoy it properly."

"I'm enjoying it now."

"Are you sure you're not hungry?"

He'd asked me if I wanted food while we'd waited in line for our drinks but my appetite was dulled even after our climb. The unpredictability of the day was unsettling.

I glanced around to make sure we had privacy. "Any more surprises?"

"Sure you want me to ruin your fun?"

And then I realized. "You turned the app back on?"

"Yes, us meeting with Eli will be on our terms. Though it won't look like this to him. He'll believe he's breeched my phone's GPS. The plan to get your paintings back is underway."

I'd left his side for a few minutes to visit the bathroom and assumed he'd turned it back on then. "But they won't have time to catch us if we leave now."

"We're not leaving."

My mouth went dry and I tried to swallow past the lump.

"If we get separated, call me." He nodded toward my handbag.

"Shouldn't we go?"

"The point is to make Eli believe he has us trapped. He'll think that coming here personally to deal with us was his idea. His ego will be fed if he takes things into his own hands." He rose and carried our empty cups over to a trash bin and threw them in, and then gave a confident nod for me to follow.

We walked along the outside of the statue's pedestal and I crooked my neck to peer up and admire the woman who was at first meant to represent an Egyptian peasant welcoming the refugees to safety. It was hard to focus with the thought we were just waiting around until the threat found us.

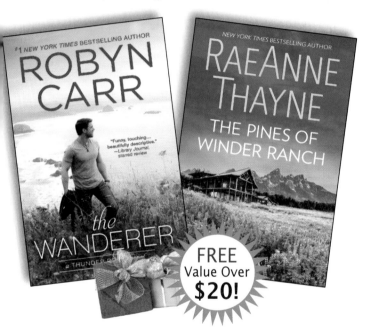

Dear Reader,

IT'S A FACT: if you answer 4 quick questions, we'll send you **4 FREE REWARDS!**

I'm not kidding you. As a leading publisher of women's fiction, we value your opinions… and your time. That's why we are prepared to **reward** you handsomely for completing our mini-survey. In fact, we have 4 Free Rewards for you, including 2 free books and 2 free gifts.

As you may have guessed, that's why our mini-survey is called **"4 for 4".** Answer 4 questions and get 4 Free Rewards. It's that simple!

Thank you for participating in our survey,

Pam Powers

To get your 4 FREE REWARDS:
Complete the survey below and return the insert today to receive 2 FREE BOOKS and 2 FREE GIFTS guaranteed!

"4 for 4" MINI-SURVEY

1 Is reading one of your favorite hobbies?
☐ YES   ☐ NO

2 Do you prefer to read instead of watch TV?
☐ YES   ☐ NO

3 Do you read newspapers and magazines?
☐ YES   ☐ NO

4 Do you enjoy trying new book series with FREE BOOKS?
☐ YES   ☐ NO

YES! I have completed the above Mini-Survey. Please send me my 4 FREE REWARDS (worth over $20 retail). I understand that I am under no obligation to buy anything, as explained on the back of this card.

194/394 MDL GMYP

FIRST NAME	LAST NAME

ADDRESS

APT.#	CITY

STATE/PROV.	ZIP/POSTAL CODE

Offer limited to one per household and not applicable to series that subscriber is currently receiving.
Your Privacy—The Reader Service is committed to protecting your privacy. Our Privacy Policy is available online at www.ReaderService.com or upon request from the Reader Service. We make a portion of our mailing list available to reputable third parties that offer products we believe may interest you. If you prefer that we not exchange your name with third parties, or if you wish to clarify or modify your communication preferences, please visit us at www.ReaderService.com/consumerschoice or write to us at Reader Service Preference Service, P.O. Box 9062, Buffalo, NY 14240-9062. Include your complete name and address.   ROM-218-MS17

READER SERVICE—Here's how it works:

Accepting your 2 free Romance books and 2 free gifts (gifts valued at approximately $10.00 retail) places you under no obligation to buy anything. You may keep the books and gifts and return the shipping statement marked "cancel." If you do not cancel, about a month later we'll send you 4 additional books and bill you just $6.74 each in the U.S. or $7.24 each in Canada. That is a savings of at least 16% off the cover price. It's quite a bargain! Shipping and handling is just 50¢ per book in the U.S. and 75¢ per book in Canada*. You may cancel at any time, but if you choose to continue, every month we'll send you 4 more books, which you may either purchase at the discount price plus shipping and handling or return to us and cancel your subscription. *Terms and prices subject to change without notice. Prices do not include applicable taxes. Sales tax applicable in N.Y. Canadian residents will be charged applicable taxes. Offer not valid in Quebec. Books received may not be as shown. All orders subject to approval. Credit or debit balances in a customer's account(s) may be offset by any other outstanding balance owed by or to the customer. Please allow 4 to 6 weeks for delivery. Offer available while quantities last.

▼ If offer card is missing write to: Reader Service, P.O. Box 1341, Buffalo, NY 14240-8531 or visit www.ReaderService.com ▼

BUSINESS REPLY MAIL
FIRST-CLASS MAIL   PERMIT NO. 717   BUFFALO, NY

POSTAGE WILL BE PAID BY ADDRESSEE

READER SERVICE
PO BOX 1341
BUFFALO NY 14240-8571

NO POSTAGE
NECESSARY
IF MAILED
IN THE
UNITED STATES

"Same man who designed the Eiffel Tower in France," said Tobias, pointing up at her. "Alexandre Gustave Eiffel designed the structure and Frédéric Auguste Bartholdi designed the statue."

"She looks like a goddess."

"They went with a Greco-Roman goddess of liberty in the end."

I flexed a bicep. "They came to their senses and realized it's the women who save the day."

Tobias pounced forward and tickled my ribs, and I laughed and struggled to get away from him. "Yeah, the truth hurts, mate."

"Mate?" He tipped up my chin. "What are you, a pirate?"

"I'm a warrior." I beamed at him.

"I'm going to kiss you."

"I'll allow it."

Something in the way he looked at me sent a stab of doubt as his mouth crushed mine, but having his body trapping me between him and the stone sent a shiver of pleasure that was impossible to deny and I weakened in his arms. I'd never be able to resist him like this, the way his tongue stroked mine tenderly, the way his lips forced mine wider and the way his kissing made me feel we were two souls entwined in a timeless embrace.

He broke away and kissed my neck. "Oh, the things I want to do to you."

"What kind?" I ran my fingers along his shirt collar.

"If we weren't in a public area I'd kneel at your feet and worship the goddess before me." He beamed brightly. "You take my breath away, Zara."

"Maybe I'd insist on kneeling before you—"

"I'm going to have to stop you there." He pressed a finger to my lips and something in his gaze changed.

A jolt of fear hit me. "Are they here?"

He pulled me along the stone wall and down the steps. "Don't look back."

We rounded the corner and we ran down more steps. All the way to a grassy bank.

"Wilder!"

"Follow my lead," said Tobias darkly.

I turned and a jolt of terror chilled my veins—

I recognized the pretty face concealing Eli Burell—that brown hair parted in the middle into a foppish style and that velvet jacket and black slacks worn to round out his arty arrogance. There, beside him, stood four men and all of them were dressed in dark suits. They looked like well-scrubbed mercenaries who'd tasted murder and liked it.

This was what Tobias had struggled to protect me from.

"What a surprise to see you here," Tobias announced with a chilling composure. "Great minds think alike."

"I was just thinking the same thing, Wilder." Eli glanced over at me. "Romantic setting. Nice to see you two are still together. Two birds and all that."

"Ever the charmer, Eli," Wilder taunted. "How did you find us?"

Eli shrugged. "I put it down to luck."

If Tobias was scared, he didn't show it. He merely moved closer to me.

"We missed you both when you left my party abruptly." Eli tugged at his shirtsleeve. "I for one was hoping you were dead when you leaped off the roof."

"I was hoping you were going to jump after me." Tobias grinned. "No such luck, apparently."

"It's over, Wilder."

"Funny, I thought things were just getting good."

"Let's have that chat."

"I don't believe we have anything to talk about," said Tobias.

Eli scoffed. "You brought the FBI to our door when you gate-crashed our wedding in Arizona—" He glared at me. "Juliet, I mean Zara Leighton, employee of Huntly Pierre."

"How's Noodle?" I sounded calm even though my heart was jackhammering.

"Our Bengal tiger has developed a taste for fresh blood." Eli raised his brows. "And I love to see him happy."

Tobias straightened. "Maybe we could set up a meeting with your dad. At a time that is more convenient to us? Cut out the middleman."

"Stop wasting everyone's time." Eli turned to go. "I'm going to let my men have that chat on my behalf. If you'll excuse me."

"Let us go," snapped Tobias.

"After all the trouble I've gone to in finding you?" Eli sneered.

Tobias looked at me and I knew he was waiting for my permission before he replied to Eli; he needed my blessing on the darkest deed I'd ever committed.

"Eli." I turned to face him. "I've seen *her*."

Tobias gave a nod to clarify. "Let us go and we'll share what we know on this rare piece."

"That's why you're in New York?" Eli narrowed his gaze on us.

Tobias gave a nod. "This insider knowledge will come with a caveat."

"Sounds fucking boring," snapped Eli, but his irises were dilated and his jaw tense and his neck flushed with intrigue.

"I'm giving you an insider scoop," added Tobias.

"My family owns everything there is that's of interest. We own all the juicy artwork, leaving places like your gallery with the dregs." Eli threw me a glare of triumph. "We have the greatest private collection of art in the world."

That wasn't true, but Eli seemed to want to believe it because he was a prisoner of his own ego.

I prayed the tourists stayed around to witness what they did to us. "Ever going to share your art with the world?" I asked.

"Fuck no." Eli glared at me. "The public wouldn't recognize a masterpiece if you put it in front of them. Did you see that social experiment where one of the most famous violinists, Magnus Mayburn, played his Stradivarius in Central Park? People just walked by. No ear for genius. The fucking hoi polloi have no comprehension when it comes to art. The fuckers don't deserve it. It's up to the leaders of the world to hide it away and protect it. We get to enjoy it because we know its worth."

"Art is more than the money it's worth," I told him. "It's the language of the soul."

Eli gave an arrogant smirk.

Tobias drew his words out slowly. "Leonardo da Vinci's other *Mona Lisa* has surfaced here. And I know where she's being auctioned." He raised his hand in caution. "This is a private affair. No one must know."

"This isn't strictly legal?" Eli shifted his feet. "If you're bullshitting me I will end you."

Tobias continued unfazed, "Tomorrow evening after my charity ball, a select group of art collectors will be invited to personally rub shoulders with the other *Mona Lisa*. If the offer is right the seller is open to parting ways with her."

Eli swapped a wary glare with his men. "If she was here I'd know."

"Apparently not."

"Who is this man?"

"The owner has requested to remain anonymous," I piped up, and it was the truth at least. "The painting is not without its complications."

Eli tilted his head with intrigue. "Are you going to bid on her?"

"If I can liquefy some assets," said Tobias. "I'm offering you a fair shot at the prize."

"I want in that room," said Eli. "This is not a request, Wilder."

"I'm sure I can persuade them."

"Where's the auction being held?"

"Private room at The Rose Club at The Plaza." Tobias shoved his hands into his pockets. "She'll be guarded heavily. Staff will not be given access to the room when she arrives. No one will know she's there. Take my view time of 10:00 p.m. You'll be the first person in—"

"Might as well cancel the other bidders, Wilder." Eli sneered at him.

"You're free to bring an authenticator. One only."

"I'm gonna want to run some tests."

"Which is permitted." Tobias gave a nod to let him know we were done.

"Can we leave now?" I asked.

"Do you have any idea who you are dealing with?" Eli grimaced his annoyance. "My father can wipe you off the earth if you sneeze wrong."

"If I get you in the room." Tobias scratched his head as though mulling over his offer. "I'll have one more condition."

Eli narrowed his gaze. "What?"

"We both benefit from this."

Eli didn't look convinced. "Have you seen her?"

"Yes." I gave an assured nod.

"And?" he pushed.

My back straightened. "She's remarkable."

"Has she passed an X-ray?" asked Eli.

My nod was to clarify she most certainly would.

"Paint samples?"

"Match the decade," I said, since they'd pass that test too because Wilder's skills ensured it.

"Her molecular structure checks out?" Eli narrowed his gaze on me. "So that's why you're in New York under such secrecy?"

I gave a thin smile. "I'm uncomfortable with her going to a private collector." And that wasn't a lie, either.

Tobias stiffened his spine beside me. I'd not exactly lied for him but I had twisted the truth. Until him I'd always colored within the lines and followed the rules and every word I'd spoken had been infused with integrity.

Until now.

I gave a confident nod. "She looks real to me."

Eli looked triumphant. "Make it happen, Wilder."

"I'll do what I can," said Tobias.

"I'm not the only one with an interest in da Vinci.

If you think you can trick me into missing the date of this auction you're wrong."

Tobias sounded calm. "If I get you in that room—"

"If my father learns a da Vinci auction went down without our involvement men will die."

"If I get you in the room," Wilder repeated, "you'll forget Arizona ever happened. We'll forget all of it too. You let us get on with our lives, and we let you get on with your weasel existence."

Eli gave a sinister smile. "I'm looking forward to putting this behind us. Ms. Leighton, my family's aware that there is a rumor circulating our Romanov collection once belonged to your father. Your old paintings are not ours. Yours were destroyed in a house fire decades ago. Ours have nothing to do with that insurance scandal."

A wave of nausea welled that he'd dared to mention my father. Still, he'd just confirmed what Tobias had told me. They really did have them.

Tobias's tone was certain. "We want this over."

Eli took a step forward. "Let's talk more about this."

"We have somewhere to be." Wilder reached for my hand and interlocked his fingers with mine. "If you'll excuse us."

"We're not done." Eli gestured to his men.

Tobias led me away and I hurried beside him down the pathway with my throat tight with tension.

"There's no getting off this island, Wilder," Eli called after us.

I gripped his hand tighter.

Tobias threw me a wink.

I cringed when I thought of the slowness of one of those boats leaving the harbor, and sensed Eli's men closing in.

CHAPTER TWELVE

My CHEST WAS tight with dread when we ran past the dock, missing the entry to the ferry. Then I saw it— the speedboat. Waiting for us at the helm was the captain and he threw us a wave when he saw us. We bolted down the steps and I leaped into the boat. We hurried to sit at the back. He snapped the order for us to go—

The engine roared to life and we sped out of the harbor, rocking over the open water with the wind blasting my face and billowing my clothes. Daring to look back, I saw Eli standing on the edge of Liberty Island dock with his men beside him.

"He won't find this suspicious?" I asked Tobias.

"He probably expected us to take off in a helicopter."

"So us having a speedboat ready…?"

"Is something I'd do."

"Right. Do you think it went well?" I didn't want to say any more with the skipper a few feet away.

Tobias gave me an assured nod and called out to our captain, "I appreciate this, Dan."

"Always a pleasure, Mr. Wilder," he called back.

Tobias scooted closer to me. "Dan's a coast guard. Getting on and off the island is monitored because it's a national monument."

"How did you make that happen?" I nodded toward the island.

Tobias leaned toward me and lowered his voice. "Eli's been waiting for me to pop up on the grid. Marshall saw him boarding a boat and let me know he was on his way."

Grateful for the ever-growing distance between us and that island, I realized every moment on there had been orchestrated. Tobias had set a trap for Eli so our meeting would happen at that exact time. Eli had been right on our heels. The only other time I'd felt such terror was when I'd fallen through a trapdoor in Arizona, with the threat of drowning all too real. My heart was still hammering in my chest.

Tobias pulled out his cell and I watched him turn the GPS off.

As we zoomed along I clutched the side of the boat carrying us fast toward the mainland.

I'd verbally unleashed the painting into existence and even though it would only be seen by Eli and his father, my heart constricted that I was part of its cruel mystique. I wouldn't rest until it was destroyed. Back during my student days when a fake painting had surfaced it had been perfectly acceptable to destroy the artwork and keep it out of the hands of dealers who duped unsuspecting collectors. My colleagues had seemingly enjoyed being part of eradicating fakes. I, however, refused to be present when the deed was done. Something inside me couldn't bear to see art destroyed even in the name of ethics.

Tobias rested a hand on my knee. "You okay?"

I gave a nod and stared out at the city view, not wanting to show any doubt until I could resolve these complex feelings.

"You did great." His expression revealed he was relieved to be away from that island too, but the way he kept glancing at me proved his concern for me was growing.

Off in the distance, dark clouds rolled in and threatened rain and my body stung with the chill. Tobias went to remove his jacket for me but I stopped him. This sting of cold kept me focused and served as a form of punishment for my misdeeds.

I closed my eyes and took in a deep breath trying to calm down.

Within half an hour I was happy to be back on dry land ascending the steps of the Manhattan marina.

Outside the dock Marshall was waiting for us in the SUV.

After pulling my seat belt on in the backseat I exhaled a shaky breath and it felt like the same one I'd been holding since being threatened by Eli. While in the New York Ballet Tobias had tried to persuade me to go home and not face this. Still, I'd been an asset to him, and the authenticity I'd provided would see Eli chomping at the bit to see our *Mona Lisa*.

Our Mona Lisa, I mused, guilt dripping off me for what I'd done.

"Marshall." Tobias gestured to him. "Take us to my favorite haunt."

"Got it, sir," he replied, and shared a smile with his boss in the rearview mirror.

The glass divider rose between us.

"Sure you're okay?" Tobias gave me a look of concern.

"I'm fine."

"I've got it from here. You've done more than enough to help set this up."

"I'm glad I was with you."

"You dealt with Eli well. He's a prickly bastard. Rules don't apply."

Resting my head back, I stared at him. "You knew when we stepped on that island he was heading our way?"

"Once I turned on the GPS I knew he'd find us." He shook his head. "We're dealing with the devil, Zara. I'm uncomfortable with you being exposed to him. Let Marshall—"

I reached for his hand. "I feel the same about you."

"Me?" He looked surprised.

"Eli won't find it suspicious that we were on that island?"

"Who would allow themselves to be so vulnerable?"

I forced a smile. "Someone with nothing to hide."

"Exactly."

"So Coops is more than just your driver?"

"He's my right-hand man. He's my Q, my quartermaster. I trust him. That's why I had him drive you home that first night you visited Oxfordshire."

Because Tobias had other plans that night, namely flying his helicopter across the country to deliver a Titian to its original owner.

"Eli took the bait," he said. "And you looked surprised when you saw him. That you can't fake."

"How about you?"

"Poker face. You reveal your emotions easily." He squeezed my hand as though needing further reassurance I was okay. "Our invite to see the *Mona Lisa* needed to appear reluctant."

"I get it. It had to be *her*. No other painting would have enticed Eli."

She'd also been an extraordinary diversion that for now kept us safe.

Tobias leaned toward me. "She's our last hope, Zara. I want us to have a future where we are safe. I want you to get your paintings back because I can't stand that family having them. Eli dangled them in front of you just to see your reaction. He taunted you like the psychopath he is."

"Will he ever leave us alone?"

Tobias frowned as he turned away, and it was the kind of look that carried a burden of knowledge.

"Don't do anything foolish." I grabbed his forearm. "Promise me."

"You know how methodical I am."

Though what we had set in motion verged on insanity. We'd compromised everything we held dear to find our way out the other side of the storm. It was a cruel irony that I had to lie about a painting to restore my father's legacy. My family's history was still playing out.

I was grateful for this interlude where we got to just be with each other while holding the devil at bay. Peering out at the city view I enjoyed these moments of calmness and wanted to savor the hours before tomorrow when the stakes would be raised even higher. For the first time, pulling off this wild scheme seemed possible. The question was, could I live with myself afterward?

I looked out at the New York skyline, this metropolis exuding a unique vibrancy I'd not felt from other cities. There was an excitement here, a sense of daring possibilities at every turn.

We drove for just over an hour.

When I saw the sign for the New York Hall of Science I felt a jolt of happiness that Tobias was bringing me to an important place to him. He purchased our tickets, and the way he walked through the building made me wonder if he'd come here as a boy with his grandmother. I didn't want to ask, didn't want to break the spell and see his brightness diminish.

He guided me into the hall of mirrors, and I spun round to see my reflection from every angle. It was quirky and the playfulness we needed.

Tobias came up behind me. "Look at you. You're perfection."

I leaned my head on his chest and held his gaze in the mirror. "'The true work of art is but a shadow of the divine perfection.'"

"Ah, you're quoting Michelangelo."

"I am."

"'I saw the angel in the marble and carved until I set him free.'" He whispered it.

I sighed at Michelangelo's poetic words. "Art through his eyes was seen as already existing. He merely chipped away to reveal what had always been."

"Everything that is has always been."

"I can never get my mind around the metaphysical," I admitted. "Like trying to grasp four dimensions."

"We're advancing at lightning speed. I believe soon we'll discover evidence of a higher-dimensional realm beyond space and time."

"Mind blown." I flashed my hands.

My thoughts carried me back to the way he'd conducted himself on Liberty Island. Tobias had impressively parried and even now exuded a quiet confidence. Unlike me, he wasn't thrown by the threat of tomorrow. That was both reassuring and a little unnerving. After all, Tobias had more than proven his self-assurance and right now even his gentleness was glinting through his steely armor.

The image of him naked beneath that hot shower yesterday was soldered into my frontal cortex and therefore easily replayed at all the wrong moments. His strong arm wrapped around me, pulling me into a perfect hug of possessiveness.

"Let's practice your poker face. For when you need it." He made a playful expression.

I liked this side of him, this cute, approachable side that he seemed to reserve just for me. Or maybe, I reasoned, that was the whole point of making me believe we had something special going on when the only thing in common was an endgame that I wouldn't see coming.

I played along and mirrored his smirk. "How's this?"

"Can't wait to take you again, Zara."

My jaw dropped at his brashness.

"Right there you showed me what you're thinking." He gave a cocky smile. "Try again."

"Okay, I'm ready."

My brain warned that Tobias had artfully drawn our enemy into his complex web. Maybe I too was caught up in this finely woven plan and just couldn't see it, didn't want to believe I'd fallen for the famed Icon. Maybe it wouldn't be until all this was over that I'd know for sure.

He whispered. "I'm counting the seconds until I can taste you again."

I held his reflection with my best poker face, but the thought of his mouth on me caused me to lick my lips in a tease.

"Try again."

"Okay, I'm ready."

"I've never felt this way about anyone," he said softly. "You are my one obsession. All I want is you."

"Don't," I said, turning to face him.

He cupped my face. "What if it's the truth?"

This teasing felt cruel. "Why are we here?"

"If you understand science you'll understand me." He stepped back and reached out his arms in a gesture of sincerity. "I want you to see *me*."

"Science is honest?"

He lowered his gaze. "Science strikes into the heart of truth and doesn't compromise."

"That's a little cold."

"Maybe that's where you come in?"

"How?"

"I'm the science and you're the art and this was what da Vinci was trying to tell us. That without one the other cannot exist."

I swooned at his words, wanting to confess my feelings for him and blurt out that I'd fallen in love with him, but the sting of rejection would cut too deep. I wasn't ready for him to push me away and remind me he "didn't do love."

This will have to be enough.

We hurried from exhibit to exhibit, and Tobias relaxed more and lit up with happiness when he came to a hands-on section of virtual reality where he could show off his tech genius. It was as though a switch had flipped on and my serious alpha had morphed into a playful boy who loved to laugh.

Tobias showed me the room with the large hoverboard and helped me climb onto it before the surface rose a foot off the ground. The board felt unstable beneath my feet and I fought for my balance, half listening to him explain the mechanism of fighting gravity. I giggled as I clung on to him. This was so damn fun and I loved this side of Wilder, the same side that had inspired him to set up crazy golf in the garden and give us some much-needed downtime.

This place showcased the most recent innovations in math, science, technology and engineering, and these subjects were so much fun when seen through Wilder's eyes. I loved every second with him as he led me around with a renewed enthusiasm, making me forget this pause in our high-risk day.

"I have a surprise for you," he said.

I rubbed my stomach to hint I was hungry, though the thought of more time in the car made me antsy.

Tobias grinned. "Come see."

I followed him out the back of the building to an open plan area of concrete where there were a few more exhibits, and jolted to a stop—there, on the tarmac, was a sleek-looking helicopter. "Is that for us?"

"Otherwise we'll be fighting traffic." Tobias made it sound like this had been easy to arrange and led me toward the helicopter.

Marshall climbed out and, after a few minutes of talking, he guarded our departure from the ground to keep the eager tourists at a safe distance as they took photos of our ascent. I was impressed with how Tobias took us up into the air with the ease of an experienced pilot. He'd once told me he also flew his own jet from time to time and I was again reminded Tobias was good at so many things.

Kind of intimidating, I silently mused, staring out at the incredible view as we banked over the city.

We landed at the downtown Manhattan heliport and

a stretch limo was waiting for us. The drive along the scenic route of the FDR Drive had a view of the east river and Tobias told me this was a pretty sight at night. Within half an hour I saw the gorgeous architecture of the Metropolitan Museum of Art and hoped that was our destination.

When the limo pulled up to the curb I almost squealed with joy. "Seriously?" I asked him, my heart pounding with excitement.

He beamed at me. "Yes."

We hurried up the stone steps and I could hardly wait to enter. However, as we entered the main foyer, a wave of doubt settled in my stomach that being here was a bad idea. Those cameras would follow our every move.

"Shouldn't we be staying away from art galleries?" I whispered. "They have face recognition software."

"Zara, we have nothing to hide."

"What if the FBI warned the museum about you?"

"That would be slander," he replied with confidence. "Which is a crime."

Suppressing my frown, I didn't want to spoil the moment and blurt the obvious. "Are you sure it's safe?"

"I know the curator. Sarah Belle's expecting us."

"She is?"

"Yes. We're free to enjoy the Met."

Being here soothed my soul and I couldn't wait to explore the gallery. I turned to look at Tobias, reminding myself not to let my guard down and to keep an eye on him.

He neared me. "You go into withdrawal if you're away from art for more than twenty-four hours."

"That's true." I did get jittery if too much time passed and I couldn't bathe in the beauty of the old masters.

"I got my science fix. This is for you." He pushed me against a marble pillar, trapping me between the stone and his hard chest. "Give me permission."

I drew in a sharp breath. "What for?"

"This." He crushed his lips to mine, kissing me hard on the mouth, and passion surged through me as his tongue lashed feverishly, alighting every nerve. My body pulsed with pleasure as his cologne cloaked me in his seductive mastery and made me forget we were in a public place. He pulled away and grinned revealing that familiar warmth in his gaze. "I love seeing you come alive like this."

"We're still in the foyer," I chuckled.

"You are home, Zara," he growled into my ear. "In my opinion you're the masterpiece."

We'd caught the attention of a crowd of tourists who were looking our way and they giggled at us.

Don't pull away...

The pressure of his body lifted from mine and instinctively I grabbed his shoulders to hold him to me. With each passing day, I'd sensed him tuning into my needs and being here was proof of that. Breathing in the gallery air felt like normality had returned even if it was temporary.

With my arm in his we strolled along the endless rooms of the Met, pausing here and there to savor a painting and swoon at the talent that had brought it to life. Within the heart of a top-floor exhibit, a French Renaissance display opened to us. I settled on the leather seat in the middle of this grandeur to admire the fantastic imagery of *The Last Judgment* by Hieronymus Bosch. A terrifying painting on three panels, the first of the Garden of Eden, the middle depicting God in heaven casting out his rebel angels and the right panel where Jesus judged the souls of the damned. The vision was hard to turn away from.

"Current mood?" He sat beside me and gestured to the panels.

"I'm a little scared, Tobias."

"Don't worry about Burell—"

"No, I mean you and I have loved art all our lives. What will this do to us?"

"When you're reunited with your paintings you will feel different about all of this. I will see to it that our creation has a brief existence. It will be as though she never existed."

"You're asking a lot from me." I wrapped my arm through his. "And I'm asking even more from you."

"I'd do anything for you, Zara."

I buried my face in my hands. "I want it over."

He caressed my back and we sat quietly and savored the peace of this quiet room and I tried to imagine how things would be between us after this.

He turned to face me. "You didn't say it."

"Say what?"

"When I confessed how I feel about you."

I turned to look at him. "Are you talking about what you told me in the New York Ballet theatre?"

"Yes."

Was he really referring to his words *I sense how easy it would be to love you*? "You were pretty vague."

He pulled me into him and crushed his lips to mine sparking an erotic aliveness within me, and I swooned as the tension in my shoulders that I'd been carrying for so long relaxed. These flashes of his affection were dangerously convincing.

I nipped his lip. "Security is watching."

"All part of our ruse."

I felt a wave of vulnerability. "So that kiss meant nothing?"

"It meant everything." He leaned back a little to try and read me. "What I meant was I don't care what the world thinks."

"You called it a ruse."

"There must be truth in every subterfuge for it to be believed. I refuse to hide. And I'm happy to be with you here."

I brought my hands up to cup his cheeks to convey how I felt about him, and he narrowed his gaze as though mulling over my confusion. We still had to face so much uncertainty and were holding on by a thread with everything just one snap away from falling apart.

Tobias rose and walked away.

I went to call after him and then realized from the friendliness of how he greeted her that he was heading toward someone he recognized. I assumed the pretty forty-something was Sarah Belle. Pushing myself to my feet I remained a little way back as he chatted with the woman who carried herself like a curator. She threw me a wave and I gave one back.

Walking in the opposite direction I neared a closed door with the gold lettering above announcing beyond was the Edgar Degas exhibit. A memory hit me—aged seven years I'd pirouetted before a Degas trying to mirror the elegance of a ballerina. *Oh, God*, I'd believed that painting had been destroyed all these years. My memories felt tainted.

"Wait for me," Tobias called over.

I wanted to be in that room, wanted to cleanse myself of this uneasiness and my feet kept walking until my hand was on the door.

Why is it closed?

Tobias cut me off. "It's not ready."

I tried to pry my arm away from his hand that had stopped me, and doubt rose in my chest for why we were here.

"Please, Zara, give us a few minutes before we go in." He turned and waved goodbye to Sarah Belle.

A wave of panic. "What is this?"

He faced me again. "When I create a hologram or a three-dimensional world it's only a reflection of the authenticity it strives to reflect. I was reminded of that when I saw your expression during the demonstration back at the house. You loved the art I'd captured with my virtual reality but nothing equals being at a gallery. Right?"

"That's just it, Tobias." My gut twisted. "With you I'm never sure what I'm seeing. You have this facade that's challenging to penetrate. I've seen a side of you I always believed was there, a good side, but then it's gone."

"Don't let *Mona Lisa* curse me for the rest of my life."

"Whatever incantation you're casting to catch the Burells is rubbing off on me." I pointed to the room. "More mysteries? More smoke and mirrors?"

He hung his head in frustration.

I twisted the door handle and gave it a shove—

Hurrying in, I stopped in the center of the room when I saw the dinner table set up with a pristine white cloth and two plate settings. Soft lighting threw dramatic shadows around the romantically set room. Making my way in farther my breath caught in wonder at the art adorning the walls and all of them were dreamy renditions by Edgar Degas.

I'd been away from my beloved art for too long.

I exhaled a long breath of surprise for what Tobias had pulled off, and when I filled my lungs again it was with awe at the portraits surrounding me. Ahead of me, I spotted *The Ballet Class*. It was painted around 1874, revealing Degas's privileged access to the backstage area of the opera house where he'd observed dancers rehearsing and had masterfully captured them in a moment of time.

I absorbed the vision of Degas's 1874 *The Ballet Rehearsal on Stage*, and admired his choice of colors, that gorgeous blue, the dancers immortalized midmovement, and allowed myself to be absorbed into the canvas and have these seconds selfishly dissolve.

I'd discovered something else about Tobias, not only from being in this setting that he'd chosen specially, but from our easy access to watch a rehearsal at the New York Ballet, and that was he had a fondness for dancing. He truly was a Renaissance man.

He gave a wary smile as though gauging what I thought of his surprise. I looked upon this complex man, a mosaic of many layers, and this was why I'd struggled to define him. His gaze wandered from painting to painting and his expression was full of adoration. Yet when his eyes found mine again they turned fiercely protective. Staring into each other's eyes, time stood still and at that moment I was seeing *him*.

He'd been right, I had needed my art fix and no matter where I was in the world art would always be my anchor. That Tobias had known this touched me deeply.

He felt like my safe harbor in the storm. Words failed me as I shrugged my apology for how I'd just spoken to him and he responded with a grin to convey all was forgiven.

He held out his hand and escorted me to the table.

A young waiter served ravioli pieces drizzled in lobster sauce as an appetizer. It would have been easy to forget we were in a gallery and not a fine restaurant. After pouring champagne into two flutes the young man laid a serviette on my lap.

Tobias thanked him.

He made a quiet exit and closed the door to the exhibit room behind him.

I smoothed out my napkin. "This is lovely."

He glanced up toward the cameras. "They only have visual coverage so we can talk freely."

I gave him the look that deserved. "And you know that how?"

"I Googled it." He gave a wry smile.

"I once Googled you."

"Anything interesting?"

"You know your public image."

"I'm interested in hearing how you perceived it."

"You have a beautiful woman on your arm in many of the photos."

"And?"

I tilted my head to say the rest.

He gestured with a wave to make his point. "I've experienced a dramatic shift off my axis after meeting you." He raised his brows playfully. "You've affected me in unusual and somewhat existential ways."

"Somewhat?"

"You've given me a reason to live, Zara."

My hand rested on my chest to soften the effect of his words.

"Do I frighten you?"

"I've given you the power to decimate my life, Tobias."

"What do you need to hear from me to know my affection for you is real?"

"Tell me why you find it hard to love?"

He set his knife and fork down. "You want to do this now?"

"Yes." I gestured to the paintings. "This is an incredible setting. I know you went to a lot of trouble to make it happen. Still, you are more important than any painting."

"It gave me a great deal of pleasure arranging this for you." He raised his hand to insist. "I made the calls, not Coops, in case you're wondering."

"It has your touch."

He cut into a square of ravioli and gestured for me to eat mine. It tasted delicious and the flavors tingled my taste buds with their creamy tomato sauce. I was hungrier than I realized and tucked into my food with gusto.

"This is perfect." Tobias set his cutlery down on his plate. "We should do this every night."

"It's a date. The visitors will just have to walk around us."

"Maybe I'll buy it."

"The Met?"

He gave a shrug. "Maybe I'll buy it for you."

"First, it belongs to the people, and second…"

He peered over his flute and held my gaze. "Go on."

"If you and I are to work, Tobias, there must be no walls between us." I sat back. "So let me in."

He blew out a sigh. "What do you want to know?"

"What drives you?"

"Bringing new concepts into the world. But you know that about me. More recently you inspire me, Zara. Your bravery. Us being here is my way of rewarding your courage."

"Because I went with you to Liberty Island?"

"Because you're giving me a chance to prove who I am."

"I know why you're closed off," I said softly. "Once you're in survival mode—"

He went to say something but changed his mind.

"Do you trust me, Tobias?"

"I find that I do."

"Why did you hold back so much from me when we first met?"

"Other than the obvious?" He arched a brow to remind me who he was.

"Something is holding you back from happiness."

He pushed his plate away. "Loving someone leads to pain. That was my experience. During the hours after my parents died I felt a shift and since that day I've been reluctant to open up."

"Tell me about that shift."

"After the plane came down I knew what had to be done. I searched for water and food on the plane. I tried the radio. It was broken. I made a fire. What kept me going was getting Annibale Carracci's *Madonna Enthroned with Saint Matthew* to Sydney. I vowed to complete my parents' mission."

"And you fulfilled your promise."

"And I hardened my heart against the agony. I felt

guilty I'd made it and they hadn't. I made the promise never to allow vulnerability near me again."

I swallowed past a lump of sadness.

"I was nine when I made that pledge to myself. Nine when I lay beneath the stars in the Outback in the dead of night and promised never to get close to anyone."

"You love your uncle?"

"My heart is impervious to a relationship." He raised his gaze to meet mine. "I believed that right up until I met you. My feelings for you are complicated."

"Complicated?"

"My heart tells me you're The One." He reached over and took my hand. "You've asked me to give up the only thing that made sense of all that happened to me. You're asking me to suppress that part of me." He looked around the display as though mulling over that thought. "I promise you I will. I'm ready for the next chapter in my life."

And I was ready to tell him how much I loved him, because he deserved to know. *I've always loved him.*

He let go of my hand and gestured to let me know the waiter was behind me. The server removed our plates and set down two entrées of fish and chips.

I'd missed my chance.

Tobias smiled as he motioned to the paintings. "This was to soothe your homesickness for England—" He pointed to our meal. "This is mine."

I blushed a little, having been so close to saying that four-letter word that would have left me vulnerable.

"Zara? Everything okay?"

"Yes, of course. You miss London?"

"I love my home in Oxfordshire. The countryside in England is like nowhere else. The quiet."

"Do you miss your foxes?"

"Rascals that they are."

I popped a chip into my mouth and it tasted deliciously salty and made my mouth water. "Sometimes you are annoyingly perfect."

"I'm going to aim to impress you for the rest of your life." He grinned. "As you can see I'm an open book when it comes to you."

"There is something else."

"Ask away."

"You're sure?"

"Yes."

"How old were you when you found out Elliot Burell sabotaged your parents' plane?"

"Nine." Tobias's gaze locked on mine. "I overheard my uncle Fabienne arguing with his lawyer. They were discussing the findings from the investigation surrounding the crash. I was meant to be asleep but I'd come down for a glass of water and I heard the tension in his voice. He was being advised to hide me away. I didn't see my grandmother for five years after that."

I felt dreadful for him. "How did they find out the plane had been sabotaged?"

"When they examined the wreckage, they found evidence the fuselage had been tampered with. They went back to check the hangar's surveillance and it showed a man working on the plane who wasn't authorized to be in there. They matched his fingerprints. He was a hired mercenary who worked for Elliot Burell."

"Why didn't your uncle prosecute?"

"The man disappeared." Tobias reached for his glass. "Burell's lawyers threatened my uncle with a defamation lawsuit. We went to live in France." Tobias drank the rest of his water as though trying to quench a thirst that would never relent.

"When you became a public figure, weren't you scared Burell would come for you?"

He leaned forward. "I kept away from that family right up until I discovered they'd stolen a Titian. I admit to outbidding them for paintings in auctions from time to time to entertain my dark heart. Zara, that heist changed my life. Not only did I achieve my goal, but I also found a collection that belonged to the most enigmatic woman I've ever met. And here we are. Dining within the company of Degas."

I turned my gaze to a Degas in a golden frame. "Do you ever wish you could just slip inside one of these and stay there?"

Tobias pushed his chair back as he stood. "I already have."

Staring up at him I tried to read his next move. I shoved a fry into my mouth nervously.

"Stand up, Zara."

Slowly, I rose from my seat, wary of Wilder's next move. I licked salt off my fingers, my heart thundering at the change in his tone. He walked around the table and neared me. "What would make the evening perfect?"

"Chocolate pudding?"

He lowered his chin. "Think grander."

"Tobias," I said breathlessly as a jolt of fear ran down my spine for what Icon was about to do next.

He leaned in and kissed my ear. "Trust me."

"I do." My voice sounded shaky, uncertain.

"Then why are you looking at me like I'm Icon?" His irises glistened under the soft light.

"I trust you." My lips pressed his tenderly.

He smiled against my mouth. "I want to bring the room alive for you." Tobias stepped back and gestured his thanks when the waiter cleared the table. Two more staff helped carry the table out.

Bring the room alive?

My heart soared when three ballerinas trotted in and all of them wearing blue leotards and lush tutus with fresh yellow flowers in their hair, gliding elegantly toward the center of the room. My palm flew to my mouth to suppress my gasp of joy. Tobias lit up at my reaction and took my hand and led me toward the far wall so we could watch them from there.

As the piano music flooded in from hidden speakers, the dancers performed their classic ballet, sweeping around the room, pirouetting, their toes pointed to the floor as they artfully danced and they rose and dipped in a continuous movement.

"This is beautiful, Tobias." My breath caught at the majesty of the dancers who quite suddenly posed to mirror the extraordinary 1889 masterpiece known as *Blue Dancers*, bringing to life a living, breathing Degas.

"I've never seen anything so beautiful." My eyes stung with tears.

"Oh, Zara, I knew you'd love it." He hugged me into him.

Tobias had reminded me of the profoundness of art, how it soothed and brought devotion back into my life, proving once more that human expression was pure in all its forms, and I felt my faith soar and my heart ascending to new heights.

Tobias rolled his eyes playfully. "And to think you would have been happy with chocolate pudding."

"You certainly know how to raise the bar," I whispered.

A dizzying altitude that leaves me breathless.

Tobias's surprise was awe inspiring and my heart was filled with gratitude for this incandescent performance. When the dancers ended their exquisite performance I thanked them profusely, so grateful they'd honored us by being here tonight.

After thanking Sarah Belle for helping him pull together this evening, we headed down the steps toward the waiting limousine.

"Let's go home," Tobias said as he sat beside me on the leather seat. "I want you all to myself."

We sat at opposite sides of the car, him with his long leg crossed over another and staring out at the Manhattan view, and me on the other side, reeling from the most incredible date I'd ever experienced. Tobias took all this generosity in his stride as though spreading fairy dust over everyone was as easy as it looked. I knew he'd gone to great lengths to make tonight happen.

The divider slid up between us as this unknown driver navigated the evening traffic.

I was still reeling from the day, mesmerized how something so terrifying had turned into a wonderful memory and as I looked over at Tobias I swooned at all he'd done for me today and all that he was doing.

"Tobias," I whispered.

He turned to look at me as though rising out of a daydream. "Come here."

Scooting over, I fell against his hard chest and breathed in his sultry cologne that comforted and I reveled at how we fit so devastatingly well together. The strength of his arms wrapping around me, the kiss of his lips to my forehead, his deep sigh reassuring me all he'd told me tonight was true.

CHAPTER THIRTEEN

WE LEFT THE HOUSE with the midmorning sun bearing down on Manhattan. This crisp day had forgotten it was autumn. The drive to 5th Avenue was the brightness I'd craved and I rested my head back and watched the way the light refracted off the high-rises.

Yesterday's near escape from Eli on Liberty Island had left me shaken and the thought I'd have to face him again caused a wave of dread. When Marshall pulled up outside The Plaza hotel I felt that same adrenaline surging through me. Tonight, our *Mona Lisa* would be snuck inside here and placed on show for one person to see it and believe her real.

And it would be done.

Tonight could go one of two ways. I'd either let that masterpiece slip into the hands of that dreadful man, or I'd snap and hack at the canvas with the first sharp object I could get my hands on in a fit of madness. I chose to keep that crazy thread of thoughts to myself.

Tobias had told me we were here to check on the final arrangements for his charity ball, the event that provided him with an excuse for his trip to New York. I turned my gaze to look at him and he was predictably relaxed and swoon worthy in the fine cut of his pin-striped suit. Even his seductively ruffled hair reminded me of when he'd visited Huntly Pierre to discuss hiring me from my firm. He'd taken my breath away when I'd strolled into our London conference room and lain eyes on a devastatingly gorgeous man, unsuspecting that he was about to break down the walls of my reality.

His erotic cologne was doing crazy things to my senses and reaching me in ways only Wilder could with that alpha stature threatening to burn up everyone who circled his stratosphere.

My formal black dress and heels matched his business attire and together our appearance would convey we were all business and ready for our prearranged meeting with the hotel staff.

"My number's programmed into the phone I gave you. Do you have it on you?"

"It's in here." I tapped my purse.

"Will you give us a moment, please, Marshall?" Tobias was asking him to leave the car.

Marshall exited the vehicle and I could see him wait loyally a few feet away. "What's going on?"

Tobias turned in his seat and took my hand. "This next part isn't going to be easy for you."

"How do you mean?" I wondered if he'd picked up on my dark musing.

"Zara, I invited Adley here for drinks."

I pulled my hand from his. "Why didn't you warn me?"

"Didn't want you to worry."

My gaze shot to the hotel door and my stomach tightened as I realized my boss was in there. "Abby?"

"She's with him."

"What about our plan?"

"The ball is set for tonight. Look, I don't want you

anywhere near the secret auction that will go down afterward."

"You'll face Eli alone?"

"It's for the best. I want to keep you safe. Knowing you're well away from this place will ensure my focus. Eli is unpredictable."

A valet opened my door and I glanced back at Tobias, needing more time to talk about this.

"I'll be right there with you," he reassured me.

I climbed out of the car and waited for Tobias to join me. He gestured a wave of thanks to Marshall and led me into the hotel.

Opulence had a new meaning at The Plaza with its Beaux-Arts style and a luxury that made it easy to forget this was not the real world, with its pristine decor, luscious furnishings, grand touches of splendorous satins and the plush carpeting flattering each step.

The Rose Club exuded privilege with its dimly lit atmosphere, red walls, leather sofas and Persian rug glamour. I wondered if Tobias had chosen this place to case it for tonight. This would be where Tobias would bring our scandalous lady and he'd set in motion a series of events that would make history. Only the world would never know about what had gone down here.

Strangely enough, it was easier to think of that then this, the imminent meeting with my boss who had flown all the way from London to berate and then fire me.

I turned to Tobias, conveying my dread. "Should I face them alone?"

"No, it's best if I do all the talking."

"You're sure?"

"They're expecting an arrogant billionaire who always gets his way and that's what I'm going to give them. Let me take the fall, Zara. What I need from you is your poker face."

My gaze shot around the room for anyone who looked like they could be from the FBI. "What are you going to tell them?"

Tobias was already walking off with his usual stylish swagger, emanating the kind of charisma that might work on Adley and Abby who were seated at a corner table. I couldn't grasp why he'd not warned me they'd be here and uncertainty returned to shake my confidence.

He shoved his hands into his pockets as he weaved around the large leather chairs and sofas, following the pathway leading to them. When Adley saw him he pushed to his feet and it pained me to see the worry lines etched deeply in his brow. After being given a chance to work at his firm I owed him to put this right. Adley had known my father and perhaps this was why he hadn't fired me yet.

I bloody well deserved it.

My feet reluctantly followed and I gave a welcoming smile as I approached their table. Abby forced a smile and even in these circumstances I was relieved to see her. She looked pretty in her black lace dress having styled her hair a little differently. In her eyes I saw suspicion.

She pulled me into a hug and it felt like a warning. "How are you, Zara?"

"I'm fine, thank you. And you?" I braved to look at Adley.

"We've been better," she answered. "Jet-lagged but we'll survive."

"Zara." Tobias gestured where he wanted me to sit and this move was his way of controlling the narrative.

Our small talk was polite and the mood not unpleasant. It would have been easy to forget we weren't close colleagues enjoying this fine hospitality. Tobias ordered a bottle of P2 champagne and within minutes we were holding tall flutes of bubbly as though I'd not failed my company on the grandest level.

Tobias lifted his glass in a toast. "To old friends."

Adley looked uninspired. "Well, I'm here. Ready for answers."

Tobias conceded with a nod. "I owe you an apology, Adley."

His gaze drifted to mine and then returned to Tobias. "To say the least."

"I respect that my actions have been unconscionable," added Tobias. "First, I wish to point out Ms. Leighton's behavior has been consistently professional."

Adley's expression became marred with confusion as he tried to process this. Abby's laser focus zeroed in on me. My heart missed a beat because we'd not discussed any of this.

Tobias drew out the tension by taking a few sips of champagne. "This is good." He looked at me. "Can I get you anything else?"

I shook my head, trying to work out what he was doing.

Tobias continued with a nod. "I'm showcasing the work of a man who has been hailed as the next Rembrandt."

Adley didn't flinch. "Where did you discover him?"

"A monastery here in New York," Tobias replied. "Brother Bay is a monk and his art is extraordinary."

"Why did you need Zara for this?" Abby asked brashly.

Tobias's hand rested firmly on mine. "*Sfumato* is a dying art. Not many artists have the talent or the patience for it. Zara accompanied me to meet with the artist and validated he was indeed creating these masterpieces."

Adley's stare found mine. "Is this true, Zara? Why not let us know?"

"The last time Ms. Reynolds interacted with Ms. Leighton she accused her of having a connection to Icon." Tobias held Abby's gaze. "I felt responsible for her reputation. I wanted to clear her name." He leaned forward and rested his elbows on his knees. "My reputation is important to me too, as you can imagine."

"This was all to protect her?" asked Adley.

"Completely." Tobias's tone was infused with kindness. "Zara works by the book. You have a stellar employee, Adley. Don't let her go."

Abby slid her glass aside having not taken a sip. "Can we discuss the evidence of her being at the Burells' home in Arizona?"

"She's good isn't she?" Tobias faced Abby. "What occurred the day after her appearance in Phoenix? I believe the discovery of *The Storm on the Sea of Galilee*, a Rembrandt that remains hanging in Burell's Arizona estate—unless he's moved it, despite it being proven to be a stolen piece. Zara led the FBI to a gold bullion collection worth a fortune with a shady history. Garnered from warmongering."

"That painting was never authenticated," replied Abby. "And the investigation into the gold is ongoing."

"Because Burell shut you out." Tobias tilted his head. "He's locked down, Abby. There's not going to be a continuation of that investigation. Burell won. Bravo for being part of that disaster."

"Tobias," I chastised him.

"How did you find out the painting was even at Burell's home in Arizona?" Abby's gaze narrowed on me.

"Tip-off." Tobias gave a tight smile. "I'm glad we've gotten this all behind us."

"This has been a serious breach in our protocol." Adley caressed his jaw. "The FBI is ready to speak with you."

"I know," said Tobias. "My next meeting is with them."

A jolt of fear slithered up my spine and yet I refused to look around the café to search them out. If Tobias was arrested, it would be down to me to pull off this evening's event and I wasn't sure I had it in me.

"Tobias." Adley used his first name as though trying to connect on a deeper level. "We must follow rules. There are ethics to consider."

"I wanted to be here," I piped up. "I want to restore my reputation and I knew that if I returned to London too soon I'd not be given the chance to do that."

"We're gathering more evidence," said Tobias. "All of it will clear Zara's name."

Adley sat back. "This is quite something."

"We're still in town tonight," said Abby.

Tobias realized where she was going with this. "I'm afraid the guest list for tonight is locked down." He turned to me. "We would have loved to have you join us but we're at full capacity in the ballroom."

My gaze held his, realizing he'd just uninvited me.

"Zara." Tobias reached out for my hand. "I'll be in touch as soon as I land in London."

"You're leaving?" I couldn't keep the tension from my voice.

He pushed to his feet. "Have a safe trip back to London, Ms. Leighton, it's been a pleasure."

My throat tightened as my brain tried to follow what was happening.

Abby rested her hand on mine. "Zara, we can fly back to London together."

"But what about the ball?" I asked on a shaky breath.

"I've got it from here, Ms. Leighton." Tobias reached for my hand and brought it to his lips. "Hopefully you've had fun?"

I'd either been played by Wilder or this was his way of making sure I was out of danger. Being part of another *Mona Lisa* being released into the underworld weighed heavily, but this to-and-fro, this keeping me on the outside hurt more than my fear of scandal.

"If you'll excuse me—" Tobias shook Adley's hand "—I'll see you back in London. Have a safe flight back."

"Tobias?" I peered up at him.

"I have an appointment with my lawyer. This should be interesting, and by 'interesting' I mean it's good to have the best representation money can buy."

"And why would you need that?" asked Abby.

Tobias rested his hand on the back of her chair. "Because rumors spread and lies ferment and when you own a company like TechRule and rake in billions you're vulnerable to unwanted attention—" His green gaze locked on mine. "I will call you."

All I could manage was a nod, hoping that last comment was a secret code to reassure me things were still good between us. If it wasn't, all that running around the city, all those nights of unbridled passion had fuddled my brain and confused me into committing the worst act of my existence.

He walked away.

Abby waved to the waiter. "Zara, let me get you some water."

Adley headed off toward the restroom as though intuitively knowing I needed a quiet moment alone with his more rational employee who was currently staring me down.

"Will you give me a moment? I'll be right back." I sprang up and walked in the direction of where I'd last seen Tobias and turned the corner into another room. He was chatting with a smartly dressed man who I assumed was his attorney Reynard.

When Tobias saw me, he made his way back. "Over here." He led me to a quiet spot before the unlit fireplace.

I searched his face for the truth. "What changed?"

"Eli Burell will be in this hotel. I don't know when he'll arrive. I'm not putting you in that kind of danger."

"Are you forcing me out of this?"

"You're in the clear. I've got this." Tobias flicked a stray hair out of my face and tucked it behind my ear. "You don't have to compromise your integrity ever again."

"I've come this far."

"Go back to London." He glanced over at the man he'd been chatting with. "I'm sorry, Zara."

"Am I just to do nothing?"

"Yes, that's exactly it. I want you out of this city. I want you back home safe. Wait for me. I will find you." He tapped my arm and walked away.

"Why?" My question was infused with a sense of betrayal, and that tension must have reached him because he stood with his back to me, mulling over his answer.

Tobias turned to face me and lowered his gaze. "I should have told you the truth last night. It was the perfect setting. I was about to say it and that damn waiter came back."

My throat tightened with the threat of his words that had the power to destroy me.

"I'm in love with you, Zara." He gave a nod as though he'd not just delivered the words I'd craved to hear, words that both lifted me and decimated me at the same time because they changed everything. He stepped closer and cupped my cheek with his palm. "I would do anything for you, anything." His expression turned pained. "That means I must ensure your safety."

"What are you going to do?"

"Finish it."

"What about us?"

"When all this is over and the dust has settled and you've had the chance to think without the stress of wondering if you'll survive and you're still willing to give us a chance, send a message to me. I will come to you." He shook his head. "For God's sake, I will be by your side when all you've done is formed the thought of me."

"Oh, Tobias."

"Go back to London." He shrugged. "Marshall will watch over you. You will be a constant in my thoughts. You're my reason to take my next breath, Zara."

Stunned, I watched him turn on his heels, with the same mastery in his stride that he reserved for every aspect of his life, and head out of the bar with Reynard beside him.

Tobias loved me.

With shaky legs, I made my way back to Abby. "Sorry about that. It's been a bit of a whirlwind." The realization hit me, that interaction served as Wilder's goodbye.

She followed my gaze. "What did he say?"

I drew in a shaky breath and sat beside her. "He thanked me for all I've done."

I hoped all I'd done wasn't the worst mistake of my life.

"You should be there tonight." She sat back. "I mean, you're the one who authenticated that monk's work. Why don't you get to enjoy this new Rembrandt?"

"He won't be there."

"But his art will, right?"

"It's fine."

"None of this is fine."

My gaze shot to hers.

"Icon's still out there." She picked up her glass. "He's gone quiet for now, but something tells me we'll see a new heist from him soon."

I feigned those words hadn't shaken me to the core. If Wilder was setting me up he'd be free to continue as Icon.

No, don't doubt his words, I begged myself, *believe that you're deserving of such a love.*

She whispered, "I'm going to save you from yourself."

"I don't need saving."

"Let's go dress shopping." Abby threw back the rest of her champagne.

"Are you going to gate-crash his party?"

She pointed at me. "Oh, we're going tonight, Zara."

"It's by invitation only."

"Adley can get us in."

"What about the FBI?" I looked around furtively. "Are they going to speak with me?"

"Tobias offered full disclosure and you get immunity. Isn't that something? God, you dodged a bullet there. Looks like he's taking one for you."

"What's he going to tell them?"

"I'm assuming everything." She gave my arm a comforting squeeze. "Adley is very forgiving. Me, I need more convincing. There's something else going on here with Wilder, and I want to know what it is."

Cringing inwardly, I hoped to convey she hadn't rattled me.

"Icon's still out there, Zara. And I find it particularly interesting Wilder didn't bring him up."

I ignored her innuendo. "I need to find a hotel."

"We're staying here. I can get you a room here too if you like?"

"Yes," I said confidently. "That's a great idea."

London could wait, my life was placed back in this holding pattern because I refused to let Wilder get to my paintings first. They were my responsibility. Getting them back gave my life meaning. And not losing them to anyone—including a fast-moving billionaire with a penchant for art history—was my priority.

CHAPTER FOURTEEN

I NEEDED TO believe Tobias's confession of love was real. My heart fluttered whenever he was near and all I had to do was trust these feelings. His words gave me strength.

Too many times I'd expressed my concern for what he'd created in that Manhattan home and maybe that influenced his decision to send me away.

I sat on the queen-size bed, trying to rally my courage to ask him all these questions. This lavish Plaza hotel might have been enjoyable if I wasn't personally in the worst place of my life. No matter how gorgeously decorated this room was with its soft pastels and chic design, I couldn't settle. I was either pacing or peering out of the window, trying to think of all the things I could have done differently.

Rising to face the mirror above the fireplace, I realized my fraught expression was revealing too much and inhaled a steadying breath to present nonchalance. I smiled when I fondly recalled how Tobias told me to hold a poker face. I'd never played the game, never needed deceit or tricks, or clever schemes to get by. That was not my world.

Abby's room was inconveniently adjoined to mine and I suspected her spontaneous visits were to make sure Tobias wasn't sneaking in. I needed to know his meeting with the FBI had left him in the clear. My gut twisted with the kind of questioning he'd endured. He'd saved me from this experience and that alone reminded me how much he cared. Or maybe, I painfully mused, he could talk more freely with them and set me up.

I'm in love with you... My heart clutched at these words.

I was going against Tobias's wishes. He probably assumed I was heading to the airport by now. That burner phone was off and I'd delayed calling him to let him know I was still here.

I wasn't done with this city yet. Leaving my paintings didn't feel right.

I was okay with staying clear of The Rose Club, and maybe by tomorrow I'd have some knowledge of where my paintings were. The GPS tracker had been inserted into *Mona Lisa*'s canvas. She may have been a beautiful abomination but she'd lead me all the way to my heritage. It made my stomach ache to think locating them was the easy part. Retrieving them... I couldn't even think of how that was going to go.

You still need Wilder, I berated myself.

And that thought burned up my brain all the while Abby and I had visited Fifth Avenue earlier. I'd bought a blue Zac Posen gown with a satin skirt and beaded bodice that clung to my figure. With all this uncertainty, I'd use the armour of glamour. My auburn locks tumbled over my shoulders, and my eye makeup shimmered to hide the redness of the tears I was holding back, and my lips were full with a natural pink.

A knock shook me from my daydreaming and I turned to see Abby dressed in her gorgeous Ralph Lauren gown and her makeup emphasized her all-seeing eyes highlighted in gold. She wore a bloodred lipstick.

She entered via the adjoining door as though she had a right to. "You look lovely."

My gaze snapped to the small device she carried and that roll of tape. "You too. What is that?"

"Pull down your dress."

"Are you putting a wire on me?" If I spoke with Tobias he'd no doubt say something to implicate himself. "Why do I have to wear that?"

"This is what's called a *compromise*."

A shiver of cold slithered down my spine. "What do you mean?"

"Help me help you."

She was trying to entrap Tobias and wanted me to help her. "Who will be listening?"

"Just me. Turn around."

Her nimble fingers worked the catch at my nape.

"Face me." She ordered.

I turned around to look at her and tugged down my dress, exposing my bra, and self-consciously crossed my arms over myself.

"Feeling vulnerable, Zara?" She glared into my eyes. "Feeling unsure? Betrayed?" She eased my arms to my sides. "Do you have any idea what you put us through?"

"I'm sorry."

"What is going on with you? You risked your career because of a stupid infatuation. You didn't call us once."

"Mr. Wilder believed that—"

"You're naive if you think this relationship is going anywhere. I saw the way he looked at you. It was with indifference."

"Please."

"All he cares about is his reputation."

I raised my chin. "How do you propose we get into the ballroom without an invite?"

"Adley made it happen. Told you he would."

I wondered if Tobias knew we'd been added to the guest list.

Abby looked unfazed. "I doubt he'll notice us. Everyone will be fawning over the great Tobias Wilder and jerking his ego."

I turned my face away because if she saw the truth of what was going down later, she'd punch me.

"Don't take this the wrong way," she said, her tone softening. "I'm on your side. I've watched him destroy your life. This is what Wilder does. Leaves a trail of brokenhearted women behind. You've seen what he did to Logan, his attorney? Don't let that be you. Wilder plays with the aesthetically pleasing and when his victim is out of his system he moves on."

"That's unfair." *And cruel to me.*

"He's certainly got you defending him."

"I have a great respect for Mr. Wilder."

"I'm reining you in, Zara." She reached for the roll of tape, pulled a strip out and bit a piece off, leaving a smudge of lipstick on it. "I'm keeping tabs on you."

I was too humiliated to speak and with no choice I stood still for her as she taped the wire between my breasts.

She rubbed the tape flat and eased the straps of my dress back over my shoulders after pulling up my bodice. "Unlike Adley, I'm not enamored with your royal heritage or in awe of your father's legacy. I've had to stand beside our boss and see what this did to him. He gave you a chance."

"I'm sorry, really I am." I felt her scrutiny as she read my expression.

Abby rubbed between my chest to check the wire. "Did Wilder tell you he'd get your paintings back?" She whispered into my ear, "Is Wilder Icon?"

"Are you?"

"Don't be ridiculous."

"Well, that's how it feels when you're accused of something." My gaze dropped to the carpet because I couldn't let her see the truth.

She looked around for my purse and saw it resting on the coffee table. She opened it and reached inside, pulling out my phone. "What's this?"

"It's temporary."

"I can see that. Where's yours?" She placed the burner phone on the table. "Anyway, you won't need it."

She'd just prevented me from texting Wilder to warn him I was wearing this.

She handed me my purse. "I'm going to help you put your life back together. I'm doing it for Adley because he asked me."

"You liked me once."

"Whatever reason you've got for keeping shit from the good guys is going to backfire. Honesty is always the best way."

"Abby, I'm not going to forget Elliot Burell has my paintings. No matter how inconvenient it is to Huntly Pierre. You're the one who told me the FBI had found them in Arizona."

"A lot has changed since then. Look, Burell denies they're part of your father's collection."

"Consider the source."

"Your father filed an insurance claim. Millions were payed out. Why not just let it go?"

Let them go...

My mouth went dry with the thought of losing them forever.

"Ready?" she snapped.

I gave a wary nod and followed her out, and as we rode the elevator down in silence the tension rose. Abby stared ahead ignoring me. I reassured myself this was a good thing as she'd not see my rising discomfort of being trapped in this claustrophobic box.

"You're going to be okay, Zara," she muttered. "You're set to inherit a lot of money next year. Looks like you'll be set for life."

"Did Adley tell you that?"

She shrugged. "I'm an investigator."

Such a violation of my privacy made me feel off kilter but despite everything I had to focus on tonight.

Out of the lift I calmed a little until I remembered Eli would be checking into this hotel later. Even though we'd be surrounded by people, knowing he could be in The Plaza sent me reeling.

When we turned the corner, and made a beeline for the Terrace Room, I needed a second to catch my breath. The vast ballroom was a statement of all that was lavish with its white and gold, with splendorous towering pillars, and ornate ceiling inlaid with dramatic art. As we made our way in, I admired the swooping chandeliers shining upon the glamorous guests of men dressed in their tailored black tuxedos and the flowing gowns of the women with their blinding diamonds to scare off the ordinary.

And there they were—

Brother Bay's stunning paintings, all ten of them, were resting upon easels at the front of the ballroom, and they all exuded an ethereal beauty with the subjects looking out at us with a startling consciousness that the *sfumato* technique always delivered. All of them offered a tenacious honesty.

Later, while many of the city's art dealers would be distracted in here, Tobias would be entertaining Eli in the Rose Club.

Wilder's web weaved the darkest ruse.

"Did you see him?" Abby tapped my arm to get my attention.

"Who?"

She rolled her eyes. "Wilder?"

"Not yet."

"Do you want to come see them?" She gestured toward the paintings.

I felt a pinch where the device pulled my chest. "Later."

As Abby studied my reaction, I realized my mistake. "There are too many people around them." And this wire was making me claustrophobic.

"There you are." Adley stepped out from the crowd and he looked handsome in his black tuxedo. He squeezed me into a warm hug while balancing an amber drink in his left hand.

I felt a dreadful regret all over again for the distress I had caused him. "Adley," I began. "I want to apologize for everything."

He gave a nod. "Art is not without its complications."

Abby threw him an incredulous glare.

"We're in the presence of greatness," Adley re-

sponded as he peered back toward the front of the ballroom at the paintings. "Have some fun, Abby."

"That's not why we're here," Abby insisted.

A waiter came by and I snapped up two flutes of
champagne off his tray and offered one to Abby. It was
a peace offering of sorts or if I was truly honest it was
courage in a tall stemmed glass for me.

She raised her hand to refuse. "I'm not drinking."

"Oh, come on," chided Adley, taking it from me and
giving it to her. "We get to enjoy tonight in the finest
company of a modern-day Rembrandt."

"I quite agree." It was Tobias.

He oozed refinement in his tailored black tuxedo
and his hair was styled with a sexy lushness. Though,
as he locked eyes with mine, he exuded an intense dis-
pleasure.

"I came tonight." I gave a shrug that stated *obviously*.

He replied with a tight smile.

"We're leaving tomorrow," Abby told him. "Thought
we'd have a bit of R & R."

"Good for you." Tobias didn't hold back. "I'm sure
you'll be happy to be back in London."

"What are your thoughts on this new talent you've
discovered?" asked Adley.

"Actually, Brother Bay was featured in *Time* magazine but the article didn't attract much attention. I'm
hoping this event changes that. All proceeds go toward
the renovation of Bay's monastery."

"A wonderful cause," I interjected.

"You do love your art, Mr. Wilder," chided Abby.

He shoved his hands into his pockets. "Art lets us
see into the heart and therefore the truth."

I raised my chin proudly. "And they really are beautiful."

Wilder gave a warm smile. "And one must protect such profoundness at any cost."

Abby seemed to pick up on the tension. "I'm going to check them out. Want to come, boss?"

Adley gave a nod and patted Wilder on the back with affection and then followed Abby through the sea of guests surrounding Bay's paintings.

Tobias's wary glare settled back on me. "We talked about this."

"Change of plan, obviously."

"Stay close to Abby at all times."

Eyes widening, I tried to convey I was wearing a wire by trailing my fingers to rest at the center of my chest.

Tobias leaned in to whisper huskily. "You like misbehaving, don't you?"

Sparking an ill-timed arousal.

He gave a nod. "I'm conflicted. On the one hand, I didn't want you here, and yet seeing you…you look stunning, Zara."

"I feel the same way." I blinked at him. "I mean, you look nice."

"Nice?"

I rubbed my eyelid, careful not to smudge my makeup to secretly signal we were being recorded via my wire.

He looked amused. "Something in your eye?"

"If you'll excuse me, Mr. Wilder, I need to go to the loo." I spun round and made a beeline for the exit and on the way out I set down my glass.

"Zara?" Tobias was right behind me.

I scurried around the corner and along the hallway

and felt the tight grip of Tobias's hand wrap around my wrist. He led me toward a door and opened it to peer in first to make sure it was empty before pulling me in.

I got his attention and mouthed, *I'm wearing a wire.*

I know, he mouthed back and broke into a dazzling smile.

My tight fist punched his bicep and he caught it and brought it to his lips. He kissed my hand, sending a tingle through it. He shoved a mobile coatrack against the door to prevent anyone from bursting in and disturbing us.

"The event seems to be going well." I tried to keep the thrill of seeing him out of my tone.

"It's good to see you, Ms. Leighton." He arched a brow. "Did you enjoy your visit to Fifth Avenue?"

"It was fun." I wondered how he knew about it.

How did it go with the FBI? I mouthed.

Turns out I have a great lawyer, he mouthed back, leaning in to trace his lips along my neck. It tickled deliciously and his breath caressed my skin, making me swoon as he pecked kisses along my jawline. Power flashed across his face and he grabbed my wrists and pinned them above my head and crushed his lips to mine, his teeth nipping at my bottom lip. *What the fuck are you doing here?* he mouthed.

Abby insisted.

He broke away and stared into my eyes. "I'll miss you when you return to London, Ms. Leighton. Let me arrange a car to the airport for you."

"That would be wonderful. When I'm ready to leave."

Tobias's hand slid down the center of my dress and

felt for the wire. *Stay away from The Rose Club*, he warned.

I intend to. I snapped his hand away from my chest. "It's certainly been an interesting experience, Mr. Wilder."

He stepped back. "You've exceeded my expectations, Ms. Leighton."

I reached for his shoulders and shoved him downward to let him know I wanted him on his knees to punish his brashness.

He went down until he was kneeling before me and tilted his head with intrigue as his green eyes sparkled with mischief. "There's another asset I'm interested in. I may need your assistance on this precious find." His hands slid up beneath my hem and trailed their way toward my panties.

Only I wasn't wearing any.

"Let me know when you see something you like." My voice provoked the danger.

"Would you be interested in joining forces with me to explore this untamed piece I have my sights on?" Wilder shot me a look of approval that I was pantiless and buried his face between my thighs and his tongue swept along my clit.

My body shivered with arousal. "I'd certainly love to hear more about your expectations."

He separated my folds with gentle fingers and kissed tenderly. "It's a piece often worshiped from afar."

I suppressed a giggle. "How about close up?"

"Ah, when explored close up—" his tongue lavished me with luxurious flicking "—it's even more beautiful. It's ethereal. One might even go so far as to say that when tasted it elicits a euphoria that is unrivaled."

"Could it be Venus?" I played with his locks and then gripped a scruff of hair.

"She's worshiped no less devoutly." He was sucking now, sending me closer to the edge. "But no, she is more, so much more…" His mouth found me again and he lavished strokes furiously.

"Worth keeping, then? Should you be so lucky to possess her?"

His mouth took me savagely, his tongue tearing into me with a controlled violence that forced my orgasm to endlessly unfold, my shaky thighs weakening and my internal muscles yearning for him to fill me. Squeezing my eyes shut, I savored my pleasure and claimed this erotic scene as my own as I tightened my grip on Wilder's scalp. Slipping out of time, my climax stole me away and wooed me into her blissful void, and I pressed my fingers to my lips to prevent a revealing moan.

He continued his gentle kisses, and then pulled my gown down to cover me, resting his forehead against my abdomen as though needing this moment as much as I did to recover, needing this closeness. Time dissolved as we selfishly stole these moments.

Tobias rose to his feet, tipped my chin and mouthed, *I am in love with you, Ms. Leighton.*

Dragging my teeth over my bottom lip, I basked in his beauty, this affection and his words that meant so much.

"When you need me again, Mr. Wilder, I'll be here for you."

He reached into his jacket pocket and pulled out a room key and handed it to me with a smile. *For later*, he mouthed. *Penthouse.*

I took it from him, hoping I'd be able to evade Abby. I tucked it into my purse.

"Let's celebrate our wonderful union—" he arched a brow "—art collector and authenticator working in symbiotic perfection."

I went to return to the ballroom.

Tobias grabbed my wrist. *Go back to your room.*

"I have to say goodbye to Abby." I eased my arm away. "I have to let her know I'm leaving." *Is he here?*

Not yet. He flashed a reassuring smile and pulled me toward the dance floor, and when I tried to pry my hand out of his Tobias gripped tighter. I glanced around for Abby.

Tobias rested his left hand on my lower spine and yanked me toward him with his right hand holding a firm grip of my hand. It was as though he didn't want to let me go.

Don't dip me, I warned—

He dipped me and my back arched dangerously close to the ground and my hair spilled behind me.

"Wilder!" I burst out.

"Tell me."

"Tell you what?" Yet even off balance with him I felt safe.

"You know."

"It's been the greatest pleasure working with you."

He lifted me upright and yanked me against him and I rested my cheek on his chest, aching for privacy, desperate to be alone and able to talk freely. I breathed him in, his heady cologne, his presence, his love, wishing I could stay in his arms forever.

"Well, as you're here," he said, "at least let me have your last dance."

"Fine."

He gave me a knowing look. "I hope you had fun."

"This was a blast."

"I'll call you later."

"Promise?"

"Yes."

"How do you feel?" He wasn't referring to the ball.

"Optimistic." My palm cupped his cheek as I conveyed my concern for his safety.

He responded with a devilish smile. "I'm looking forward to seeing how our beauty and the beast play out. Personally, I like the idea of having a front row seat."

I rolled my eyes to chastise him even if he was vague.

"Zara," he whispered into my ear, "if the meaning to life had a taste you would be it."

I reveled in this moment and clutched him, wishing this romantic dance wasn't an illusion.

He broke away. "Time for bed. Nightcap?"

"Bombay martini, please."

"What have I done to you?" He beamed a smile and disappeared into the crowd.

I felt the loss of him too easily and moved away from the other dancers. Exhaling, I let out a contented sigh that we always found our way back to each other. No matter what, we found each other in the storm and it comforted me knowing this would soon be over. Though my heart quickened when I remembered Eli would be entering The Rose Club soon.

Moving closer, I admired Bay's paintings with their extraordinary beauty, marveling at their realism. They were being adored by a large crowd who'd gathered around them. I closed the distance between me and the artwork, aware of the honor of being in the same room as a rare talent that rivaled some of the greatest in history. Brother Bay was a living, breathing master of our time.

"Having fun?" Abby nudged me.

I ignored her innuendo. "How's Adley?"

"He's just found his East Coast buddies. How are you holding up?"

"I'm okay. You?"

"Having fun, actually. Where's the man of the moment?"

"He's getting me a drink."

"I can't believe you're still talking to him after he tried to ditch you earlier." She let out a long sigh. "Maybe I misjudged you."

"How do you mean?"

"Maybe you go after what you want too."

"Look, Abby, please don't get the wrong idea about me. Yes, I come from a famous Russian family but I'm not a princess. Nor do I act like one."

"I wouldn't say that. Lately you've been acting spoiled with no thought to anyone else. And you need to let this Burell obsession go."

"Can you blame me for wanting my paintings back? My family faced a great danger to get them out of Russia. My happiness is their happiness. My fate is their fate. This is about making their deaths mean something."

"That was a long time ago, Zara."

"No, I refuse to forget the past. I refuse to forget the names of those who gave their life so I could have a better one. Do you know the story of what happened to the royal Russian family?"

"They were killed."

"In the dead of night, they were marched down into a small dark basement and reassured they'd soon be moved to a safer location. Minutes after Czar Nicholas, Czarina Alexandra and their five children were imprisoned they were under siege by an execution squad and warned that their deaths were imminent. That's right, their murderers were considerate enough to put the fear of God in them first. Seconds later, the entire family were shot, bayoneted and clubbed to death. The children took longer to die because they'd stashed a few of the family heirlooms beneath their clothes in case they needed to sell them later to buy food. The bayonets kept bouncing off the heirlooms and missing their flesh. Their bodies were then mutilated and buried in unmarked graves." I swallowed the agony of knowing this had been the fate of my ancestors. "Their crime? They were born into royalty. A prejudice you hold against me, Abby."

Her expression softened, perhaps because she too imagined the screams of the children that night.

My voice strained. "My family risked their lives to get those paintings to safety. They believed in something greater than themselves. These are the same paintings that belonged to my father and were stolen from us and to hide the fact our home was set on fire. Those paintings are more than canvas and paint and profound talent and a treasure trove of art. They are hope, and faith, and love that endures. So, don't tell me I should forget them."

Abby swallowed hard and turned to face Bay's paintings. In the aftermath of those passing seconds of my outburst I saw understanding in Abby's eyes, sadness even. I turned to look upon the portraits, and it made me wonder if Bay had chosen these very subjects because all of them exuded a certain wisdom.

"Apparently, it took Rembrandt years sometimes." Abby's voice was infused with respect. "I wonder how long each one of these took."

"They are beautiful." My thoughts carried me all the way to mine, stashed somewhere so that no one could see them. My family had sacrificed their lives for them, and I was sacrificing my integrity to get them back.

She gestured with her chin to the other side of the room. "Wasn't that drink meant for you?"

Tobias was talking with a pretty blonde and from their closeness they seemed to know each other. He gave her the drink he was carrying—my Bombay martini.

Then I recalled where I'd seen her before—

Wilder was talking with Elliot Burell's granddaughter and though I'd only ever seen Paige Burell once, other than in *Vogue* while researching her family, it was that vision of her in a wedding gown whooshing along a hallway in that Arizona estate that had stayed with me.

My gaze dragged around the room as I searched for Eli, and my attention snapped back toward Tobias. I watched him chatting politely with her.

My gut warned me to tell Abby who Paige was, but I put this down to my ego not wanting to get bruised from her assuming Wilder was womanizing. I wondered if Eli had sent his niece instead. He and Paige were around the same age which had confused me at first, but Eli himself had explained he was Elliot's son. His father had him late in life with a third wife, or so I vaguely remembered.

Perhaps, I reasoned, Tobias was asking her if Eli was here, after all the fake auction was set for just after

10:00 p.m. I wondered how she'd gotten in past security. Tobias caught me staring and his eyes flittered to the ballroom exit in a subtle gesture to warn me to go to my room. My gut wrenched because that meant Eli was here.

"Come on." Abby grabbed my arm firmly and led me toward the bar. "You need a drink."

I assumed she thought I needed to drown my sorrows after we'd observed Tobias talking with a pretty blonde.

Abby got the attention of the barman and ordered two glasses of Chardonnay. Tobias could handle the Burells, I was certain of it. Still, it wouldn't hurt to flit the occasional glance his way to watch his back. Sitting on a bar stool I observed the barman pouring our drinks and at the same time I used the mirror to survey behind me. Paige whispered something into Tobias's ear—he whispered something back and she smiled.

Dread sent a cold chill through me as my gaze scanned the guests for her uncle.

This was really going down.

Vaguely, I noticed a glass of white wine being placed in front of me and a wave of nausea washed over me. I wasn't sure my stomach could take much more. I slid off the bar stool. "I need to go to the loo. Will you be okay?"

"Sure." Abby squeezed my arm. "I'm here for you. I know I can come over as a bit of a bitch sometimes. You had us all scared."

"I'm sorry for all of that," I admitted as my guilt burrowed deeper. "Hurting Adley hurts me too. It was never my intention."

"If you need a shoulder to cry on." She shook her head. "What am I saying, you're stronger than this."

"I am."

"At least you got to see him before you left." She pointed toward Wilder.

I headed out of the ballroom and glanced back toward the bar and saw Abby was distracted by the barman. Tobias was still deep in conversation with Paige.

The hallway was empty.

Strolling along the plush carpet I searched for the restroom. I quickly found it and made my way into a stall, admiring the posh-looking everything that was The Plaza's loo and trying to think of anything other than this rising nausea.

A pinch came from my chest and in a fit of annoyance I slipped my hand down my bodice to smooth the offending tape, though when it pinched again I ripped at the wire and kept tugging until I was holding it in my hand and staring at the thing. I tucked it into my purse and carried on as though I'd not just compromised Abby's attempt to entrap me. I peed and headed out to wash my hands.

Staring at my frazzled reflection, I took a moment to reapply my lipstick and fluff my hair in the mirror—

A tall man loomed behind me.

I turned to face him and almost fell backward when he grabbed my forearm and painfully pulled me out of the restroom.

"Let go." My throat constricted in terror.

"Scream and you're dead," he snapped.

Ahead was a door and he dragged me into a deserted hallway. My aggressor yanked open another door and shoved me in, and I staggered forward, dropping my purse and almost tripping—

Across the room, Eli was dressed sharply in a black

tuxedo with that arrogant fop of hair over his right eye, and beside him were four of his men and all of them were also camouflaged in black tuxedos to conceal their savagery.

I drew in a terror-drenched breath—if he opened my purse and found that wire the event Tobias had carefully planned in The Rose Club wouldn't happen.

"Hello, Zara." Eli strolled toward me. "I'm here for my painting."

CHAPTER FIFTEEN

ELI SHOVED ME against the wall.

My heart pounded violently and I was terrified he'd find the wire, even if I needed Abby to hear this. Glancing around, I realized this was a conference suite and no one would have any need to come in here.

"Zara, I'm glad I got to bump into you." Eli towered over me. "As you work for Huntly Pierre, you work for my father—" his breath warmed my ear "—you work for me." His fingers wrapped around my throat and he squeezed. "Wasn't it your job to find our Titian?"

"There are leads." I trembled. "Your father is being updated."

"But you're here? In New York? You're not doing your job." Eli gripped my face and pain shot into my jaw.

I turned my head away when Eli's hand ran along my collarbone and lowered to my chest.

The door burst open and Tobias stormed in. "Get off her."

"Well, thank you for joining us, Mr. Wilder." Eli stepped back.

"Zara," snapped Tobias. "Out, please."

Eli's arrogance overflowed as he grabbed my shoulder. "She was enjoying our private party."

I suppressed my panic. "Let us go."

Eli sneered. "Or what? I won't get my painting?"

Tobias gestured left. "Your painting is waiting for you in The Rose Club."

"I'm not interested in bidding on it." Eli straightened his back.

Tobias gave a nod. "I'm sure I can assist with what you need."

Eli waved his command and his men attacked Tobias.

He broke free—throwing a punch at one of the burly men who staggered back. He fought well, but there were too many of them and they manhandled him into a violent restraint. One of the other men landed a fist on Wilder's lip and split it open.

His head fell forward; dazed.

And then I saw the gun with the barrel pressed directly on Tobias's temple.

"Put the barrel in his mouth if he speaks." Eli waved his order. "That should work."

I suppressed a sob and threw Tobias a reassuring glance that we were going to be okay, all we had to do was stay calm until Abby got here with backup. If I could just convey this to him.

Tobias squeezed his eyes shut in frustration. "Don't touch her."

"Unless you want to eat metal, shut the fuck up, Wilder." Eli sauntered back toward me. "I have so many questions and something tells me you know the answers."

"Listen, Eli—" Tobias sucked his bleeding lip. "She has nothing to do with this. I hired her to help me with tonight's event. Let her go."

The man holding the gun hit Tobias's face with it and almost knocked him out.

"Don't," I cried.

"It's time to track down my Titian." Eli loomed over me.

My back struck the wall as he neared and I felt that nausea returning. I tried to breathe against my dread of that gun. "I'll find your Titian." My voice cracked with emotion. "I promise."

Tobias struggled against his captors.

"If he moves again, shoot him." Eli turned back to me. "Don't worry, it has a silencer. Tell me who owns this *Mona Lisa*?"

"We went through his emissary."

"Name?"

"I can put you in touch with his staff—"

"Can you put me in touch with Icon?"

"I…I think so."

"Well, we know he's in New York. The FBI are looking for him here. Huntly Pierre are on his tail. He's here. And there's a rumor you're in contact with him."

I shook my head. "I don't…"

"Okay, shoot the fucker." Eli turned and flicked the order to kill Tobias.

"Wait!" Blood roared in my ears. "I can get a message to him."

Eli calmly waved his hand. "Hold off." He turned back to me. "Who is he?"

I shook my head. "I can contact him. I will."

"Well, that's fantastic. This is what I want. Get Icon to steal me that *Mona Lisa* in there." He pointed in the direction of The Rose Club. "Tell him to deliver her to my room at 7:00 a.m. We'll have breakfast and chat about all things art related. By the end of tomorrow Icon will be working for me."

I threw a glance at Tobias. "Please, let him go."

Eli looked fierce. "If Icon fails to turn up with that painting, Wilder dies."

"No!"

Eli smirked. "Wanna see your boyfriend again? Alive? It's best we throw that detail in."

"I can get you money."

"I thought you were a researcher, Zara? Have you no idea who you're dealing with? We are the wealthiest family in America." Eli turned to his men. "Can you make sure he doesn't make a scene?"

They went for Tobias and attacked him, knocking him out cold. I bolted toward him but my head jolted painfully when Eli grabbed my hair and dragged me back. He slammed me against the wall and my legs buckled beneath me as I leaned on it with panic-drenched breaths causing waves of dizziness.

"Everyone out." Eli barked the order.

"No, you can't," I screeched.

Tobias was dragged out with his feet trailing behind him and I ran to stop them but two of Eli's men blocked my path.

I was alone with Eli.

He slammed me against the wall and a jolt of pain reverberated through my skull. "I know where you live, Zara. Where you work. I know your weakness is Wilder."

I turned away. "I'll do anything. Please, don't hurt him."

He pulled my focus to his dark gaze and his eyes were as cold and black as a shark's. "If you tell the FBI about this, Wilder dies. If you tell your friends at Huntly Pierre, he dies. If Icon fails to bring me the *Mona Lisa*…

you get the gist." He tipped up my chin. "I look forward
to spending more time with you, Zara Leighton."

He took a sideways step and left.

I flew after him, scooping my purse from the floor
and following him into the hallway—one of Eli's men
blocked my way.

I couldn't speak, couldn't think straight, all I saw was
that brutal image of Tobias with a gun in his mouth. I
tried to sidestep around the man. He shoved me backward knocking me to the floor and I dropped my purse
and the catch flew open. I grabbed it and hugged it to
my chest, staring up at him.

"7:00 a.m., have Icon come to The Marlborough
Suite with the painting," he said. "Don't fuck it up."

He headed off down the hallway and I clambered up
before anyone saw me. In a daze, I headed back to my
room, no longer caring about that claustrophobic box
I had to endure to get there. All I could think of was
Eli's threat and if I told anyone...

Digging my fingernails into my palms to focus, I
should have listened to Tobias, should have realized
Eli would do anything to own the rarest of paintings.
He'd never have risked losing a bid in an auction room.

The chill from the air-conditioning hit me when I
reached my hotel room. I dropped my purse and key
card to the floor, ran to the bathroom and dry heaved
into the sink. I was being asked to achieve the impossible to save him. Tobias had arranged the presentation.
My name wasn't on the paperwork. I couldn't imagine
what had to be done to get to that painting in The Rose
Club. The security I'd have to get past was going to be
impossible.

I dabbed my face with a napkin and caught my reflection in the mirror—pure terror etched so deep it would never leave.

I'm coming for you, Tobias, I sent a silent message to him. *Hold on.*

Stay alive.

Exhaling a shaky breath, I headed out of the bathroom—

Abby was in the drawing room. "You okay?"

I coughed past the taste of bitterness and my brain ran through every scenario; every word, every physical signal had to be carefully mundane so as not to arouse suspicion.

"I heard you," she said.

Panic fluttered in my chest. "Oh?"

"Throwing up." She came toward me and rested her palm on my forehead. "How are you doing?"

"Fine."

"You took off your wire?"

I glanced at my open purse with the wires sticking out. "I'm in for the night."

She knelt and scooped my purse off the floor, pulled out the wire and placed it on the coffee table. She opened my purse farther and peered in. She pulled out Tobias's gold penthouse key card.

"For the gym." I headed over to the minibar and found a bottle of water in there and offered it to her, trying to suppress this trembling. "Want one?"

"No, thanks." She flipped over the key card.

"I'm going to have an early night." I twisted the lid off. "Did you enjoy tonight?"

Her gaze rose to meet mine. "Yeah. Wish I could afford one of those paintings. Maybe I'll end up with a print instead. If they make them." She frowned as she contemplated and it was the kind of rumination of someone putting the pieces together. "Can I ask you something?"

"Sure."

"He broke your heart, didn't he?" She gave a look of sympathy. "That's why you're feeling sick?"

I set the bottle down. "I have a lot to think about."

I am ruined from what I've done and the risks I've taken.

This is all my fault.

She handed me the key card. "I'm here when you want to talk."

I clutched it in my palm, stepped forward and hugged her, suppressing my need to beg Abby for help.

I couldn't risk it.

The rigidity left her body as she hugged me. "I've been there."

I have to put everything right...

Abby headed toward the dividing door to her room. "I'm going to leave this open in case you need me."

"I appreciate that," I lied.

CHAPTER SIXTEEN

WITH MY FACE buried in my palms I willed myself to think straight.

I knew what facing great odds meant because I'd grown up surrounded by heroes painted on canvases who appeared all too real with their all too authentic pain reaching beyond the centuries. These old souls conveyed they'd found a way.

I could do this.

I would find a way to save Tobias.

Elliot Burell may have tried to steal that hope from me when he'd stolen my paintings or when he'd attempted to burn down my family home or when he'd sent my father to an early grave, but the memory of those paintings taught me what the human soul could endure.

Though I was on my own this time to face off with this deadly adversary who threatened everything I held dear, I had to move forward.

I had to get the other *Mona Lisa* to Eli.

Sitting on the edge of my hotel bed staring at the wall, I waited until I hoped Abby had fallen asleep, and then set off for The Rose Club, bringing my purse with me. My brain processed every possible scenario of getting the painting out of there without any hassle from security.

The ride down in the lift was nothing compared to how terror-struck I felt. Within minutes I was entering the place where an hour ago Tobias was meant to have met with Eli in a cordial fashion.

Within The Rose Club a few well-dressed hotel guests sat chatting on the leather furniture with the extra privacy of the lights having been dimmed for the evening. From around me came clinking glasses and vibrant conversation. Following the natural curve of the sitting room I came to a hallway. At the end a young man in a smart suit guarded a door. This had to be it. What other reason would there be for a room to be protected from anyone entering? Tobias had hired this private space for the exchange and even though he knew he was dealing with the devil, even he hadn't anticipated the extent of his cruelty.

Maybe this entire time Eli was just trying to get to me. Persuade me, bully me to give up the search for my paintings and all the while I'd led Tobias into danger. The thought of having to face Eli alone in the morning chilled my flesh. I could always ask Abby to accompany me, but then I'd be putting her in danger and threatening Tobias's life.

Making my way down the hallway, I mulled over the best approach that would get me in that room.

With my head held high I greeted him. "I work for Mr. Wilder."

The guard looked me up and down. "Hello, ma'am, are you here for the viewing?"

"Yes, Mr. Wilder wanted me to inform you there won't be any exhibit this evening. There's been a change of plan."

"I was wondering why no one turned up." He seemed

to suppress a frown, though he gave a nod as he opened the door for me and I felt a rush of adrenaline that I'd made it in. That wasn't how I'd expected it to go. Once inside my heart jackhammered against my ribs—

The glass case atop a thin marble podium was empty and my legs almost gave way.

Where the hell was the painting? Another guard checked his cell phone at the back of the room and quickly shoved it into his pocket. "Ma'am, can I help you?"

I threw him a friendly wave. "Just checking in." I pointed to the glass case. "Making sure everything is in order."

"I'm waiting on the guests." He didn't sound too sure. "Do you know how long they'll be? I was told this would end at eleven. That's half an hour ago."

"It was canceled, I'm afraid."

He looked astonished. "I've been paid to guard nothing?"

I hoped Eli hadn't stormed in here and taken it away.

"Has anyone been in this room other than me?" I asked.

He shrugged. "Mr. Wilder."

My blood pressure spiked. "When?"

"Around eight."

Those hours since seeing him dragged violently away felt like decades.

"Did he say anything?"

"Paid us."

"Okay, good. That's taken care of." My brow was spotted in perspiration. "Nothing was brought into this room or removed?"

"No, ma'am."

"And you've been in here all evening?"

"Yes, ma'am."

"Mr. Wilder sends his apologies." I backed up toward the door. "Sorry for any inconvenience." I gave a nod of thanks to the guard outside and hurried back into the lounge of The Rose Club, making my way to the elevators. Once inside, I opened my purse and pulled out the key card Tobias had given me earlier and with trembling hands shoved it into the panel to give me access to the highest floor. All the way to where Tobias was meant to be staying in the penthouse.

To my relief, the key card worked and I was in his room and searching for that damn painting, my hands shaking and my spine locked in dread. The vast suite was a luxurious haven of the best of everything this hotel had to offer—though now the gold-and-burgundy-themed room felt nauseatingly with its over-the-top luxury, the colors burning my eyes with the glare of opulence, and the amount of space was nothing but an impossible challenge.

I ran into the bedroom.

One of Tobias's white shirts hung over the back of a chair and I raised it to my nose and breathed him in, that heady mixture of power and passion, and I buried my face in the softness of the material connecting me to him.

Give me the strength to find this.

I had to think like Icon.

I threw my purse on the bed and looked around. Tobias favored neatness, and with that in mind I knew his suitcase and the holder for the painting would be tucked away. I found a few clothes in the wardrobe and there came a stark terror he may never wear them again. I should never have left his side. We'd used the wrong strategy with Eli. He liked to win. Period. There was never going to be any negotiating, no reasoning, because in his twisted mind it was acceptable to exchange a life for a painting.

There was a large chrome case in the wardrobe and I dragged it out and lifted it onto the bed. Each side had four silver locks that would need a combination to open. I needed to crack the code, needed into this case.

Think.

I entered the year of my birth on the left and his on the right. I swapped this over when it didn't work. Several attempts of another idea failed too. I paced while dragging my panicked thoughts back from what Eli might be doing to Tobias.

What if the painting wasn't even in here? What if Tobias was having Coops deliver it and I had no way of getting in touch with him. Unless… Tobias had programmed his number into my burner phone? No, Tobias had told me he didn't want to implicate Coops or Marshall, and their roles were designed to protect them as well as him.

A flash of inspiration hit me. Entering my name on the left of the catch and his on the other side but this time abbreviating his to Toby. When that failed too, I stubbornly tried swapping them out—

The case clicked open and there came a jolt of victory. After throwing the lid back, I was staring at *Mona Lisa*'s portrait adorned within a wooden gold frame. I froze in awe at the realness of Italian beauty Lisa Gherardini staring back at me.

Wow—

Mona Lisa was before me and her authentic appearance threw me for a second as I tried to grasp that she'd been created so fast. If I wanted proof no man would have been able to pull this off, all I had to do was remember she'd been created by a computer. Tobias's hand was behind the technology, but this was an act of science, a natural philosophy that stretched the boundaries of what I'd believed possible.

This could work. *No*, it had to.

I carefully slid the painting into a pillowcase and with my mouth dry with nervousness, I left the penthouse and returned to my room. I hid the painting beneath my bedcovers in case Abby came to check on me.

The night would come and go but there'd be no sleep for me, merely pacing, my thoughts consumed with Tobias. All I could think of was how he was coping, what he was thinking and if he was going to be okay.

In a flash of panic my hand rested on the hotel phone as guilt possessed me for not contacting the police. This dread of making the right decision was tugging at every cell in my body until fatigue sent pain into my bones.

A compromise was needed; finding the hotel notepad, I wrote to Abby and left the message on the coffee table next to the wire she'd made me wear.

I'll be in The Marlborough Suite. If anything happens to me, I went to meet with Eli Burell.

By 6:45 a.m. I was heading to Eli's suite.

The painting was heavy despite her size and even if this had been the real *Mona Lisa* that I'd shoved inside a pillowcase, I felt no guilt for exchanging her for Tobias. Seeing him safe was all I cared about and the need for reassurance that he'd not been hurt owned every thought. I willed myself not to show fear. More than anything, I'd come to terms with giving up on those precious paintings. He was worth my life and nothing was going to come between us.

My knock brought the sound of footsteps and the un-latching of a lock. The door shot open and I stared up at a burly man who I recognized as one of Eli's guards. He'd been one of the thugs who'd beaten Tobias last night. My jaw tightened with a need to reciprocate the same kind of violence for what he'd done to my lover. I peered past his bulky frame into the suite.

"In," he snapped.

Clutching the pillowcase to my chest, I made my way down the short hallway and entered the luxurious space and my gaze darted around for Tobias.

"Well, hello, Zara." It was Eli appearing from a hall-way and I'd never seen him casually dressed before, those jeans and that sweater disarming. That overly privileged fop of hair, a reminder of his cruel arrogance, caused bile to rise in my throat.

He looked astonished at the pillowcase. "No way."

I stepped forward. "Where's Mr. Wilder?"

"Well this is unexpected."

Doubt circled my gut. "I need to see him first."

"It doesn't work like that." He snatched the painting.

"It's the *Mona Lisa*," I said. "I kept my end of the bargain."

He reached inside and slid out the painting and dropped the pillowcase. As his gaze swept over the canvas, awe flashed over his face, morphing into cruel amusement. "She's so small."

"Tobias!" I called out. "I'm here."

Eli set the painting on the table behind him. "I was expecting someone else."

"I did the best I could."

He smirked. "How did you pull this off?"

"Why does it matter?"

"Where's Icon?"

I gave a confident nod. "*I* stole her."

He glanced over at his burly bodyguard. "Do you believe her?"

I sucked in a nervous breath. "Where is he, please?"

"Have breakfast with me." He gestured to the hallway. "I had invited Icon but as he stood me up it will have to be you."

"I did what you asked."

"What I asked for was for you to inform Icon he was expected here." He stomped a foot and yelled, "Now."

"I'm sorry, I did the best I could." I pointed to the painting. "I brought you that. Doesn't she count for something? She's priceless."

"Let's talk about Arizona." He smirked. "What did you make of my mousetrap?"

Terrifying.

"You handled it magnificently." He came closer. "A true inspiration. Though just before you became my guest in my art piece, Wilder placed a GPS tracker on the frame of *The Storm on the Sea of Galilee*." He glanced at the *Mona Lisa*'s frame.

"We fell through the trapdoor—"

"Let's talk about *St. Joan*."

My gasp revealed my connection.

"My dad gifted her to Paige. Some fucker stole it from her home in Switzerland and somehow it ended up in London at Christie's. Icon was the thief. I'm sure about that. Didn't your father own that one?"

"Maybe it's not the same one."

"Something tells me it is."

My thoughts shoved me back to that day at Christie's when I'd been escorted into the room where *St. Joan* was awaiting. This was how she'd made her way there. And this was how Tobias knew of her location. Icon stole her from Paige. Icon placed her at Christie's.

And now I knew for sure Icon had stolen her.

Eli shrugged. "Dad wants his Titian back. Paige wants her *St. Joan* back." He shortened the distance between us. "Know what I want?"

I shook my head as panic rose.

"Icon."

"I can get a message—"

"Where is he?" Eli's eyes filled with disbelief. "I mean, we're talking about the other *Mona Lisa* here. How the fuck did he steal her?"

"I just…"

"This is the work of Icon. Who is he? I want a meeting."

"I risked my life getting that for you. Please, where's Tobias?" I bolted toward the back of the suite and searched the other rooms. "Tobias?"

"In here." Eli's voice carried from another room.

Warily, I made my way in that direction with my thoughts scattered like fireflies in the blackest night—

The door slammed behind me and Eli stood between me and the exit. There was a bed in here and the sheets were ruffled, and the wardrobe open and empty.

"Come here. I'm hankering for some entertainment."

I snapped his hand away. "Don't."

"Do you know what happens to the human body

when it's deprived of oxygen? You actually get high. Right now, your Tobias is flying high on hypoxia."

My throat constricted. "You promised you wouldn't hurt him!"

Eli knocked me backward and I slumped onto the bed. My screaming was muffled as his palm slapped to my mouth to silence me. His hand struck again. "Shut the fuck up."

My lungs fought for air—

I bit his hand and he slapped me across my face again, and the shock of pain stunned me still.

"Anything to do with Leonardo da Vinci is mine. If you see a da Vinci, you call me. If you hear of a da Vinci, you let me know. If you suspect a da Vinci is in your neighborhood, I want to know. Do you understand?"

"Yes."

He reached for my zipper. "Let's have some fun."

I struggled, fighting with everything I had and managing to snap his hands away from my trousers.

The door burst open—

Abby flung herself at Eli. "Get off her."

He scrambled off the bed. "Sean!"

She reached out and grabbed my hand and pulled me up. "Zara!"

Eli grinned, as though he'd not just attacked me, and walked backward toward the door wearing that disgusting smirk. He spun around and ran.

I staggered off the bed and bolted after him into the sitting room—

Eli was gone.

The *Mona Lisa* was gone too. Turning slowly, I saw

his bodyguard slumped on the floor and moaning, and my gaze snapped to Abby.

"The fucker deserved it," she snapped. "What happened? Why are you in here?"

I yanked away from her grasp and bolted out, sprinting down the hallway and flying between the open lift doors and striking my palm against the panel.

The doors closed—

Abby raced down the hallway toward me.

"I'm sorry," I called out.

The doors shut before she reached me. These four walls closed in and my breaths rasped for air…

When the elevator landed, I ran toward the revolving front door, bursting out to the street and scanning the faces for Eli or any of his men. Desperate for a sign of Tobias. My limbs felt like lead as I paced up and down, trying to look for a car or anything that would help me. Panic incapacitating me with the realization I'd messed up. I'd misjudged; I'd failed Tobias in every conceivable way. If anything happened to him I'd die from the agony.

The sting where Eli had struck my face burned like fire and this whiplash proved my recklessness.

I'd flown into the center of the flame.

CHAPTER SEVENTEEN

I'D MISCALCULATED WHAT the Burells were capable of.

The family who specialized in mass murder. Our rules were no match for their rigged game. This was never going to be played fair, though I had foolishly acted as though it was. Tobias had tried to protect me from all of this and that's why he'd not wanted me at the ball last night.

In a blur, I left the hotel and caught a taxi back to our Manhattan home that had been our refuge, the place where the seeds of our plan had been sown and now I regretted not talking Wilder out of it.

After hurrying into the drawing room, I pressed my palm to get access to Tobias's workshop. The door opened and I was let in. I sprinted down the ramp and between his workbenches and made a beeline for Jade. She sat on her charger.

"Jade, I need you. Wake up." I tapped the top of her.

The drone rose from her base and hovered before me as that green power light flickered on.

"Tobias is in trouble. Do you understand? You have to help me find him. Can you do that? I need you to help me find his equipment. This is an emergency."

Jade floated off toward the back of the workshop— all the way toward a chrome door.

"Open it," I ordered.

It clicked and the door swung wide and I stepped through—

What the hell?

Lined up along the left-hand wall was a row of fifteen drones, and all of them looked exactly the same as Jade. Why would he need so many? The door slammed shut behind me, sending me into blackness. Arms out, I made my way toward the door.

It was locked.

"No." I slammed my palms against the chrome. "Open the door."

In a flash of inspiration, I remembered Jade, the one on the other side of that damn door, could track Tobias with his wristwatch. I'd seen him talk directly into it and give orders to Jade back in Arizona. Tobias was connected to that drone.

I turned and with outstretched arms fumbled for one of the other drones resting on that chrome shelf and hoped to God they worked. I tapped the first one I came to. "Wake up."

A green light flickered on the front.

"Make me a coffee." I said the first thing I could think of.

Within the darkness there came the humming of the drone lifting. A green light floating in the dark and I followed it. There came a click and light flooded in from the open door. I burst out, following the drone, with panic reaching a fever pitch at the time I was wasting. It headed away and up the ramp.

I ran to Jade. "Tobias needs you." I bit back my anger.

She hovered past me and into the room, and when she reappeared she was dragging a duffel bag. I knelt and unzipped it and peered in at the climbing gear, tool kit,

a flashlight and all the gadgets a thief might need. Jade
hadn't locked me in there on purpose. She'd wanted me
to find this and the door had shut by accident.

"This is good." I stared up at her. "Follow me."

Inside the satellite tracking room, I studied the control panel. "Turn this on, Jade."

The screen lit up. "Connect to Wilder's wristwatch,
Jade."

The images flipped from one screen to another until I
saw New York projected via a satellite image in a gray-
and-white blur.

I tried to make out what I was looking at. "Show me
where Wilder is at this very second, Jade."

The screen zeroed in until a small dot moved along
Interstate 81.

"Is that Tobias?" I snapped my gaze back at the
screen.

The image went blank.

"No, no, no." I held my hands together in a prayer.
"Where did it go?"

"Hey, sweetheart." It was Tobias's face enlarged on
the screen and he was staring at me. He looked well
with no sign of injury or expression of distress or anything to hint something was off…

"Tobias, where are you?"

He gave a warm smile. "If you're watching this, it
means I'm seriously indisposed. Nothing to worry
about, I'm sure."

My mouth went dry as I realized this was a recording.

"Get your passport. I showed you where it is. Ask
Jade to call Coops and he'll arrange for my jet to be at

your disposal. I'll meet you back in London. And, Zara, I love you, okay. I'll see you soon."

"This is all my fault," I called up to the screen. "Jade, you're coming with me."

Dragging the duffel bag behind me, I made my way up the ramp and into the foyer, and on the way out remembered Tobias had the key fob for the Aston Martin. It was probably still in The Plaza's penthouse. If I couldn't get the car to start I'd have to think of something else and fast. *Jesus*, please don't make me have to get on that motorbike.

I rested my palm on the outside panel to lock the front door and Jade floated alongside. After pressing my thumbprint on the Aston Martin keypad, I was relieved it clicked. I yanked open the passenger door and gestured for Jade to float inside. She settled on the front passenger seat. When I looked up, several early morning joggers were staring at the drone with their jaws slack in surprise.

"She's a pet." I threw the duffel bag into the trunk and hurried around to get in.

Although driving on the other side of the road was going to be challenging, I reassured myself I'd get my confidence up and the car was an automatic, after all. I'd driven his car in LA. That hadn't been a disaster and with the painfully slow traffic I'd not be going too fast at first. I hoped the car transporting Tobias was also slowed by the rush of commuters.

I pressed my thumb onto the key panel just as I'd seen Tobias do. The Aston Martin purred awake and I breathed a sigh of relief that Tobias had seen to it I could drive this. I sent silent thanks his way for his forethought. I strapped a seat belt around Jade and then pulled on mine.

"Bring Tobias Wilder's location up on the GPS, Jade."

I'm coming for you, hold on.

The tracker flashed awake and went through a series of screen changes.

If Jade was wrong she'd direct me farther away from where I could help Tobias. All I had was his technology to rely on. I'd observed him interact with his devices and they'd always interpreted what he'd requested whether it was to bring him a drink or clean up broken glass or hail a helicopter at a moment's notice. Never had this need for his tech savvy been more vital.

Abby had witnessed Eli's attack and by now she'd have reported that to the authorities, I was sure of it. She had solid evidence on how dangerous he was. I felt dreadful that I'd run out on her like that but after what she'd seen Eli do she'd probably be on the hunt for him too.

The blip slid up I-81.

I had never imagined that trusting in one of Tobias's AI units would ever be an experience I would have to contend with. Even though she was quiet and still, Jade brought some comfort, and I wondered if this was why Tobias had created her, because in some way she pushed aside the loneliness. She certainly provided some comfort for me.

"Jade." I glanced her way. "If anything happens to us you must find and destroy the painting you created. Understand?"

The only response was that green light flickering which was no response at all, really.

"I know it seems harsh," I reassured her. "But in our world only real things can exist." I cringed at how that might have come over. "I mean, when it comes to art." Me caring about an AI's feelings proved how damn tired I was. "You know my dad once threw a boiling hot cup of tea over a fake. That brown liquid and heat just ruined that painting, and I still can't get the image out of my mind. It wasn't real though. Someone was pretending it was and in there was the problem." There, I'd sufficiently explained that away to my inanimate friend and proven to myself just how stressed I was to rattle on about nothing to nobody.

Within half an hour I was out of the city and heading north, and if Tobias's captors kept going they'd be in Canada. I'd never be able to cross the border. Fatigue soaked into my limbs and caused my stomach to churn as nausea welled.

I breathed another sigh of relief when the dot stopped. Judging from the map I was fifteen minutes away from their current location. My frantic speed had made up the lost time between us. I turned my headlights off and rolled along the road with its tree line of a private estate.

In the distance, I made out a country shingle colonial mansion that was surprisingly small compared to Burell's other homes. I didn't want anyone to hear the engine so I pulled onto a grassy bank to park behind several trees.

I leaped out and popped the trunk. Rummaging in the back inside the duffel bag, I grabbed what I might need. Days ago, Tobias had shown me how a few of these contraptions worked and I'd been filled with annoyance and not believed I'd ever need these skills.

I considered the many scenarios for when entering a

home. No, this was not happening. I wasn't trained for this. If I messed up, I'd place Tobias in terrible danger and possibly...

Focus. Get him out of there.

This was the nightmare I'd never seen coming.

Okay, climbing harness, just in case. Spare rope hooked across my chest. If I got caught wearing this getup I'd be in bloody trouble. Gritting my teeth with tension, I continued to pull out what else I'd need and clipped each item onto the belt including a flashlight, wire cutter and a pick for a lock.

I opened the passenger door and leaned down to get Jade. "Take me to Tobias." I unclipped her seat belt and she floated out.

My heart leaped when a small metal arm protruded from her side and she pointed to the house. Maybe, I mused in the craziest part of my brain, she missed her boss? It was obviously the same area of my brain that had gotten me into this mess.

She floated beside me as I made my way toward the mansion. There were three large SUVs parked outside with blacked-out windows. This sinister convoy gave me hope I was in the right place. Tobias had to have been transported in one of these.

Peeking through a window at the front I observed the stylish decor. It seemed like it had been decorated with a woman's touch. Maybe this was one of Paige's homes? It would make sense for Eli to bring Tobias to a place that wasn't his father's or even his.

What I vaguely remembered from what Wilder had taught me was the garden lights could come on at any time, even in the day should motion be detected. I'd noted the skylight as I'd approached and felt a sick feeling that would be my only option. Trying the front door was reckless. Yet entering through the roof was suicide, surely?

With Jade above me, I reached up and hooked my fingers through her base. Tobias had told me he exercised with her like this by doing pull-ups and she was capable of carrying his weight. This was the mother of all experiments because I had no idea if he'd been joking.

Jade supported my weight.

I let go and knelt to draw in deep breaths, rallying my courage to pull off the most demented stunt of my life. *No*, that was me coming to the States, I mused darkly. *Next time stay at home. Order takeout like a nice chicken tikka masala. Read a good book; something by Jane Austen or J.K. Rowling. Why not read it in the bath? With a bloody big glass of Chardonnay.*

Screw it—

I rose to my full height and wrapped my fingers around her base again. "Entry point is the roof, Jade. Don't fucking drop me."

With my legs dangling and my body fighting this drag of gravity, I felt the rush of air blasting my face and the strain in my hands was agony as they trembled with the tension of being carried up and up and up…

These were the longest seconds of my life.

My feet met the roof and I let go and crouched—*I was really doing this.*

I was breaking into a private home off the meager intel I'd gathered from a drone that couldn't speak and wasn't able to convey meaning. This was a practice in trust like no other. Ironically, the trust I'd always sought was coming from a machine. A device Wilder had created. I wondered if he took Jade with him on his adventures too.

I pointed to the skylight. "I need to get in there."

I'd always wondered how Tobias cut the glass of the Burells' rotunda in Amboise. It wasn't a power tool as the police had reported, it was Jade who was providing a demonstration of her laser skills as she cut a hole in the glass big enough for me to get through. Out of her bottom protruded a suction cup and it connected to the glass and tugged the central piece out and placed it carefully to the side. There was no time to gawp in wonder at this impressive technology.

Grasping Jade's base again I used her to lower through the hole and glanced down as I descended.

Two men appeared beneath me.

"Stop," I whispered.

The drone held me halfway between the ceiling and the ground hovering over them. My hands were numb. My heart banged furiously against my rib cage. I drew strength from Wilder. He'd tell me to breathe slowly to endure the pain, to center myself, to calm, and he'd tell me it was all worth it.

The way of Icon.

I recognized one of Eli's bodyguards who had attacked Tobias. There was too much pain in my fingers to feel the relief of being in the right place. They went in separate ways and I was lowered to the ground. I let go of Jade before my feet hit the carpet, and doubled over, hugging the pain out of my hands.

Then hid in an alcove.

Following Jade's lead, I trailed after her toward a staircase. The sound of a television came from one of the rooms. A morning talk show with an audience from the sound of it. With my back against the wall I hurried down, alert and ready for anyone who might try to stop me.

Halfway along another hallway we came to a stop and Jade pointed to a door. After turning the handle and peering inside I saw a staircase leading down. With the door closed behind me I tiptoed, praying the floorboards wouldn't creak.

This basement had an eerie feel to it and the atmosphere worsened when the scent of bleach hit my nostrils and it reached the back of my throat. I counted ten doors either side with round windows. Jade pointed to the end one. I was so close I could feel Tobias's spirit, I was sure of it.

Inside the room, I was filled with horror at what looked like a clinical setting with a medical chair. Jesus, what did they do in here?

The room was empty.

Tobias's wristwatch was on the floor. I picked it up and suppressed a sob as I hugged it to my chest. Jade's arms lowered to her side and if I believed she was capable of emotion, that looked like defeat.

Dear God, tell me I'm not too late.

I shoved his watch into my rucksack and made my way out and ran from door to door, peering into each room.

I saw him—

My heart soared with relief. Tobias was slumped in a corner on the floor and was shackled to a wall, his face bruised, his eyes closed, and his shirt and jacket stripped from him.

I tried the door and it opened. "Watch for anyone coming, Jade." I ran toward him and knelt close. "Tobias." I shook his arm, feeling as though I was inhaling air for the first time since I last saw him.

He moaned and slurred, "Fuck Picasso."

"Tobias, it's me."

He raised his head. "Zara?"

"Yes."

He pried his eyes open. "You have to get out."

"What did they do to you?"

"Run."

"I'm here to get you out."

"What time is it?" His body was covered in bruises and his hair was soaking wet.

"Can you walk?"

He shoved himself up on his elbows. "Zara?"

"Yes, it's me."

"Remind me to kill Eli Burell when I see him." He moved his right foot and there came a clang of a shackle.

"Oh, God."

"That doesn't sound like a vote of confidence, Leighton." His voice was husky.

My hand cupped my mouth at the horror of what they'd done to him. "I have to get you out."

"The Manhattan house is safe. Wait there—" He tugged on the shackle.

"We have to cut you free."

"You gave me something to live for."

"I'm not leaving you."

"Unless you brought a power tool." His head crashed down in defeat.

"Jade's with me."

He peered through one eye. "Why didn't you say?"

I sprang up and opened the door. "Jade, come in. Hurry."

The drone floated in and sped up as she approached Tobias.

He patted her affectionately. "I know, buddy, I've looked better." He pointed. "Do your thing and cut the metal to free me. Fast as you can."

Jade hovered near his ankle and a laser shot out toward the metal cuff linking Tobias to the wall. Sparks flew as a blue line trailed along the metal.

"Are the police coming?" Tobias shuffled onto his side.

"No, but Abby knows Eli's dangerous."

He frowned. "Does she know about the painting?"

"No." I gave a shrug. "Eli has it now. For what it's worth."

"How?"

"I found it in your room and gave it to him."

"He better not have touched you." Tobias glared at me.

"Look at me, I'm fine."

His gaze stayed on me trying to judge if this was true. "Maybe your paintings are here."

I waved that off. "Let's just get out."

"Yeah, before his experts tell him he owns a piece of shit."

"She's beautiful because you created her."

He arched a brow. "Who are you?"

Even now he made me smile. "Can you stand?"

"I think they broke a rib. Remind me to not check in to this shithole ever again. They don't even offer room service."

"Can you walk?"

His leg jolted. "Careful with the sparks, Jade. If my pants catch on fire I'm firing you."

"She helped me find you."

He smiled and it turned into a grimace. "She's good like that. Makes great tea and leads you to boyfriends. If I put her on the market she'd make me a fortune." He sat up and pulled the metal shackle apart. "Good job."

I helped him up. "If this doesn't slow Icon down, I don't know what will."

"If this is your elaborate plan to persuade me to give up this life you're a fucking genius."

"Maybe Jade can shoot a laser out if anyone tries to stop us." I pulled open the door.

"She's not wired like that. She's programmed using Isaac Asimov's Three Laws—" He hobbled beside me as he whispered, "A robot can't harm a human. Nor can it allow a human to be injured through inaction. All orders from humans are to be obeyed except if a conflict arises with the First Law. She must protect her own existence, though this law of self-preservation can't conflict with the first Two Laws. That's the short version." He brought his finger to his lips, gesturing for us to be quiet.

I rolled my eyes to hint that was all very fascinating. Tobias couldn't help himself—science would always be his safe place. Stealthily, we made our way up the stairs and out into the main house.

I pointed upward and mouthed, *The roof.*

He mouthed back, *How long has Jade been off her charger?*

Why?

He pointed to her flickering green light and I couldn't believe what he was insinuating. We had to move fast. With Tobias's arm around my shoulders I supported him up the staircase and retraced my steps. Even if my paintings were here I didn't care. All I wanted was to get him out. Once on the top floor we hurried to the spot beneath the skylight.

"You first." He pointed upward.

"You should go."

"Jade." Tobias snapped his fingers and then reached for me positioning my fingers to wrap around her base. "Go."

Gravity pulled as I was lifted upward, and I counted the seconds until I was through the window and standing on the roof looking down at Tobias.

Jade descended to go back for him.

I watched with horror as Tobias snapped a hand signal for Jade to stop and then disappeared from view. Voices trailed below and I froze, staring down with my heart beating frantically. One glance up and they'd see our drone.

The way was clear again and Tobias gestured for Jade to lower to him. She reached him and he gripped her from beneath, rising in what felt like a painstaking slowness until he was standing beside me on the roof.

"Jade led you to me?" he asked.

"I tracked your watch." I pointed to my rucksack. "It's in here."

"I'm sorry, Zara. The plan fell apart. I let you down."

"No. Eli has our *Mona Lisa*."

"How did you get it out of the case?" He waved that off. "Let's just get out of here and talk about it later."

"Car's over there." I pointed in that direction.

Jade's green light was out.

Tobias knelt beside her. "Her power's dead."

"We have to bring her with us. She's part of the team."

"Yes, I don't want them to reverse engineer her."

"And no man left behind and all that."

He gave a smile and gestured to my climbing gear. "The old-fashioned way, then."

Tobias secured the end of the climbing rope to the window frame and I used the carabiner and rope to abseil down. With my feet firmly planted on the ground, I sent the gear back up to Tobias, with him pulling on the rope it was attached to. He clutched Jade to his chest on his smooth descent.

We ran toward the car.

Within minutes we were in the Aston Martin and speeding along the road, with frequent glances in the rearview mirror for any sign we were being followed.

I watched Tobias connect a wire to Jade and it looked like he was recharging her and then he set her down on the mat between his feet.

He turned the air-conditioning panel on himself. "How did you crack the code to the chrome case?"

"I used the most logical letters."

"Our names?" He shook his head in disbelief. "Hopefully that serves as something, right?"

Yes, using our names as the code to get into the painting had meant so much. I'd not had time to wallow in his romantic gesture.

"It was nothing." I threw in a wave as though it really had been that easy.

"I believe it." He squeezed his eyes shut for a second. "I've put you through this—"

"You can make it up to me. But it's going to have to be better than a new phone this time."

Tobias laughed weakly and jolted when the pain hit him. "Looks like we're all clear."

"If you say that was fun, I'll hit you."

"It was everything it should have been."

I glanced his way. "How do you mean?"

"I was in a room with no view and all I had were thoughts of you." He reached over and took my hand. "It was enough, Zara. Just the thought of you was enough."

"Tobias." I breathed out a sigh of relief.

"Self-drive on," he ordered and reclined his seat and closed his eyes. "Sixty-Ninth Street residence."

The wheel shifted, and cautiously I waited to make sure the car was self-driving. Resting back a little, realizing the strain of the last few hours was lifting, I let the car take us home.

Tobias carried Jade back into our Manhattan residence. Inside his workshop, he set her down on her base to continue charging. I left him there and went upstairs to use the restroom and then wash my hands and face, trying to scrub this day away and wondering if I'd ever shake this dread.

Tobias needed me. After drawing him a hot bath I returned to the workshop.

He was asleep and slumped over his workbench. He was too tired to resist when I grabbed his hand and pulled him out and up the staircase and led him to the bathroom. I helped him strip off his shoes, trousers and underwear, and there came a well of relief that Tobias wasn't seriously injured and was here with me again. Touching him, being this close meant everything, and every second, every chance to brush my hand over his body felt like an answered prayer.

He climbed into the tub and water whooshed around him as he laid back and rested his head on the edge. His eyelids closed but still came that sweet smile. This wasn't the time to ask what they'd done to him or what he'd endured at the hands of those men.

Kneeling beside the tub, I leaned over, reached for the body wash and squeezed the rich scented liquid onto a sponge and bathed him, caressing his long limbs, easing up over the bruises and lovingly nurturing him, enamored by his masculine curves that had endured such cruelty. I washed his hair, running my fingers through his already damp locks, and he let out a sigh. He lowered all the way into the bath and let me rinse the soap out of his hair.

Afterward, I dried him with one of the plush towels and got him to sit on the edge of the tub so I could use another towel to dry his hair. He looked up at me and gave another smile of contentment. Taking his hand, I guided him to his bedroom. I peeled back the duvet and helped him climb beneath the sheets. Sitting beside him on the bed, I caressed his dark golden locks to soothe him.

"I told you to leave." His voice rasped with emotion.

I was sure he was talking about the event at The Plaza, when I'd not only defied him by being there but also not left when he'd warned me to go. Guilt washed over me that because of those decisions I'd almost killed him. "I'm so sorry." That memory of seeing him beaten up and tethered by a metal cuff to the wall would haunt me forever.

"I don't care about me." He brushed a stray hair out of my eyes. "If anything had happened to you…"

"Try to relax."

"I'm not giving up, Zara," he whispered.

"What was that?"

"I need you." He pulled me down beside him and clutched me to his chest.

Snuggling in, I rested my head against him and breathed in the happiness of being back in my man's arms.

"I have a great idea," he muttered. "But you're not going to like it."

"Go to sleep." I kissed him.

"Okay, we'll talk tonight."

"Sounds like a plan."

"Zara, be my wife…"

"Tobias?" I raised my head to look at him but he was already asleep.

CHAPTER EIGHTEEN

DRENCHED IN THE darkness of Tobias's bedroom, I reached out and my hand brushed over an empty sheet. I sprang up and listened out for him, and then grabbed my wristwatch from the bedside table. It was close to 8:00 p.m., proving I'd slept all day. When I saw the note left on his pillow, a sinking feeling settled as I read it.

Sweetheart, we are close to this being over. I'll be back soon. Believe in me.

What was he thinking?

Earlier he could hardly walk and now this? My heart pounded as I realized what this was, Tobias asserting his authority and leaving me out of the decision. After the last twenty-four hours I deserved a medal. Things were different now. I was different. I'd experienced too much not to see this resolved.

I shot out of bed and my feet hit the hardwood floor. Surely he wasn't heading out to recover the paintings? Not after seeing what that family was capable of. I wrapped the sheet around me and padded toward the staircase. Peering over the banister I let out a sigh of relief when I saw Tobias. He was carrying a box through the foyer toward the door.

"Hey!" I called down.

He closed his eyes, realizing he'd gotten caught.

"Where are you going?" I hurried down.

"Go back to bed."

"We slept all day. Well, I have, anyway." I closed the gap between us and reached up to press my palm to his forehead. There was no fever but he looked pale.

He put the box down and grimaced.

I gripped the sheet to my chest. "Where are you going?"

Though with him dressed in black, I knew what this meant.

"It's nothing." He reached for my other hand and kissed my wrist. "Go get something to eat. You must be starving. I've got this."

"Eli mentioned something about hypoxia? Did he use that torture on you? Because there's clearly something wrong with your brain."

"What can I tell you? I'm a long-distance swimmer. I can hold my breath for extensive periods of time."

A jolt of panic. "What did he do?"

"Really want to know?"

"No. Yes. Tell me."

"He used water torture. But I'm fine."

"What!"

"Look at me. I'm fine now. It was kind of refreshing if you're into that." He joked, but his face revealed the strain.

"Call the police."

"Not yet."

"Don't do this."

"Listen—" He gestured for me to follow him toward the staircase.

I sat beside him and he pulled me into a hug and kissed

my nose. "Zara, this won't be over until the Burells are stopped from funding foreign wars. By now they'll know I'm gone from that house. The chance of them moving your paintings is high. If I don't act now, they may never find their way back to you. And if we call the police and they happen to find them and by some miracle get them out of Burell's hands, these issues get complicated once lawyers get involved with their international laws."

"What are you going to do?"

"End this."

"Where are you going?"

He stared off, reluctant to say.

"What's in there?" I pointed to the box.

"A drone."

I'd already seen his secret stash of drones. I brought my legs up and hugged myself.

"What's wrong?"

"I saw them."

He looked half amused and half concerned. "Okay."

"Why do you have an army of drones?"

"How did you get in that room?" He tried to read me. "Jade gave the game away?"

"I'm serious." I leaned back to look at him.

"Jade can be annoying like that. Look, I planned on doing this myself."

"Doing what?"

"They're the manpower I need to pull this off."

"That's why you have so many?"

"What's the other explanation—(a) I'm planning to take over the world, or (b) I have a drone fetish, or (c) I'm a lonely bastard who needs the company of an AI who always agrees with me?"

I arched an amused brow. "Maybe *c*?"

He pounced on me and tickled my ribs, and then flinched at the pain from moving so fast.

"You shouldn't be out of bed," I snapped.

"This is happening."

"Okay, then I'm coming with you." I pressed a fingertip to his mouth. "You don't get to push me aside on this one. You trained me for stuff like this. I was there for you."

"I can't do that to you again." He shook his head. "You risked your life for me. It's unconscionable that I exposed you to danger."

"You trained me."

"For self-defense. This is different."

"We make a great team."

"It's too dangerous, Zara. Anyway, I work better alone—"

"Going alone is reckless. I saved your butt, remember?"

He closed his eyes. "If anything happened to you."

"We go together or not at all, Tobias. This is the only way. Let me do it for my dad. Please, I need to prove I'm carrying on my family legacy. I'll be part of the mission to get them back."

"Your dad would hate me."

I wrapped my arm around his and rested my head on his shoulder. "My father would be proud of you for what you're doing to restore his paintings. It's my turn now. Please, let me do this." How could I live with myself, knowing he was out there risking his own life again because he knew what those paintings meant to me? "I'm ready."

He sighed heavily and pushed himself to his feet. "I'm leading the mission. Understand?"

"Don't underestimate my superpowers."

"Let's put your superpowers to work. Go make coffee and grab a bite to eat, and then we'll go over the schematics."

"If you sneak out I will find you."

"I know." He gave a nod. "I'll prep the kit."

Within ten minutes I'd dressed in a black tracksuit and a T-shirt and pulled on well-fitting sports shoes. Then I headed off to the kitchen. I took several bites out of a cheese and tomato sandwich that I found in the fridge, while brewing a pot of coffee. I carried our two mugs into Tobias's workshop.

He was in the room with the satellite tracking on and had brought up the map of New York. He turned and gave me a big grin as he accepted his mug. "Thank you."

"Careful, it's hot. Do you need a painkiller?"

"Already on it." He stretched and tried to hide the pain.

I could see he'd been beaten up, and was glad I'd caught him in time from leaving on his own. Was that relief I was seeing in his expression? Pride, maybe? Either way he seemed to have come round to me working with him.

I dare to believe I'm doing my bit to balance out the evil in the world.

These words felt like a sacred mantra that he'd once spoken to me and I was proud to be part of this.

"Okay, this is where we're going." He turned a dial and zoomed in to Manhattan, and the image closed in on an old building. The large rotunda was like the one belonging to the Burells' home in Amboise, France. The same one Wilder had broken into when he'd seen my paintings. He'd come out of there with more than just a Titian. He'd left with the truth of what they were hiding within their dark chamber. He'd left Amboise with more than hope, Tobias had left with a link that would lead him all the way to me.

He pointed to the screen. "The signal for our GPS on our *Mona Lisa* is coming from here."

"Where is it?"

"Right under our noses. Cloisters, it overlooks the Hudson River. Don't be fooled by the ancient architecture, this place will be challenging to infiltrate."

"Dear God, let the paintings be with our *Mona Lisa*. Let this be worth it."

"You still have an out, Zara." He turned to face me. "I've got this."

"Tell me what we're up against?"

"I've researched the security. Though we need to get in there to see what we're looking at. Elliot Burell's place in Arizona was fucked up, so something tells me this will be too. When I hacked into the company email there was an interesting revelation."

"Oh?"

"When you don't want an email to be traced, you write it and leave it in Drafts. It never leaves the email. It looks like a member of the Burell family gave a contractor his password for this email address so he could access the messages. It was an order of a large shipment of steel. I'm trying to imagine why he'd need so much steel going into Cloisters."

"A steel door?"

"And a lot left over." He turned to the screen. "This is going to be my most challenging job yet."

I rested my hands on my hips. "Do we have all the equipment we'll need?"

"The best money can buy. We must be prepared for anything. The Burells are merciless."

"How long will it take?"

"An hour, maybe. Zara, it could be a trap for Icon." He set his mug down. "I want you to promise me that if we get in there—"

"If either of us are in danger we leave."

"That's the plan."

"This is a good day. I'm getting my paintings back and you get to expose this family for what they are."

He drew in a deep sigh. "I want to whisk you away afterward to a private beach on a deserted island. We'll kick off the celebrations for our new life together."

I wrapped my arms around his chest. "Hold that thought."

That flinch reminded me of his bruises.

He tapped my back for me to step away and pointed to the screen. "I'm going to show you what we have ahead of us."

I threw a salute. "I'm ready."

After twenty minutes of Tobias's detailed presentation I was eager to go.

We finished loading the white van Marshall had dropped off outside the house. It was apparently a rental and could hold all our equipment in the back and, should we be successful, the paintings we rescued too. With caffeine surging through our veins we stepped out into the chilly night and Tobias secured the front door.

By ten we were heading along Harlem River Drive, which was the longer route but meant we'd approach from Broadway and be less conspicuous. We parked just off Margaret Corbin Drive and Tobias prepared the equipment. I watched him turn on all fifteen drones.

He gave a cheery smile. "Once we find the paintings we hail the gang." He nodded to the shiny drones. "Cutting the paintings out of their frames could harm them."

He was right of course. Bringing just the canvases would be easier, but the precision needed to extract each one from its frame would take us too long with the kind of care needed to protect them from tearing.

If Tobias pulled this off it would be the heist of the century.

"Let's hope no one tries to steal our drones." I hated leaving them unsupervised.

"Actually—" Tobias pointed down the quiet dark road toward a cyclist heading our way.

"Coops?" Although it was good to see him, there came concern that if we were caught he'd be dragged into our drama. Still, he looked happy to see us.

We greeted him with a warm hug and I was amazed when Coops watched his boss prepare the gear. We pulled on our climbing equipment and attached our tools. After that adventure we'd shared around the city days ago I'd suspected Coops might have some knowledge of Wilder's shenanigans. This was more than I realized—this was full disclosure.

"If we're not out of there in an hour, make the call," Tobias told him. "The police and FBI."

"Got it." Coops threw me a wary glance. "Last one, boss?"

"Last one," Tobias agreed.

I watched them both interact, realizing this friendship went deep and this exchange proved that Coops had to have an inside knowledge on what Tobias had been up to over the years. I wondered if he knew he was Icon.

The night-vision goggles we put on were part of an elaborate headset and we nudged them up onto our foreheads for now, and waved Coops goodbye. Staying close, I followed Tobias across the street toward Cloisters, the property nestled in the center of woodland and conveniently camouflaging our trek to our entry point.

We made it to a Gothic chapel and I was taken aback by the intricate carving of the ancient stone. I wanted to seem as calm as Wilder, but my trembling hands gave me away.

Tobias whispered, "This part of the building was transported from Burgundy. It's nice, huh? This is where we access the old chapel."

"Okay, good, we can ask for forgiveness on the way in."

"Is that meant to be funny?"

"I'm trying to lighten the mood."

He frowned with amusement. "Cute."

I gave a nod, ready for this to be over.

Tobias studied me. "At no time touch my butt. No pinching. No admiring. Just don't go there. Got it?"

He made me smile and I dipped my head as he re-adjusted my headset.

"No shenanigans," he added.

"What kind?"

"I'll give you a demo to be clear." He pulled me into a kiss and I felt my headset bend against his forehead. He broke away and grinned as he nudged aside his headset to return to his passionate kiss, his tongue sweeping in a way that was both reassuring and inspirational. This burst of affection meant everything. He was letting me know how proud he was.

I was about to break into a property with Icon himself to steal paintings. *My paintings*, I mused, so technically this wasn't a heist but more of a process of retrieval.

Tobias pointed to his own headset as he fitted it around his ear. "If we get separated we can communicate with this. If there's anyone else down there with us, the visor will detect their body heat and a blue light will appear in the corner of your eyepiece for a second. Hide until you get a signal from me that it's safe. The night vision kicks in when needed." He looked me up and down. "Suits you."

I swallowed hard and, after taking several deep breaths, gave a nod I was ready and watched him work the lock on the French carved door.

Terror flooded through my veins.

Everything had changed and I tried to comprehend how this once careful girl had flourished into a courageous woman. These unfolding moments were about me taking my life back. Never had anything felt so right, and there came the sense there was an invisible thread between me and my paintings leading me to them.

Tobias tapped my arm to get my attention. "Here's the bad news—"

"Bad news?"

"On my mark, I'll cut the power and we'll only have sixty seconds to find the entry point to the underground network. Any more than that and the guards get suspicious—" Tobias directed his wristwatch toward the building. "Don't dillydally your slow British arse."

This was how Icon deactivated the power during the heists, and right now I was receiving the mother of all demonstrations on his methods. The kind of evidence a member of Huntly Pierre would crave.

All those weeks of tracking him down, and here I was breaking and entering into a building with him as an accomplice. With my heart pounding, my adrenaline surging and my breaths sharp on each inhale, I realized what I was doing.

A thought flashed into my mind and it stunned me into silence. What if Tobias took my paintings and left me in there? What if all this was merely the endgame that I'd not even considered until now?

"Jesus," I muttered.

Don't take your eyes off him.

"They'll think it's a glitch in their system." He raised his hand and counted down. "Three, two and one."

We burst in and I watched Tobias secure the door—

I was stunned by the beauty of the four stone tombs lying flat and upon them were carved effigies of mysterious women, each a Spanish masterpiece of sepulchral art decorating the resting place.

Tobias hurried over to the statues at the front of the chapel and moved from one to the next, exploring each as he went. We were desperate to find a mechanism that would reveal a doorway. The schematics had shown this was the entry point to the underground tunnel but not specified exactly where. This had a Knight Templar feel to it and I guessed that was the point. Some secret society where access was granted to the privileged and the doorkeepers were the Burells.

As we searched for a clue, the seconds dissolved and the strain made me feel as though oxygen was lacking. The cause was a heady mix of dread and adrenaline.

Kneeling before one of the stone burial tombs I ran

my fingers along the gap between the base and the stone body of a carved woman. I made the mistake of glancing up and seeing a flash of frustration on Wilder's face. I leaped to my feet and ran to another tomb. He quickly joined me on the opposite side of her and we both ran our fingers along the edge. My hand bashed against solid resistance and pain shot into my fingers.

Pull, mouthed Tobias.

I tugged the stone protrusion and nothing happened. At this rate we'd be running for the door and getting out of here. I tried pushing the protrusion and there came the noise of stone scraping against stone filling the chamber. The carved woman slid off her base revealing stone steps leading into darkness.

Tobias glanced at his watch. "Go."

I sprang into the unknown and turned sharply to make sure Tobias was right behind me. As he followed me down the steps, the entryway grated above us returning to its base and casting us into blackness. Sealing us in.

Wilder flicked a light on his headset and lit the way down. Fine hairs prickled on my forearms from the drop in temperature, and I hoped there'd be a way out and we'd not become buried down here where no one would find us.

It could be a trap for Icon, came Tobias's words to haunt each step forward.

Or the cruelest trap for me.

The only noise was our careful shuffling downward. When we finally reached the end of the stairwell we peered down a very long hallway.

His hand came down onto my shoulder. "I'll lead."

Tobias was eerily serene and I put this down to him

acclimating to these adventures where so much was at stake. At the very end he approached a keypad with the confidence of someone who'd done this before. He removed a gadget from his rucksack and used it to scan over finger pads with a blue fluorescence revealing what numbers had been punched by someone else. He repeated the combination and the door clicked open—

Inside the room was an easel holding our *Mona Lisa*, her haunting eyes following us as we made our way toward her proving how authentic Tobias had crafted her. There was nothing else in here.

Tobias narrowed his gaze as he studied her. "They changed the frame."

"Do you think Eli will try to resell her?"

"Doubt it." He leaned forward and examined the canvas. "Hey, *Mona Lisa*, your job is done." He frowned as he noticed something on his watch. "The GPS isn't coming from her."

A jolt of fear hit me. "You don't think they found it?"

"It's pinging in this vicinity."

I threw him a wary glance because something felt wrong with her or perhaps everything felt right. The mystery reflected in *Mona Lisa*'s gaze was uncanny, the way she followed me as I walked around Tobias to take a closer look at her, the way her perfection screamed authentic.

Tobias's fist shot toward the canvas—

I punched his hand to redirect it and almost knocked him off balance. He steadied himself and glared at me in disbelief, and then his expression turned to horror. "No way."

"I'd need my magnifier but…" Shaking my head. "She looks real."

"Jesus, I nearly punched a hole through her face. I thought she was ours."

"She's the other *Mona Lisa*. She really exists." My words came out full of awe.

"Thank God for you, Leighton."

"Eli must know ours is a fake?"

He shrugged. "There's meant to be three that Leonardo painted. Maybe Eli wanted the other one?"

"Where's the GPS coming from?"

Tobias raised his wristwatch to look at the screen. "That way."

"Shall we take this with us?"

He examined the frame. "Sure, why not? Let me make sure she can come out easily first. We don't have too much time."

Within a few minutes he had the canvas rolled up and tucked inside his rucksack. Following the blip on his wristwatch, he led me toward the only other door in here other than the one we'd come through. With a turn of a handle it opened and we stepped out onto what looked like a high ramp that led to a stairwell.

Impossible; I blinked to take in the vast view of what looked like a giant roller coaster without a tram, trying to grasp what I was looking at as my gaze scanned the enormous cavern beneath it, all the while recalling the large wheel in Arizona.

What lay ahead was monstrously spectacular in comparison, the profound life-size design of a Rube Goldberg constructed in steel. This contraption was so complex with one mechanism promising to cause a domino effect on another should it be triggered. This was where all the steel had been used and it could only be navigated on foot.

We'd never make it to the other side.

My pulse quickened when I saw the enormous steel ball that was at least six feet in diameter. It looked like it was designed to come rolling along after you to knock you into the endless chasm.

"It's impossible." I let out a shaky breath.

CHAPTER NINETEEN

TOBIAS TURNED TO face me. "Go back."

"Together or not at all."

His gaze swept over the design. "We've come this far, right?"

"What is this?"

"Part of their elaborate safe system, I suppose. That wheel back in Arizona looks like Eli was dipping his toe in the water of what was possible. This looks new."

"This looks finished."

Tobias pointed to the end where, should one be lucky enough to survive this madness, there was a doorway that might just lead to a vault. Oh, God, we'd come so close.

"Bloody hell," I said. "I hate them."

"My thoughts exactly." He gave my arm a reassuring pat. "This is him trying to compete with Leonardo da Vinci. I told you he's obsessed."

"How could anyone compete with such a master?"

"Someone with daddy issues, evidently." We walked to where the staircase ended and the Rube Goldberg device began. "This is mathematics and art cobbled together."

To walk on it we'd have to navigate the thin rails and if that chrome ball came loose we'd be screwed. One wrong move...

Tobias stepped closer. "Leonardo da Vinci's dying words were 'I have offended God and mankind because my work did not reach the quality it should have.'"

"That's modesty."

"Unlike Crazy-head here."

"It doesn't make any sense. The wheel in Arizona was simple. Rudimentary in design. If Eli is advancing this would have taken longer to create."

"This is his dad."

"Elliot Burell's design?"

Tobias shot me a wary look as he realized. "Shit."

A small blue light came onto my headset directly before my left eye. Then snapped off.

The sound of clapping from behind us.

I turned to see Elliot Burell wearing a smug look on his face. He was dressed in a tailored suit and yet it did nothing to hide the monster wearing it. He reached into his jacket and removed a handgun and pointed it at us.

"The FBI know we're here," I said.

Burell gave a sly smile. "Let's have that chat you've been hankering after."

"Well this is cozy," said Wilder. "Love the contraption. Very Freudian. Looks like karma to me."

Elliot's gaze swept from Tobias and back to me. "Have a grudge, Wilder?"

Tobias shrugged. "There's just so many of us out there."

"Is it because I have the biggest collection of Leonardo da Vinci artwork and unique pieces ever collected?" Burell looked triumphant. "You always were jealous."

Tobias's back stiffened. "That's not it at all."

"I thought to myself how threatening can a nine-year-old be? After that unfortunate crash of your parents' plane I assumed you'd be kept occupied by a lifetime of therapy."

"I found my own way of getting over what you did to my family." Tobias drew in a sharp breath. "So far it's been quite the success."

"Ah, yes, your entrepreneurial exploits are quite the inspiration. Love the keyboard-in-the-air thing. Though I'll be sticking to a conservative approach. What a waste of time."

"You never did have any vision."

"That is my finest work." He gestured to the Rube Goldberg.

"Look," I said. "I just want my paintings back. The ones you stole and exchanged for fakes so my dad wouldn't notice."

"He knew." Elliot Burell closed his eyes for a second and it looked like pride. "Bertram couldn't prove it. He chose the insurance money so you wouldn't be thrown into poverty trying to fight a case he couldn't win."

I hated being this close to him and knowing the kind of pain he'd caused.

"You can have your paintings." He gestured to the structure. "If you can get to them."

There was another way. We just had to find it. This man of seventy wasn't ever getting on that thing.

"How did you discover this place?" Elliot asked.

"I stuck a GPS on a fake *Mona Lisa*," Tobias said flatly. "Eli was stupid enough to steal it and generous enough to lead us here."

"Masterful job, Wilder."

"Integrity is important. Well, to me, anyway."

Elliot was unfazed. "I think we're probably both relieved this is over."

"Let Zara go."

"You've compromised my privacy."

"And you might want to revisit your online security. I'm willing to send the message to our accomplice to delete the files I copied off your hard drive. If you let us go."

"Files?"

"I hacked into your computer and gathered all the intel detailing your illegal activities in the Middle East. Namely, breaking the Geneva Convention."

"I bend the rules. It's the kind of specialty that requires a steady hand and the ability to do what must be done."

"You profit from war, Burell," Tobias snapped. "Children are dying beneath the rubble of houses your planes bomb."

"Collateral damage."

"Let us go," said Tobias.

"And why would I do that?"

"If you murder us the feds will know."

"I will bury you both so deep not even the worms will find you." He pointed his gun at me.

"I'm really hot." Tobias turned to face me. "Are you?"

I shook my head; my body was too encased in fear.

Tobias ripped open his shirt and I stared in horror at the wire attached to his bare chest. It looked like the one Abby had stuck on me in the Plaza hotel room.

"The FBI is listening in," said Tobias. "Hearing every word."

Elliot's jaw tightened. "I've done nothing wrong."

"You just admitted taking down my parents' plane in Australia. You also admitted to burning down Zara's home after stealing her paintings, and then admitted dead children are collateral damage. I imagine the FBI's popping the champagne as we speak. Think of all those cold cases connected to you they'll be able to close. Probably half their workload, considering the damage you've left as your legacy."

"And you are Icon," said Elliot. "You wouldn't be so damn stupid."

"If I was I'd be proud of it."

I was terrified Wilder was about to confess to being Icon and alter the trajectory of our future.

He tightened the strap of his rucksack. "Icon returned the paintings you stole. He reversed the damage."

Elliot waved his gun at us. "Move."

I backed up, terrified of what was behind us. Three more steps and we'd be on a path that would lead to a catastrophic fall.

Elliot wielded his gun back on Wilder. "Off you go now."

Tobias grabbed my hand and pulled me into a hug. Elliot's gun shot off, barely missing Tobias. He ducked and covered his left ear, where the bullet had flown by, and at the same time shielded me.

"Now!" Tobias yelled.

We turned and leaped onto the Rube Goldberg.

"Hold on tight," Tobias shouted.

The device tipped and we dropped with it—

If I was going to die it would be with him beside me. I was comforted by the vague thought that if anything happened to us the feds would at least find the paintings.

But what if they didn't...

Hurtling downward—

The air caught in my throat as I was flung forward and bashed my forehead against the railing when we bounced to a stop, and there came a jolt of pain in my hands and knees. Reaching out, I had a white-knuckle grip on the edge and felt a pinch to my back where Wilder had grabbed a fistful of my shirt to hold on to me.

Squeezing my eyes shut so not to see the cavern below, sucking in a desperate breath, I said, "What's that noise?" I refused to look.

"Let's pick up the pace."

We were on our feet and running down the bouncing frame.

"Hook your carabiner onto the rail. We have to jump." Wilder hooked his carabiner and I did the same. The gate closed on my silver mechanism and I gave it a tug to check that it would take my weight.

"Now!" he yelled.

I glimpsed a blur of movement as that enormous ball barreled toward us with blinding speed. We leaped into the air and there came a jolt through my body of being caught by my rope, and I swung beneath the rail, tethered beneath the bar—then came a rumbling overhead as that ball rolled within feet above us and continued fast down the track, setting off a chain reaction.

Dangling midair, we swapped a glance of relief that we'd missed it.

Following Tobias's lead, I lowered myself to the level beneath and the frame bounced again when we found our footing. I unhooked the other end of my carabiner and grabbed another one from my belt to make ready if we needed to leap again. We hurried downward, knowing the unpredictability of another threat that could catch up with us.

Ducking when a wood panel swung round and nearly took our heads with it. Tobias led the way to a large chrome stand and we landed on it with a thud. It took us up and over to another level. We navigated the series of steps taking us down.

"This way." Tobias gestured ahead.

When we made it to firm ground, I managed a quick glance up toward where we'd left Elliot Burell and saw he was no longer there. A shudder of cold ran down my spine.

Against the brick wall was set a metal ladder leading up into the darkness and it reached all the way to a dizzying height of at least five hundred feet. This was how far we'd fallen.

My body trembled; my breaths raspy as I tried to grasp what we'd faced.

"Well done, Leighton." He shook his head and his voice softened. "Zara."

I turned to face him. "Yes?"

"You're fucking amazing. You know that, right?"

"I'm not leaving without them," I said firmly.

Up was the only way out. I went ahead and Tobias followed me onto the metal ladder. Halfway up the arduous trek my palms were raw from the tension of each bar I gripped with fading strength.

Eventually, we made it to the same level where we'd been standing. This was the other side.

Tobias set to work on the door. A trickle of sweat stained the back of his shirt but other than that he continued to exude the calmness I knew him for. Even after that threatening shot from Burell's gun Tobias was self-assured. Waiting for him to decipher the combination to the large chrome door felt like a lifetime.

He stuck a small flat square against the keypad and threw me a smile. "How are you doing?"

"You're wearing a wire?"

He lowered his voice. "Coops is recording everything. Just in case."

"Not the feds?"

Tobias looked amused. "No. They'd slow us down." He nodded to the room. "The GPS is pinging from in here. This is it."

I wanted him to open the door right now.

No, that was a lie, I didn't want him to open the door, because if my paintings weren't in there we'd risked our lives for nothing. And I loved this man with all my heart and nearly lost him—

"Zara?" Tobias had gone on and was standing inside the open doorway and he was holding his hand out to me.

My heart sensed them before I even turned the corner, this invisible thread tugging me ever closer to those paintings.

Here now, seeing them again for the first time in years I comprehended their profoundness, their sheer existence validating everything Tobias had told me.

As I pivoted around and around, my gaze found each painting, each masterpiece: the Degas, the Rembrandt, the Picasso and more, like old friends from my past. These were the paintings my family had risked their lives to save, the paintings my father had given up on to protect me. The paintings that deserved to be enjoyed by many. Over there was our fake *Mona Lisa* hanging on the wall and staring back with her subtle smile as though approving of us having used her to find this lost treasure.

There were other paintings here too.

My soul sang out when I set eyes on the others stolen from Boston's Isabella Stewart Gardner Museum, their Rembrandt, a Vermeer, a Manet and sketches by Degas.

"There's too many," I realized.

"Help me stack them." Tobias snapped the order. "Take them off the wall and rest them against it. Line them up ready. Hurry, Zara."

There was the delicate Renoir that Daddy had kept in his office… *She reminds me of you, little one*, he'd once told me.

"Zara!"

I rose out of my daydreaming and tried to fathom how Tobias was going to get them out of here.

"Coops," Tobias spoke into his watch. "This is our location. Send in the drones."

From here I could see the text appear on Wilder's watch in reply, and Tobias's nod confirmed Coops had gotten the message.

With all the paintings secured at one end of the room, I watched Tobias head over to another door. He turned to me. "We have about ten minutes when I cut the power."

"What are you going to do?"

"Open the door. We'll secure two paintings to each drone."

I wondered how strong the drones were for this feat and then remembered they could manage someone of Wilder's weight or mine.

"This is insane." I couldn't help but say it. "The guards will see the paintings on the security cameras."

"I'm cutting the power. I've got a security breach set for the Egyptian exhibit. That'll keep them busy. The police will be notified of the alarm and will respond all the way at the other end. We'll be cutting it tight. Coops is ready to receive the paintings and stack them in the back of the van."

"Burell didn't call the police on us?"

"He's probably heading for his plane. That shit I have on him will put him away for life."

"Tobias." I looked at him with awe.

This was art and science coming together just as Leonardo da Vinci had intended, and this was us, a symbiotic relationship that would have received his blessing.

Tobias stared at me.

I let out a laugh of relief and joy and wished with all my heart my father could see this, see me here, now, doing what had to be done and reclaiming our legacy.

Tobias ran at me and pulled me into a leisurely kiss and I melted in his arms as though we weren't midway through a heist, and time dissolved as I went with this spontaneous show of love.

The drones floated into the gallery one after the other, all fifteen of them, and Tobias and I worked fast to attach two paintings to each drone. Securing the frames to them, two arms on either side that held our precious cargo. The vision of them floating off outside in a convoy was mesmerizing. Each drone rose above the trees, making their way toward the van.

"Zara, go. I'll take care of the others." Tobias pointed

to the paintings from Boston's Isabella Stewart Gardner Museum. "We can't leave them."

"I'm not leaving you."

"Get to Coops. Help him stack the paintings." He pulled me into a hug. "I run faster."

"Be careful." I gave the room one final last glance and then grabbed our *Mona Lisa* off the wall and followed the drones out into the night.

I quickly made it to Coops and helped him stack the rest of the paintings in the van. Coops sent three drones back to Wilder.

"What happened in there with Burell?" he asked breathlessly.

"He tried to shoot Tobias." I raised my hand quickly. "He's fine."

"Does he need me?"

"He's right behind me."

The sound of a helicopter flying overhead startled us and we watched it bank left and disappear into the clouds above the Hudson River. I'd never get used to this.

"I'll go back," I said.

"Wait." Coops grabbed my arm. "There's a car."

We slammed shut the van door and pretended to be talking, though at this hour we'd look suspicious no matter what we did. Coops's eyes widened and I turned to see what he was looking at. A drone was making its way over the tree line with two paintings in its grasp. Coops ran to the front right wheel and pretended to be looking at it.

The Toyota slowed to a stop and the driver's side window lowered, revealing the friendly face of a young man.

I peered in at the couple. "Hi."

"Are you okay?" the young woman asked.

"We're fine. Thank you."

Coops tapped the wheel. "Changed the flat. All good now. Thanks, guys."

I tried to keep my gaze on their faces and not be drawn to the vision hovering three feet above their car. It took all my willpower not to look at the striking 1880 *Chez Tortoni* by Édouard Manet. The portrait depicted a man wearing a top hat, and he appeared to pause for a moment from writing a letter to look up. A thin glass of beer before him.

They drove off down the street.

My shoulders slumped and I turned to face the van. I tried to fathom the miracle of what we'd pulled off.

Not yet...

Tobias ran into the opening of trees with the last drone hovering above him. Two more miracles saved, the first *The Concert* by Vermeer and *Landscape with an Obelisk* by Govert Flinck, and the visual of those floating paintings in a drone's clutches looked surreal.

I let out a deep breath when Tobias leaped over the wall and landed smoothly. He hurried over to us and swept me up and twirled me. "Told you it would be fun."

I slapped his chest playfully. "You and I have different ideas of fun."

Tobias broke away and gave Coops a grateful hug. He climbed onto his bicycle and with a wave he sped off.

"I hope you pay him well." I watched him go.

"I do but you can't pay for that kind of loyalty, Zara." He winked. "Let's get these back to the house and prep them to fly to England."

I reached out and grasped his forearm. "I have another idea."

"We'll talk on the way." He opened the passenger door for me and I heard him check the back was secure before he climbed into the driver's seat.

He navigated the van away from the curb and back toward Harlem River Drive.

When we'd put enough distance between Cloisters and our van and I felt confident we weren't being followed, I allowed myself to dream of seeing those paintings showcased in an art gallery where they'd be enjoyed by so many.

Tobias reached out and squeezed my hand. "Zara?"

Perhaps he'd guessed where my thoughts had carried me. "If I'm going to be living here I want them near me. I want their home to be The Wilder."

Wonder swept over Tobias's face. "We'd be honored to host your collection. But I'd insist on having you to watch over them as my senior curator. This is what you meant, right? By being near them?" He dragged his gaze from the road to look at me.

"Isn't Maria Perez your senior curator?"

"She's retiring. So we have an opening."

Senior curator sounded so much like me. I'd be finally taking that leap of faith, upending my life and leaving a job I loved with the prospect of transporting myself to a country I hardly knew.

But I knew Tobias.

All I'd seen had provided me with a window into his soul and I loved everything about him.

Everything.

My thoughts drifted to *St. Joan of Arc* and I sent her a silent message into the ether: *we did it.*

Adrenaline still raged through my veins when we pulled the van up outside the Manhattan home. It took us just less than an hour to cover each painting with cloth to conceal them and then carry them carefully into the house. The drones were boxed up one by one, and Tobias and I brought them in too and secured them once more behind the steel door in his work space.

Tobias stood back and watched as I spent a moment with each painting, admiring the canvases and reminiscing about the memories each one brought, allowing my heart to contemplate us pulling this off.

"Zara?" Tobias grabbed my attention and his gaze moved over to our fake *Mona Lisa*. "Want me to do the honors?"

I gave a wary nod and pulled my gaze from the painting as though Lisa Gherardini Giocondo herself was staring back at me, aware of her fate. "Make sure she's the right one."

"Over there." He pointed to the canvas he'd pulled out from his rucksack. "Never tell anyone how we got her out."

"We didn't have any choice." I made my way over to the real painting, the other *Mona Lisa* that had remained hidden all these years and looked so similar to the one in the Louvre, and leaned in to study her. "What a find, Tobias."

"You're going to need to forgive yourself for stealing her."

I gave a tight smile. "Collateral damage."

"Indeed."

"Let's find who really owns her."

"Don't get addicted to the rush, Zara. It's a slippery road."

"I'll get us a drink." I headed up the ramp.

Within the kitchen, I placed the kettle onto the stove

and pulled out two mugs ready to make some decaf tea.
I clicked on the gas and popped a tea bag into each mug.

My body ached and adrenaline still bubbled beneath the surface. I wanted to get those paintings to The
Wilder as fast as possible where they could be guarded
by state-of-the-art technology. I was glad it was over—

My body froze as a wave of terror drenched me in
sweat. I was going to just stand by and allow it to happen. What if he'd done it already? I flew out of there,
raced into the foyer, and jolted when I made it to the
bottom of the stairs and saw Tobias heading along the
landing.

I bolted up the stairs after him. Tobias continued into
the master bedroom. I caught up with him in time to see
him pulling off his shoes and falling back onto the bed.

He lay there with his clothes on and his hands resting behind his head and yawning. "Let's go to bed."

"Where is she? The *Mona Lisa*?"

"You'll never see her again, Zara."

"Tell me you didn't burn her."

He pushed himself up onto his elbows. "No."

"Then how?"

He patted the bed. "Sit down."

"Tobias?"

"I didn't want you to think of me as the person who'd
destroyed her. Didn't want you looking at me that way."
He gave a shrug. "I delegated."

"Who to?"

"Jade."

"What if she misunderstands? What if she destroys
the wrong one?"

He sprung up off the bed. "She wouldn't do that."

I read doubt in him, I was sure of it, and turned on

my heels and bolted along the hallway and down the staircase, through the foyer and all the way into his workshop.

I yelled when I saw the authentic *Mona Lisa* was gone. All of the paintings were gone.

Tobias caught up and followed my stare.

"Where are they?" I burst out.

"Here." He hurried through and quickly made it to the chrome door at the back. "Open the door, Jade."

Barging past him I needed to see them all before I took my next breath. They were all stacked neatly, and there at the end lying on a flat board was the authentic portrait of the *Mona Lisa.* Approaching her, I peered down at the painting, needing reassurance there was no foul play going on here, no smoke and mirrors, no betrayal that I'd been too dazed to catch.

Tobias wrapped his arms around me. "See, everything's okay."

A chill washed over me as I turned to look up at him. "How is it to be done?"

"I thought this was what you wanted?" He frowned. "Having her do the honors lets us both off the hook."

That was true at least, but all I could think of was how beautiful that painting was, how mesmerizing, how profound an existence.

Running from the house, knowing the others—the ones we couldn't carry—were burning up.

I shoved Tobias aside and ran back into the main workshop. "Jade."

"Jesus, Zara." Tobias was right behind me. "I thought this was what you wanted."

I jolted to a stop when I got to the kitchen and saw Jade hovering over the stove before the kettle. Tobias bumped into my back and I staggered forward toward the central island, and my gaze saw the painting lying flat on the granite. She was fine. The painting was in one piece and Jade hadn't destroyed her.

Jade's long arm lifted the kettle and tipped boiling hot water into a mug and filled it to the brim.

"She couldn't do it, either," I muttered.

"That's sweet of you, Jade," Tobias said. "She's making you tea. Wow, that's a new one. Usually she needs an order for something like this. Next time leave enough room for milk, Jade."

"Okay, good." I sat on the bar stool and Tobias sat beside me.

I threw him a reassured smile and he threw one back.

"I know it has to happen," I whispered. "It's just that I'm not ready. I mean, you created her and that means something." I gazed down at the canvas. "She's the first painting by an AI and this is a landmark event. Perhaps that alone should be taken into consideration. Maybe what I've viewed as an abomination all this time should be seen as a technical achievement."

Jade lifted the mug with one of her metal arms and carried it toward us. She'd failed to add milk this time but I didn't mind, not really. She floated above the granite counter and hovered a few feet above the painting— and tipped boiling hot tea over *Mona Lisa*'s canvas, merging and melting the colors, and we flew backward to avoid the splash.

"What the fuck!" yelled Tobias.

Jade paused midtip, seemingly assessing his reaction.

My chin quivered. "In the car, I told Jade on the way to rescue you, I needed her to destroy it."

"Still." Tobias gestured his shock.

Slowly, I turned to face him. "I told Jade the story of my dad doing this very same thing when he discovered a fake. She remembered."

His gaze moved to the painting. "She did the right thing."

I read that from him, no regret, no sadness, merely his acceptance and I breathed out a breath of relief, realizing we had fought for her, given her a second chance and somehow, someway fate had intercepted.

"Fancy a nice cup of tea?" Tobias asked as he neared me, wrapping his arms around me and giving me the biggest hug.

I nuzzled in to him and breathed out a long sigh. "Let's go to bed."

We turned and hand in hand headed off to the bedroom together.

CHAPTER TWENTY

Two days later

EVEN THOUGH I'D been in that underground chamber of Cloisters when Elliot Burell had confessed all the evil he'd unleashed, hearing his sinister rant pouring into the conference room at The Wilder Museum sent a chill down my spine.

Tobias and I had flown back to LA last night and he'd used his remarkable resources to ship the art collection to this hilltop gallery without detection.

Behind us upon an easel and covered in a veil of black silk ready to be revealed was a jewel in the crown of the art world. Knowing she was in this room with us felt surreal.

Burell's words were being replayed for Abby Reynolds, Adley Huntly and Special Agent Pearson, along with Tobias's lawyer Reynard Linde. They swapped wary glances with each other at Burell's confession. He was admitting on that tape to stealing my father's artwork and the monstrous act of taking down Tobias's plane. He'd shown pride at being the cruelest warlord and admitted illegal acts against humanity.

Tobias raised the remote and stopped it. "This was recorded in New York so it's admissible in court. As you can hear, that's my voice and Zara's."

Reynard looked up at him with pride. "We'll prosecute to the max."

Tobias gave a nod. "Hopefully this will shut down the family's foreign affairs and cease the murder of the innocent..." His words trailed off with the ease of a man who knew he'd achieved the remarkable.

The pathway to peace was within our grasp after years of agony, and all because of him.

Special Agent Pearson piped up. "We received an anonymous tip related to Burell's dealings in the Middle East. The intel is with the Pentagon. Someone from the inside accessed all his data and forwarded it to us. His days of warring are over."

"Well, that is good news," said Tobias and he reached out beneath the desk and squeezed my hand.

"And that other matter?" I asked. "His son keeping an endangered animal?"

"Who keeps a Bengal tiger as a pet?" asked Abby. "Haven't they watched those TV shows where the bloody thing turns on them?"

Agent Pearson agreed with a nod. "Eli Burell has received a $25,000 fine and will be getting jail time."

I let out a slow steady breath. "Noodle."

"I'm sorry?" Adley gave me an inquisitive look.

"That's what he calls his tiger," I said remembering it had been a gift for Paige though I left that detail out.

"And don't forget that assault charge on Ms. Leighton," said Abby. "I witnessed Eli Burell's attack on her and I'm ready to testify. Add a few more years to his sentence."

Tobias's hand became rigid in mine and he stared at me in horror.

"Abby was right," I told him. "She stopped him from hurting me."

Tobias's grip tightened on my hand. "I hear the Boston's Isabella Stewart Gardner Museum also got its paintings back?"

"Also?" Abby narrowed her gaze on Tobias.

"Didn't you hear? The Wilder Museum received a shipment of paintings just this morning and they are from the Romanov collection. My experts confirm the provenance rests with Ms. Leighton. If anyone has questions, please address them through Reynard. The Wilder will not be making a statement. The issue is over."

"Weren't these the paintings discovered at the Burells' house in Arizona?" asked Abby.

I sat up straight. "Elliot Burell denied his paintings were connected to the Romanov collection. I believe you'll hear that in his transcript."

"Where did they come from, then?" asked Abby.

"I'm looking into it," said Tobias.

"And of course, I will be paying back the entire insurance payout as the paintings were not destroyed in a fire as first thought."

"Ms. Leighton," said Reynard, "with your permission?" On my nod he continued. "We wish to discuss the subject of Icon."

"I was wondering when we were getting to that." Abby's tone was sarcastic.

"My client Icon," said Reynard with a controlled cadence, "who will continue to remain anonymous, has a gift for you. Mr. Huntly, as an act of good faith this *gift* will be proof he was at all times working for a higher purpose."

"This is going to be good." Abby flashed a glance at Agent Pearson. "It doesn't work like that. Right?"

"Actually," said Adley, "it does appear that Icon was restoring art to those who it was stolen from. These are our findings back at Huntly Pierre."

Abby looked exasperated. "Still, these were crimes and any illegal act must be prosecuted."

Adley reached over and rested his hand on Abby's. "All the paintings are with their owners who hold full provenance."

"What about the families who believed they were theirs?" she added.

"They were in possession of stolen property," said Agent Pearson. "No charges will be pressed as it appears many of them had no idea of the illegal holding. Not in the States, anyway."

"Are you even a bit curious?" Adley used his chin to point to the painting behind the veil upon the stand.

Abby rolled her eyes. "Go on, then. I know Adley's itching to see what this is."

Tobias pushed himself to his feet. "I'm honored to have worked with Ms. Leighton. Here is what her expertise uncovered." He whisked off the veil—

It was the *other Mona Lisa*.

The same one we'd rescued from Burell's hands.

My thoughts flashed back to the portrait Tobias had created and then unwittingly destroyed by Jade and it felt right to have witnessed it and seen for myself it was done. This authentic painting felt like a rush of fresh air, and I soaked in this moment as my gaze wandered over her knowing eyes and wistful smile.

"Is she real?" asked Agent Pearson.

"We believe so. We're hoping Adley can confirm

this?" Tobias grinned at him. "Maybe you can track down her provenance and find out who owns her."

"We'd be honored," said Adley, standing to make his way over to the portrait. "Well, I'll be."

"Where did you find her?" asked Abby.

"We came upon her during a hunt for another painting," I told her.

"This will make history," whispered Agent Pearson.

Adley gave me a reassuring smile. "Come back to work, Zara. Start back as soon as possible."

I did my best to ignore Tobias's stare that fixed on me.

"Thank you, Adley, that means the world to me," I said. "I'll give your offer serious consideration."

"Make sure you guys get to see the Terra-Cotta Army exhibit," Tobias offered. "Before you fly back."

"We've already had the pleasure of seeing it," Adley told him. "Quite something. Very impressive achievement getting it here."

"I have an amazing team." Tobias winked my way.

"I'm glad everything is resolved." Adley's frown softened. "Things were a little touchy there for a while."

Tobias faced the *Mona Lisa*. "A greater purpose was hailing us and we responded to the call. She's one of history's greatest finds."

"And the dealer who had her?" asked Abby, throwing me a wary glance. "He's just willing to give her up for the sake of letting her go to her true owner?"

"He came around," said Tobias.

And with this painting having been obtained illegally by Elliot Burell, he'd have no recourse to complain. I prayed the person he'd stolen it from was still alive and could experience being reunited with such a treasure.

We hoped whoever once owned her or inherited her would share *Mona Lisa* with the world.

With the meeting wrapping up I held back to watch Abby secure the painting into the specialized carrier provided for them.

She handled it carefully. "We'll accept Mr. Wilder's offer of a security escort to accompany us to London. He's also offered for us to fly on his jet."

"I'm glad." I helped her seal the carrier.

She threw me a glance. "So many unscrupulous thieves out there ready to run off with a masterpiece."

"It's over. I promise."

She gave me a knowing look. "Has Icon really given up his heroic deeds?"

"According to his lawyer, yes."

"I'm pretty good at sussing people up, Zara. You surprise me."

"Really? How?"

"I thought you were a wallflower when I first met you. Assertive, yes, but not someone who would face off with the likes of Elliot Burell."

"Life presents challenges and we can either step up and face them or face the consequences."

She leaned in and whispered, "'If the meaning to life had a taste you would be it.'"

I jolted back and stared at her.

"I listened to the recordings from the wire put on you," she said softly. "That's what Wilder told you in the ballroom while you were slow dancing."

My face burned like fire that she'd heard him say it.

"I want a man who talks to me like that." She shook her head. "That was pretty smooth."

"He was joking." My fingers traced along my necklace and settled on the emerald.

"No, Zara, he wasn't. That man's infatuated with you. I can see why. You know who you remind me of? You're like a modern-day Joan of Arc. That painting really does deserve to be with you. I hope she turns up too."

I held her gaze to hold the lie that *Joan* was already with me again and right now she was in Tobias's home waiting for me.

She looked wistful. "You're not coming back to London, are you?"

"I never did thank you for saving me from Eli in The Plaza."

"That was nothing."

"It was brave and you seriously kicked his bodyguard's butt."

She laughed. "You sound American already."

I smiled at her fondly.

"Come here." She pulled me into a hug. "I'm going to miss you. You're one to watch on the art scene. Something tells me you're going to be a leader in this profession."

Tobias appeared in the doorway. "Ready?"

I gave him a nod and turned to Abby. "Say hi to everyone for me."

"I will." Abby looked over at Wilder. "Look after her."

"Always." He held out his hand for me.

After saying an emotional goodbye to everyone, we headed out of the office area of the gallery and made our way toward the exhibit room that would become the final home to my paintings.

Four of my collection would remain in England a while longer. The National Gallery would continue to show the Vermeer, the *Cannon Gun* sketch by da Vinci and that breathtaking Michelangelo. My *Madame Rose* was still safely housed at The Otillie, and I silently promised to visit her every time I went back. When the time was right, I'd bring them over to join the others to complete the collection. My father would be filled with joy if he knew.

When we were out of earshot Tobias pulled me aside. "What did Eli do to you?"

"Nothing compared to what he did to you."

He scowled. "Tell me."

"He shoved me. That's all, really." Saying any more was unwise, I didn't want Tobias running off to find Eli.

The thought he was going to jail provided some comfort. Justice had been served and maybe it would prevent him from following in his father's footsteps and becoming a warlord.

"Just say the word, Zara—"

I pressed a fingertip to his lips. "This is our time. Don't let them invade our happiness. Let's put this behind us."

His jaw tensed in contradiction. "If I find out he hurt you…"

The memory made me nauseous and I was done letting that family steal one more thought from me. This was a new start where happiness would be ours.

"Come on." Tobias pulled me down the hallway. "Show me how you want your paintings displayed."

The security guard gave us a respectful nod as we approached and granted access to the exhibit room. My paintings were resting on temporary tables set up in the center and my gaze roamed over them. My heart soared that I was in their presence again. Each painting carried a memory of a conversation I'd had with my father about each one of them, and his words stayed with me.

Maria approached cheerfully. "Let's discuss what you want written on the plaques beside each painting, Ms. Leighton."

"Call me Zara, please." I gave Tobias's senior curator a big hug.

"I hope your answer is yes." She watched my reaction and added playfully, "Mr. Wilder won't let me retire."

"Maria, that's because your skills are hard to replicate." He flung an arm around her shoulder. "Do you approve of our new candidate?"

She leaned into him. "I think you'd be lucky to have Ms. Leighton as your new curator. The Wilder would be in good hands."

"You're so kind." I exhaled a shaky breath at the responsibility and my attention fell once more on the collection.

I'd never believed this day would come. That wasn't exactly true. On that day in Wilder's penthouse I'd been full of hope that we might pull this off and here we were.

I steadied my emotions, looking upon my beloved works of art and ready to spend quality time with them. Back in New York, we'd packed them up carefully into crates and transported them with us to the private airport where Tobias's jet was waiting to return us to LA. We'd flown back with our precious cargo. I'd slept soundly on that flight, knowing they were with me.

Memories of my father flooded back as I strolled along the line of paintings and I sighed in wonder at the Vermeer, the Renoir, the Sandro Botticelli, all of them wonderful to my eyes, all thirty of them ready to be enjoyed by so many.

Tobias kissed my cheek. "I have to make a call."

"See you soon." I watched him walk away.

"So cute." Maria gave an endearing smile.

I didn't want to pull my gaze away and let that image fade. Wilder was the most gorgeous man I'd ever met and even after all this time I was enamored by him and in awe he was mine. Every moment had threatened to pull us apart and yet a greater purpose had fused the bond between us and strengthened us.

I love him.

This man had overturned a decade of travesties and righted the wrongs of a family who until now had run rampant on the world stage. His safety had always been more important than these paintings, and I knew what he'd risked for me to make this a reality.

"Zara?" Maria pulled my attention back on her.

"Yes."

"I like seeing him smile," she said warmly. "He deserves you."

"Thank you, Maria. I've never been happier."

"You studied at The Courtauld?"

"Yes, I loved it there. I worked for Huntly Pierre for a while and now hopefully here. I've applied for a work permit."

She gave my arm a squeeze. "We want you here."

"That means the world to me."

"Come on," she said. "Let's decide where to hang these."

Oh, my God, I was staying in America. A rush of blood to my head brought a wave of dizziness and the last few days caught up. I leaned against the table to steady myself.

"Are you okay?" she asked.

"A little overwhelmed." I gave a confident nod. "Let's dive in—" I pointed to the Degas. "Let's start with this one. My father loved it."

It was a silly thing to say because he'd loved all of them.

When I checked my watch again I could hardly believe two hours had passed. I headed off to Tobias's office. When he wasn't in there I pulled out my phone and texted him.

I'm taking a break. Would you like some tea?

When there was no answer, I tucked my phone into my jacket pocket and wandered off to find him. Knowing I was going to be spending my working days here was fantastic and I sent out a prayer of thanks.

Tobias's voice rose from a hallway around the corner. I paused before the double doorway to the Terra-Cotta exhibition. His voice came from down there. Tobias had told me he wanted to give me a personal tour of this very exhibit, so with him already in there this felt like perfect timing. The security guard gave me a nod of permission that I could head on down.

"Hey." I took the steps toward him.

Tobias was standing to the left of the stairwell and he turned and looked up at me with surprise. "Hey, sweetheart." He gestured to the guard. "Close the doors, please."

The doors banged shut behind me as I descended and we were cast into dimness within the vast cham-

ber. The Chinese Terra-Cotta Army with its long line
of soldiers, horses and carriages looked spectacular in
its life-size design. Being in their presence felt surreal.

I squinted until my eyes adjusted. "Everything
okay?"

"Yes. How did it go?"

"Great. The exhibit is going to be spectacular."

"We'll call it the Leighton exhibit for now."

He made me smile.

His expression turned conflicted. "I was making
some final travel arrangements."

"Oh?"

"I'm going away for a few days. I'll be back for the
unveiling of your collection. Everything is set. Invites
have gone out—"

"Where are you going?"

"Europe."

My throat tightened at his vagueness. "What for?"

"I want it to be a surprise."

"What kind?"

He grabbed my wrist and pulled me into a hug. "I'm
working on something very special for you and want
it to be a surprise. You're just going to have to wait."

"You told me Icon was done."

"Zara."

"I'm serious."

"So am I." His frown deepened.

I gave a tight smile. "Your eyelid twitched."

"You know me by now, surely?" He nudged me until
my back met the wall. "Don't be irrational."

I shoved at his chest but he didn't budge. "Let me
go with you."

"I agree we need to take care of your flat. We can do that next week."

"Why can't I fly back with you now?"

"First, you need to complete your exhibit and second I want this to be a surprise." He leaned in and pressed his lips to mine and possessed my mouth, kissing furiously. "We'll honor your legacy." He reached low and his hand slid beneath my skirt toward my panties and he caressed me through the material.

Arousal sparked every cell in my body and my sex felt a rush of pleasure. "Don't go." I couldn't stand to be away from him.

"Time for some make-up sex." Tobias spun me round, and I reached out and rested my palms against the wall for balance.

My jaw slackened at his cheeky resistance and, no, I wasn't going to let him manipulate me with that bad-boy seduction. I stood straight in rebellion, though when his fingers slipped into me I was walking a tightrope of need. Damn my body for giving me away. As he drove his fingers deeper I yearned for all of him.

"How long have you been wet, baby?" He crooned in my ear.

"Awhile."

"You were thinking of me?"

"Yes." I turned my head slightly. "Why now?"

"Last-minute opportunity."

I pushed back, and he grabbed a lock of hair and tugged it in a show of erotic possession and there came a sting at my scalp. His right hand was delivering masterful strokes inside me as the tip of his thumb stroked my clit with precision causing me to rock against his strumming. My orgasm was so close I was riding its first wave.

"Come hard for me." His husky voice exuded danger. "Understand?"

My sighs echoed as I squeezed my eyes shut, shielded by darkness, here in the quiet corner of the museum Tobias wielded his control over me with the mastery I'd become addicted to. I became one with his hand, quivering in this seemingly endless bliss as I gave myself over to his control. Lost to the world, gone from time and space, I became his willingly and shattered into a million pieces with his name on my tongue.

I gasped for air as his fingers slowed, bringing me down and bringing me back to now. When I finally managed to stand straight, he readjusted my skirt and gave a nod of approval as though he'd not just sent me hurtling into outer space, my thighs still shaky, my panting giving away I'd was wrecked from his dominance.

"God, you're beautiful, Zara," he soothed. "I'll miss you."

This discussion wasn't over. I just needed to gather my thoughts after coming off this climatic pinnacle that still had my clit panging with pleasure.

He gave the kind of nod that would win in the boardroom. "Marshall will drive you home."

"Excuse me?"

He gave a heart-stopping grin. "Don't try that attitude with me, Leighton. You work for me now."

My hand slapped to his chest and my glare matched my annoyance.

His smirk revealed his mischievous side as he nudged me up against the wall. "My Zara, *my* curator."

I was too far gone to defy him, too turned on to deny my body what it had been craving from the moment I'd met him. How would I endure being this close to him every day and not bending to his will?

I lifted the hem of my skirt in contradiction to my outburst, as though daring him to do me right here was perfectly acceptable and proving this was what I'd wanted all along. My fingertip ran along my cleft in a daring enticement.

His jaw tightened when he looked down at how wet he'd made me. "I can't deny you anything. You know that."

"I want you inside me."

"Say it."

"Your cock," I said breathlessly. "I need it. Fuck me, please." I moaned the last word.

Mesmerized, I watched him unzip his pants and offer his length, sculptured exquisitely and so hard, and when he pressed against me and slid between my thighs in a tease I moaned wantonly.

"Anything for you," he whispered and lowered to slide his full length inside me.

I gasped when his sheer size filled me entirely, stretching me, owning me. He lifted my left leg to hook around himself and held it there. His mouth met mine and he smiled against my lips. "Zara, you will love your surprise, I promise." He leisurely fucked me against the wall. "Doing this is important to me." He grinned. "This too."

I wrapped my hands around his neck and, as he lifted me up, both thighs wrapped around him and I clung with my heels crossed behind him. He banged me against the wall and each thrust felt like home and my body trembled from this blinding pleasure, feeling wild and safe and captured by him willingly, caught in the slipstream of this breathtaking orgasm.

He whispered into my ear, "You are my way forward."

I inhaled sharply as his words settled into my heart.

Tobias lowered me and my heels hit the stone with a scrape and my ankles wobbled from this giddiness. He held me until I'd gotten my balance again. Breathless, I tried to get my hair under some control before having to face the staff again.

Tobias stepped closer and pressed his body against mine. "I will call you every hour until we're together again." He kissed my forehead. "I love you, Zara Leighton."

"I love you." I pressed my lips to his.

"Don't forget you're mine."

I raised my chin, still dismayed he was leaving me so quickly.

"Come on," he said. "I'll walk you back."

"I'll stay here for a while if that's okay. I want to look around some more." This place had a serenity to it and I liked the idea of being able to think things over on my own time.

"Okay, enjoy." He pulled me into the biggest hug.

When he broke away I felt the loss of his arms.

"Zara, say you're mine."

"I'm yours."

He flashed a smile. "Right answer. I'll reward you as soon as I get back." The vision of him in that finely cut dark suit taking two steps at a time toward the door made him look like a king on an unstoppable mission.

The door closed behind him.

He'd left me reeling and with an uncertainty for his

need for secrecy. My head crashed against the wall and I stared out at the terra-cotta horses. They were striking and it was a remarkable accomplishment to get them here and display them so magnificently.

I let out a sigh of frustration. I'd needed to see Icon was behind us.

Tobias had just brought doubt.

CHAPTER TWENTY-ONE

THE SCENT OF roses filled the house.

Before Tobias had left for Europe four days ago he'd filled his Malibu home with flowers. I'd walked from room to room, breathing them in and wishing him back with me again. Now he was here and planting kisses to my forehead every five minutes, proving he'd missed me too. Upon his return this morning, he'd swept me up into his arms and carried me to the bedroom. We'd rolled around the sheets, making love and laughing with joy at being reunited.

He'd promised he'd make it back in time for the unveiling of my exhibit, and here he was looking tall and dashing in his black tuxedo as he finished dressing in the bedroom. I was relieved to have him home.

Still, there were secrets between us, and I couldn't wait to hear him share why he'd had to go away so briskly.

I watched him from across the room fiddle with his cuff links, and I was enthralled by the way his fingers twisted them into place. Those hands had been on me not half an hour ago and I could still feel the tingle of his touch. After a quick tug of each shirtsleeve he threw me a big smile.

His green gaze caught me in its steely sights. "You look gorgeous, Zara."

I neared him and straightened his bow tie even though it didn't need it. "Very handsome, Mr. Wilder."

"I love that color on you." He dragged his teeth over his bottom lip seductively.

I'd chosen the Stella McCartney gown especially for tonight with its soft pink, a plunging V-neck and elegant skirt that felt soft against my skin. I liked the way it flowed around my ankles with an ethereal splendor. It was fitting for such an important night—the unveiling of the Romanov collection at The Wilder.

There'd been tension when Tobias had left, but during those long days he was away I had time to think. If we were going to have a future, then trust between us was key and I owed my man this. He'd always come through for me. *Always*.

I'd spent my time sunbathing by the pool, reading my Kindle, taking dips in the heated pool, and pausing now and again to admire the striking view with gratitude. All this beauty was captivating and it felt like our long-awaited reward.

I'd explored Tobias's home and had one-way conversations with Jade. I'd sat her beside me on the living room couch and we'd watched a couple of movies together. I told her what I liked about the film and she sat there with her little green light on in what felt like quiet contemplation.

I was glad my Tobias was home.

We headed out to the waiting black limousine and set off for The Wilder, and it felt like normality had returned, with me snuggling up to Tobias and him holding my hand and staring out at the passing scenery.

"You pulled this event together so quickly," I mused.

"That's Maria's influence. You have big shoes to fill, Zara. She's a beloved curator. And loyal to a fault."

I hoped I'd be as liked by the staff as her.

He pulled me into a tight hug. "You'll do great."

"I have to sort out my flat." I turned to face him. "I need to pack up everything."

"I'll help you." Tobias's stare lingered on me. "Marshall," Tobias called out to him and the black glass divider rose to provide privacy.

Tobias eased my head to rest on his shoulder. "Words aren't enough."

Breathing him in, I allowed myself to finally exhale his essence. "I missed you."

"Missed you more." He looked into my eyes and tipped up my chin. "I want to enjoy this before I have to share you with everyone." He leaned in for a kiss and his tongue darted into my mouth and he moaned. "Zara, you really are made of all things nice."

My fingertip brushed along my mouth to savor his kiss as that dreamy fantasy lingered. "Kiss me again."

His hand lowered to my knee and he slid my hem up and over my thighs, and he leaned over to kiss my mouth. "These lips are mine." His hand trailed higher along my thigh, electrifying my skin beneath his touch. He dipped his head between my thighs and eased my panties aside. "And these lips are mine." Stroking my clit with his tongue.

My head rested back and I went with his delicious teasing, my fingers playing with his hair. Relaxed and letting go I became lulled by his kisses of affection.

"I could worship you all day like this." He let my hem fall and pulled down my dress.

"You've rendered me speechless."

He smiled and pulled me into a hug. "God, I love you."

My body trembled in the wake of his words. If it wasn't for the profoundness of what this evening meant, I could stay in this car all night with him.

When we reached our destination, we walked down the impressive walkway leading to The Wilder Museum. I turned to look back at the limousine and gave a wave of thanks to Marshall. He waved back.

In this very spot Tobias had tried to have Marshall drive me to the airport. Yet I'd refused and that one decision had led me all the way to this moment and all the way to finally being reunited with my paintings. All the way into Wilder's arms.

"Forget something?" He followed my gaze.

"No." I beamed at him and soaked in his intoxicating beauty.

The doorman welcomed us in and I was wowed by the impressive crowd already gathered in the foyer. This black-tie event to celebrate my collection felt like the final part of our journey and a wonderful way to reveal what had remained hidden for too long. My emotions were all over the place. I was sad my dad wasn't here to see it.

Tobias turned to face me. "Just say if you need me to whisk you off to a quiet place so you can catch your breath."

Weaving my arm around his I gave a thankful nod.

I gasped when I saw Clara, my best friend who'd flown all the way from London. My face flushed with happiness. She was chatting with my old professor, Gabe Anderson, and his boyfriend, Ned.

"Tobias?" This had to have been his doing.

He followed my gaze. "She flew with me from London."

This was the most amazing surprise and I couldn't quite believe I was seeing her. She came toward me wearing the biggest smile and her ebullient welcome reminded me of home. She'd dressed in her favorite halter-neck dress and oozed glamour. She swept me up in the biggest hug and her scent of lavender embraced me.

"This is too wonderful." Tears of joy stung my eyes.

"You had me scared there, missy," she said.

I blew out a long breath as an apology formed on my lips. "I'm sorry for making you worry."

"Tobias told me everything." She threw him a grateful nod. "I got to fly on his private jet," she giggled. "And no way was I missing being here for this." She held my gaze as her eyes widened with wonder. "You got them back?"

"Yes, all of them. They're here, Clara. I can't wait for you to see them."

She glanced at Tobias. "It's a bloody miracle."

"I know." I grinned and had to pinch myself.

We flew into a flood of words and she caught me up on her news of her family and her latest work in London.

Tobias gave a knowing smile. "I told her she could stay with us."

"You must, Clara," I insisted.

"I have to fly back first thing tomorrow," she apologized. "But I'm coming back for a holiday first chance I can get."

I was overwhelmed to see Gabe and his partner, Ned, and they looked dashing in their black tuxedos. Gabe was eager to revisit the Terra-Cotta Army exhibit, and although it was closed tonight Tobias told him he'd arrange a private visit and called over Maria to make it happen.

I was giddy with seeing everyone and I almost forgot why I was here. Tobias was pulled away from me and before long he was deep in conversation with the other guests. I watched him suavely navigate the guests who swarmed around him.

Savoring the sophisticated architecture of the museum, I let my gaze wander over to the corner where a terra-cotta horse and carriage was displayed as an inviting piece for those here to see the exhibit. Not that long ago I'd stashed my phone in there and run off to Arizona. Tobias had followed and his actions had saved my life. Days ago, I'd risked my life to save him too. We owed each other the greatest debt and I wanted to spend the rest of my life repaying it.

After chatting with Clara for a while I realized I'd not seen Tobias for at least an hour and told her I was going to go rescue him. I found Maria chatting with the receptionist at the foyer desk and asked her, "Do you know where Tobias went?"

"The east wing." She gave a smile. "He'll come back soon."

"Wasn't he visiting that new painting?" the young receptionist piped up.

Maria widened her eyes in a warning. "I'm not sure about that."

A tremor of uncertainty. "Thank you, Maria." I went after him, wondering what new exhibit she was referring to.

Inside the eighteenth-century Spanish gallery I didn't see anyone and turned to leave—

La Maja Desnuda was looking back at me.

This striking nude painting by Francisco José de Goya—the same one Tobias had taken me to see to authenticate for him in Blandford Palace in Oxfordshire. It was my first adventure with him. All air left the room as I realized he'd used me to case the palace for him. Right in front of me was evidence of Icon.

I inhaled a sharp breath of terror as my gaze wandered over the canvas portraying a beautiful naked woman lying down with her arms resting beneath her head in a manner conveying comfort with the man painting her. She emanated eroticism, the way her head rested on plump pillows and her legs together in a dignified pose. This was the work of Goya, one of Wilder's favorite artists. He'd yearned to possess her.

But at what cost...

Strong arms wrapped around me and I stiffened in Tobias's embrace as his cologne wafted over me lowering my defenses.

"There you are," he purred into my ear. "Have you quite finished dazzling everyone with your beauty?"

I spun round in his arms. "How?"

"*La Maja Desnuda* went up for auction at Sotheby's yesterday in London. I purchased her. She's authentic according to you so I felt confident to buy her. All aboveboard, Leighton."

I exhaled in a rush, knowing there'd be a bill of sale and this would be easy to cross-reference with a few strikes of a key while visiting Sotheby's website. "This was why you left me? To buy her?"

"No, actually. She was a happy coincidence." He pulled back. "Do you doubt me?"

I glanced back at her, hoping what I'd find would reassure me.

He leaned close to my ear. "You thought this was Icon's doing?"

I cringed inwardly realizing I'd messed up the mood of the evening.

"After everything?" His voice cracked with emotion.

"It's a big day for me. Just give me a moment."

He kissed my cheek to comfort me. "I get it." Though his eyes reflected hurt.

"I'm still getting used to being here," I explained. "This place."

He caressed his chin thoughtfully. "I was going to tell you *La Maja Desnuda* was here. Your nosy nature proved unwavering. I thought you were still with Clara."

"I came to check on you."

"Spy on me?"

"I should have waited for you."

He mulled over that. "Want to see your surprise?"

"The reason you went to London?"

"There's a price to pay for your mischief." He swept me up, flung me over his right shoulder, carried me out of the room and waved to the guards who looked on seemingly not sure what to make of us.

I laughed at his playfulness.

He smacked my bum. "You might want to shut your eyes for this part."

"What are you going to do?"

"Rock your world. The thing I was put on this earth to do." He put me down and crushed me between himself and the wall. "The reason I went to London was not predominantly for the Goya. Or to have Clara here." He gestured to the door beside us and I realized we were outside my exhibit.

"Then why?" Unable to wait a second longer I burst through the door—

The paintings looked incredible adorned along pristine walls, and as I wandered along tears welled at their beauty, each one was awe inspiring with its polished brass plaque set beside its frame detailing its painter.

And then I saw her—

My beloved *Madame Rose Récamier*, the 1803 Jacques Momar I'd donated to The Otillie, and the reason for Wilder being at the gallery that same evening. She looked just as vibrant as when she'd adorned my bedroom and only survived the fire because she'd needed restoring, and had found herself in my father's office on that dreaded night. They were all here and safe...*almost*.

I turned to face Tobias. "How?"

"You signed off to me being a custodian of all your art, remember?"

He knew what *Madame Rose* meant and had gone out of his way to bring her here.

Tobias stood beside me. "I tried to bring over the others from The National Gallery. They've already had the brochures printed. All ten thousand of them for the Michelangelo exhibit. Magnus Needham begged me not to remove them from the gallery just yet. I tried."

"Oh, Tobias." I turned to face him. "Thank you." I soaked up the profoundness of what was within this room. "The others will join us eventually."

"We'll keep your *St. Joan* out of the limelight for now."

"That's a good idea. Let everything settle first."

He pressed his palm to his chest. "I will be the most honored museum owner in the world to have your entire collection here."

"These are here because of you, Tobias. All of them. My father would be so proud of you."

"You too." He looked thoughtful. "Before I let in everyone I wanted to do this in here. It feels appropriate because these are the paintings that led me to you." He gestured his sincerity. "This is how I found you."

There came a crackle of electricity between us.

"Zara." His face brightened. "Marry me."

There came a rush of happiness on seeing his enduring smile.

Tobias lowered himself onto one knee and looked up at me. "Zara Elizabeth Leighton. Will you be my wife?" He reached into his tux pocket, removed a black velvet box and held it up to me.

Of all the things I expected to happen today, this wasn't one of them.

He flipped open the lid and within lay a sparkling princess-cut diamond set in a platinum band. "Promise me we'll have forever." He removed the ring from the velvet cushion and slid it onto my left ring finger and it fit so well.

Tobias rose and pulled me into a hug. "Say you'll be mine forever." His lips crushed my mouth as he sighed and I swooned against him.

"Yes." I nuzzled in and held him to me.

"I'm going to spend the rest of my life making you happy, Zara."

Our love had won out.

"Come on." He led me out. "I want us to get a blessing."

Out the door and down the hallway we hurried, soon arriving in the vast room displaying a series of masterpieces from the late 1800s. There, directly in our line of sight was Jean-Jacques Henner's 1879 *Madame Paul Duchesne-Fournet*.

Tobias stared off down the walkway toward her.

"She's smiling at us," I whispered.

"That looks like a blessing to me."

"It sure does." I looked up at his beautiful face flooded with happiness and savored these passing seconds.

All these years of being immersed in art had taught me how to live, how to fight and how to love, and I knew with certainty that home would be anywhere this man was.

EPILOGUE

Six months later

FROM THE BALCONY of Tobias's Malibu home, I enjoyed the endless ocean view and inhaled the fresh air. When I lowered my gaze another spectacular sight came into view. Tobias was taking his afternoon swim and cutting swiftly through the water in his heated pool. Though it was more fun to watch him climbing out with water dripping off his sculptured torso, and he looked like an Olympian put on this earth to tease. He turned his gaze toward the balcony and threw me a wave while delivering a dashing smile I'd never get over.

Yes, it really was my favorite view.

I'd missed him terribly during his trip to New York just a few days ago and was glad to have him home. I'd lived here for the last six months in utter bliss and each week had flown by with the ease of a sun-drenched life. We'd shared our first Christmas in this house, our first New Year's Eve, and even now I tried to grasp how much life had changed for the better.

Working at The Wilder meant my hours were filled with assisting in acquiring new art, exploring potential exhibitions that would be a good fit for us and wandering around the museum. Spending time with my beloved paintings and seeing Tobias during my day was my greatest pleasure.

In a month, we'd head off to Italy to tour the city and purchase pieces for the museum. We also planned to visit the Uffizi Gallery in Florence to see the other *Mona Lisa*, the painting we'd rescued and then entrusted to Huntly Pierre. They'd situated her at the Uffizi after her true owner couldn't be located but her provenance had ended in Florence. The hunt would go on for those who she truly belonged to. This Tuscan gallery had seen an increase of visitors since her arrival after we'd sent her home.

Each painting was more than a sum of its parts, it felt like a living breathing entity with a history reaching back to its original creator who first breathed life into the canvas. I loved being part of this profession and knew the privilege of seeing art every day.

My world felt even safer since the arrest of Elliot Burell, who'd been deported from Germany and sent back to face justice. His thirty-year prison sentence meant he was never getting out alive. His war mongering days were over. Tobias's mission was successful and had brought him the kind of peace he desperately deserved.

A boat sailed by on the horizon, drawing me back to the present. My wedding was hours away and I couldn't remember having been happier about anything. Of course, graduating at The Courtauld was a highlight but nothing came close to becoming Mrs. Wilder.

A view like this was worthy of capturing. I'd encouraged Tobias to bring his paints out here and have a bash at that seascape. I wondered if he missed his English foxes. He'd reassured me his jet was on standby if ever I became homesick and needed my London fix.

My fingers swung the chain of my necklace back and forth across my throat as I watched Tobias stroll over to a lounger. This single emerald was a reminder of how much his father had loved his mother. He'd given her this necklace when she became pregnant with Tobias as though sensing the miracle of the kind of man he would one day be.

I never wanted to take it off.

And goodness, this engagement ring was exquisite with the way it caught the light, its diamond refracting colors with its endless promise of serenity.

Tobias gestured for me to join him. I turned and headed into the bedroom, taking a detour along the hallway to the spare room, the one Tobias was forbidden to enter. Inside, my body thrummed with excitement as I neared the elegant white Monique Lhuillier wedding dress, with a delicate lace-trimmed overlay, ready to be worn this evening. Everything I had dreamed was coming true, starting off with a private beach wedding with just him and me beneath the stars at the foot of our home. Reaching out to touch the material, running my fingers over the charmeuse slip dress, I was eager to put it on and become his bride.

Heading down the staircase, I paused when I saw a flash of movement to my left. The only visitor due was the hair and makeup stylist who wouldn't arrive for several hours. Tobias and I both wanted a low-key wedding and after much contemplation had decided it would be just us and the officiate as well as the artist who would capture our day in the pastel tones of a watercolor. I turned the corner and saw Coops carrying a large wrapped piece of art in white paper and he hurried around the corner with it.

Tobias had decorated this place with his extraordinary taste and I loved walking barefoot on the Spanish terra-cotta tiles and sitting near the fountain in the foyer. It wasn't unusual for him to switch out his art from time to time or move them around to provide variety, though I wondered what new piece Tobias had purchased without me.

A painful thud hit my chest as Coops ran right into me, heading too fast back around the corner, his hands now empty.

"Careful, Coops." I caught my breath. "Are you okay?"

"I'm so sorry." He looked distraught. "Didn't think you were back from the market."

That took me back because I wondered how he knew I'd visited the farmers market in Santa Monica earlier, purchasing fresh seafood, fruit and heaps of salad for tonight as we'd planned on preparing food by ourselves too. Still, it made me wonder why it would be an issue for Coops.

I smiled at him fondly. "What was that?"

"What?" He looked nervous.

I pointed toward where he'd just come from. "That thing you were carrying?"

He gave a nod and hurried off. "Not sure what you mean."

"Coops?" I called after him but he was already at the front door. Turning sharply on his heels he called back, "I never did ask you if the footage was clear?"

"I'm sorry?"

"When I converted Mr. Wilder's videotape? You

mentioned not wanting anyone to see it so I had a private firm take care of it."

"Oh, Tobias's birthday party?" I realized. "Yes, you did an amazing job. It's preserved perfectly on a digital file."

We'd watched it a month ago, and this time Tobias had managed to see the entire footage as he sat beside me scooping vanilla ice cream out of a china bowl and reminiscing about his childhood, sharing cute stories that made me laugh.

"Have an amazing evening," he said. "Call me if you guys need any last-minute help with anything." Coops hurried off.

"You're always amazing." Though right now he seemed unusually nervous.

Intrigued, I retraced his footsteps and went looking for the painting he'd just dropped off—my feet stuck where they stood—the painting he'd just denied carrying.

Vaguely, I recalled the kind of work Coops conducted for Tobias. He'd been his right-hand man for years and though young, had a maturity beyond his years and was fondly described by his boss as a tech genius. How had Tobias described him? He'd nicknamed him Q, as in *quartermaster*, because that was the term used in the military for men who provided the equipment needed for soldiers when they went into battle.

A chill washed over me that there was a new painting in this house that I knew nothing about. A secret that shouldn't be. I was sure there'd be a perfectly good explanation and with a mouth dry and thirsting, I strolled into the kitchen, suppressing my old doubts that had no right to linger. I found my sunglasses on the granite island and slid them up to rest on my head and then poured two ice teas and adding a dash of lemon.

I carried them out into the garden and handed Tobias his drink. "There you go."

"What would you say if we delayed our honeymoon by a day?" He looked thoughtful. "I want to spend our wedding night here. Have this place be our first memory of us as husband and wife."

"You changed your mind?" I tried to read where this had come from, after all he'd painstakingly planned every detail of our wedding and all he'd talked about was that private island and how he couldn't wait to get there.

"Zara?"

"Sure, I think that's a lovely idea." My thoughts flashed back to seeing Coops disappear behind the corner with that tall frame. I hesitated for a beat, wondering when would be a good time to broach the subject.

A buzz went off on Tobias's phone. He reached for it and read the text and cringed, then flipped over the phone.

I'd not caught the sender's name. "Who was that?"

"I'm turning it off for the rest of the day." With a slide of a finger over his screen it was off and he placed it back onto the glass table.

"I hope it wasn't bad news."

"It's fine. Come grab some rays." He patted the sunbed beside his. "We have time."

"I love it when the sun is out."

He laughed. "It's always out in Cali."

Lying facedown on my towel, I got comfortable and unclipped my bikini top and threw it over to him. "Look what you won. Lucky thing."

"Don't mind me while I lick your top." He grinned.

I rolled onto my back and smiled, and it was one of those grins that showed that everything was just as it should be. "We might need to pour that tea over your head to cool you down, buddy."

"Buddy?" His admiring gaze swept over me as he reached for the tube of sunblock and squeezed a white blob between my breasts. "Just doing my bit for prevention." His fingers paid special attention to my nipples, causing them to perk. "You can thank me later for my forethought."

His massage was a reminder of how amazing his touch felt, both arousing and comforting, and my body ached with a need that would never be quenched by this incredible man.

My body stiffened as a thought gate-crashed my mind. What if Tobias had brought me to Malibu to live because lulling me with his affection and keeping me busy at his museum was all an elaborate ruse to ensure his work as Icon continued?

Don't do this to yourself. Not today. Not ever.

Still, if I allowed myself to consider the possibility of it, I had to admit the dark fact that I'd never be any wiser. That trip he'd taken to New York to take care of his grandmother's home in Manhattan had been without me because he'd wanted to explore her personal items and he'd expressed he didn't want me to get bored even though I'd offered to help. I'd been kept busy at The Wilder Museum with our new exhibit of artifacts from the Mayan civilization, a passion project for both of us.

These were irrational thoughts and probably stirred by wedding day nerves. That's all this was, I reassured myself, the normal kind of jitters you'd expect from the imminent commitment I was about to throw my-self into headfirst.

"Relax," he cooed. "The house is shielded. I made sure of that when I purchased the property."

"Paradise." I tried to let go and almost purred as he caressed me in rhythmic circles.

"I want to buy you something. Name it."

"I don't need anything." I popped an eye open. "Have you seen this place?"

"Jewelry?"

"I have your mom's necklace. I love it and never want to take it off."

That made him smile. "Ring?"

I raised my left hand to show off my blinding dia-mond. "Hello."

"Are you really happy? You have no regrets, right? I know how much you loved your job in London."

"I'm in heaven, Tobias. This is nirvana."

"You're my reason to breathe."

My heart melted all over again.

His hands slipped to my stomach and he worked his circular motion there, and I tried not to sulk at my near miss of bliss when a ringtone disturbed the quiet. Rais-ing my head off the lounger, I glanced over at Tobias's pained expression.

"I'll get it." I pushed myself up. "You relax."

"Sure." He raised his hands in defeat. "Otherwise you'll be wondering who called you. I want your thoughts to be only on me for the rest of the evening. As selfish as that sounds."

I reached for a towel, wrapped it around myself and returned to the house, closing the sliding glass door behind me so as not to disturb Tobias. There, on my laptop screen, was a missed call from Huntly Pierre.

Maybe they'd heard about our wedding and wanted to wish us all the best for tonight. In the name of public relations, considering Tobias was still a client, I clicked the return-call button.

Huntly Pierre's logo filled the screen and then Abby's face appeared. "Hey, Zara," she said brightly. "Thank you for taking my call."

"Of course," I said. "Anything for you. How are you?"

"Not bad." Her gaze slid behind me. "You alone?"

"Yes."

"Where's the man?"

"Outside."

She drew in a sharp breath. "How's the weather?"

I peeled off my sunglasses. "Sunny. How's London?"

"Rainy." Her wary gaze jumped to someone behind the screen.

She wasn't alone but was pretending this friendly chat was merely between us. The hairs prickled on my forearms. "Everything okay?"

"You look sickeningly healthy." Abby laughed. "Lots of downtime?"

"I'm working hard. You know me."

"How's Wilder?"

I needed to know the reason for her call on a Saturday. "To what do I owe the pleasure?"

"We have a situation." Her playfulness dissolved. "There's been a major art theft at Buckingham Palace."

My throat tightened as my brain went into overdrive. "Oh?"

"I don't want to say too much." Abby glanced behind

her. "Look, we've been commissioned by the Palace to find this one. This is big. Like a major masterpiece has just vanished off the face of the earth. It's the queen's all-time favorite. We've hit nothing but dead ends. The queen's personal secretary hasn't told her yet as he doesn't want to alarm her."

"How can I help?"

Abby leaned in closer. "I can't believe I'm even saying this—"

"Seriously?" I managed before she'd finished her statement.

She seemed unfazed. "We believe it's the work of Icon."

With a trembling hand, I tilted the screen to ward off the sun's reflection bursting through the window.

"Don't hate me for asking, Zara."

"You want to know where I was?"

"Tobias, was he with you last week?"

Lying felt wrong but not protecting Tobias felt even worse. "What day?"

"The staff are pretty vague. As you can imagine the palace is huge and they have a ton of art over there, but the painting went missing between last Wednesday and today."

A chill washed over me. "What was stolen?"

"I know this is difficult for you."

"I'm okay, what was the painting?"

"A West."

"Which one?" Though my brain was asking what size this masterpiece was before it disappeared.

"It was taken from the State room. *Queen Charlotte* by Benjamin West—"

"That's a nice painting."

The size would match the very one Coops had just dropped off.

I feigned not to be shaken to my core. "And the provenance?" Though she knew I was really asking if there'd been a suspicious break in ownership. A history that might make it a target for Icon.

"It was painted for King George III and Queen Charlotte." She sounded solemn.

"No break in provenance? Doesn't sound like Icon."

"There's always a first."

My throat tightened and my gut wrenched at her insinuation. "Not sure how I can help?" I pined for that glass of ice tea waiting for me by my lounger.

"This one was against the queen." She widened her eyes suggestively. "This one hits at the center of everything we hold dear."

"I get that." I gave my best apologetic smile.

"Do what you can at that end."

What she was asking of me cut to my core.

"Are you up for it, Zara? Are you willing to do what is right?"

"Always." Though my heart ripped into pieces at the thought of it.

Doing what was right was searching this house for that painting and then calling off my wedding. Then setting the authorities on the man I loved. The only person who got me. The only one who'd broken down my walls and shown me how to live.

"I'll be in touch." I snapped closed the laptop.

Pushing to my feet, I stared out the glass door at Tobias. He looked like he could be asleep behind those shades, seemingly guilt free because he believed what he did to be right.

"You promised me," I whispered into the ether.

Looking around, I soaked in the glamor and the coziness. I'd let my guard down here, finally trusted and allowed myself to believe I deserved to be happy.

I jolted—

Tobias stood before the glass window staring at me and he looked like he was trying to read me from there, and even though he still wore sunglasses I could see he was concerned.

He stepped forward and slid the glass door open. "Everything okay?"

"Yes."

He pulled off his glasses and set them on the kitchen island. "Sure?"

"Absolutely."

His gaze drifted to my laptop. "Who was it?"

"Abby."

He pulled me into a hug. "What did she want?"

Tobias felt so good crushed against me, his natural scent mixed with his sexy perspiration from having sat out in the midday sun wafted over me and sparked all the wrong responses, the same ones that rendered me boneless in his hold.

"I need to take a shower." He stepped back. "So do you."

"Last week," I managed, "you were in New York the entire time?"

"Yes, why?"

"You didn't need to pop over to England?"

"Without you?" He strolled over to the fridge and opened it, peering in and seemingly looking for something. "I would have told you."

"Right."

"Will you forgive me?"

"Why would I need to forgive you?"

He laughed and brought out an oyster shell. "Come here." When I didn't move, he neared me. "Open." He lifted the dark shell to my mouth and tipped in the oyster and a blast of the ocean melted on my tongue.

"Forgive you?" I repeated, wiping away a trickle of juice, though my hand stayed pressed to my lips to hide my terror. I'd been wrong, I'd been used as a pawn in Tobias's carefully orchestrated plan.

He took an oyster for himself and tipped it into his mouth. "I meant, forgive me for diving into the seafood early. God, I love oysters."

"Love that farmers market."

"You can always be assured the produce is fresh."

"Yes."

"It's true what they say. These suckers are an aphrodisiac." He planted a kiss to my neck and then pulled away. "I know what this is."

I gasped and stepped back.

"And I know the cure." He reached for my hand and led me out of the kitchen.

"Tobias." My voice sounded shaky.

"This is what's expected."

As we climbed the steps, my hand trembled in his. "How do you mean?"

We made it to the top of the stairs and he brushed a hair out of my face. Out of the corner of my eye, I caught the steep drop down those stone steps and instinctively stepped back from the edge.

"This is prewedding nerves, sweetheart." He tugged my hand and we entered the master bedroom, walking through it and entering the bathroom en suite.

He led me all the way into the shower, and I stood before him naked now with my arms covering my breasts, huddled in the chill until he got the water running.

He reached out and pulled me against him. "Body warmth." He planted a kiss to my forehead and then turned to work the dial.

Hot water showered over us and though it heated my chilled bones I couldn't seem to think straight. I should have made an excuse, should have gone off to find that West and gotten this over with. Right here, now, I was beneath the same roof as one of the queen's most treasured possessions. I was betraying everything I held dear.

Tobias pressed me against the glass. "Where are you?"

"Here," I lied, but my thoughts were anything but in this shower with him.

"You're not scared about marrying me, are you?"

"It's all so fast."

"We've lived together for six months. I know you're The One, Zara. There's no one else for me. God, I've never loved anyone the way I love you."

My gaze rose to his. "I love you so much. I'd do anything for you."

His lips crushed mine and he owned my mouth as he swept his tongue against mine, finding every crevice, every stroke one of possession, and his hands pressed against my cheeks to hold me in his grip. I surrendered in his arms and went with this rush, having been captured by this man the first time I saw him.

He pulled back. "You saw it, didn't you?"

My lips trembled as I tried to deny it.

"Oh, baby." He yanked me against his chest and hugged me tight. "You weren't meant to see it."

"I don't know what you mean."

His frown deepened. "Coops?"

"He chatted awhile but couldn't stay."

Tobias's eyes were assessing mine. "What's going on?"

"Nothing." Though I was the one with the right to ask him that.

"What did Abby say exactly?"

Her words flooded back and scorched my heart.

"Zara, you must tell me what's going on."

"I did see it," I blurted. "The Benjamin West. How could you? Tobias, you promised me." I shoved open the glass door and leaped out and ran for a towel.

"What West?" He was behind me, dripping water and not caring about reaching for a towel himself.

I turned to face him. "The one you stole from Buckingham Palace."

He pulled away and closed his eyes as he realized he'd gotten caught. "I made a promise to you. I kept it. Whatever was spoken on that call is not true. I'm sure there's a perfectly good explanation."

"Tell me the truth."

"On our wedding day!" He sucked in a sharp breath. "Of all the days you choose to do this it's today? You're infuriating."

"I'm infuriating?"

He caressed his brow. "This must be the last time, Zara."

"The last time for what?"

"We ever mention that name."

"Icon?"

He stomped over to the landline, picked up the phone and punched a number set to speed dial.

"Who are you calling?"

He calmed. "Adley."

"Why?"

"Because today is our wedding day and no one is going to ruin it." He listened to the person on the other line. "Adley, it's me…Yes, fine, thank you. The Palace, that missing painting. Don't take this the wrong way, but I'm guessing it went for cleaning or there's a perfectly good explanation. Has anyone asked Her Majesty?… Sounds like a plan. Call me back…Great, thank you, and you too." He slammed the phone down and turned to face me. "Happy now?"

"You think that's going to be enough?"

"All this sun's gone to your British brain." He grinned and came toward me. "I thought you'd changed your mind about me."

Trying to suppress a frown. "Let me go."

He stepped back and grabbed a towel, then wrapped it around himself.

"What am I going to do?" I whispered.

"Come on." He took my hand and pulled me down the stairs and along the hallway, retracing the steps Coops had taken. "In here."

We burst into the living room. He let go and went inside a cupboard. He pointed to the large painting wrapped in white. "This is what you saw?"

"What is it?" My throat was sore from tension.

He rolled his eyes. "Zara." He lifted it and carried it over to the far end of the room and rested it upright against the table. "My wedding present to you." He rested his fisted palms on his hips. "I wasn't expecting to give it to you like this. I had this day planned out. Me dressed as your groom and you in your wedding dress while we sipped champagne as husband and wife. Still, you and I will never follow the rules or live by tradition to such an extent that it comes before our feelings."

Staring at the wrapping paper, my thoughts raced with what was beneath the white luxury wrapping.

"Do you want to do the honors?" He gestured to it.

Wary still, I shook my head.

"Allow me, then." He stepped toward it and yanked at a corner and pulled. "Coops collected it from the framer. He was meant to get it into the house without you seeing it. This was meant to be a surprise." Ripping farther he revealed a canvas and the faint image of a woman's red gown. I recognized those strappy black shoes as the paper tore away. This was no Benjamin West; those colors and tones weren't his style, though I did recognize the masterful strokes of the *sfumato* technique—

The painting was of me wearing a red gown and red-and-golden bodice that hugged my curves. Though I'd never posed for this, I had been photographed in this very pose with my auburn locks tumbling over naked shoulders, and my smile was the same one I'd held for Tobias when he'd snapped this shot at a gala at The Wilder two months ago.

"Recognize his work?" Tobias beamed at me.

"Brother Bay?"

"It took me a lot to persuade him to paint from a photo but I twisted his arm in the end." His gaze swept over the canvas. "You are sublime, Zara."

My voice was still shaky. "This was why you didn't want me in New York?"

He came toward me and gently eased my hand from my face. "Feel better?"

"It's beautiful."

"That's because it's you."

I waved that off as I held back tears. "No, I meant it's an incredible gift. I don't know what to say."

"Remind me to thank Coops for his suspicious behavior that sent you into a spin."

"It was my fault. I'm sorry, I—"

"Doubted me." He pulled me into a hug and squeezed me into him. "I have a lifetime of proving my honesty to you. You're about to marry the man who was... I deserve your doubt. Don't be hard on yourself."

I reached for his face and read forgiveness in his eyes.

"Still, I'm going to need to punish you." He picked me up and carried me out of there and up the stairs fast and all the way to our bedroom, where he flung me onto the bed.

He pulled off his towel in the style of a matador as though trying to break the tension, and he made me laugh as he climbed onto the end of the bed like a prowling panther. He leaned low to kiss the inside of my ankle and trailed kisses up toward my inner thigh, teasing, kissing and licking close to my sex but not there yet and making me writhe for his touch.

He grazed his lips over mine and then pulled back and stared into my eyes, seemingly reading something, his expression changing, his frown deepening.

"What's wrong?"

"I know what you need. I always did and I always will."

"What are you saying?"

"Let's play," he cooed close to my ear.

Pushing myself up onto my elbows, I watched his well-toned naked suntanned body saunter across the room, his skin shimmering from the light streaming in from the late afternoon sun. He slid open a drawer and removed red silk ties and gave them a tug to test their strength. He returned to my side, where he dipped the mattress as his knee pressed in. Reaching up for my wrists and holding them tight, he brought them above my head, and several knots later he'd tied me to the bedpost. Those same ribbons were used to secure my feet, only he spread them wide, leaving me exposed and vulnerable. Tobias brought another one of the red silk ties and lifted my head to wrap it around, pulling it around my mouth and gagging me.

Looming over me, he admired his handiwork. "You're my addiction, Zara. Erotic and exquisite and everything a man desires. There is one trait, though, that we need to work on. And that is trusting me implicitly."

Raising my head off the pillow I tried to read him and made an indecipherable moan.

He raised a finger to silence me. "Hold that thought."

My body was chilled from the breeze finding its way in through the door that Tobias was exiting.

"Wait for me." He flashed a smile. "Not that you have any choice."

What the hell?

Pulling the cords, I squirmed to escape my bindings, and when that didn't work I gave a yank, trying to pull up my legs but it was no use. They were secured too tightly and I strained against the binds frantically, my heart thundering, my panic rising.

Tobias reappeared and his expression was calm as he carried himself with that steely pride I'd seen on him that first day we met. "Zara."

I mumbled against this gag.

"Good point." He reached for the discarded throw over a high-backed chair and pulled it up to cover me. "I know your body better than you know it yourself." His voice was low and seductive. "Every curve, every angle, every taste. I've journeyed over you a thousand times and mapped every inch and when you fail to give yourself to me completely, I know."

Swallowing nervously, I gave my wrist another pull.

He whisked out his cell phone and pressed a number.

I moaned my fear.

Tobias pressed his index fingertip to his mouth to silence me. "Yes, Adley, it's me again. Just checking in on that issue you're having at the palace." Tobias frowned as he listened. "Oh, I see. That is interesting."

My body trembled and my eyes widened as I tried to comprehend what he was doing and how crazy I'd been to let him tie me up. Tobias strolled closer and brushed away the blanket covering my foot and caressed it tenderly, pinching my toes and running a finger up my sole to cause a horrible tickle, only I couldn't jerk away and his torment of my foot was maddening.

He waggled his eyebrows, proving he was enjoying doing this to me. Tobias broke away and slid his thumb over his screen.

Adley's voice rose from the phone. "We can't believe it, either," he said. "Turns out the queen personally gifted the painting of Queen Charlotte to her grandson and forgot to report it. They literally stuffed it into the back of their Land Rover and drove off with it to Kensington Palace."

"The Benjamin West has been accounted for?" Tobias clarified and widened his eyes at me to make his point.

"Yes, how did you hear about it going missing?" asked Adley.

"A rumor found its way to us. We're glad it turned up. Have a lovely day. Oh, and Adley, if you ever need any help with a case don't hesitate to reach out to me. I may even be inclined to lend you Leighton. You know what a resource she is." Tobias told Adley goodbye and hung up. "Someone has been very naughty. Notice I'm looking at you, Leighton."

My head crashed onto the pillow and I squeezed my eyes shut in embarrassment.

"As I told you earlier." He pulled off the blanket. "I'm going to have to chastise you." His mouth closed over my big toe and sucked. "This is what I have in mind. You're not allowed to come until I say. Sound fair?"

I gave a reluctant nod.

He slipped into a grin. "You weren't relaxed. This is our day. Ours—yours and mine—and I want it to be everything you dreamed of." He reached over and pulled down the gag.

"I'm sorry."

"Accepted." He gave a roguish smile.

It was all okay and I swooned as uncertainty left me.

Sighing contentedly as his hand cupped my sex, I raised my head to watch the way his fingers trailed over me and then slowly circled my clit. He dipped his fingers into my wetness to use it to lubricate me fur-

ther and then played with that little bud tingling beneath his touch.

"You like this?" he asked huskily.

"Oh, yes," I moaned.

He rose off the bed. "No more sex until we're married."

"What!"

He turned and came at me fast. "I can't even follow
my own rules anymore. You've destroyed my willpower
completely."

My back arched when he leaned low between my
thighs and plunged his tongue inside me, fucking wildly
in the most delicious way and then lapping and circling
my folds until he had me shuddering violently through
a blinding orgasm as his tongue lavished me with attention. He rose and came to rest over me, and he controlled his hardness, dipping the tip by sliding his cock
along my sex. The need for him was too great and I
cried out for him.

He responded, plunging inside me deep and sure,
rising on his elbows to peer down at me and hold my
gaze as though trying to read me, seemingly needing to
see I believed him, believed all of it and, most important, see there was no doubt left in me that he'd given
up being Icon.

Somehow, someway I'd tamed this amazing man.

A jolt of pleasure surged through me as his pelvis brushed over my clit, and I wrapped my fingers
around the headboard, gripped it with white knuckles
for traction, and shuddered against the pleasure surging through me. I wanted to throw my legs around him
and cross my heels to capture him against me but they
were still bound by those silk ties. If he broke away now

I'd die from this need, yearning with every cell for this connection that I never wanted to end. My soul soared with all the emotions that were dissipating after they'd ravaged me day after day since knowing him.

His mouth was on mine, hungry and unforgiving, his tongue owning every corner as he savagely kissed. And with the same force I kissed him back, nipping at his lower lip, and biting down on the flesh of his right shoulder when the pleasure became overwhelming and I could no longer hold back, no matter my promise to control my release. "Please," I begged.

"Not yet," he ordered, lowering his head to catch a nipple between his lips and dragging his teeth over the sensitive skin, sending ripples of bliss through it. That sensation tugged at my clit to torture me more.

"Oh, God," I yelled. "I can't."

"You can and you will." His voice was demanding as he plunged into me with powerful thrusts that went deeper than he'd ever gone, his hips working me like a powerful piston, his hard chest striking mine. His mastery was gentle and then savage as he collided his heat-soaked body against me.

His firm chest pressed me into the mattress and then he pulled back and stilled, holding my gaze. "I'm giving you my oath now, Zara. My vow to you is my loyalty and my love, and I will spend every day making you happy."

"I love you," I managed through this rising orgasm, my channel owning him fiercely and pulsing around his full length until ripples of pleasure snatched the air from me and I gasped my next breaths until he spoke the words that would save me—

"Come together, Zara."

I screamed, convulsing with his name on my tongue, caught in the quake of this climax, finally allowing myself to surrender, giving myself over and opening like a flower in full bloom, no holding back, no selfish desire to keep anything for myself. Instead, I let him in entirely, trembling through the devastating sensations surging like a tsunami to sweep me away without the chance of ever going back and drowning in the pleasure of him as we merged as one.

We collapsed in each other's arms and I slipped into nothing but peace.

Afterward, we bathed in his enormous marble bath with bubbles and soapsuds pouring over the side in abundance and soaking the floor as we neared the time we'd soon have to separate, though briefly, to prepare for the rest of our lives.

Within an hour, I had been pampered and prepared with my makeup flawless and my hair a mass of spiraling waves over my shoulder, and as I stared at myself in the bedroom mirror I saw someone new. I'd never felt more right about anything and becoming Mrs. Wilder filled me with joy. Soon, I'd be joining Tobias on the beach of this sanctuary that had become our home, and with these daisies in my hair and happily barefoot, I would say my vows and become his wife. There'd be no guests today, it would be just us, promising to love and to cherish.

Lifting my bouquet off the side table, I brought them to my nose and breathed in the sweet scent of red roses filling the air with their perfume and reminding me of the flowers Tobias had first given me. Nostalgia carried on the breeze and found me, and though my mum wasn't here to cheer me on or my father to give me away, I was content with the thought they were with me in spirit nonetheless.

Making my way down and out of the house, I drew the ocean breeze into my lungs and spoke a quiet prayer, thanking God for delivering me.

From the end of the garden, I savored the sea view stretching out in a glorious deep blue with the promise of a sunset on the horizon. I turned my gaze, wanting to remember this moment forever, wanting it fused onto my consciousness. I inhaled a sharp breath at the way the lush roses twisted around the wedding arch and there standing beneath it was Tobias, wearing a white shirt and beige trousers and he was barefoot too.

With the soft sand melting beneath my feet I headed toward him, greeted by his wide grin and eyes brimming with elation as he admired my dress from afar.

"You look stunning, Zara," he called over and padded toward me.

I was vaguely aware of the officiant standing a little way back and past her, the woman sitting not that far away holding a paintbrush with an easel before her, ready to capture our service in a painting. The dreamy idea, all Tobias's, of us being immortalized in watercolors.

He closed the gap between us, reached out for my hand and kissed my wrist, and then wrapped his arm around my waist and dipped me. "Tell me you want me," he purred into my ear.

As my hair tumbled beneath me I felt safer than I ever had. "I want you." I whispered it, feeling like a beloved damsel in his strong arms.

"Tell me I make you happy."

"You make me happy."

"Tell me you are mine forever."

"Yours forever."

"I love you, Zara." He let out a long sigh and nuzzled into my neck and lifted me up before him. "Let's go have our happy-ever-after."

"I love you, Tobias." I followed him toward the scent of roses.

He beamed back as he reached the shade of the trellis.

My heart fluttered as I walked beneath the arch of flowers and I turned toward him—my love, my future, the man who made me giddy with happiness.

In the depths of my soul I had discovered within me an invisible strength, and as I spoke my first sacred vow to him, my heart soared as this truth became my reality—love is the greatest art of all.

* * * * *

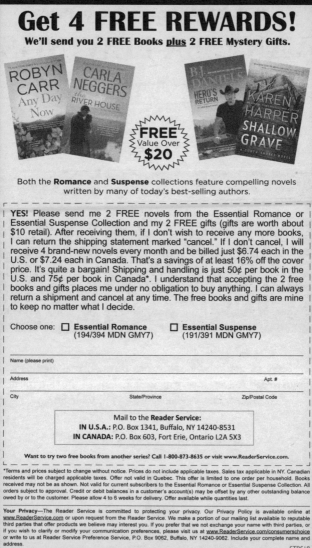